THE ALBUM

Xulon Press
2301 Lucien Way #415
Maitland, FL 32751
407.339.4217
www.xulonpress.com

Printed in the United States of America.

ISBN: 9781545613283

February 2019

To Norm -
Always seek the
Truth, and you will
be free! Mary Ellen
Blake

John 14:6

Preface

I did not plan to write this book. If I could not write the Great American Novel, why bother?

However, characters and situations kept visiting my mind in the dark hours of the night with stories to be told. Finally I began turning on the light and scribbling furiously as the ideas came. Such has been the case for several years, day and night, as I have lived with this book.

All characters are completely fictional and bear no resemblance to anyone, living or dead. However, many of the situations are based on fact, things that I have heard of, read about, or experienced. Truth indeed is stranger than fiction.

The themes of this book were entirely unplanned. They developed naturally as the characters began to emerge, coming together in ways that amazed me.

Special thanks are due to my husband Jim who gave unlimited encouragement, support, and even help with household duties to free me to write. His suggestions about the writing were invaluable.

I wish to thank my friend Charalene who gave hours of her time to try to retrieve my first writing when I accidentally sent it into cyberspace. Her efforts were in vain but the loss proved to be a blessing in disguise. The re-write turned out to be a big improvement. She continued to help me save my work, and she offered vital editorial comment. I am grateful to many other friends who read early drafts and had helpful suggestions.

Thanks also to my friend Cheryl who helped in innumerable ways to give me the time to write.

Mary Ellen Blake

Chapter 1

"Hey, be careful! You could hurt him!"

"Don't worry, I won't. But he'd never know. What difference would it make?"

"It's wrong, that's what."

"He's as senile as his roommate. They'll make a great pair. Nut-cases, both of them."

"Man, that's disrespectful!"

"You know it's true. You heard him ranting and raving when he came in."

"So what? He's a human being! Treat him like one. Besides, you could be in one of these beds someday. How would you like to be treated?"

"Me? No way! When my time comes, I'm out of here. A quick injection and it'll be all over. That's what these guys should do, get out of the way and make room for younger people. They shouldn't even be here."

"That is so wrong. Why do you work here, if you feel that way?"

"It's a job. And I'm good at it. Don't you forget it."

"Well, you have a lot to learn about old people."

The old man tried to open his eyes but it was too much effort. He shuddered in the darkness as he listened to these two young men. He labeled one Nice Guy and the other Mean One, and tried to memorize their voices. He might hear them again. *You never know.*

"Good morning, Mr. Douglas," said the social worker the next day as she settled into a chair next to his bed. He looked at her through a blurry haze. *I need to locate my glasses,* he thought.

"My name is Ms. Jackson," she went on, "and I want to welcome you to Sunset Gardens. So sorry about the circumstances, though." She paused, then asked gently, "Do you know what happened?"

"Uh...the fire?" He remembered the screech of the smoke alarm, the acrid smell, gasping for breath, his eyes burning, being jostled around. He closed his eyes, trying to forget.

"Yes. It was very bad. Bright Horizons burned to the ground. You're lucky to be alive. You spent a few days in the hospital, and now you're as good as before."

"Sunset Gardens? Where is it? I'm not familiar with it."

She named a city some distance from his previous location. *I might as well be in another country*, he thought. *Who would ever come all the way here to visit me?*

"Did anyone else make it? Ed Kellerman and Ron Evers?"

She thumbed through some pages. "Um...No, no, I'm afraid they both...uh, lost their lives. Smoke inhalation." She nodded kindly. "You were very lucky, you know."

Lucky? My only two friends, my card-playing buddies, gone! Such good times we'd had...we used to joke that we kept each other from dying of boredom. He turned away, unable to respond.

"We took in a few women. Do you want names? Everyone else went to other places."

"No...no, that's all right." *I hardly knew any of the other residents.*

"I see that you lost your glasses. We've scheduled you for an eye exam today and you should have new ones in a week."

A week! Can't read, can't even see....for another week. Oh well, I'll just stay in bed. No reason to get up.

"Ms. Jackson. Do you have my bag?"

"Do you mean the pillow case? Yes, you were clutching it. There's something big and heavy in it. We didn't look. It's in your closet. Do you want to keep it there?"

"No, I'd like it in my nightstand. Just as it is."

"Hmm. We'll see if it fits. It reeks of smoke, you know. Do you want us to wash the case?"

"No, no! But....thank you."

"We'll take care of it right away. And with that, Mr. Douglas, I must go. Again, welcome to Sunset Gardens." With a wave of her hand, she was gone.

He lay stiffly in the darkness, unable to sleep. *Now I really am alone*, he thought bitterly. *Kate and Allen, gone so long, and now the only two friends I had left in the world. I hardly remember people from my other life. Before the nursing home. Oh... I mustn't say nursing home. They don't want you to, they have fancy names now, but it's all the same. Once you're there for a while people forget about you. And I'm ready to forget about myself. What's the point*, he thought grimly, *who cares if I live or die?* The darkness called him, inviting him, and he began to surrender to it. *Ah, welcome darkness. Oblivion.*

'*He's a human being.*' The memory jarred him. *I don't feel like a human being..... 'Treat him like one.'* From a distance he saw, or rather felt, a pinpoint of light beckoning him. It warmed him, and he felt himself straining towards it. It began to envelop him, but the darkness pulled him back. He struggled against the darkness. *Ah, my faith,* he thought, *it's calling me. What good is faith if I give it up in the hard times? I am a human being! God is in control, he loves me; I have to believe that. He wants me to live*. Yielding at last to the light, to God, he fell into a deep and dreamless sleep.

He met Nice Guy a few days later. "Hello, I'm Rob Carlyle," he said with a smile. There was no mistaking his voice. "Your own personal Nursing Assistant. You and a few dozen others," he joked. "Glad to have you here, though I'm sorry about the way it happened." His tone changed and he gave Mr. Douglas an understanding look as he patted his arm. "I can hardly imagine...." He shook his head. "Terrible about the loss of life. Did you know any of those who died?"

Mr. Douglas looked away. "Yes...." he muttered, "my two best friends." *My only friends,* he thought, unable to say any more.

"That's tough," replied Rob, squeezing his arm sympathetically. "I'm sorry. Well," he brightened, "I think you'll make some new friends here. It's a good place."

"Maybe." *I doubt it,* he thought. *It's not that easy.* He was ready to change the subject. "You were with me the night I was brought in, weren't you?" He decided not to mention Mean One. *I'm brand new here, I don't want to get off on the wrong foot.* "I'm sorry for my ranting and raving. I probably wasn't very nice to you. They moved me in the middle of the night." He shook his head, embarrassed. "I was disoriented."

"No problem. You were fine," he smiled reassuringly. "Yes, you came in at 6:00 in the morning so I can imagine what time they got you up! Hospitals are famous for that, right? Well, speaking of '*up*', they want you out of bed," he said, taking his hand, "and into your wheel chair. We got you a new one, see."

Up to now he'd protested that he didn't feel like getting up but he realized he wanted to do as Rob asked. "I guess I'm ready for a change," he admitted as Rob helped him into his chair.

"I'm supposed to show you around. I'll give you the Grand Tour!" With a flourish Rob started off. He showed him the dining rooms, the lounges, the rec room, a little kitchen, the garden, and then the library.

"Ah, home," Mr. Douglas sighed, "I'll stay here all day. Right now I can't see what's here – though I do recognize that good set of encyclopedias."

"They're pretty old," Rob commented as he opened one up. "Twenty years old."

"That's not a problem." *Why, that's just yesterday*, he thought. "I'll read them from start to finish, just you wait and see."

"Okay, we'll set your bed up here," he joked. "Just be sure to come to meals. Now, time to get you back."

"Thanks. Whew, I'm tired already."

"Better get rested up! I'll be around first thing tomorrow morning to get you up."

"You mean it, don't you," he grumbled. Rob shrugged and smiled.

I might as well give in gracefully, he decided.

The next morning he managed a smile for Rob and they began to get acquainted. After that he was on his own. He went out and about the halls, giving a brusque '*hello*' as he went along, not stopping to talk but stopping now and then to rest. Several times through the day he lingered at one of the picture windows that looked out into the garden. The bleakness of the January landscape matched his mood, yet he found that the peacefulness of nature began to stir something within him.

This became his daily pattern. When his glasses arrived he began to do his reading in a quiet spot overlooking the garden, watching the scampering squirrels and the occasional bright cardinal, drawing strength from the ever-changing view.

"You look as if you've seen a ghost!" exclaimed Rob as he entered Mr. Douglas's room a few days later.

"Oh…uh….must be the new glasses."

"That bad, huh? I guess I shock people. You were better off not seeing me," he laughed.

"No…uh…you reminded me of someone, that's all." *What's the matter with me,* he wondered, *Allen gone so long, any handsome young man…..*

"How do you do it, Rob, three twelve-hour shifts in a row?" he asked.

"Lots of people do," he replied. "Not a problem. I go to school during the week, pre-med, my senior year, and I get a week's work on the weekend. Seven AM to seven PM. I like it."

"Yes, if you don't need to sleep," Mr. Douglas remarked dryly. "No Friday classes? No social life?"

"Not in my schedule."

"So why work here?"

"I wanted some medical experience, to see if it's right for me."

"What do you think?"

"I like it. I look forward to coming in here. Not to say there aren't the bureaucratic frustrations, but you get that anywhere. I like the people. Giving care. I think this is right for me, the medical field."

He'll make a good doctor, Mr. Douglas thought. *It's different from nursing, but he'll give good personal care. That's important.*

He found himself looking forward to weekends when Rob would be working. He began spending weekends in his room with a volume or two of the encyclopedias so he could converse with him, though he would not have admitted it if asked. They talked as if they'd always known each other, about almost anything....sports, world events, history, science, music, though not religion. Rob shrugged it off, '*It doesn't interest me.*' They talked freely, vigorously, intelligently, not always agreeing but always respecting each other.

By common consent they avoided talk about family. He knew only that Rob's father had died when he was a baby; his mother always had a new boyfriend and had no time for him. His grandparents had raised him and they had passed away recently. It was a bare outline, casually told, with no details. It was obvious he didn't want to say any more. There was a touch of sadness shadowing him, behind his outgoing nature. *Well of course*, Mr. Douglas thought, *why wouldn't he be sad, with what he's gone through? It certainly would help if he talked about it.*

Ha, he thought with a shake of his head, *it's not that easy.* He had his own painful memories which he chose to keep to himself. But he was happy to talk about his career as a civil engineer – '*I'm a roads and bridges man – that is to say, I was, in my other life,*' and his love of the out of doors. He told about being part of a Big Brothers group and bringing city kids to hike and camp with them.

Because of Rob's sympathetic interest he told about the spinal cord injury a dozen years ago that had left him paralyzed and how he had struggled to retain his independence, living alone. Then, when he and his peers were planning carefree retirements, he had fallen again. Independence gave way to assisted living and eventually to full time nursing care. He was younger than most of the other residents but he found his niche. "I adjusted to it all," he said, "each step of the way. My faith has carried me through. But this last change….coming here….this has been the hardest," he groaned, shaking his head.

"Maybe because it was so traumatic," offered Rob.

Hmph, he thought, *so were the other changes*. "Well, Rob, whatever it is, I'm done. Through. No more changes for me."

"I can understand that. I hope you'll be happy here."

"I'll do my best." *Whatever that is*, he told himself.

He often thought of Rob's sad past and marveled at the success he'd made of his life. He hoped his friendship with him, if he dared call it that, would be helpful. He respected his wish for privacy and tried to avoid asking personal questions. Yet it was only natural to ask if he had a girlfriend.

"No….but then, I've never met any girl who interested me," he replied with a shrug. "I hope I do, someday."

"It doesn't hurt to be choosy. Be careful, you don't want to fall for the first girl who smiles at you with her eyes." *What am I saying*, he chuckled to himself, *didn't Kate win me with her eyes?*

"Not likely," he replied, "and besides, I'm too busy for a girlfriend. It would just mess me up. Med school first. When I'm thirty or so…."

"Good idea! Now's the time to concentrate on school."

He didn't know whether he'd met Mean One or not. Finally he decided he was the surly young man who worked the night shift. He talked very little and never gave his name. Mr. Douglas always breathed a sigh of relief when he left the room, though he couldn't say why.

"Say, Rob, what's a young guy like you doing, working with us old people?" Mr. Douglas asked one day. "Surely you could earn more money somewhere else."

"Since you asked, this is as good as it gets, right now." He frowned. "I worked second shift in a factory for a year, longest year of my life! But the factory closed down and that was fine with me. Then a buddy told me I could get trained pretty fast as a nursing assistant. So I did. I've been here about six months. I like it. I guess it's because of Granny."

"Hmm....your grandmother, who passed away?"

"No, my grandpa's mother, my great grandmother. I always called her Granny. She lived with us while I was growing up. She spoiled me outrageously – with her time and attention, you know – and I just naturally accepted old people. Oh – sorry about that," he laughed.

"I'll have you know," he declared, "I'm actually a young person disguised in this old body."

"I believe you are," Rob agreed with a smile. "Well," he went on, "because of Granny, I'm very comfortable with...um, older people." He stopped to reflect. "I've learned something since I've been here. You older people are a national treasure. You're the greatest natural resource we have."

Mr. Douglas shook his head, touched. "Rob, "he finally replied, "I'm glad you feel that way. Not everybody does." *Mean One would not agree, I'm sure.*

Rob worked efficiently and they didn't linger over conversation, though in each brief encounter they could pick up where they had left off. One day, a conversation about politics and history led to a sharp difference of opinion that surprised them both. Each was sure he was right. Neither was willing to budge, even when they came back to the subject good-naturedly throughout the day. At the end of the day the subject was unresolved. *But I know I'm right,* Mr. Douglas told himself. *After all, I lived it.*

When Rob returned the next week, Mr. Douglas was ready for him. "Rob, do you remember our discussion last week?"

"Oh, yes," he laughed, "that was a good one."

"Well....I did some checking. Went to those old encyclopedias. What do you think I found?"

"I have a feeling you're going to tell me," Rob said with a grin as he tightened the blood pressure cuff.

"You were right," he replied with a nod. "The facts are on your side. Much as it pains me to admit it," he sighed as he yielded his position to Rob.

"Ha!" Rob laughed. "You don't say! Well, I did a little checking of my own." He pulled a paper from his pocket. "Found some stuff online. Actually, you were right. The encyclopedia was wrong. New information has come out. Take a look."

Mr. Douglas looked it over with surprise. "Isn't this interesting! Well, well. That's what I thought all along. Just couldn't prove it."

"I'm glad the truth won out. That doesn't always happen."

"Thank you, Rob." He reached out and shook his hand. "Thank you for taking the time to check it out. I can't tell you what that means to me."

There was a tear in Mr. Douglas' eye.

Chapter 2

'Don't get involved.' Rob had learned that in training. It was a dictum he chose to ignore. Not to be crass about it, but – they die. Yes, he had lost some in his care. Some deaths were expected, others were a surprise, but it always brought a touch of sadness. It didn't stop him from offering his own brand of friendship and respect, listening as he worked. He cared and they knew it.

There were those who had to be told the same thing over and over, and those who were not pleasant. But there were those who added new dimensions of interest to his day, responding to his warm manner with friendliness and sharing of their life stories. And then there was Mr. Douglas, who seemed in a class by himself. If he was closer to him than anyone else he didn't let on. He would not play favorites.

Harsh sounds: banging, curses, ugly words, wakened Mr. Douglas out of his sleep. He recognized the voice of Mean One who was tending to his roommate, angry because the man had been sick in the night. With as much strength as he could muster he rose up in bed and called out, "Leave him alone! He can't help it!"

The next moment Mean One was standing over him. "Shut your face, old man! You'll be next if you're not careful!" He turned away, snatched the curtain shut and completed his work. Then he exited the room.

Mr. Douglas lay trembling in the darkness, unable to sleep.

He told Rob about it the next day. "I think he was with you the morning I was admitted," he added.

"That would be Damien. Damien Sanders. Yes, he was with me. We had a number of admissions and I came in early to help. Normally I don't work with him. But," he reflected, "that doesn't sound like him. I see him at meetings, and he's very professional. I can't believe he would behave that way." He shrugged. "Not that I'm doubting you, though."

"He was not professional. He needs to be stopped."

"Right about that. I'm glad you challenged him. A lot of people would have just shut their ears."

"I wish I could have done more. I couldn't stop him." He told Rob what he remembered of Damien's remarks that first day. "You spoke up for me, by the way. I appreciated that."

Rob shrugged. "That was nothing. But now that you mention it, I remember. His remarks were pretty bizarre." He frowned, shaking his head. "It seemed out of character for him. He's a nice guy, a college student. A bit older than me. He has a good reputation here. Among the staff. I don't know what the residents think about him."

"He wasn't nice," Mr. Douglas insisted. "I think that's his true character. Loosened up with a little alcohol, is my guess. I smelled it."

"That's a shock," he nodded. "But you've got to report him. This incident."

"I intend to. Today. Rob, would you also make a report? Call it '*patient abuse*'. That's exactly what it was. I know it's second hand, but you might carry more weight."

"Yes, I will. But still...." He shook his head. "I can't believe it. I wouldn't have thought it of him."

"Rob, people aren't always what they seem."

Rob forced himself to remember Damien's chilling words and what they revealed about the man. He wasn't naïve, he'd heard that point of view before. But it was unnerving to hear it from a colleague. *Well*, he wondered*....is Damien right? These old people – should they be here? Not Mr. Douglas, he still has his mind – but what about the others, who have lost theirs? In fact....why am I here?*

His mind flashed back to Granny. He had been ten or eleven when he began to notice that Granny was changing. He complained to his grandma that Granny forgot things as soon as he told her. Grandma had explained that Granny's mind was changing. It was shutting down, and she needed Rob's love to help her. Rob had taken willingly to the task and had been rewarded by a relationship that depended not on words and memories but on something deeper, on love and kindness. Granny never lost her kindness, and Grandma said it was because of Rob. *'Someday'*, he had told his grandparents, *'I'm going to be a doctor and take care of people like Granny.'* His grandparents told him that if he were in Granny's position he'd want somebody kind to take care of him.

No, he concluded, *Damien's got it wrong. And I'm glad I'm here.*

Is Damien right, Mr. Douglas asked himself as he tried to sleep that night. *Everything in me says no. It's against everything I believe. Yet if there ever was a useless life, it's mine. I'm no good to anybody. What good does it do to read all day? I can understand why somebody would want to end it all, if they lived this kind of existence. But that's not the same as ending someone else's life. That's another matter entirely. That power*

could be abused so easily! No, he concluded, *no one should have that power.*

Well, do I have the right to end my life? Why not? He pondered. *No, no, that's God's business, not mine. I can't see the whole picture, and He can. Even if I were helpless, like my roommate here....no, I wouldn't have the right. But....I can understand those who think they do. It's a terrible thing, to be useless.*

If I'm useless, it's my own fault. I am too dependent on Rob. He won't be here much longer. I need to get out of my shell, talk more, socialize a bit.

"Say, Rob, what do you know about Damien?" Mr. Douglas asked one day. "He hasn't been in for a couple of weeks."

"Funny you should ask. The news broke yesterday. He was busted – arrested – for getting into the drug supply. But that's not the worst of it."

"Oh – there's more? Why am I not surprised?"

"Well, I can understand stealing drugs for your own use – but he was caught with lethal drugs. Nobody's saying what for. I'm stunned. The staff is in shock."

"I'm not," he stated matter-of-factly. "It all fits."

"You must see something I don't," Rob replied. "It's hard for me to comprehend. Lethal drugs? That's not Damien." He shook his head. "Why – why in the world?"

"Nothing good, I'm sure. Rob, think about it."

Rob could think of little else over the next few days as stories swirled about the case. There were suspicious deaths in other places Damien had worked, and now, allegations he was involved in deaths here. *Could this be true? Damien? A colleague? Could he be responsible for any deaths here?* Confusion gave way to anger as he considered that possibility.

He had reported the incident with Mr. Douglas's roommate to the Director of Nursing. She had already heard it from Mr. Douglas. '*Thank you, we'll check it out,*' she had replied. *How do you check something like this*, he wondered. *It would be Damien's word against an elderly resident who might have been having a nightmare. After all, Damien was well liked and had an excellent reputation.*

His words to Damien when they were admitting Mr. Douglas came back to him. *'You have a lot to learn about old people.' No,* Rob mused, *that's not the problem. He knows how to treat people, old or young. He can charm anyone, anytime.* He forced himself to face the facts. *Underneath his charming façade, he doesn't care about people. That makes it all the worse. That's it. That's the real problem*, he concluded.

It was all very troubling.

Rob and Mr. Douglas offered to give testimony to the police about what they had heard from Damien. The detectives took a statement from Rob and then came to see Mr. Douglas, causing no little excitement among staff and residents. He told them of his two encounters, adding soberly, "I could have been one of his victims." He hoped it would help establish motive. Only time would tell.

"Rob, you're good," Mr. Douglas commented as he watched him work swiftly and efficiently with him and his roommate. "Why don't you stay on after you graduate, until you start med school?"

"Thanks for the kind thought, but I've already got a job lined up close to school. I'll be a server at one of those fancy steak house chains, DeGeorgio's at the Lake. I'm sure you've heard of it. They're busy during the summer, the tourist crowd. Tips are good, especially at the parties afterwards."

"No, I don't know the place." He shook his head. "I'm not from around here, you know. We'll be sorry to see you go. It will be a loss to us all." He tried to conceal how much a loss it would be to him. He didn't want to presume upon Rob's friendliness.

"Also, I'm looking for an apartment closer to med school," Rob went on. "It's about an hour from here, you know, in the city."

"I understand. Just thought I'd ask."

He doesn't want me to leave, Rob thought. *In a way, I don't want to. I'll miss him.*

"I'll stop by once in a while to say hello."

Both of them knew it would not happen.

How can I say goodbye to Rob without embarrassing him, Mr. Douglas wondered. Graduation was fast approaching and with it the end of what had become a warm and comfortable relationship. He hesitated to call it a friendship. *After all, I'm one of dozens he takes care of. He can't afford to be a friend to anyone. No, this has meant more to me than to him. I'm going to miss him more than I should. I don't want to say goodbye to him.*

If there's anything I've learned in life, he thought, *it's that people come and go. You say goodbye to them and move on. Ha! If you're lucky you get to say goodbye,* he thought with a twinge of bitterness, remembering Ed and Ron.

Rob had just gotten Mr. Douglas up from a nap and was getting him settled in his wheelchair.

"Well, Rob, are you looking forward to graduation? It's just a couple of weeks away."

"No, I'm not," he replied brusquely, his jaw set. "It means nothing to me."

"That's a strong statement." He was taken aback by the force of Rob's words.

"I'm glad to be finishing. But the actual graduation," he gave an indifferent nod, "I might not even go. There won't be anyone attending for me."

"No one, Rob?" he asked with surprise.

"Not my mother. I don't even know where she lives. It doesn't matter to me. I have no other family."

"That's sad." *Dear Lord, I wish I could help him. But what could I say?*

"Don't worry about me. I'm okay. It's strange, though – I miss the one person who couldn't be there anyway." He stopped working and folded his arms across his chest, shaking his head. Mr. Douglas gave him a curious look. "My father. It's on these landmark occasions that I think about him. I wish for what I can't have. That's pretty dumb, isn't it? Considering that I never even met him. He died when I was a baby."

"No, it's not dumb," he replied warmly, meeting Rob's gaze. "Not at all."

"Would you like to see his picture?" Rob asked, to Mr. Douglas's surprise. "It makes me feel close to him, to carry his picture in my wallet."

"I would be honored. Thank you." Touched by Rob's gesture he decided to ask a personal question. "Rob, how did your father die?"

"He died in the First Gulf War. In Kuwait, 1991. He was in the Marines." Rob handed him the picture.

"Rob." A strange look convulsed his face. "Rob, what was your father's name?"

"Robert Allen Douglas. Ha, Douglas, like you. I never thought about it. I'm named after him, I'm Robert Allen Douglas too but a stepfather adopted me so now I'm Carlyle. I never think of myself as Douglas –"

"Quick, Rob!" Mr. Douglas interrupted him with urgency. "Go to my nightstand and get that pillowcase! It has a book in it."

In a moment the book was in his hands, a large album stuffed with unmounted photos. Hurriedly, clumsily Mr. Douglas rifled through the pictures until at last with a cry of satisfaction he held one up. "Rob, look at this!"

"What!" he exclaimed, shocked. "It can't be...." It was a picture of a young man and woman in a romantic pose. The young man bore a striking resemblance to Rob. "It's the same picture!"

Clutching the picture, Mr. Douglas said proudly, "This is my son, Robert Allen Douglas, Jr." He choked out the words. "He died in Kuwait in 1991."

"That's my father!"

"And I am Robert Allen Douglas Sr...."

They looked at each other. "Rob," Mr. Douglas began, taking his hand, "That means I am your –"

"My grandfather?" Stunned, he was momentarily frozen. In a daze he leaned over and wrapped his arms around the old man, unable to speak.

"And you are my grandson – my grandson." Tears spilled from his eyes. They held each other close. He looked at him fondly. "Allen's son! I never thought to see him...."

Laughing, crying, they could scarcely believe what was happening. "This can't be....it can't be....it's unbelievable!"

There were no words to be said. Then Rob's face lit up with sudden inspiration. "Mr. Douglas – Granddad – will you come to my graduation?"

Unable to speak, Mr. Douglas held tightly to Rob's hand and nodded his head, then he stammered, "Yes....yes....I would be honored!" He pulled back, reached for a tissue and blew his nose. "My grandson." He shook his head in wonderment and smiled. They embraced once more. "My grandson....Rob! Yes, yes! God is good."

They didn't want to let go of each other. They lingered as long as they could but Rob had a shift to complete, so with difficulty he took his leave and returned to work. As he stopped at the nursing station a co-worker, noticing his dazed expression asked him if anything was wrong. He blurted out a few words of explanation, then went about his business.

Long after Rob left, Mr. Douglas sat alone in his chair, hardly able to grasp what had just occurred. *How can this be? This fine young man, who I've tried not to love, is Allen's son! What has God done? My God, who brought me back to life when I was ready to give up, my God, who I've ignored these last months – my God still loves me and has given me new life, new hope!* He could not eat, he could not face anyone. His tears flowed freely and he made no attempt to stop them. He sat for a long time, smiling through tears.

There was a tap on his door and the Administrator, Mrs. Markowitz, asked if she could come in. "Good news travels quickly! I wanted to find out, is it really true?" They shared the gladness of the moment. "My dear Mr. Douglas," she told him with pleasure, "it couldn't have happened to two finer people."

The next day when Rob came into work he was greeted with happy bedlam; everyone was celebrating the amazing news. He was hardly able to complete his rounds. Mr. Douglas, who Rob now called Gramps, was an instant celebrity. In the afternoon a nurse came to take him to Mrs. Markowitz's office. Rob was there and came over to him, seizing his hand. "Gramps! A reporter is here, from the local paper. She wants our pictures."

Mr. Douglas drew back. "No, no. I don't want any publicity. We don't need that."

"Mr. Douglas, Mr. Douglas, this story is too good to keep. It's such a heart-warming, human interest story. Won't you please agree?" pleaded Mrs. Markowitz.

He didn't want to disappoint Rob, who seemed so eager, so he agreed to a few pictures. But he had very few words for the reporter. "No, we had never met. His father was deployed overseas when Rob was very young, and then he was killed. I never knew where he was. That's really all there is to it," he said with finality.

As they left Mrs. Markowitz's office he expressed his misgivings to Rob. "I'd much rather the press wasn't involved. Things can get out of hand."

"Gramps, it's a story. People like that."

"It's a wonderful story! Don't get me wrong, I'm walking on air. In my wheelchair! But as for the press, you never know what might happen." He smiled in resignation. "Never mind, it will be fine," he said as they bade each other goodbye.

I don't like being the center of attention, he thought. *I'll be glad when things get back to normal. But what is normal? My son's son walks this earth! I thought I would never see him.... and now he is here with me! Such a fine young man, who I'd come to love even though I knew I shouldn't. Now I can love him with all my heart.*

Rob didn't know what excited him more, to acknowledge Mr. Douglas as his grandfather or now, at last, to learn about his father. *I don't know anything about my father, nothing, nothing,* he thought. *Now I will get to know him! Mr. Douglas, Gramps – what a wonderful old man he is – he is my father's father!*

Another amazing thought.... *someone in my corner! Someone to love me, someone I can love, to cheer me on. I didn't know how important that is until now, now that I have it. I have him! My family, my own flesh and blood. He had no one, and I had no one. Until now.*

Graduation day. Rob came for Gramps early in the day, proudly escorting him through the lobby and out the door to the cheers and applause of staff and residents. In the weeks between their discovery until now they had tried to maintain a professional staff/resident relationship in public, but now Rob was very much the loving family member. "It will be a long day, Gramps. Do you think you can make it without getting too tired?"

"I'll make it whether I get tired or not! I'm going to enjoy every minute of it," he declared happily. *It's also my first social outing in a long time*, he thought, *but that's my fault. I'm going to make up for lost time*. Rob had arranged for a nursing assistant to sit with him during the time he would have to leave until he could rejoin him afterwards. He would take her back when they were done. "Rob, you thought of everything," he said appreciatively.

When the ceremony was over Rob proudly introduced Gramps to his friends and professors. After returning the aide to Sunset Gardens he drove him around campus, then showed him the city with its many landmarks and attractions. "It's unbelievable to be out like this!" he exclaimed, overwhelmed.

"Most of all, to be out with my grandson. Another 'Grand Tour' – remember that, Rob?"

Rob shrugged his shoulders and smiled, enjoying Gramps' pleasure. It didn't matter.

Gramps took his hand. "I never thought I could be this happy." Rob smiled in agreement.

They enjoyed dinner in a fine restaurant. Gramps insisted on treating him. "Rob, I am so proud of you," he told him, his face displaying his pride. "You outshone them all!"

Now he felt more comfortable in asking him about his college life, his friends and his classes, though not yet about his family. Rob responded with stories and anecdotes, laughter and joking until at last he looked at him and exclaimed, "Gramps, your eyes are glazing over. Time to go back." They parted with a warm embrace and promises to keep in close touch.

Ah, thought Mr. Douglas, *life will never be the same again! And I like it.*

Chapter 3

Jolted out of his sleep, Rob rolled over and punched the alarm clock. *Why doesn't it stop ringing?* He tried again but it continued to ring, rhythmically and incessantly. His eyes focused and he looked at the time. *Eight thirty*. It felt like the middle of the night. *Oh, that party. It broke up in the small hours of the morning and I had to stay to clean up. Why doesn't the alarm stop ringing? Uh oh, it must be the doorbell.* He rolled out of bed, hurriedly pulled on pants and a shirt and stumbled to the door. Peering through the peephole he saw a woman of middle years of nondescript appearance standing there, her face in the shadows. *Hmm, I don't quite recognize her. She's probably harmless*. He opened the door.

"Robbie! What took you so long? Shame on you, you should be up by now," she said sharply. "Your neighbor told me you were home so I kept on ringing."

"Oh – Mom. What are you doing here?"

"A fine welcome that is! Can't I come and see my son when I want to?"

"Uh – sure, of course. Come in and sit down. Can I get you some coffee?"

"Yeah. I'll take a cup. But you're the one who needs it. What were you doing, partying all night?"

"You have no idea," he replied, groggily. *Oh, if she only knew. And she's the one who needs coffee, she's hung over*. He went into the little kitchen, made a couple of cups of instant coffee and took them into the living room. He took a seat on the couch in front of her.

"Aren't you out a little early yourself?"

"I was in the neighborhood."

"The neighborhood! How did you even know where I live? I just moved here."

"Mmm....I have my ways," she said pointedly. "I'll tell you if you're nice to me."

"It doesn't matter to me," he shrugged. *I'm not going to play her game*.

"Well!" She took out a cigarette.

"Mom, you can't! This is a non-smoking building."

She lit the cigarette and began smoking. "You won't tell on me."

Stiffening with anger, he didn't know what to say.

"I know somebody who works with you. At DeGeorgio's, right? Quite a talker, he is." She mimicked him, " '*Oh, my buddy Rob Carlyle, you should have seen him the other night! The way he handled this patron who was drunk. It was so funny!*' Now, how many Rob Carlyles are there? I knew it was you." She laughed as if she'd witnessed it herself. "Oh, it was so funny –"

She's more than hung over, she's drunk, Rob thought with disgust. "Okay, Mom," he broke in, "who is it who knows so much about me?"

"Rob," she rolled her eyes, "he knows you. He lives the next building over. He knows where you live."

"Mom," he said loudly, "I'm not interested!" *A drinking buddy? I'll bet she doesn't even know his name. Why is she here? Not to see how I am, that's for sure. Better not make her mad, then I'll never know what's going on*.

"You don't need to raise your voice at me! Now, aren't you wondering why I'm here?"

"All right, all right." He stopped, making sure he had her attention. "Mom," he asked deliberately, "to what do I owe the honor of this visit?"

"Well!" Dramatically, she pulled a newspaper clipping out of her purse and waved it in front of him. "Here's my son – on the front page – with him!" Her voice rose with anger. She poked the picture with her finger. "Your grandfather!" The headline read '*Grandson and Grandfather Find Each Other.*'

"Well, Mom, if you read the article you'll know that I just graduated from college," he said coolly. "A week ago." *Now why did I say that? I don't care if she knows or not.*

"Oh, I'm sure you did yourself proud."

"Yes, I did. Too bad you missed it," he said sharply. *She can't even congratulate me? Someone was proud of me*, he thought. *Gramps was positively beaming!* "All right, Mom. What's this all about?"

"It's him. Your grandfather. So! He surfaces at last! I came here to tell you, Rob, don't have anything to do with him. He's a bastard. He broke your father's heart."

"Mom – what do you mean?" he asked, shocked, incredulous. "He's not like that! You're wrong."

"I'm sure he's wonderful to you. Came to your graduation, did he? Well, he didn't even come to your father's graduation from basic training. He couldn't be bothered."

"I don't believe it! I'm sure there's a good explanation."

"Oh, it's true," she sniffed. "Rob, I'm telling you for your own good. He broke your father's heart and he'll break yours."

He felt a wave of anger roll over him. "That's enough! I don't want to hear any more! I've got things to do. You'd better go." He took her arm and pulled her up as he guided her to the door. "Now, goodbye."

"All right, all right! Don't say I didn't warn you."

"I'll handle this myself, thank you. And Mom," he glared at her, "next time you come – try to be sober, please."

She looked at him with disdain. "What do you know about it?"

Closing the door behind her he drew a deep breath, then paced to the window and back, swearing loudly. *Why is she doing this to me? Why does she have to ruin my happiness? It's always something*. He dropped onto the couch, head in his hands, trying to steady himself. He tried to think. *What is going on here? What could she mean? Can I trust anything she says?*

This couldn't be true. It couldn't. He'd come to know Mr. Douglas, Gramps, for many months. He was a kind-hearted man. *But wait, hadn't he told me, 'people aren't always what they seem'? There's a mystery to him. Gramps simply won't talk about his family, which now is my family too.*

He'd had such high hopes after they discovered each other, hopes that Gramps would take out that album stuffed with pictures and tell Rob all about his family. About his father! He knew nothing, he'd always felt bereft. *Now at last,* he thought, *I'll learn my past*.

It didn't happen. After graduation as they sat in the restaurant he had asked Gramps questions about his father and the album. There was a distant look on his face, and he changed the subject. The door was closed.

So, is Mom right? Is there some bad blood between Gramps and his father? I should talk to him. Ask him directly. But – what if it's true? What if I lose him? Do I want to take that risk? He shook his head. *It's all so confusing*.

A week or so later he was standing in line at a fast food place when he became aware someone was looking at him. *Well, I can look too,* he thought, *she's worth looking at!*

"Say, aren't you the guy who discovered his long-lost grandfather? Your picture was all over the front page. That's such a wonderful story!"

"That's me," he replied self-consciously, and then he was struck dumb by the beauty of her eyes. In a daze he placed his order as she waited for him, and a few minutes later they were seated in a booth in the back of the restaurant.

"Well, I have the advantage," she began. "You're Rob Carlyle, and you work at a nursing home. I read the article about you and your grandfather."

"Right, that's my name," he replied, flattered that she had remembered it. "And you are?"

"I'm Aimee." She smiled warmly. "Rob, that's such an unforgettable story. I've thought a lot about it. It's not just that you found a long-lost relative....it's that he had no one else in the world. Now he has you."

"Yes, that's it! Actually, I don't either," he explained. "Have any family, that is."

"No family?" She looked at him with surprise.

"Well, I was raised by my grandparents, and they passed away. Now it's just me," he said lightly. "Maybe some great-aunts and uncles I don't even know – but no, just me."

"That is sad." She smiled sympathetically. "Well, then, how wonderful that you have each other. I'm glad for you. For you both." She smiled invitingly. "Rob, what was it like to discover him? To discover each other?"

"Unbelievable...." He tried to find words. "It was incredible! Amazing – you see, he wasn't a stranger. We had come to know each other pretty well. I liked him, loved him, I think, although I wouldn't have admitted it. You can't love your patients, you know."

"But you did. He sounds pretty neat. And so do you." She smiled again, and he felt encouraged to go on.

"Another thing....I needed someone to be proud of me. I didn't realize how important that was, until I saw him waiting for me after graduation. That meant a lot," he nodded, "a whole lot." He blinked back tears as he looked away.

"It must have." She waited for him to regain his composure. "I'm sure you would have handled it alone, but it means so much more to have family backing you up." There were tears in her eyes. "I'm happy for you."

Reaching across the table, she patted his hand.

He felt warmed by her understanding. Impulsively he took her hand and kissed her fingertips.

"Ohh... I've never had anyone kiss my hand before. You must be from another planet."

"Yes, yes I am," he nodded, "from another planet! And I hope it's not the last time I kiss your hand," he replied as he let go, unwillingly.

"Umm....what an amazing story, you and your grandpa. Rob, I think good things will come of it."

"I sure hope so." *But I'm not so sure*, he thought. *What do I do about Gramps? Where do we go from here?*

"What is it like, seeing him every day – as your grandpa, not a patient?"

"Well, I don't, that is, I don't work there anymore. I left after graduation."

"Where are you now?"

"I'm at DeGeorgio's at the Lake; I'm a server –"

"I'm impressed! They're known for their handsome servers. '*Extra Special Service by Extra Special Servers'*.... you know their ads."

He groaned. "It's a job. Nothing special, believe me. But, let's talk about a more interesting subject." She looked at him questioningly. "You. I don't even know your last name. You are Aimee....?"

"I'm Aimee, that's A-i-m-e-e. Aimee Love."

He laughed. "You have a very strange name, you know."

"I like it. I'm glad to be strange."

"Aimee.....that's French for love, right? That's Love – Love."

"Well, my parents were a little strange. They loved being Love. They always said my name was a private joke –"

"Or maybe you were the private joke."

"Ha, ha. Maybe. Anyway, most people don't catch on. My middle name is Eileen. You can call me that if you like."

"Oh, no. I like '*Aimee*'." He smiled at her and her heart did a flip. "So where do you work?"

"Looks like we're both in the food business, but just for the summer. I'm at The Bread Oven down the road, the sandwich place. So tell me....do you have anyone special?"

He gave her a puzzled look.

"You are from another planet," she said kindly. "What I mean is, are you in any relationship?"

"Oh....I'm definitely an alien. Another planet, you know. Probably a bit naïve when it comes to girls," he laughed. "No, I don't have anybody special, that's not in my plans right now." *But that could change pretty fast*, he thought. "I'm just starting med school."

"There's no one in my life either." *But that could change in a heartbeat*, she thought. "I've been holding off till I finish grad school."

They talked easily, like old friends. He had found his voice with her. He told her about Gramps and the accusations of his mother, his own confusion and discomfort. "So," he concluded, "I haven't asked him about it. We've talked a couple of times on the phone, and – it's awkward. It's like a wall of glass between us."

"Rob – that's terrible!" She shook her head in disbelief. "You and your grandpa, you're barely getting started in your new relationship – and she comes along, and....and...ruins everything!"

"She popped my balloon, that's for sure."

"More like an arrow through your heart," she responded darkly.

He looked away, angry at the emotions welling up within him.

"Rob," she replied firmly, patting his hand, "you've got to find out for yourself. You need to talk it out. In person. As you say, the phone is too awkward."

He brushed tears away. "Well....he's an hour across town, and with my online classes and my job....I just haven't had a chance to visit him...."

"You're afraid....no, you're worried that she may be right?"

He struggled to answer. "I'm making excuses. I can't be evasive with you, can I...."

She nodded understandingly. "You'll do it. One of these days."

"I hope so." He shook his head. "Now…..let's get back to something more interesting..."

"What is that?"

"You. Remember?"

"Not me! I'm terminally boring. Happy family life and all that," she laughed. "Are you sure you want to hear this?" He made a face at her. "Okay….I was the apple of my parents' eyes, the darling only child for seven years, and then my twin brother and sister were born, Jason and Jacquie. So I should have been insanely jealous, right?"

"That's how it is in books."

"Actually, I loved those babies to pieces. I was my mother's right hand girl. But they're in their own world and I'm in mine. So we get along fine."

"Aimee, that's not normal. You must be from another planet."

"Ha, ha! I wasn't the typical rebellious teen, either. Guess I missed out on that too."

"Sounds too perfect." He shook his head.

"No, we're normal, not perfect. Sisterly squabbles and all that."

"I thought you got along fine…"

"We do, just the normal sister stuff. Little sister jealous of big sister, thinks she's the Queen Bee because she has privileges; big sister thinks little sister gets away with murder…she does, too! Things I was never allowed to do."

"Ha, ha. And you're the Queen Bee?"

"No," she laughed, "of course not!"

"Ah, the normal sibling rivalry. I wouldn't know because I'm an only kid."

"Our family is very close," she went on. "In some ways our family is different. My dad was a career Army man. He's retired now. We lived around the world; dad was often deployed. I respect my parents and they respect me. But I don't have to answer to them. I'm my own person, believe me."

"I can believe that," he nodded. "Do you still live with them?"

"Yes, my dog and I. We're inseparable."

"Ah....does anything come between Aimee and her dog?"

"Not so far." She shrugged her shoulders. "Who knows?" She suddenly caught sight of the clock on the wall. "Oh, my goodness! I'm half an hour late for my job! I'll be canned for sure."

Reluctantly she got up and left, giving him a quick good-bye and leaving him feeling as dazed as when she first smiled at him. *What just happened to me?* He looked at his phone.

How was I smart enough to get her number, he asked himself. *Or did she suggest we exchange numbers? When can I see her again?*

"I forgot something." He looked up to see her standing there smiling at him. She put her hand on his shoulder and placed a kiss lightly on his cheek. "Bye now!" With that, she was gone.

Shaken, he asked himself, *what is happening to me?* Twice in the past month his quiet life had been interrupted by the bright burst of fireworks; first, the revelation that his favorite patient Mr. Douglas was in fact his grandfather, now, meeting this beautiful girl he felt he had been waiting for all his life, who seemed to understand him better than he understood himself, who brought out the best in him. And he wanted only the best for her. *How can this be?*

He knew his life would never be the same.

Chapter 4

A couple of days later they met again for lunch, early enough that they could spend as much time as possible together before Aimee went to work.

"Wow – I almost didn't recognize you! Your hair...." Dark curls framed her face and fell softly over her shoulders. He hadn't noticed her hair before. He guessed it had been pulled back or pinned up. "You should wear it that way all the time," he said approvingly.

"I don't think so," she shook her head. "Not when I'm working out, or on the job. Not in the summer. Usually just special occasions."

"Then this is a special occasion." Their eyes met. "Well, Aimee," he smiled disarmingly, "if I make every occasion a special occasion.....you'll have to wear it that way every time you're with me."

"Oh, Rob..." She was flustered in spite of herself. "You've got me there."

He took her hand and kissed it. "Just be sure to get it all pinned back before you go to work, right?" He smiled at her and her heart refused to behave.

"Yes....of course," she replied, regaining her composure.

"Thanks for getting food," he nodded, "more time for us. Now, what happened when you went to work? You said you didn't get fired."

"No, by some stroke of luck! I practically had to promise my first-born to the manager, and he ever so kindly let me do all the dirty work that night. Ugh! But at least I have my job."

They talked, they listened, sharing their interests and dreams. She told about her Master's program in History. "It's not calculated to make me rich," she acknowledged, "or even find me a job."

"But you must love it or you wouldn't be doing it...?"

"That's true! I want to make history come alive for children so they can love it as much as I do."

"Kids will be lucky to have you as a teacher! My teachers seemed to go out of their way to make history boring. Then, a few years ago I picked up a biography and I enjoyed it so much, I was hooked!" He laughed. "Now I'm always learning something new."

"Too bad I couldn't have taught you back then. You would have loved it." She spoke earnestly and without any flirtatiousness.

"Well, Aimee....you're the teacher and I'm the student. I think we could learn a lot together," he replied, flirting shamelessly.

"What do you want to learn?" she laughed. "I love to teach. Now – I know you're a med student. How did that happen? Where do you want to go with this?"

"I've always been interested in medicine. In science. I like older people. I've learned not to call them '*the elderly*' – they don't like that. Nobody's elderly anymore. I also feel drawn to the military, to the Marines." He had told her about his father.

"Interesting....you might work with aging Marines. My mom does, she's a nurse at the V.A., a psychiatric nurse."

"Hey, that's neat."

"You might do that. Psychiatry."

"Nah, that's not me. I'm hands-on, not a head-doctor."

"Hmm, strange are the mysteries of life. You might decide on pediatrics."

"Well…." he reflected, "you may have called that one. We'll have to see."

She had to leave for work. He insisted she allow herself plenty of time, earlier than she thought necessary, but he warned, "You can't be late, you won't get a second chance," as they left the restaurant. Taking her arm he led her to the side, took her in his arms and gave her a tender kiss. "Aimee," he said, kissing her again, "you're the first girl I ever kissed."

"Umm…." she murmured, yielding to his embrace, "you're doing fine…."

"Yes," he said, brushing her hair from her face. "But I need practice…lots of practice!" as he kissed her again.

"Well….Rob…." she kissed him in reply, "practice makes perfect…." She pulled back. "You're pretty clever, you know –"

He grinned. "You like my surprise?"

She nuzzled her face against his, ending with a kiss.

"Sweetheart…." He kissed her face. "Happy, Aimee?"

"Mmm….yes…."

"You need to get to work," he whispered in her ear, kissing her again.

"I need to get to work," she replied, not leaving his arms.

"Yes, you do." He pulled away. "You can't be late. Aimee, I don't want you to be late." He loved saying her name. Letting go, he gave her one last kiss. "Here, take this with you."

"Rob, goodbye…." She turned to go to her car.

"Don't forget to put your hair back up," he called as she got into her car.

She sat behind the wheel trying to compose herself. *What is happening to me? Am I ready for this?*

Rob watched her drive out of sight, scarcely able to contain his joy, then turned and walked back to his apartment. Not until then did he realize he'd driven to the restaurant. His car was still in the parking lot.

He texted her later that day. '*Come run with me.*'

'*Where 2?*' she texted back.

'*Another planet. Meet at the campus track, 9 AM?*'

The next morning they had a vigorous run, then ran hand in hand to a large tree near the track where they tumbled to the ground laughing, leaning back against a tree. He wrapped her in a hug.

"Rob, sweetheart, you are –" He stopped her mouth with a kiss. "Um…." she welcomed his kiss. Breaking away, she patted his face. "No more, not now. I want to talk a while, and you said you need to study before you go to work."

"Right, I do," he agreed, "but one last kiss…." He settled back against the tree, pulling her close to him. "Now, you wanted to talk."

"I was wondering, have you heard anything more from your mother, since she showed up at your apartment that day?"

"Ah, Mom." He shook his head. "Not my favorite subject. But you deserve to know."

Aimee nodded sympathetically. "The answer is no, I haven't heard from her. And that's fine with me," he declared. "I used to tell Gramps I didn't care if I saw her or not, but now," he said with rising intensity, "I don't want to have anything to do with her, ever!"

"Not ever? Why now? "

"Ever since she said what she did about Gramps!" he said, clenching and unclenching his fists. "She sowed seeds of suspicion and doubt about him. I can't think of anything good that's ever happened when my mother was involved. Why should it be different now?"

"Yes….she sounds like trouble." She held his hands, comforting him. "Hmm, you said she'd been drinking. Is she an alcoholic? Does she have a problem with drinking?"

"Well, she can't live without alcohol," he said grimly. "And that's a problem, definitely."

"Yes, that would mean she's an alcoholic. It explains a lot," she replied with a knowing nod.

"You seem pretty well informed. How do you know, if you don't mind my asking?"

"That's okay," she shrugged. "I do know a lot, but only indirectly. My Gram, who used to take care of us, used to be a drinker, but not when I knew her. She'd been sober for a long time. Now, let's not talk about your mom anymore. Honey..." she looked at him, "what's happening with your grandfather? Are you still talking to him on the phone?"

"Yes....we still talk. And no, I haven't visited him. I will when I'm ready." Lips tight, he swallowed hard and looked into the distance.

"I see," she replied sympathetically. *Better not go there*, she thought. "Well then.....what about your other grandparents, the ones who raised you? What were they like?"

He shook his head, frowning. "I....I can't. I don't want to –" He took a deep breath. "It's hard to talk about."

Two painful subjects already. I should quit now, she told herself. *But he needs to talk*. She smiled invitingly. "Will you tell me about them? I'd love to hear."

She looked deeply into his eyes as he struggled with his emotions. "All right," he began slowly. He paused to frame his thoughts. "Grandpa and Grandma Ferguson. They got custody of me when I was about six, after I was taken from my mother." He nodded slowly as he began to remember. "They were good people. They gave me a happy home. My great-grandma, I called her Granny, lived with us for years. I was very close to her....then she passed away." He stopped. "Are you sure you're interested in all this?"

"I wouldn't have asked you if I weren't," she replied, holding his hands tightly.

"I don't want to bore you with my life story." He didn't want to tell his life story.

"No, go on. I'm interested. I want to know you."

"Okay....just for you." He sighed and thought for a minute. "I lived at home for my first couple of years of college. That was good because I could do stuff, track and band and orchestra. I didn't have to work. I never expected that to end." He stopped and took a deep breath. "I never expected to lose them." She looked at him with sympathy. "An auto accident, head-on collision, and they were gone, just like that! A drunk driver. My grandpa, he was like a dad to me." He turned away, head in his hands. "I can't talk about it. Not yet."

"Oh Rob....how awful." Tears filled her eyes. She put her arms around him, stroking his back. As he regained his composure she squeezed his hand. "Losing someone you love, suddenly....I know how hard it can be. I lost my Gram about a year ago and it's still hard to talk about. It's not the same, it's not as bad but....I know the pain."

He nodded gratefully. "Thanks."

"So....was that the end of your carefree life?"

He was silent a minute. It helped, talking to her. "Hmph! My carefree life. Yes, that was the end, all right. It was my growing up. I lost them – the only people in the world who loved me – and I lost my home. That was a hard loss too. No place to go back to. I had to find my own place, get a job, be independent. So now....I think I've done pretty well."

"I think you have too. But Rob, you make it sound easy. Was it really?"

"Well, no." He stared off into space, re-living it all. "No, it was difficult. Incredibly difficult. I can't believe I lived through it." He shook his head. "The family next door, the Brannigans – I'd known them all my life – they took me in. I couldn't stay in my house alone. I couldn't do it. They helped me get on my feet, make decisions. Like – selling the house. I didn't want to but I couldn't live there, it was all I could do to go in there –" He stopped, overcome, head in his hands.

"Oh, Rob," she said with feeling, wrapping her arms around him. "I am so sorry. I am so sorry."

He was undone. He struggled to hold back tears, angry at himself. "You know, I've never told this to anybody! I feel like an idiot." His shoulders heaved with sobs as his tears flowed freely.

"You're not an idiot to me," she whispered, waiting until he was able to speak. "I'm glad you could tell me."

Wiping his eyes on his arm he went on. "So, the Brannigans, they helped me get established, sell the house – my grandparents had left it to me, it's paying for my education. I decided I had to work to pay my expenses. They taught me everything I needed to know – except cooking, I've always cooked. Well, it's been almost two years. I'm doing fine now." He nodded with satisfaction.

"Yes, yes, you are!" She held his hands tightly. "You know, Rob, I don't do pity. Nobody's a victim. We play the cards we're dealt – but you are amazing!" Lots of people in your situation would have given up." Looking at him closely she asked, "What kept you going? Did you ever consider giving up?"

He looked away. "No. No, I never considered it. Why," he shrugged, "I don't know." He thought about it. "I grew up with family stories of pioneers, immigrant ancestors who left family behind and came here to start a new life. With a legacy like that, I couldn't let them down. I always wanted to make something of my life, to live up to my ancestors. And now, to my grandparents."

"What a story! That shows the power of history, to inspire a person."

"Well, well, the history major speaking!" he laughed. "I hadn't thought about it that way, but you're right. Also, I remember Grandpa saying, '*where there's life, there's hope*'. I always felt as long as I have my life I have hope." He stared straight ahead nodding his head. "Looking back I think I was pretty lucky, because I haven't needed any student loans. It won't last forever. Pretty soon I'll be in hock up to my teeth."

"Yes, you are lucky. It's not my business, but wouldn't your mother have inherited the house?"

"My grandparents were too smart for that. I think there's a trust fund for her, but she has to be sober for a while. That's not likely. Actually, it was a surprise to me, inheriting the house."

"They were wise people. You deserve to benefit. Rob, what about the Brannigans? Do they keep in touch?"

"Yes, they used to have me for holiday dinners, but not lately, he died last Christmas and she moved out of State to be near the kids. They're all grown and far away."

"My goodness, more losses!" He shrugged his shoulders. "Rob, I have a strange thought. I never would have wanted your grandparents to die. But if they hadn't, then you wouldn't have gone to work at Sunset Gardens, and you wouldn't have met your grandpa."

"Or you! Yes...." he frowned, "good things can come out of bad, but why do bad things have to happen first?"

"Oh, Rob. Strange are the mysteries of the universe."

"Now, Aimee." He put his arm around her, ready to change the subject. "It's time for a much more interesting subject. You." She frowned. "Remember?"

"Oh, Rob, you remember. I'm terminally boring! I could tell my life story in one minute. I've told you most of it, already."

"Well, go ahead." He smiled encouragingly. "Here I am, listening, full attention."

She shook her head and laughed. "If you insist....okay. I grew up in Germany and France where Dad was stationed. He was deployed, saw some combat. That made us closer, we were concerned for him, we learned to depend on each other. Then, when he came home we were a whole family again. It was wonderful....though sometimes it took a while for him to adjust. I went to school on base but then for high school I went to a school in town. A little German town. Whenever we could, we traveled all over Europe, camping, or staying in hostels. It was a great life."

"That sounds like fun! You must have great stories to tell –"

"Oh, it was, chasing my brother and sister all over Europe!" She rolled her eyes. "Aimee, the built-in nanny. But yes – it was fun. I'll tell you my stories someday, just wind me up –"

"Ha, I'll do that. So – that might have something to do with your love of history?"

"You either love it or hate it. For me, it's one great on-going story. Helps explain the present. My senior year Dad was transferred Stateside to D.C., so I went to high school in Virginia. A big switch from the German school. Talk about culture shock! Then I went to a community college for a year. Just as I was getting adjusted, we came back here, Mom and Dad's home town."

"Another community for you."

She laughed. "Well, by now I was used to adjusting. Mom kept up her nursing license all those years in Germany so she was able to get a job at the V.A. and go to school for her R.N. That's when Gram, her mom, came to live with us, to look after Jason and Jacquie. It was neat, I got to know her, and we got really close. I also got to know Dad's parents. So all at once I was rich in grandparents. But as you know," she sighed, "Gram passed away and Grandma and Grandpa Love moved to Florida."

"You've had your losses, Aimee. So that's how you understand……"

Tears filled her eyes and slipped down her cheeks. "Aimee…. honey, what is it?"

"Gram," she replied in a faint voice. "My Gram." She buried her head in her hands.

"Oh….of course." He put his arm around her and drew her head to his shoulders, kissing her hair. "Now it's my turn to comfort you."

"It was just a year ago….a heart attack….I miss her so much…"

"Of course you do."

She dried her eyes. "I feel better now. Sometimes it just…. comes over me."

"When it does, I hope I'll be there to comfort you." He held her and kissed her cheek. "By the way, your life story, that was…..um, ten minutes, maybe? One problem, though." He frowned. "It wasn't boring. Short and sweet. Very interesting."

"Good. Now, let's do another run." She grabbed his hand, giving him a peck on the cheek as they got up. "Then, study time."

"Not if you keep kissing me."

Chapter 5

They met again the next day. After their run they sat to relax under a tree. Aimee took his hands. "I couldn't sleep last night, thinking about you. What you've been through." His face clouded over and she hastened to add, "Not pity. No, it's just that, you've been through so much and done so well –"

He pulled away and looked off, his jaw set. "I didn't tell you the whole story. I can't lie to you."

"What do you mean?"

He shook his head. "I wish I could." He gave a little laugh. "Lie to you."

Gently she brought his face towards hers, then caressed his hands. She waited for him to speak.

He looked away, unable to meet her gaze. "I did so well, did I? Ha! Suppose I told you I went on a month-long drunk?" His voice rose. "Does that shock you?" He couldn't read her face.

"No, not at all," she shook her head sympathetically. "Only a month? If it had been me – I'm not a drinker, but I think I would have become one, very quickly. To ease the pain."

"Maybe six weeks, or more, I don't know. I didn't keep track, it's all a blur." He put his head in his hands. "I drank every night, so I could sleep, then drove into school the next day. I don't remember a thing."

"Dear Rob." She took his hand. "What stopped you?"

"Hmph! My friend Matt, Matt Brannigan, he came home on leave from the Army. He found the bottles. I was staying in his room. We fought about it. He ratted me out to his parents."

"Uh oh. Then what happened?"

"They sat me down, said losing two lives was bad enough, they didn't want to lose a third, not if they could help it."

"Then what?"

"They went with me to a grief group. Not a help. I didn't fit in. So they asked me to go to a counselor –"

"Sounds like a good idea."

"I didn't think so. She told me I was angry, I told her she was crazy. I went for a while to please the Brannigans, then I told them I was better and I quit."

"Were you better?"

"I told them I was. I knew I wasn't going to drink anymore. Like the Brannigans said, I owed it to my grandparents' memory to make something of my life. They'd lost so much to alcohol already –"

"Oh, yes. Your mother."

"So I just put it out of my mind. Death happens. Life goes on. For a long time I couldn't talk about them……basically, I put them out of my mind. Then along comes Aimee…." He managed a faint smile. "Hey, you're the only one I've talked to. You know, I'm starting to remember some of the good stuff – but if I start feeling bad – I just put it out of my mind."

"Not for long, I hope. Sooner or later, you have to talk about it. Now, listen here. Like I said, I don't do pity. But I still think you're wonderful. And Rob –" she smiled, nodding her head, "if you ever want to talk – you know where to find me."

"Oh, yes!" He gathered her in his arms. "Right here." He kissed the top of her head, then found her lips. His tears were on her face, to his embarrassment. He turned away.

She kissed his eyes. "These are good tears, honey. Good tears."

"Thanks, honey." He spoke almost in a whisper. "Thanks for listening to me. It does help."

"I'm glad of that." She patted his face. "Any time."

"Thank you. And thank Grandma Ferguson too."

"Grandma Ferguson? Why are you thanking her?"

He leaned back against the tree, pulling her head against his shoulder and kissing her hair. "Grandma Ferguson was a very smart lady. Shrewd."

"Well, Rob, go on. This sounds interesting."

"Don't know about that. I don't want to bore you…."

"Oh, just go ahead!"

He gave a little laugh. "Grandma taught me not to cry alone. Not to hide in my own misery. See, when I was with my mother, and I was feeling bad about something, I never talked to her or her boyfriend-of-the-month. They wouldn't have been interested, so I just kept it inside."

Aimee listened with her heart in her throat. *How terrible, how lonely for a child!*

"When I went to live with Grandma and Grandpa Ferguson, they were strangers. I sure wasn't going to talk to them. So when something bad happened, like at school, I would go to a spot in the living room against the wall and sit on the floor, my head on my knees, my arms wrapped around my legs, curled up in a ball. Grandma would come over, all sweet and mothery and ask me what was wrong. I'd tell her, '*go away, go away!*' And she did, until one time she wouldn't take no for an answer. I don't know how she did it, but she got me onto the couch – ha, I was a big kid –"

She slid on to the grass in front of him, holding his hands, studying his face.

"She put her arms around me, rocking me, rubbing my back, and she said we would stay there until I could talk about what was wrong. Finally I did, I probably cried a little, but I remember that I talked with her and I felt a lot better. She told me if I was feeling bad about something I should always talk to someone I loved. She said when I was miserable it made her feel bad too but if we talked it could get better. So that was the end of my '*misery spot*' on the floor, and she was right, I did feel better."

"Wow," Aimee exclaimed, quietly, "she was one smart woman."

"Yes, she was, but I got back at her," he said with a sly look. Aimee looked at him with curiosity. "One day I saw her crying in the kitchen. I told her she should talk to me. She said it was a grown- up matter, she couldn't tell me. So I said, *okay then, if you won't talk to me you have to talk to Grandpa.*"

"Ah, ha. Smart kid, weren't you!"

"I think she was crying about my mother."

"I can believe it." She put her arm around him, then whispered in his ear, "Robbie, you can talk to me any time."

"Yes, Grandma."

They held each other, then she pulled him up. "Let's do another run."

"Yeah! I need it."

They were enjoying the morning runs, going out almost every day. With Aimee working the afternoon shift and Rob working late at night, this was their best chance to be together. Sometimes they ran the campus track, sometimes in the city park.

"Why won't you come to my place to clean up before work?" he asked one day. "The offer's always open."

"Thanks but no thanks. Not to change, anyway. Rob, your apartment is so small we'd fall all over each other," she laughed. He'd shown her his place one day when she had driven him home.

"That's not such a bad idea," he said with a devilish grin.

"The campus gym is fine with me," she laughed. "Thanks anyway."

They went to Aimee's work place for lunch. "I had stopped eating lunch here," she told him.

"Ha! And you work here. Do you know something we don't?"

"No, nothing sinister! I was eating at a different place every few days. I was looking for you, to meet you, after I read about you in the paper," she confessed with a laugh. "I figured a man has to eat....and just maybe I'd run into you."

"Seriously? And here I thought it was coincidence that you recognized me...and you knew my name, too." He frowned and shook his head but he was flattered. "How many weeks did you do this?"

"A couple of weeks. I lucked out, I met you on my fourth fast food place. My family thought I was crazy," she laughed, "but I had the last laugh."

"We both did," he said, taking her hand. "You know, that is strange. Really strange. I don't normally eat out. That day was the first time in months I'd eaten at a fast food place. I just happened to be there on the day you were there…."

"It must be fate! But I don't believe in fate. Now, tell me something. Am I really the first girl you've ever been serious about?"

"Well, my embarrassing secret is, you're the only one. The only girl I've ever gone out with."

"I would never have thought that. A handsome guy like you."

"But Aimee, the class nerd never gets the girl."

"You? A nerd?"

"Yes. And proud of it."

"That's okay, you're the nicest nerd I know! And you got me. My dad says I'm a force to be reckoned with."

"I'll say you are!" he said approvingly.

"Rob, you mean to tell me no girl has ever tried to get her hands on you? Chased after you?"

"Ha, ha – girls like that turn me off."

"You can't be flattered, huh?" He shrugged. "Now you've got a girl who chased after you – what do you say to that?"

"You hypnotized me," he laughed as he kissed her hand, looking deeply into her eyes. "How else would we have met?" He shook his head. "I hate to admit it, but I was scared around girls. Except as friends."

"I don't get it. What's the difference?"

"Well…." He thought about it. "I've had friends who are girls, but not girlfriends. Not by choice, exactly. I just never met any girl who interested me….until you."

"I'm glad you were scared around girls. It kept you from being stupid around girls."

"Give me credit, Aimee. That's a game I didn't want to learn, that phony stuff. I could have if I'd wanted to."

"That's one reason why I love you," she declared. "You know what you want….and what you don't want."

"What scared me was, I thought most girls expected that…. that game playing."

"I couldn't say. But I'm not '*most girls*'."

"And that's exactly why I love you!" he exclaimed.

"Isn't it amazing that we found each other?" She took hold of his hands.

"With a little help from you. Hmm," he said, holding on to her hands, "You don't want to eat, do you?"

"We could feed each other." Holding each other's hands, they tried it.

Then, "Nope!" he said, putting her hands down. "A man's gotta eat. As you said."

A few days later they took their lunch to a nearby park where they found a bench beside a small pond where ducks and geese swam serenely.

"Rob," she began tentatively, "how are things going with you, your memories of your grandparents? You know what I mean."

"Oh –" his lips tightened, "I'm managing."

"Is that good or bad?" She took his hand in her hands.

"Well….I'm thinking of them now, which is good, I guess. Good memories." She smiled in agreement as she stroked his hand. "But at nighttime, it used to be I'd fall asleep as soon as my head hit the pillow. Now I find myself pounding the pillow asking *'why?' why?'* " he shook his head, "that's stupid. Really stupid."

"Oh, baby –" she brought his face to hers.

"I tell myself, '*Grow up, Carlyle. They're gone, get over it,*' he said bitterly. *'Remember the good times.*"

"That's right, Rob. That's all you can do. That's all anybody can do," she said in a pained tone. "I don't have any answers…. but, I think it's good that you're facing it."

"Probably. I have to sooner or later. So I tell myself."

"You don't blame me?" she laughed, anxiously.

"No, of course not," he kissed her cheek, "You mean well. Someday I'll thank you."

"That's something to look forward to. Honey," she asked brightly, "do you have any pictures of them?"

"Not to look at." She looked puzzled. "I have a good picture. It's in my box of important papers. I – I haven't been able to look at it," he admitted. "But now...." He thought about it, "maybe I will."

"Suppose you bring it to me tomorrow?" she asked eagerly. "They're part of you, I want to see them."

"Oh, baby...." He squeezed her hand. "You put me on the spot, don't you!"

"Is it framed?" He shook his head no. "Well, then, we could get a nice frame – and you can put it on your nightstand –"

He laughed and held her. "Aimee, what am I going to do with you?" He kissed her hair. "You know how to get what you want! And make me want to do it. But that's okay, I love you for it," he said with a shrug. "You're not doing it for yourself."

"Oh, Rob. I know it's hard for you, I do. But I can't wait to see their picture! Oh....would you believe it's almost time for me to get to work."

"You can drop me off at the library. I've a ton of studying to do."

She took his hand. "Let's have a run!"

As she dropped him off and headed the car to work she thought, *That turned out well. But what about his other grandpa? How long is he going to put him off?*

Chapter 6

Another day….

"So, when did you know you were in love with me?" she asked, teasingly.

"When you looked at me! That first time, in line."

"That soon? Rob, that's not possible," she laughed.

"That's what my buddy Bryan said; he said that was very '*junior high*'. He said I was a late starter and I'd feel that way a hundred times before I settled down."

"Some buddy he is! I hope you don't feel that way about anybody else." She seized his arm possessively.

"Only with you, Aimee. Every time you look at me, you hypnotize me. So, what about you?"

"Oh….I took a lot longer. The day we met, when I went into work late my boss said, '*What happened to you? You're an hour late!*" I told him I'd just met the man of my dreams –"

What she really said was that she had just met the man she was going to marry.

" '*The man of my dreams*', huh? I like that!" He laughed and rolled his eyes. " '*A lot longer?*' " he repeated.

"And he rolled his eyes and said, '*Wonderful. Then you don't need a job.*' I had to talk fast to get him to keep me."

"So you knew then?" His voice was stern but he was smiling. "You sure made it rough for me. I didn't know where I stood with you."

"How did I make it rough?" she gave a quizzical look. "You know I love you!"

"That kiss! The day we met. It seems like that's all I'm going to get from you."

"I don't know what you mean." She shrugged. "You've gotten more than that. But that kiss…." she took his hand, "I felt I had to go back and let you know I liked you."

"I loved it! But Aimee, it was a promise but no delivery. I suffered – for a long time! I didn't know where I stood with you." He shook his head with exasperation, squeezing her hand.

"Make you suffer?" she asked, tenderly. "Rob – how?"

"How can I believe you're in love with me? You keep me at arm's length. You're still keeping me at arm's length. You won't spend the night with me, you won't even eat lunch at my apartment…." *with a little fun afterward before we have to go to work*, he told himself. "What am I to think? Are you playing games with me? I don't want to think that."

"Honey, I've been clear from the beginning. You know that. I'm not playing games. Rob, I'm an all-or-nothing woman. We've talked about it. It's marriage or nothing at all."

"Marriage? But why?" he asked, perplexed. "I still don't understand. You haven't really said why. Why not just move in with me? Or spend a night once in a while? I'm not ready to get married. Not now, not yet." He shook his head… *I didn't expect this!* "Honey, we love each other! We need to live together to find out if we're compatible, before we even talk about marriage."

"No, Rob. It's marriage I want. If we lived together, why would we ever want to get married?"

"Maybe we wouldn't. But why marriage? What's so special about marriage?"

"I'm not exactly sure," she said with a half laugh. "I just know it is."

"Now, Aimee," he nodded seriously, "that's a tough argument to answer."

"Okay, okay," she laughed. "There's a permanence to marriage."

"Permanence? You've got to be kidding!"

"Sure, marriages fail. But people usually take marriage more seriously than living together."

"Sometimes they do, sometimes they don't."

" 'Living together' is casual, trial and error," she went on earnestly. "You know that. I'd never relax. I would always be wondering, *is this going to last?* Rob, what do people do when things don't work out? They just go find somebody else. In fact –" she stopped as a new thought occurred to her. "You know what they're doing? They're preparing for divorce."

"How is that?" he asked skeptically.

"Most people, when they're living together and it doesn't work out, they just give up, call it quits. Now what kind of preparation is that for marriage, learning how to make it work?"

"Okay....you've got a point, but that wouldn't happen to us. We'd stick with it and make it work, because we love each other!"

She looked deeply into his eyes, nodding slowly. "I agree. I think we would try to work out our problems –"

"So!" He seized her hands, smiling.

"No." She shook her head. "No. Rob, if we're that sure of each other, why not get married? Honey, I want the permanence of marriage! People are more likely to work at marriage. Usually. And when I get married," she looked at him pleadingly, "I want to be sure. Ready – ready to make it work."

He shrugged his shoulders and shook his head. "I don't know, honey. Look, we're going around in circles!" *I don't want to fight,* he thought. *I don't agree with her but I love her.*

Enough of this, Aimee thought, *this is not something to argue about*. She patted his hand. "I don't want to argue. How about a change of subject?"

"Fine with me," he replied, relieved.

"I was wondering....what does your buddy Bryan say about your weird girlfriend?"

"Oh, oh...." he laughed as he considered what to tell her, "you don't want to hear!"

"Some friend he is."

"Look, Bryan's a good guy. He and I have been best friends for, like, a dozen years. He's faithful to his girlfriend –"

"Glad to hear it. So he's not a '*player*'."

"No he's not. He and Natasha have been together for a couple of years. I'm the odd man out, so I don't see the two of them very much, just when she picks him up at the gym on Saturdays after we play racquetball. And we used to watch Monday night football together."

"So what does he say about us? Maybe we could get together. As couples."

"Well....about you. He said he was glad I had finally found a girl friend."

"Good man."

"Beautiful and brainy."

"Okay...." She smiled and nodded her head.

"He said I should respect your convictions."

"Yes! Good man."

"He said I shouldn't try to persuade you to do something you're not ready for."

"I don't know about that. Forget the '*not ready*' part."

"Then he said, '*Too bad, Rob, you'll just have to suffer.*' "

"That doesn't sound too bad. Now, Rob, you're not the odd man anymore. Why don't we go out together?"

"We could do that. I'd like you to get to know him. I'm sure you'll like him."

"He's a friend of yours. I'm sure I will."

He smiled in agreement. But he hadn't wanted to tell her his actual conversation with Bryan.

"Hey, man, I'm glad you finally found yourself a girlfriend. She's beautiful too, so I hear. Now how did you, Rob Carlyle, manage that? Did you hypnotize her?"

"Actually, I think she hypnotized me. But I'm not complaining," he said with a grin.

"Okay, when are you moving in with her? Or she with you? In your tiny little apartment you two should just fit. Hand in glove."

"Ha – that's not going to happen." He tried to put Aimee's ideas in as favorable a light as possible.

"Good grief, man, couldn't you have found yourself a friendlier girl? Oh, I forgot, she found you and hypnotized you. I can believe it."

'Look, Bryan, Aimee's the girl I want. She's everything I want.'

"Well, sooner or later she'll change her mind. They all do. In the meantime you'll just have to accept her ideas, if you care about her as much as you say you do. Maybe she's not ready. You have to, you know, make her ready. I can help you."

"Bryan, no, forget that. I'm not trying to change her mind. But – it's rough."

"Don't be a fool. If she doesn't change her mind, lose her. I would if I were you, it's a dead end. In the meantime you'll just have to suffer!"

"Thanks a ton, Bryan! See you next week."

'Suffer?' Oh, yes, he was suffering. *Love is supposed to make you happy,* he told himself. *Well, I'm happy when I'm with her and miserable when we're apart! Why can't I be with her all the time? She fills my thoughts during the day and my dreams at night. It's a good thing I didn't meet her when I was at school, I'd be Rob Carlyle, college flunk-out....*

"Rob, where are you?" She snapped her fingers. "Earth to Rob...."

"Oh – I was thinking things through....Look, honey, I won't try to talk you out of your convictions." She smiled in appreciation. "That's who you are. Believe it or not, that's one thing I love about you. You're a strong person." He put his arm around her, drawing her to himself. "I'm curious, though....does anyone else think like you do?" He laughed. "Weird?"

"Oh....yes. My good friend Julie, Julie Prescott. You met her last week. I'm going to be in her wedding later this summer, you know. Also – some girls online, a chat group."

"So you're not the only weird one in the world! I wonder what her fiance thinks about this, what's his name, Zach?"

"Yes, Zach Carter. He didn't understand at first. But he loves Julie and he respects her. They're committed to each other. But hey, you can ask him yourself. Remember, we're going out next week, the four of us."

"Oh, yes, the Comedy Club. Okay, I'll talk to him then." He gave a sly laugh. "Zach and I, we'll just, uh, disappear. But watch out, your ears will be burning! Both of you. I'll see what he has to say about our '*weird girlfriends*'."

"You do that. Honey….." she took his hand, "remember this. Aimee may give you the cold shoulder now and then, but…." she smiled affectionately, "Aimee isn't cold."

"I hope to find out someday," he said resolutely.

"I hope you do! Now," as they said their goodbyes to each other, "time to get back to the real world…."

Frustrated, confused, disappointed, Rob considered his situation. *How ironic is this? I waited so long for a girlfriend, and now I've found her! We're so right for each other – and she keeps me at arms' length! Well almost,* he admitted. *What's wrong with a night or two together or moving in together? If it doesn't work out, well, then we move on. Find somebody else, until we find the 'right person'. But that wouldn't happen to us, we love each other,* he told himself. *We would make it work. She's right about the apartment, though; it's so small we'd fall all over each other. If we lived together we'd get a larger place and I'd pay for it.*

He envied Bryan and Natasha's comfortable, convenient life together. *They're doing it right. Why not Aimee and I? But no, it's not going to happen! When I'm with her I understand her reasoning, it kind of makes sense, but when we're apart it seems so unfair. Even so…..I have to respect her convictions. It's all very frustrating.*

The next day they relaxed on a bench after their run and fed each other strawberries Aimee had brought from home.

"Um, delicious! And so are you," he said. "Tell your mother she grows very good strawberries. And a beautiful daughter," he laughed. "Seriously now, not to dispute anything you said yesterday, but all those dire warnings about living together, they wouldn't apply to us. We love each other. So why not?"

"Rob, darling, I think you didn't hear me. It's marriage or nothing. We need to keep the brakes on." She patted his face. "You've been good about that. So, even if you don't agree with my point of view –"

"Right," he nodded slowly, "I'll honor your wishes."

"Good! Now, another thing. There's the 'B' word to consider."

" '*B*' word? What are you talking about? I would never call you that. Don't even think it!"

She laughed. "Oh, no! It's '*Baby*'. I don't want an accidental baby."

"Ha, ha! Not a problem, honey," he assured her. "Birth control."

"No, Rob," she shook her head. "It's unreliable."

"It works for Bryan and his girlfriend."

"Well, every girl I know who got pregnant was using birth control. I don't want to take that chance."

"If we had a baby we'd manage," he said.

"Oh, this from the man who's not ready to get married! And we'd '*manage'?"*

"Of course we would."

"Rob, no. I don't want to just *'manage'*. A baby deserves better than that. I want my baby born into a home with a mom and dad who are committed to each other, who are used to being husband and wife."

"We'd make it work," he insisted.

"Oh, honey." Taking his hands, she looked searchingly at him. "Suppose it didn't work out? After all, we don't know each other that well. Who knows whether we're really committed to each other? Suppose one of us finds someone else –" he shook his head in objection –"but we already had a baby? Then what?" She shook her head. "Baby gets split between us. Baby gets a new daddy, a new mommy. Maybe two or three in a row. Baby gets confused. I've seen it many times. Friends of mine. How can I do that to an innocent child?"

"I know," he looked down, "that was my life. I had too many '*dads*' who weren't dads at all."

"That's so sad. You know, my mother's life was like that," she said soberly. "Chaotic. She never knew her father and she didn't like the men her mother brought home. She's told me about it. It's like – nobody thinks of the child."

"Honey, that wouldn't happen to us. I know it wouldn't," he persisted.

"Who knows? If we had a baby and then split up, who knows what would happen to it?"

"It wouldn't happen to us! But that happens in marriage too. Divorce, baby in the middle."

"Yes, I know. But less often. Especially if people are ready to get married. Committed to each other." Taking his hands she summed things up. "Rob….my parents gave me a gift! They gave me stability and two parents who love each other," she said passionately. "I'm a rare breed among my friends. That's what I want to give my child. So, if it means not making babies until I'm married, so be it."

"All right...." he conceded, nodding his head, "if that's your belief…." He shrugged.

"Look – if I create a life, even accidentally, doesn't it deserve the best possible chance? Don't I owe the baby that much?"

"If you bring it into the world, yes….but that would be your choice."

"No, Rob, I don't want to have to choose, I don't want to be in that position –" She looked at him imploringly. "Somebody has to think of the baby! Rob – I want my baby to have the best. That means a mom and a dad. Married." She smiled. "Happily married."

"Well, I can't argue with that." He put his arm around her and looked deeply into her eyes. "My sweet Aimee. You are one of a kind! And I love you for it."

Chapter 7

"That was some discussion you guys were having," Aimee remarked the next week at the Comedy Club. "Or were you just enjoying the bar?"

"The bar, definitely," Rob replied with a wink. "But we came back for the food. Wouldn't want it to get cold."

"Not to worry! We weren't going to let it get cold," she told him sweetly. "We'll eat it for you."

He grinned as he snatched the plate from her.

"So," Julie began coyly, "what did you decide? About us?"

"There's no doubt about it," Zach began as he gave a nod to Rob, "you two are the weirdest girls on the planet. But –"

Rob finished the thought, "we decided we'd keep you."

"Keep us?" Aimee's eyes opened wide as she shook her head at Julie.

"Keep us?" Julie echoed. "Keep us where? On a shelf?"

"In a closet?" Aimee continued, frowning.

Rob nodded seriously, lifting an eyebrow to Zach. "Maybe a box. We haven't decided yet."

"Hmph!" exclaimed Julie. She looked at Aimee. "Do we want to hear more?"

"I have a conclusion of my own," Aimee replied to Julie, nodding her head. "I think we have the two nicest guys in the world. Should we keep them?" She shrugged.

"We'll have to think about it," Julie replied, sidling closer to Zach. "Of course, '*nice*' doesn't sell magazines."

Aimee nodded in agreement. "But why would I want some magazine hunk when I have Rob?" She put her arm in his and gave him a kiss on the cheek.

"Um, yes!" He returned her kiss. "But – what's a '*nice guy*' anyway? Girls don't like '*nice guys*'. I hear that all the time."

"Obviously.... some do," replied Julie with a smile at Zach.

"They just say that to justify being jerks," Aimee explained. "I'll tell you what a '*nice guy*' is. Someone who treats me like an equal. With respect."

"Someone who appreciates that I'm a female. A woman," Julie continued. Not '*one of the boys*'.

"*Vive la difference!*" exclaimed Rob, smiling at Aimee.

"Right!" agreed Aimee, giving him an appreciative glance.

"Most guys are just sizing us up," Julie went on. "Looking us over to decide how they can get what they want. That is so insulting."

"If a girl is looking for that, fine for her," Aimee added. "Then it's just a matter of negotiation."

"I want a man who respects me as a person, with manners and courtesy, who respects my convictions –" Julie began.

"Yes," Aimee broke in, "who lets me treat him as a man. Who respects him. As a man."

She looked meaningfully at Rob.

"Now you're hitting on a sore spot," said Zach with a frown. "Men seem to be an endangered species. Like – listening to that comedian tonight –"

"Oh, you mean the rapper who calls herself a comedian?" Aimee asked.

"Ms. '*potty mouth*'?" Julie added.

"That too," Aimee continued. "She's a man-hater, that's obvious."

"Well, I'm here to stand up for men," Julie stated.

"Right," Aimee agreed, nodding to Julie, "men are not the enemy. We need to respect men, not try to change them. We think differently. After all, we come from different planets, don't we?"

"True enough," Julie replied, smiling warmly at Zach. "Men and women need each other. Like two halves of a heart."

"Ah, now you're getting sentimental," joked Rob.

" '*Need each other*'? Isn't that a bit extreme?" Aimee asked. "My mother always told me I had to learn to make it without a man. But....thinking about it....maybe you're right. In a different way....

"On an emotional level," explained Julie. "A man completes a woman, gives satisfaction as a husband, father, friend –" She took Zach's hand. "And a woman completes a man."

Aimee nodded thoughtfully. "I see that with my mother and father. I think that's why I appreciate Rob, as a man. Even though I know I can make it on my own."

"I'm glad to hear that," Rob agreed warmly.

"Aimee's right, men need women, too," Julie went on.

"You've given this a lot of thought, haven't you," Rob said.

"Yes, I have. A lot of personal observation. I notice when a man marries and is serious about it, his priorities change. He stops being a playboy. A woman can bring out the best in a man –"

"Or the worst," Aimee broke in. "It has to be the right woman."

"A good woman," Rob agreed, putting his arm around Aimee.

"Well, that rapper tonight –" Aimee waved her hand for emphasis, "she has a point, you know."

"Say, whose side are you on?" Rob asked, raising his eyebrows.

"A lot of men are jerks. Worthless. It's true, ask any woman," she continued.

"And why?" asked Julie. "Their mothers spoil them. A lot of them don't have fathers to look up to and their girlfriends let them get away with anything. No wonder they're irresponsible."

"See, it's not our fault," Rob laughed, "women are to blame!"

"Ha, ha," Julie replied. "But responsibility, it has to be taught. So often, it isn't."

"I've heard my father talk to my brother," Aimee reflected. "He's very strong about men treating women with respect."

"And you saw that in Rob," Julie said.

"Yes I did," she nodded. "Now – getting back to that rapper. She must have had bad experiences with men. So why take it out on all men? That doesn't help."

"It helps her," Rob declared. "She's laughing all the way to the bank."

"Oh, yeah," Zach agreed grimly. "You know, if a man talked that way about a woman he'd be destroyed. But people thought she was hilarious."

"I wasn't laughing," Aimee retorted. "Neither was Julie."

"I noticed," Rob nodded. "Thanks, honey."

"It's a double standard. And it's not respectful. I should have walked out." The others looked surprised. "Well, yes. My mom would have, and dad with her. They're right. I believe in standing up for my convictions."

"Ah, yes. Your convictions. That's what we were talking about earlier, wasn't it?" Rob reminded them.

"My weird convictions. Well.....are you with me, honey?"

"Aimee – honey – I respect your convictions. Do I agree?" He gestured helplessly. "Give me time."

"That's okay with me." She took his hand. "I understand. I can wait."

As they were getting up to leave, Zach took Rob aside. "A word of advice, man. You love her? Don't fight her."

Rob was silent. *I love Aimee, I do. But I'm not ready to get married. So where does that leave me?*

"I really am weird, honey," she told him the next day as they brought their food to the booth. "It's not a joke."

"That's okay." He patted her hand, nodding. "I like my women weird."

"Oh, you do?" she replied archly. "I'll be sure to find a really weird one to take over when you're done with me."

"Not gonna happen," he countered. "You're the only woman I want."

She smiled. "What I mean is, I'm out of the mainstream. That's the way I want it. It's my choice."

"That's not so terrible."

"You know how water rushes over the rapids before it becomes a waterfall? Like Niagara Falls?" He nodded. "Well, that's where the mainstream is headed. That's not where I want to go. So – I'm going upstream."

"Good for you. I'm not exactly mainstream myself."

"I tried it. The mainstream. I got my feet wet in the party scene."

"The party scene, huh? Tell me what I missed."

"My parents always told me, I don't have to try something to know it's not good for me. Like, I'm not going to try cocaine. Or even pot. What if I like it?"

"Right. I feel the same. Because of my mother."

"They used to tell me to stay away from the party scene, it's nothing but trouble. And I did, I was living at home, it wasn't too hard to say 'no', but guys kept inviting me and finally I decided, *okay, I'll go once, with a nice boy, I'll be careful.*" She shook her head. "I was curious. Not a good reason."

"And? What was it like?"

"Boring! Unbelievably boring. It was like, get drunk or stoned. Well, forget that. I could have danced all night, I love to dance, but there wasn't much dancing. Finally I thought, *I've had enough.* I looked for the boy who brought me – and he was with another girl! Very friendly with her. What a jerk."

"I'll say. He was crazy not to stay with you!"

"Yeah, right. Well, all of a sudden he was gone. Then, there were four or five boys on the prowl, drunk, heading in my direction. I knew what they wanted and I thought, *I'd better get out of here!* I grabbed my phone and called my dad and woke him up, thank God! He said he'd be there in ten minutes."

"Good for him! And you."

"Well, we lived twenty minutes away! I almost didn't find my coat. I couldn't remember which room it was in. I went in room after room, I saw more than I wanted to see. I got a real education."

"I can imagine," he laughed.

"I sure was glad to see Dad. Yes, he was there in ten minutes! In pajamas and a robe. Not even a coat, and it was winter. I told him that was the end of my party life."

"I'll say! But not the end of your social life, I'm sure."

"No. But I've done it my way."

"How was that?" he asked, intrigued.

"Oh – fewer dates, more girlfriend stuff, community work." She shrugged and smiled. "Some lonely times. That's the price I paid for being choosy. But see….I chose you." She took his hand possessively. "I have no regrets. Now, what about you? Your social life?"

"I'm a lucky man, that's what!" he exclaimed, ignoring her question. "I'm glad you were choosy." He took her hand and kissed it. "Aimee, honey, I chose you too. It may not seem that way to you but….." he looked deeply into her eyes, "I chose to stay. I don't want you to think you're some kind of default girlfriend. If I hadn't felt the way I do about you I would have dropped you by now." He remembered Bryan's words, *'If she doesn't change her mind, lose her'*. He laughed. "When you started giving me grief –" she frowned – "you know what I mean. I thought about what I wanted in a woman, with a woman….and there was no doubt about it. Aimee….darling, I chose you."

"My darling Rob…..you don't know how good that makes me feel!" She held his hand tenderly across the table. "I think we didn't choose each other at all. Fate brought us together."

"Even though you don't believe in Fate," he laughed. "I guess most couples in love feel that way."

"Hmm…..I remember when my sister Jacquie had a homework assignment to ask people the best thing that ever happened to them. She asked Mom at dinner, and Mom said it was when she married Dad. She couldn't figure out what had brought them together because they were so different, and yet they were so good for each other. It must have been Fate."

"That proves my point."

"Then she asked Dad and he said the same thing. Mom laughed and said he was just saying that because she had, and he said, *'oh, no, remember how you used to cry in the early days because things were so hard?'* Mom broke in and said, *'Yes, I thought things were never going to get any better. I don't want you kids to think marriage is always light and easy.'* And Dad said, *'You would cry, and I would tell you, just remember how much I love you.'* He said, now he knows that wasn't much help because he was part of the problem. He was spoiled and undisciplined. But he loved her, they stayed together, things did get better for them. They helped each other. It's interesting that they had the same idea, that Fate had brought them together."

"That's a neat story. It makes me want to meet your parents." He took her hands.

"You will, don't worry. As soon as we can arrange it. She withdrew her hand. "Hey, don't you want to eat? Now, I told you all about me. What about you? Your social life?"

He shook his head. "I never had the slightest interest in the party scene, I thought it was dumb. Bryan was my backup man on that. There was a group of us guys, we just hung out. We had one thing in common, we wanted to get an education, not mess up our lives. We drank beer, but we knew enough to limit ourselves. We helped each other."

"That's good. What did you do together?"

"Marathons, we called them – trivia competitions at the local pub, things like that, cards, chess, sports on TV – don't laugh! we really did."

"I'm smiling because I would enjoy that myself! Though maybe not the sports part, not a marathon. No girls, huh?"

"We were slow learners, I guess. See, I went to an all-boys school. So did Bryan. Grandpa used to tell me not to worry about it, he told me not to get into the social scene because it could mess up my life. He said when I met the right girl I would know it. He said he did, with Grandma. He was right, wasn't he!"

"He was right. I wish I could have known him."

"I wish," he sighed. "He said I ought to wait until I was at least into my residency. I figured then I might do some online dating service, because I didn't have a clue how to find a girlfriend."

"You still could," she teased, "if you're not sure."

"Hmm," he shook his head, laughing, "I'll have to think about that." He kissed her hand. "You don't have anything to worry about. But let's not talk about marriage. Not now."

"That's okay with me. What about these old friends of yours? I never hear you talk about them. Where are they now?"

"You know about Bryan. He found himself a girlfriend. Eric and Kyle, they've moved on to other schools. Ben and Joe have graduated. Actually –" He sighed. "Life changed for me after Grandma and Grandpa….um…." He looked down. "I stopped socializing."

"I guess so. Rob, you sound about as weird as me. Guess that makes us a pair, doesn't it?"

"A special pair. I never would have believed it." He took her hand in his hands, smiling warmly. "You are the special one."

"My goodness, Rob Carlyle….." She studied him. "For a guy who doesn't have any experience with girls, you do all right. You're not a shy guy at all. Am I missing something here?"

"Oh, I know how to treat a girl. My Granny saw to that. You know, if I don't treat you right, she'll rise up out of the grave and haunt me."

"Ha, ha. I'll remember that. I think you do just fine. I'm glad I'm the one to find that out."

"Did I mention Kim, and Christie, and Meg?"

"What? Who?" she asked, unbelieving.

"The girls next door. The Brannigans. We played together as kids, along with their brother Matt, and we stayed friends through high school. When I started talking with you it was just like talking with them."

" '*Just like'?"* she echoed, wrinkling her face.

"No, no, you and I are like magnets. I've never felt this way about any girl."

"I'm glad of that! What would Granny say about you wanting us to live together?"

"I know what she would say." He frowned. "Well, I'm my own person. I don't think there's anything wrong with it. But, Granny taught me to respect other people. If you say no, I've got to respect that." He looked off to the side. "Right, Granny?"

Chapter 8

They had planned a date for just the two of them, a picnic at a park on the Lake to celebrate the first month since they had met. After a canoe ride and lunch they found a bench on a bluff overlooking the lake.

"Aimee, I'm trying to understand you, your ideas, where they come from. I'm not trying to change your mind, just understand you. This isn't a religious thing with you –"

"No, I don't even believe in God. I'm not making any religious statement."

He shrugged his shoulders. "So what, then? Is it your parents? Do they influence what you do, or don't do? Would they object if you spent a night with me?"

"I'm a big girl, Rob. I make my own decisions. To be honest, they wouldn't like it but they would not interfere. They treat me like an adult." She took his hands. "Actually, it did start with something my mother said."

"So! It is your parents."

She was suddenly serious. "I've been wondering about.... what to tell you. It's very personal and private....about my mother." She looked away.

He smiled encouragingly. "You can trust me."

"Yes," she nodded. "She told me something years ago," she began slowly. "The '*mother-daughter*' talks, you know. She said she wished she and Dad had done things differently. They'd had others before they met. She wished they hadn't."

"She admitted that?" She nodded. "I'm surprised."

Aimee remembered their conversation as if it were yesterday.

"I was just entering junior high school," Mom began, *"when I gave up my virginity. It was my own idea, I was ready. After that, I gave myself to this boy and that. It was expected. Most of the other kids were doing the same. Aimee, growing up is hard enough, but this made it all the harder."*

"Gosh," Aimee replied, *"the girls say it's pretty cool."*

"Not really…it gets old. Just have them wait awhile. It plays with your emotions. I was like an emotional volleyball, up, down, and punch, punch, punch. My studies suffered, but I did get to college. There it was the party scene. And I was the number one party girl."

"Wow! That must have been fun!"

"No, Aimee, it wasn't." She dropped her head. *"It was…. degrading. And for what? Attention. A few minutes of attention from a boy, knowing that I didn't care about him and he didn't care about me. One morning I woke up with a man whose name I didn't even know. Even worse….I couldn't remember anything about the night before. It was the drugs and alcohol. Now, how cheap is that? It hit me, how cheap I had made myself. Honey, I don't want you ever to feel the way I felt that day."* She shuddered.

"Oh, Mom," she said, hugging her.

"I asked myself, what am I looking for? Up to then I would have said fun. I wanted fun, that was all that mattered. But now it left a bad taste in my mouth. And I could see, there was no future for me."

"It was pretty risky, too," Aimee observed, *"like, the drugs and alcohol."*

"Smart girl! I asked myself, what did I really want? Love, with a good man. A career, probably, but most of all, love, and a family. Commitment. I realized I'd never find it living this way. So, I found a girlfriend who felt like I did and we made a pact, to save ourselves until we had found the man we wanted to marry, and hopefully, until we were married. We wanted to be sure. You see, that would test any man."

"So, you met Dad. Did he know about your past? Did he mind?"

"Yes, he knew. Well, he had a past of his own. But he respected me, he honored my decision. He's a good man, Aimee. Then, I regretted all the 'cheap stuff' that went before."

"Mom, it worked. You've had a good marriage. What you wanted."

"Yes, but also because we worked at it. I'll tell you, though, a past like that carries consequences. We live with those consequences every day, and always will."

"What consequences, Mom?"

"Some things I can tell you, some things I can't. But not today."

"Mom... you've convinced me."

"It's not the easy way. But it's worth it. I can help you, if you'll let me. Help you learn how to say no, how to avoid the pitfalls, stay true to your convictions – and still have friends and have fun. If you'll let me."

"Yes, Mom, that's what I want."

"That's quite a story," said Rob, warmly. "I can see why you didn't tell me before. Okay, they wished they hadn't. But it didn't hurt them. You say they have a pretty good marriage."

"It did hurt them. Mom said, when you do find the right one you inherit all the baggage from past relationships. It causes problems. Dad says they beat the odds because they didn't give up. He says there's just something different about marriage, a security and freedom that come with commitment. It helped them have a better relationship. So I thought about it. I didn't understand it then, but I believed them. The more I see of life, Rob, the more I think they're right."

"Well….." he nodded slowly, "you have a point there. All this '*roommates with privileges*', like a game of musical beds, casual stuff, hookups and all that….something is missing. It's commitment….yes, but it's also love. I'm old fashioned, I guess. I want love in my relationship." He smiled at her. "Love and romance."

"Yes, yes! So do I. I've held out for love, all these years."

"And now we have it!" He looked at her imploringly. "I still think we could make it work, without marriage. But that's up to you." He thought about Bryan and Natasha. *I wonder….do they really love each other? Like we do?*

"Yes….my sweet Rob! Thank you."

"Honey –" he took her hands, "with all due respect to your mom, and I do respect her even though I haven't met her – don't you think she's making herself feel better for making bad decisions by laying an impossible expectation on you?"

"That's a fair question, but no, no, this is my decision," she told him firmly. "And it's not an impossible expectation! Look, when I was a kid, a teenager, I saw other kids cheat themselves. They wanted love so they grabbed anyone who came along. They would crash and burn, go off in directions they didn't want. I didn't want that for myself. I wanted to keep my eyes on my goals. So I decided to '*just say no*'. And I'm still saying it."

"Aimee, you're one of a kind! I love you for it," he told her admiringly. *In spite of myself,* he thought.

"Another thing, this decision made us closer, mom and I. I wasn't always trying to push the limits, she didn't have to rein me in – but I still managed to be pretty independent, pretty strong-willed. That's what it takes to '*say no*'."

"Hmm. A girl as beautiful as you must have said 'no' a lot."

"Yes I did," she replied with a toss of her head. "I learned something, too. When a guy figured out I meant it, it was '*goodbye*'. Almost every time. That told me how he really felt about me."

"Yes, I guess it would."

"So –" she asked cautiously, "will you leave me too?"

He made a face at her. "No, no – I won't, you know I won't. I've chosen you. Aimee, I love you, I do! We have something wonderful...." He held her close.

"And I love you....." They kissed, savoring the beauty of the moment......

She decided it was time to come back down to earth. She had a delicate question to ask.

"Honey, I want to talk about something."

"Not now," he replied, kissing her again.

"Rob. What's happening with your grandpa?"

"Oh, nothing, really," he replied, kissing her. "I don't want to talk about him now." But he yielded to her smile and replied, "I call him once a week, but like I told you before, it's awkward."

"I guess you run out of things to say."

"Right."

"I want to meet him."

"Sure," he kissed her again, "I'd love for you to meet him. I'll take you with me some day."

"No, no. I want to meet him soon, now." Her arm still around him, she pulled away.

"Well, I can't do it, not right away, I've got –"

She laughed. "No – I mean, go meet him on my own."

"You mean, just go, introduce yourself?"

"Of course. I'm not shy, you know."

"No. You're not shy." *No, she's not,* he told himself. He felt a twinge of annoyance. Gramps was his, and he didn't want to share him. Or lose him.

She read his face. "Rob, I'm not going to interfere. I won't bring this matter up to him. It's between the two of you. I just want to meet him. Be his friend."

He shrugged. "I can't stop you. I wouldn't anyway." He thought about it. He felt he could trust her. "All right. It's all right with me. He needs a friend."

"Okay. I'll drive out to see him one of these mornings, before work. I promise I won't meddle." *But I may be a catalyst*, she thought eagerly. *If I get to know him, it will be harder for Rob to stay away!* She gave him a parting kiss on the cheek. "Now.... we were going to rent some bikes."

Later, she re-lived the rest of her conversation with her mother many years ago.

> *"Mom, wasn't it hard, after you had.....um, a reputation, to just stop, say 'no'....um, you know what I mean,"* she laughed, embarrassed.

> *"It wasn't easy."* She shook her head. *"Not at first. I'm glad I had a friend to help. But then it was liberating. Very liberating! I began to see people differently....I focused more on myself, in a good way, I got to know myself. I*

learned not to be needy. I became strong. That's when I dropped out of college and went to nursing school."

"That's pretty neat.."

"Yes. I was off that merry go round of being used and using others. I made new friends too. Better friends. Honey, this is what I want for you and your sister and brother. To be strong, be in control of your lives, not get sidetracked."

"How long was it, before you met Dad?"

"About a year. It was worth it. I have no regrets."

"Well....you got what you wanted, a good marriage, a good husband, a home, a good family...."

"Good children," she laughed, giving Aimee a kiss.

Yes, yes, she thought. *I've come this far. I found Rob! I love him! I respect him so much, because he respects me. I only hope I can keep him.*

And keep hold of myself.

"Honey, did you have a good time yesterday?" They had spent the afternoon with Bryan and Natasha.

"Oh, yes. It's a long time since I was at a baseball game. It was fun. I'm glad I finally got to meet them, get to know them."

"So – what do you think of Bryan?" *Ha,* he thought, *that's the kind of question she likes to ask me. But I want to know, I want her to like him.*

"Well....he's bright, charming, a leader –"

"Yes, but, what do you think of him, as a person?"

"I would say, he's all that, and he knows it."

"You mean, arrogant?"

"That was my impression. Natasha adores him, and he takes advantage of that. Takes advantage of her."

"How do you figure? I've never seen it."

"Women's intuition." He frowned, and she went on. "He looked me over! He even flirted with me. Or tried to. That's insulting to Natasha. And you."

"Are you sure?" *Not Bryan. He wouldn't do that,* he thought uncomfortably.

"Women see these things," she assured him. "Of course I'm sure! Also, he speaks for her."

"What? I've never seen it."

"How about, *'Nah, Natasha doesn't want to take a walk. She wants to sit with me, don't you, honey?'* That was when she got up to take a walk with me during the seventh inning stretch."

"Well...." He didn't know what to say. "That's not right." *That sounds like Bryan,* he admitted reluctantly.

"Is that what I have to look forward to?" she asked sharply. "If so, count me out."

"Oh, no, I can't see myself speaking for you, or anyone. It isn't right. You don't have to worry about me."

"That's good to hear. Honey....was he like this in high school? With girls?"

"We didn't have girlfriends. We hung out, you know, sports, video games, dirt bikes....guy stuff. He was a good student and my grandparents liked him. I don't think he had a girlfriend till his senior year. Then....we started college, he lived with a couple of guys. His second year he moved in with a girl named Jody –"

"So he's a serial romancer." Rob made a face. "His place, her place, or theirs?"

"Um....her place. Same thing now, with Natasha."

"It figures."

"How's that?"

"He can leave. Leave her high and dry."

"Hmm! I never thought of that."

"I think he's not the same Bryan you grew up with. He would have been better off hanging with you. But he's your buddy. And I'd like to get to know Natasha better. I'm willing to go out with them again."

"Thanks, honey. He's still my friend."

A few days later Rob surprised her with an invitation to go on a walking tour. "I'm not telling you where, just be prepared to go straight to work when we're done," he said mysteriously as he turned the car onto a quaint side street.

She looked around with curiosity. "Rob, what is this?"

"It's the Old City, restored. You're going to love it."

"Oh, my goodness. I've always wanted to come here! I just never got around to it, and I've lived here for four years. Embarrassing, isn't it?" she laughed, taking his hand as they got out of the car. "How did you know about this? Did you find it just for me?"

"Just for you, yes! Actually, I was here myself, about a year ago. Before school ended. I saw a flier about it, a walking tour of the Old City. I tried to find someone to go with me. Ha, ha. It was like, '*Hey, Carlyle, can't you find something better to do on a weekend? Sleep, maybe? You are weird, totally weird.*' So I went alone."

"Good for you. Well, honey, that's what we are," she took his arm possessively, "weird! And glad of it. Now you can show me the best places."

"I'll see it through your eyes," he said with a wink. "That makes it more fun."

They spent a leisurely morning investigating old houses and streets. "I like it better on a weekday, not so many tourists," he decided.

"Yes, we get more attention from the guides. I love the costumed re-enactors. I wonder, why don't they have children do some re-enacting? It's summertime, they could do it."

"Why don't we ask?"

A while later they were eating lunch on a tree-shaded patio discussing what they'd found out. "So, they think kids couldn't be depended on and besides, they don't have anyone to work with them." She looked at him intently. "Rob, kids can do amazing things! They just have to be challenged, inspired....I want to do that, I do."

"If anyone could, it would be you!" he said admiringly. "I'll bet you've worked a lot with kids."

"Some. I tutored kids in reading when I was in high school. Then when we were in the D.C. area I ran a summer camp for kids, and I took them to historical places. That's when I started thinking about getting a Master's in history and working with children. Now, I'm more sure of it than ever. That is, if I can get a job," she sighed.

"Are you worried about it?"

"Sometimes. The important thing is to get the right internship, working with kids."

"Well, honey, like I said before, kids will be lucky to have you as a teacher. Now, tell me...." he smiled confidently, "did you have fun today? Did you like my surprise?"

"No....I didn't like it," she teased, "I loved it! We have to do it again. There are many other places we can visit," she said excitedly. "I picked up brochures. Now that you have someone to go with you –"

"I like it! We'll plan on it. Soon, while we still have mornings to ourselves. I picked up a couple brochures of my own. Next week, wait and see...."

"You're not going to tell me, are you?" He smiled secretively. "I might have a surprise of my own," she told him. "Hmm....I wonder if my parents have ever been here? They grew up in this area and they like history. I can't wait to tell them what we did today!"

His mood shifted suddenly. "When will I meet your parents, honey?" he asked with a troubled look. "The longer I wait...."

"The more nervous you get? Look, Rob, I would have taken you home the first day I met you! But remember, they work days and we work evenings. You work Sundays, too. That leaves Saturday and Sunday mornings. Dad has to be at his job Saturday mornings, and you like to sleep in on Sundays."

" '*Like to?*' " he echoed. "I need to. DeGeorgio's owns me on the weekends. Just a couple more weeks, I'll be done," he frowned, "and then it will be the insanity of med school. Hmph," he shook his head, "maybe I'll never meet your parents."

"Honey....don't worry," she patted his hand. "Dad promised to take off a Saturday so we can get together. Look, they'll love you and you'll love them. I guarantee it."

"Oh, yes. And if they don't?"

"Well, I'm independent. You know that. I make my own decisions."

Rob kept his misgivings to himself. *Aimee may say she's independent.....but, if her parents, her father especially – she's a 'daddy's girl' – if they found some fatal flaw in me, wouldn't she soon find it too? Why am I so nervous? Am I insecure? I never thought so, I've aced any interview I've ever had....but my whole future happiness depends on these two people I've never even met! They're larger than life to her, and now to me.....*

"Rob....where are you? You're a million miles away." She squeezed his hand. "Are you still worried about meeting my family?" He managed a faint smile. "Soon. It will be soon. You'll do great. All you have to remember is....I love you."

Chapter 9

Mr. Douglas sat in his chair looking out into the garden. The air conditioning chilled him but he needed assistance to get out the door into the warm air, and once out he never knew if he could find someone to help him get back in. *You hear about people who are on the outside looking in,* he thought, *and here I am, on the inside looking out.*

I'd love to hear from Rob. I was afraid I might lose him when he left here, moved across town....and it looks like I have, he reflected sadly. *In another month he'll be in med school and that will be the end. I should have known better than to get my hopes up. Oh, I talk to him every Sunday, a few minutes, then it's 'Gramps, I have to get ready for work.' It's not like before. Even though he was part of the staff and I didn't know he was my grandson, we still saw and talked to each other all the time. How I used to look forward to seeing him!*

There really hasn't been anybody to talk to since he left. For a while there were lots of questions, everybody loved Rob – but then it was back to normal and I was Mr. Douglas, the loner. Like a lid snapping on a box, everything went back to what it used to be, just like that, snap!

There was a tap on his shoulder and he looked up into the brightest pair of brown eyes he had ever seen – except for Kate's. He tried to remember his wife's eyes. "Mr. Douglas?"

she asked. He gave a nod. "Hello, how are you?" He looked at her in amazement.

"Mr. Douglas, I'm Aimee, Aimee Love. I'm a friend of your grandson Rob. Would you like to go out into the garden? The birds are giving a concert and the flowers are heavenly."

Taken by surprise, he could barely stammer, "Yes, yes, thank you!" Before he knew what was happening they were outside in the warmth of a July day, the heady fragrance of honeysuckle filling the air.

"I go to school with Rob," she explained, "and I'm going to marry him."

"Oh, that's wonderful!" *So that's what's been keeping him,* he thought. *I wish he'd told me….*

"Well, he doesn't know it yet," she confided, "we've only known each other a little while. So don't say anything, okay?"

He nodded, smiling. "Your secret is safe with me."

She shared some fruit and pastry she had brought and they began to get acquainted. She told him she was halfway through a Master's program in History. "I'll never get rich on it, but I love it," she said, and discovered that he loved history too.

"But not when I was your age," he added, "that interest came much later. Now I've read through all the history in our little library. Even the encyclopedias."

"Mr. Douglas, you are history!" she exclaimed excitedly. "Have you ever thought of recording your life experiences?"

"No!" he replied sharply. "That is, I have nothing to talk about."

"Oh, everyone thinks that. You think your life story isn't interesting," she went on enthusiastically. "But it is, it will be to other people!"

"No, I'm quite sure. I don't want to." He was adamant, so she dropped the subject.

"As you wish," she said. "Well, I can't stay – but may I come again?"

"I will look forward to it." *Do I dare,* he wondered as they bade each other goodbye.

Driving home, Aimee thought of her father's love of history and his extensive library of history books and biographies. *I'll bet he'd be willing to lend some.*

A couple of days later she was back, books and pastries and fruit filling her arms.

"Ah – food for the body, food for the mind, and you, my dear, are food for my spirit."

She blushed. "Thank you, Mr. Douglas. It truly is my pleasure. My father was thrilled to find someone who shared his interests. He's happy to lend these books."

He looked them over with delight. "I hardly know where to begin. Well, now, you must call me Gramps. Rob does, and I like it very much."

"I'd be honored, Mr. Doug- I mean, Gramps." She took a deep breath and introduced the reason for her visit. "Gramps, have you ever thought of moving? To a place nearer to Rob, and to me?"

"No, no. Thank you, but no," he replied firmly. "Definitely not."

She went on, "Sunset Gardens has a sister facility, Sunset Woods, very near to the University. They have some vacancies. I've checked."

Oh, she checked, did she. She's a fast worker! "Aimee – thank you, but the answer is no. This is my second place, and I'm too old to learn new people and places. No, I need to stay where I am."

She went on, undeterred. "I understand, I do. But you can't make an informed decision without all the facts, can you? We could take a ride over there right now, just to take a look. Then you can say no, if you still want to. And I won't say any more about it."

Well, how could he resist her charming smile? *Ha, I wouldn't mind getting off the grounds for a while....*

The room at Sunset Woods was about the same size as his room at Sunset Gardens but the window looked out on a wooded scene. *Hmm, my present room looks out on a parking lot.* He lingered a moment, absorbing the serenity of the view.

"Hello there."

He wheeled his chair around to see an older man with an impassive face, his right hand outstretched and his left hand grasping a cane. "M' name's Howard. Howard Grayson. Would you be my new roommate?"

"Oh, no. I live over at Sunset Gardens. I'm here with this young lady," he gestured to Aimee, "just visiting. I'm Allen Douglas. No, I'm not moving."

"Don't blame you. I wouldn't want to either. Too much hassle. Say, you think you can stay a while? We need a fourth man for cards."

He moved in the next week.

"Honey, where are we going?" Rob asked as she turned into an unfamiliar drive. She pulled into a parking space and stopped the car.

"We're visiting your grandpa," she replied brightly. "He lives here now."

"He what?" His voice rose.

"He moved in last week. I arranged it," she announced. "Do you like my surprise? Oh, Rob, he had so little, a few clothes –"

"You arranged it?" His lips tightened. "You told me you visited him. But not this. You could have told me!"

"I didn't plan to do it.... I...I... should have told you," she admitted. "But you'd have tried to stop me, and I...."

"You're right, I would have." He turned towards her, his eyes cold. "But you could have made your case, and then you'd have done whatever you wanted. That's your right." He frowned. "You might even have convinced me, you know."

"You're right," she replied with chastened tone. "I'm terribly sorry."

"I'd have handled it." His voice rose higher. "Better that, than behind my back!"

"Oh, honey...." She shook her head.

"And you weren't going to meddle!"

"Rob – whether you believe me or not," she pleaded, "I didn't plan to do this. It was an impulse. And then I thought, *okay, it'll be a surprise*. I thought you'd like it."

"Yeah. Well. It doesn't matter." He started to get out of the car.

Realizing how much she had hurt him she held him back. "Yes, it does matter. I am sorry." She turned his face towards hers. "I didn't trust you enough to talk it over. You're right, I should have." There were tears in her eyes as she reached for his hand. "I'm really sorry." She shook her head. "So sorry. But Rob, I didn't say anything about your issues with him."

He didn't know what to say. She smiled at him and he didn't want to stay mad at her. He took a deep breath. "Well... all right." With a faint smile he asked, "Tell me, how did you ever get him to move? He was so against any kind of change."

"I don't know...." she laughed, "I proposed, he accepted."

"Ha!" He laughed in spite of himself. "Well, we're here. We'll have to see, maybe he'll be pining for his old place." He took her hand as they got out of the car.

They had some difficulty finding him. Finally they tracked him down in the Solarium playing cards with three other men.

"Oh, hello!" He waved them over. "Rob, Rob, how good to see you!" he exclaimed, pumping Rob's hand. "And Aimee," he smiled at her. "Men, this is my girl, Aimee Love."

"My girl – too," said Rob, pointedly, putting his arm around her.

"And my grandson, Rob Carlyle." Rob and Aimee greeted the men, shaking hands with them.

"My roommate, Howard. My buddies Max, and Jerry. Say, could you wait five minutes? I'm winning."

"You think you are," retorted Howard.

They took chairs a short distance away. "This is amazing! I've never seen him like this," Rob marveled.

"Honey," she replied, "I'm as surprised as you are. He seemed so....alone, before."

He kissed the tears in her eyes and gave her a kiss on the lips, a good one. "You're forgiven," he told her.

When the game was over, Gramps having won, he wheeled himself over to them.

"Gramps, I believe you and Aimee have already met. Hey, will I have to fight a duel with you for her affections?"

"Let me decide that," she declared. "I have affection for you both."

"And a little more for me?" Rob asked suggestively.

"Well, Rob, I bow out," replied Gramps. "You're a sure winner."

He took Gramps' hand. "Gramps....I hardly know how to say I'm sorry. But I am, I'm really sorry. It's been two months since I saw you, at graduation. There's no excuse. Now that you're closer, I'll be here more often."

He graciously accepted Rob's apology.

"Now, Gramps, one other thing," Rob said importantly. "With all due respect, I have to tell you, your prediction was wrong."

"Oh? What prediction?"

"About the press. Good things did come from that newspaper article." He told how he and Aimee had met. "If there hadn't been a reporter and a camera, Aimee and I would never have met." He remembered that the article had also brought Mom. That wasn't good. And he still hadn't had that talk with Gramps.

Gramps congratulated them, then showed them around, ending in his room. "I think I'm going to like it here. I'm making a good start. Say, Rob, how's the steak house job going? I bet you don't miss Sunset Gardens one bit."

"You'd be surprised. DeGeorgio's?" He shrugged. "It's working out okay but it's not all that great."

"How's that? The money should be a lot better, and that's what you need right now."

"Yeah, the money's great and I'm doing well. Hard worker and all that. But the atmosphere is cutthroat." He shook his head. "The parties get pretty raucous. It's not for me."

"Do you wish you'd stayed on for the summer? At Sunset Gardens?"

"I thought about it, you know, '*maybe Gramps was right*,' he laughed. "But I wouldn't want the commute, an hour each way."

Ha, he reminded himself with a surge of anger, *this job brought Mom to my door. Not good. I don't need her and I don't want her*. He clenched and unclenched his fists. *But wait – this job brought me Aimee,* he remembered, his tension ebbing.

"If I had worked at Sunset Gardens I wouldn't have met Aimee," he went on. "I would have worked weekdays. I wouldn't have eaten lunch on campus that day."

"Strange, strange, strange," Aimee began,

"'are the mysteries of the universe?' " Rob added.

"I wasn't going to say it. But....now I know it was Fate."

"Absolutely!" Rob agreed, his arm around her shoulders. Gramps watched with pleasure.

"Aimee," he asked, "what brought you to work here, in the city? You live a distance away, don't you?"

"Yes, about thirty miles away in a little town you never heard of." She laughed. "It was an impulsive decision."

"So tell me! I presume Rob knows?" Rob nodded.

"Okay....I worked at The Bread Oven through the school year, part time. Then towards the end of the school year the manager offered me full-time during the summer with a raise in pay, said he didn't want to train someone new and he wanted someone dependable."

Rob nodded encouragingly. "Right."

"It was a tempting offer but I decided to tell him, '*no thanks, I have a job back home*'. Then – would you believe? That article appeared, '*Grandfather and Grandson Find Each Other....*" they all laughed, "and I decided I'd like to hang around campus this summer and see if I could run into that handsome grandson! So I told him '*yes*'. My parents thought I was crazy, of course."

"Well, you are," Rob agreed. "But I love you anyway."

"It must be Fate," she replied, snuggling up to him.

"Aimee, it was a fateful decision," Gramps said. "We're all glad for it!"

They visited a while longer, then as they were getting ready to leave Rob spoke up. "Gramps, I'd like to come and see you pretty soon. Talk some things over with you."

"Any time, Rob. I'd love to have you. Aimee too. But, call me first so I can...uh, arrange my social life."

"Oh, Gramps!" they burst out laughing.

Gramps watched them drive off. *I hope he comes*, he thought with a sigh.

"Are you coming with me when I go see Gramps?" he asked her on the way home. "I'd like to have you with me."

"I'd rather not. This is something between the two of you."

"I wish you would. You know I'd love to have you...."

She shook her head. "No, Rob."

"Well....all right," he conceded. "It's my responsibility. I've been putting it off for so long....I hardly know where to begin."

"You'll do fine. Much better without me. Just – tell him what happened."

"Yeah. I'll do it." He was quiet, thinking it over. Abruptly he asked, "I never told you about his album, did I?"

"No....you mean the one he took the picture out of, the one of your father?"

"Yes, that's the one. It's a big book, stuffed with tons of pictures, they're all loose, and he keeps it in an old pillowcase that smells of smoke. It's the only thing he was able to rescue from the fire in his old place –"

"Oh, yes! I saw that pillowcase when I helped him move. I didn't know what was in it, and he sure didn't want to let go of it."

"Aimee – my father is in that album! His life, I mean. And Gramps' life too, I'm sure. His whole family. It's my family, too!" he exclaimed, bitterness edging his voice. "But I've never seen it. I asked him about it, when we were at dinner after my graduation, I asked him if we could get together and I could learn about my father. That's fair, don't you think?"

"I would say so. What did he say?"

"He just sighed. He looked off into space....and he said something like, '*Oh, Rob, I'm not ready yet – someday –*' and he stopped. He seemed lost in thought. That was as far as we got. So now, I intend to ask him again. This ought to be the perfect opportunity."

"I agree. Let me know, I can't wait to hear!"

Chapter 10

A few days later Rob and Gramps sat together in the garden at Sunset Woods. They laughed about the change in their roles. "I'm still getting used to it," Rob told him, and agreed that the new place made the transition easier. "It would have been hard for me to visit you at Sunset Gardens and not be on duty."

"Oh, yes, the residents wouldn't have left you alone. They would want their favorite nursing assistant. We wouldn't be eating in the garden, either."

"Yeah, too much work for staff. Aimee didn't know the half of it, when she moved you. It really was a good thing."

"It's the door that makes the difference." Rob eyed him curiously. "The grocery store door, the one with the electric eye. We can go in and out easily, carry a tray.... Couldn't do that at the other place. Always had to wait for someone to help me. Little things. I like eating out here. This may be the start of something good."

Rob laughed, happy to be back with the man he had known as '*Mr. Douglas*' for so long. He felt surprisingly calm. *Now at last I can talk about my mother, those accusations she made. I shouldn't have worried about this,* he thought with relief. *No matter what I find out, we're going to be all right.*

Gramps' face changed suddenly and he looked at him with concern. "Rob, what's happened to you?"

With a sinking feeling Rob met his gaze. "Happened? What do you mean?"

He frowned. "What happened to that serious young man who was going to wait to settle down, at least until he was thirty?"

Rob laughed with relief, then shook his head. "Did I say that? In another life I did. Ha! Aimee changed all that."

"Rob," Gramps admonished, shaking his head, "don't tell me you've let yourself be taken in by a pair of beautiful eyes?"

"Don't forget the smile, Gramps. I think she hypnotized you with her smile."

"I'll say!" he laughed. "And I like to see a girl in a pretty dress."

"Right about that," he agreed. "Never too old to admire, eh, Gramps?"

"I hope not! Make that a pretty girl in a pretty dress."

"Oh, yeah! So, Gramps," he asked eagerly – "what do you think of her?"

"Rob, you did all right," he nodded, shaking Rob's hand, "I like her."

"She's in a class by herself," he began enthusiastically. "And she's not cheap. I like that."

"She's a lady. I don't know if that's the right thing to say nowadays. Some women consider it an insult."

"Grandma Ferguson told me that a lady is a woman with manners. She said '*Rob, that's what you want. Don't settle for anything less.*' Now I know what she meant."

"Right. You're a very lucky young man."

"It's a funny thing, I've met plenty of pretty girls but none I ever wanted to get to know – and now I've got Aimee! She's not just a pretty girl, she's a woman. That's what I want." Gramps smiled in agreement. "She's wonderful to know," he went on, warming to his subject. "She's got it all, beauty, brains, and a heart – I mean she's a good person, she cares about people – it's amazing, I can hardly believe it!"

"You've described her very well."

"Another thing I like about her, she's a family girl. She's close to her family..." *But I hope not too close,* he told himself.

"Grandpa and Grandpa Ferguson always said that was very important. Oh, by the way, I've met her family. It took forever but I finally did, last week. I was really nervous about it but I shouldn't have been."

"Of course not! Aimee's okay, isn't she?" he said with a grin. "Her father seems like a decent chap, though I've never met him. I've been reading the books he lends."

"Hey, that's cool. Aimee told me about that. Well, I liked them a lot. Her parents, her sister and brother. I just hope they like me," he said with an indifferent air.

"Why wouldn't they? Family, that's important. When you marry, you marry the family too."

"Yes – that's good for me. But what about her? You're all the family I have. Don't get me wrong, Gramps", he added quickly, "you're everything to me. In more ways than one."

Gramps smiled and patted his hand. "You don't know how good that makes me feel. Now, don't worry. Don't worry about family. She's lucky to have you."

"I'm the lucky one," he asserted.

"Rob, if you had met her at school, would you have asked her out?"

"No, never! She's out of my league, totally –"

"Yet she seems to think you're in her league."

"Yeah, how can that be?" He shook his head. "I still can't believe it."

"Don't sell yourself short. You've got a lot to offer." Rob shrugged. "You're a good man. That's the bottom line. Oh, and it doesn't hurt that you're good looking," he laughed, "but of course you are, you're my grandson."

"I can't argue with that, can I? By the way, did you know she looked me up? She liked what I said in our interview." He told how they had met.

"Ha, ha, I like that – she's a go-getter, isn't she! And it all started with the newspaper article. Well, it was a good interview, your part. I liked the way you talked about your job. It said a lot about you. Ha, I liked where you said you wouldn't play favorites, but in spite of that –"

"You were my favorite resident," Rob completed his thought.

"I liked that." He stopped and reflected. "It's pretty amazing, yes. Now I'm glad we did the interview. Ah, you and Aimee...." he smiled with pleasure, "I can't pretend to understand how these things happen. But every once in a while good people find each other. I'm happy for you. Enjoy what's happening."

"Oh, I will. I do."

They talked and laughed as they enjoyed the lunch Rob had brought. It was like the old days. Over dessert he brought up the main reason for his visit. "Gramps, I'll admit it. I've been avoiding you. Something was bothering me, and I....I couldn't ask you about it. That wasn't fair to you."

"Rob....what is it?" he asked with concern.

"Right after graduation," he began slowly, "I had a visit from, of all people, my mother." He poured out the story she had told him, that Gramps had broken his father's heart. "Gramps," he asked, bewildered, "what is this all about? She can't be right."

"Rob," he looked off in the distance. "Your mother is right. It's true, I did break his heart. I've had to live with the pain of it all these years."

"I know there's an explanation! You can tell me," he urged, taking his hand. "Please."

Gramps struggled within himself for a minute or so, then began slowly. "Ah.....briefly....the night before your father left for boot camp, we had a terrible fight. He left with my angry words ringing in his ears. I felt terrible, I wanted to apologize," he stopped and sighed, gathering strength to go on. "But I was stubborn. When I finally was ready, I didn't reach him until midway through his training. At first he didn't want to talk with me. But finally he did, and we reconciled. His mother and I talked with him and told him we would be attending his graduation." He smiled. "Everything was all set."

Rob nodded in agreement.

Gramps shook his head sadly. "It didn't happen. His mother had a stroke. We had to cancel the trip. I couldn't get through to him directly, so I left a message." He shook his head. "He never got it. Oh, Allen!" he sighed, remembering, "he never got it."

"Oh, Gramps!" he replied, shocked. "That must have crushed him."

"I'm sure it did. It was a while before we finally connected. He had already gone to his new assignment. We had a good talk and all was well. But yes....yes. I did break his heart."

"That really is the other side of the story," Rob said bitterly.

"There's one other thing. When we talked the first time, he was so excited. He had met a girl from home, a college student, and she was going to have his baby. '*Now, Allen*,' I told him, '*if you love her you must do the right thing and marry her.*' Well, he did love her and they got married. Then, he was shipped out to California before the baby was born. It seems she didn't go along. She had found another man."

"Why does that not surprise me?" he snapped. "She finds men the way a bee finds flowers."

"I'm sure she doesn't find what she's looking for."

"Oh, I'm sure you're right," he agreed.

"Rob, that baby was you. Your father never got to see you. He tried and tried to locate your mother and you but with no success."

"That's why I don't want to have anything more to do with her!" he burst out, banging his fist on the table. "I was taken away from her when I was a little boy. Then she would show up every now and then and make trouble, like a ball bouncing and hitting me in the head. She and my grandparents would fight, usually because she was drinking – and then I wanted her to go." He stopped for a moment, trying to calm himself down. "It was strange, I used to hope she would come and see me, and then I wished she would go. But no more. I'm just going to write her out of my life!" he declared, almost shouting.

"My boy." Gramps patted Rob's hand sympathetically. Then, "Rob – I want to meet her."

"What? Why? Why in the world?" he asked, unbelieving.

"This is how I see it. Your father loved her, and if I'm to judge by that picture we both have, she loved him too. She was once my daughter in law. And together, they produced a wonderful son." He smiled at Rob. "So yes, I want to meet her. Even just once."

"Well, that's your business," he snapped. "Just keep me out of it." His lips tightened. "I tell you, she's not worth it."

"I don't want to say that about anybody," Gramps objected.

"Hmph! I don't even know where she lives. She never gives me her address. How do you think that makes me feel?"

"I guess that settles it," he sighed. "For now."

When they met for a run the next morning Rob was bursting to tell Aimee about his talk with Gramps. But she put him off. "Oh, no," she interrupted him, "we need to run first, talk later, or we'll never get to the run." Reluctantly he joined her.

"Our best time yet, huh?" she teased a short time later, looking at her watch as they collapsed under a tree. "Now, tell me about Gramps. I'm dying to hear!"

"I'd almost given up getting to talk with him," he began slowly, shaking his head.

"So Rob, what happened?" she asked impatiently.

He paused. "I thought it would never happen –" he looked off in the distance.

"Okay, Rob, get to it!" she demanded.

"Well, you know how Gramps is –" he shrugged.

"Rob!"

"Oh, baby, I'm messing with you." He laughed and put his arm around her. "I'll tell you what happened."

She listened with rapt attention. When he finished she took his hand. "What a story! Your poor father, never getting to see his son, Gramps trying so hard to reach your father –"

"Well, he's not telling me the whole story. I know he's not." He sighed with frustration. "I never asked him about the album.

It was the perfect opportunity, but I just couldn't do it! He was...." he shook his head, "I can't explain it, he seemed so hurt. You should have seen his face when he talked about the fight with my father. He was in anguish! What was so important that they couldn't reconcile before he left?"

"I don't know. I don't know," she sighed. "Maybe you're expecting too much."

"And of all things! He wants to meet my mother. I don't know if he wants a reconciliation or what, but I don't want any part of it."

"I can see why you wouldn't. Ordinarily, I'd say family above all. Because my family means so much to me. But I hate seeing her hurt you this way."

"I can handle it," he assured her bitterly. "I've been doing it all my life."

"But why ask for it? You know, hon, I respect your grandpa so much, I really do. I think he's very wise. But just because he's old doesn't mean he's always right. In this case, I happen to disagree with him. If he wants to get to know your mother, fine. He has his reasons. That doesn't mean you have to see her again."

"You don't have to convince me."

"You need to protect yourself," she told him firmly. "Don't give her a chance to hurt you again. Forget her. Just accept what you have. You've reconciled with your grandpa, and that's what matters."

"You're right. You're absolutely right," he agreed. "I don't owe her a thing." He thought about it. "But I owe Gramps something. If she contacts me, I'll arrange for them to meet. He wants it. That's as far as I'll take it. I don't even have to be there."

"Right! Arrange it for him. Now....do you mind if I ask," she began slowly, "why were you taken from her?" She took his hand tenderly. "What did she do? Was she abusive?"

"That's okay, honey," he replied, wondering whether to continue. He took a deep breath. "I don't remember much. It wasn't what she did, she wasn't abusive. It's what she didn't do. She didn't take care of me, and that was scary. Then I went to live with my grandparents and that was scary too, because I didn't know them. I've told you about that."

"Oh, Rob, honey. How hard that must have been for you. Your whole life uprooted." She held his hand tightly.

"Well, it was, but I've made myself forget. Now – are you trying to make me remember?"

"It helps to talk, you know. And....it's important for me to know."

"But what if I don't want to remember?" He didn't want to go on but her smile encouraged him to continue.

The words came painfully. "They were loving people..... that helped. School, though....I couldn't handle it. They wanted me to repeat a year and I hated that because I was a smart kid. I wanted to learn." He stopped, unable to go on.

"Rob....I am so sorry...." There were tears in her eyes. "I am so sorry."

He withdrew his hand, his jaw set. "This is why I don't want to talk about it! I don't want you feeling sorry for me." *Not Aimee. Not again.* "I've told you enough sad stories." He looked away, sorry he'd gone this far.

Gently she turned his face towards hers, looking deep into his eyes. "Rob, I care. That's not pity. Let me care, please?" She stroked his face. "Now, what's the rest of the story? How did a little lost boy become an honors graduate? That's a good story."

He looked at her with surprise. "I've done my homework," she smiled knowingly.

He shook his head. "Okay, okay.... you win." He took her hands and held them tightly. "My grandparents said something interesting. They said I was basically a pretty well-adjusted kid. My mother must have done something right. But I still couldn't handle school, the social aspects. It interfered with my learning, so Grandma taught me at home for a few years. They saw to it that I did sports, and that helped. Sports and Scouts. Then I insisted on going back to school –"

"So you were ready –"

"I don't know about that. I wanted to be in band; I'd been taking trumpet lessons for a few years. They sent me to a private school, Oxford Academy. That helped. It was seventh grade and I was the class nerd, but it wasn't so bad. I wasn't the only one. Band was my salvation. I loved it. That helped make the transition for me. Band – that's where I met Bryan, in the band. He was a good buddy, all through school. Hey, I play a mean trumpet," he laughed. "Too bad you never got to hear me."

"I'd love to hear you!" she replied enthusiastically.

"I don't think so." Tight-lipped, he shook his head, his face a mask. "I'll never play again."

"No!" She looked at him with alarm. "You can't mean that. Of course you'll play again!"

"No. No more." He looked away.

She could see that he wasn't going to talk about it. *He's so much like his grandpa...* "Well, then, something puzzles me. You and I are the same age yet I'm a year ahead of you. Did you lose a year in the beginning, or what?"

"Yes, although that's not the reason. I dropped out of first grade but Grandma taught me at home and I went pretty fast. Then when I did go back to school I took a lot of accelerated classes and some extra subjects. By the time I graduated, I wanted to take a break before starting college."

"Sounds like a good idea. You didn't want to burn yourself out."

"Grandma said it was because I wanted to wait until Bryan graduated a year later so we could go to State together but that wasn't it –"

"Oh, no? Are you sure?" *So why are you telling me,* she wondered.

"Of course I'm sure. I wanted to work a year. My grandparents wanted me to help pay my way and I was okay with that. I didn't want to work while I was in school if I could help it, so I worked a year for Mr. Brannigan in his construction business. Earned a bundle and saved most of it. By the end of the year I was ready to go back to school. Oh, and I played in the community orchestra that year so I could keep up with my music."

"And you made first chair trumpet in Marching Band –"

"Well....eventually. How did you know that?" he asked, surprised.

"I have my ways," she smiled enigmatically. "You've left your mark around here, you know. Salutatorian.....you missed Valedictorian by a decimal, didn't you?"

"She beat me out." He shrugged. "It mattered then – but not anymore."

"That's still very impressive. Ah, Rob." She paused and shook her head. "I'm terminally boring but you are absolutely fascinating. What fun to get to know you." She smiled and again he fell under her spell. "Now....any other deep dark secrets?"

"Did I tell you I was adopted?"

"No!" She dropped his hand. "I didn't know! When did that happen?"

"Before my grandparents got me. I was adopted by one of my mom's husbands. That's why my name is Carlyle, not Douglas, like Gramps."

"Oh! What happened to him?"

"I have no idea," he said with an indifferent shrug.

"Now that is a mystery."

"It's no big deal. I only have dim memories of him. Good memories. But...." He sighed, looking off into the distance, "it's always bothered me that I was legally his, yet my grandparents got custody. Didn't he want me?"

"You wonder." She grasped his hand. "Hmph, I'm glad somebody did. It gave you a life."

"I have a brother, too," he went on. "By my mother. I don't think I ever knew him. I don't even know his name. My grandparents tried for a while to locate him but gave up. My mother had given him away, or something like that."

"Oh, Rob, how heartbreaking." She shook her head.

He shrugged. "It's in the past. It's done with. I don't even think about it."

"I agree with you there! You could drive yourself crazy wondering about it. Now I see why you don't want to have anything to do with your mother."

Suddenly he turned away from her, his face contorted with emotion. "Why? Why? Why?" he cried out in anguish, angrily punching the ground.

"Rob – darling…." She tried to comfort him, not sure what was going on.

"Why?" He clenched and unclenched his fists. "Honey…. you mean well. It helps to talk – when I'm with you. Then I get busy and forget. But –" he shook his head in despair, "when I'm trying to fall asleep, all the anger comes back. I don't want to be angry."

She took hold of his hands. "Rob…." She didn't know what to say. "Rob…."

He turned to her. "Why is Mom the way she is? Why? Why were the two greatest people in the world snatched away by some cruel hand of Fate – or God?" he demanded loudly. "Aimee – it's a can of worms I never should have opened! It was a mistake."

She held him close. "Oh, darling, I don't know." *I thought he was doing better. I thought he was over this*. "I don't have any answers. I don't think anyone does…..life can be so unfair." Tears filled her eyes. "I don't think it's a mistake, to talk about it." *I hope not….* "What I learned from my Gram – she went through so much hurt in her life – she taught me that it's better to talk about your anger than keep it inside, bottled up."

"Oh, baby," he gave a wry laugh, "your Gram and Grandma Ferguson. They would have made a pair. But – I'll tell you, I was better off when I wasn't thinking about it –"

She shook her head. "You need to talk about it. Gram had help from a counselor –"

"Oh, no. That's not for me! I'm done with shrinks."

"Okay then. But I won't be your counselor."

"I wouldn't want you to be. So –" he frowned, "what did your Gram do about anger? Did she just walk around angry all the time?"

"No, of course not! Basically, it was – talk about it with someone you trust, like you are now – then – well, you have to decide to let it go. Just, let it go. Stop blaming anyone."

"Ah, '*just let it go*.' Yeah, sure. I've heard that before! But I –" he dropped his head in his hands – "I don't want to live with anger. I'm not an angry guy. I've always been pretty positive about things....but this – I don't know." He shuddered.

"Honey – I think you're better off now, talking about it. Even though it's painful. It's like a tooth being pulled. It hurts for a while, but then you're rid of it."

"If I want." He squeezed her hand. "It helps to know you're with me."

"Darling, believe it. We're in this together. We'll keep talking." She held him close. "You know where to find me."

"Oh yes. Right here." He took her by the chin. "Honey....I'd be glad to trade my absolutely fascinating past for your terminally boring one." He kissed her on the lips.

"Oh.....oh, Rob." She shook her head. "I don't realize how fortunate I am, do I?"

"That's okay, honey. You'll learn." He kissed her as he held her close. "I could kiss you from now till Christmas....."

"Mmm....I'd love that....but I think we'd better take it easy. How about another run?"

A few days later a sudden hard rain interrupted their run and they ran to his car, laughing. Rob pulled her into the back seat with him.

"Rob, no –" she protested.

"Brrr! It sure turned cold fast – and we're soaked to the skin." Wrapping his arms around her, he kissed her. "You're shivering. Let me warm you up." He rubbed her arms. "Does that help? Oh, baby, I love you....and you love me." He kissed her face. "I want to make love to you," he said urgently. "is that so wrong?"

"No....no, it's not wrong. I feel that way too. But not now –"

"No, I didn't mean here –" He kissed her again, holding her tightly. "Let me warm you up…."

"Rob, darling, no, no. You know what I mean. We've been through this." She shook her head, her emotions churning. "I don't know, I don't know....Rob…." Burying her face in her hands she edged away. "Honey, drive me to my car, please." She got out quickly and moved to the front seat.

Slowly he got out and joined her, frustrated, angry at himself. "Aimee…." He took her hand. "Honey, I'm sorry. I was out of line. I went too far. "Look," he turned on the heater, "this will warm us up – ha! or cool us off," he said, as he was met by a blast of cold air.

"Thank you Rob. I do love you." She squeezed his hand. "I'm sorry too. Sorry to say no."

"That's okay. I understand." *I'm trying to understand*, he thought. "Honey, we can't go for a run tomorrow, I've got an on-line test. But the next day –"

"What if it rains? It's predicted, all week."

"How about a museum or two?" he asked as he pulled up to her car. "There's a lot of stuff we haven't done yet."

"I'd love it! You know that. Especially with you." Cradling his face in her hands she gave him a tender kiss. "I love you, Rob Carlyle….more than you know."

Chapter 11

At last they had a night off together for a long-planned evening at his apartment. He had prepared a special meal for her.

"Rob – how wonderful! Candlelight and wine. And dinner – you made it yourself."

"Just for you," he smiled, "to celebrate us."

When they had finished he took her hand and smiled warmly. "My sweet Aimee....." he kissed her hand, "remember when we were talking about whether to live together? And you said, '*maybe we wouldn't work out*'. I've been thinking about it. We love each other. Why wouldn't we work out?"

"Rob, Rob...." she sighed, "that's naïve. If love was enough, there would hardly be any divorces. It takes more than love."

"That's right. So doesn't it make sense for us to live together so we can find out if we're compatible?"

"You mean try on the shoes before you buy them."

"Exactly! That's it."

"Honey – There's much more involved here than a pair of shoes. Look, I gave you my reasons. I spelled it out for you. Please, please – don't make it difficult...."

"I respect your convictions. But, Aimee – darling – I just want to give you my point of view."

"I think you don't respect my convictions! Rob, we can't keep going through this...."

"Oh, baby, it's just that I love you so much...." He held out his arms to her.

"Rob, I have to leave. Right now." Hurriedly she got up and started towards the door.

"Aimee, why? Don't leave – we were going to watch a movie." He reached out to hold her back. "What's going on?"

"Rob, good night –" She left quickly, leaving him standing there, bewildered.

Why, why, she thought as she rushed down the stairs and to her car. *Rob, don't you know, if I had stayed there another minute I'd have been in your arms and never left.... I shouldn't have gone to his apartment! That was a mistake, I know it now*. She got in her car and sat for a minute to calm herself. She pulled down the visor and opened the mirror. *'Aimee'*, she asked, tears filling her eyes, '*are you crazy? Why are you making things so difficult for both of us? Is it worth it? You don't want to lose him!'*

Oh, I was so sure....When I didn't care about a guy, it was easy. I didn't feel this way. I need to think this through. She began to quiet herself as she dried her eyes. *But I can't think when I'm with him. I need to take a break, get away from him for a while. That's it*. She got out her phone and texted him that she'd like to meet him tomorrow for lunch.

The next day they were sitting in the back booth of their favorite eatery.

"Aimee –" he took her hand, shaking his head, "what's this all about?"

"I need to back off for a while. Not see you....I need to think things through."

"Honey, no! Are we breaking up?" he asked, unbelieving.

"No, no, not at all! I just need a while away from you. Can you accept that? You know, if we're meant to be, Heaven and earth couldn't keep us apart."

"No – but you are," he told her.

"Rob, we're going too fast."

"Too fast?" He shook his head. "Honey, we're not going anywhere at all!"

"My sweet Rob." She took his hands. "Do you know why I left last night?"

"No, I couldn't figure it out. Were you mad at me?"

"Oh, no, no. Far from it." She looked in his eyes, tears in her eyes. "Rob, if I had stayed, I'd have given in to you without you even asking. I'd have violated all my principles and convictions, just like that."

He looked at her with surprise. He kissed her hands. "My sweet Aimee….I don't want that. Not that way. You've got to be true to who you are."

"Honey, thank you, thank you for understanding me! That's one reason I love you. Rob," she paused, taking a deep breath, "Rob, I need to think through my convictions. See what I really believe. We can't see each other for a while. No contact. No phone, no text –"

"Not see each other?" he asked, not understanding.

"Not for a while –"

"Not even texting – ?"

"No, no contact. That would just mess me up."

"How long?"

"A couple of weeks, maybe –"

"Well….all right," he agreed reluctantly. "I don't like it….but I love you. I'll take a breather. If that's what you want."

Rob and Bryan had just completed their racquetball game and were relaxing over cold drinks.

"You say Aimee dropped you for a couple of weeks? Rob, why are you letting her do this to you? She's jerking you around, man."

"No, she's not. It's…." he struggled to find words. "It's this '*life style decision*', as she puts it, saving herself till marriage, and she wants us to cool down." He found it difficult to explain. And he didn't want to bring her mother into it.

"Oh, man!" He expressed his opinion with a few expletives. "Rob, it's game-playing. My advice is, lose her."

"Bry, no, she's not playing games. I know her better than that."

"Well, then, she's an ice princess and she doesn't want to tell you. She's not considering your feelings at all. She's only thinking of herself."

"No, Aimee's not like that."

"Well, whatever. In any case, you're getting hurt. Look, you've found your way with girls now. Some guys just take longer but now you're there. So, find yourself another girl. A friendlier girl. But be careful, find somebody who's easier to get along with. You've got a lot to choose from. It's a buyer's market."

"You crack me up! I'm not buying anything. It's Aimee I want."

"Didn't I tell you, *'you'll just have to suffer'*?"

"Man, you'll suffer again next week. I'm gonna whack you good! I'm on a roll. Look, I've gotta go. See you then."

So what's different now, Aimee asked herself as she thought about her relationship with Rob. *I love him. I want to be with him, all the time. I want him with every fiber of my being. And I know he feels the same way! This is agony for both of us*. She pondered....*my convictions made good sense, ten years ago when I was young and silly. Probably kept me from doing something stupid, even ruining my life. But now?*

She remembered meeting Julie and the pleasant shock of finding a kindred spirit. Julie had put her in touch with an online chat group, young women who had decided to take the long view instead of the quick and easy way, who had decided, as they put it, to take responsibility for their lives; to grow up, get an education, get married, have a family....in that order. Not be pressured by their peers or their boyfriends. *Well, has any of that changed? I don't know. I need to talk with Julie*, she thought. *She's been so busy with wedding preparations I haven't wanted to bother*

her with this....but we need to talk. And Mom.....it helps to talk with her. Rob may not like it, but she can help me.

She thought too of her *'someday baby'. I don't want a child of mine to come into the world without two pairs of arms to hold it. A mom and a dad. Am I so crazy to want that? Oh, yes, that can happen without marriage....*she thought of friends of hers, *but I come back to my vision of a stable marriage. That's what I want for my baby. How can I make that happen?*

So what has changed? Not my convictions. I've changed.

"Where's Aimee?" Gramps asked Rob as he stopped the next Sunday afternoon. "I was expecting both of you today. I can't imagine you without her."

"Not anymore," he answered morosely. "Not now, anyway."

"What?" exclaimed Gramps, shocked. "You didn't break up, did you?"

"No, I don't think so. She wants a *'breather'*, she says, we're getting too close, she wants to think things through...." He was less in agreement than he was when they had talked. He felt miserable without her.

" *'Too close'*? Here I thought you two were heading towards a lifetime together. It certainly looked that way to me."

"She says we're *'going too fast'*. I'd say we're going pretty slow, compared to every couple I know."

"You'd like to be together all the time, is that right?" Gramps asked with a knowing nod. Rob agreed. "Live together?"

"Why not? We love each other."

"What does Aimee say about that?"

"She says '*no*.' She has a lot of reasons, they kind of make sense, but she has no idea what it's like for me."

"Well, if she says '*no*', then that's it, isn't it? You have to respect that."

"I do, Gramps. I'm not pushing her. But hey, she doesn't understand how difficult this is for me."

"For her too, Rob. You need to know, it's not easy for her."

"Yeah, that's what she says. It's just, like I tell her, weird." He told about his conversations with Bryan.

"Oh, my!" Gramps laughed heartily. "Yes, yes. I've heard all that before. "What do you think?"

"He's no help. He's wrong about Aimee."

"Rob, Aimee's right. My dear grandson," he gave him a long look. "Go slow."

"Why?" he exclaimed heatedly, "Why? I've waited so long – for love, for a girlfriend. '*Going slow*' just doesn't cut it. I think '*carpe diem'* is what I need to do! Seize the day, the moment." He got up and paced. "But I respect Aimee. I do, I really do. I don't want to pressure her." He thought for a moment. "I think that's what I was doing, pressuring her." He threw up his hands. "It's all so confusing!"

"Confusing? Or just difficult? I'm sure her reasons make good sense." He gestured to Rob to sit beside him. "Rob, look at it this way. She chose you. Ignored every other man and waited for you to come along. That makes you pretty special."

Rob sighed. "I've thought of that. She's pretty special. But still –" he shrugged.

"So now, you can wait for her."

"Ha, ha, that's a good argument.....but it's not the same thing."

"Okay. But take it from me, you need to know each other better."

"What better way than to live together?"

"No, not really. It's like playing house. It's not marriage, not the real thing. You need to get to know each other in all the other ways. Then you'll know whether you're ready to live together for the rest of your lives. If you go too fast, it can lead to all kinds of unintended consequences."

"Gramps, if you don't mind my saying, you sound like the voice of experience." Gramps smiled secretively. "What kind of experience?" he asked with a devious smile.

Gramps looked away. "To be honest," he sighed, "I didn't know all this when I was your age. I wish! Oh yes....we had to learn the hard way, your grandma and I. Someday I'll tell you...."

"I'd like to hear! Wasn't it your generation that, you know, broke all the rules?"

"Ha, yes! My generation wrote the book on every kind of experimentation." He stopped and reflected. "I remember how liberated I felt when I heard '*if it feels good, do it*.' But, they don't tell you this, the consequences are terrible. I'm thankful that we got lucky and got out of that mess before we got badly hurt. So, I thought things through, gained a little wisdom that I wanted to pass on to my son. But.... I waited too long. Then he was gone." He stopped and nodded, "Rob....think about what I'm saying."

"So we're back to Square One. What consequences? Why not live together?" he asked impatiently. "Why not?" He shook his head. "Look, I don't want to argue with her. I won't pressure her." He shrugged his shoulders and sighed, "I want to understand her. When I'm away from her, her arguments seem pretty flimsy."

Gramps nodded his head understandingly.

"Why not live together, see if it works out? If it does, we can get married. If it doesn't, we split up. Though I'm sure we'd work out. That's what everyone else does," he exclaimed heatedly. "I'm not talking '*hook-ups*', I'm talking about people who really love each other. Like we do."

"Rob, Rob." Gramps took his hand. "You're a good man. I'm proud you're my grandson. "Look here, why don't you stay, have a meal with me and we'll talk more."

"I could do that. Sure beats eating alone."

"You may change your mind after tasting it," he smiled, taking out a paper. "Go choose something, put it on my bill."

A short while later they were seated together over a meal. "Rob," Gramps began, "if you were living together and began to have problems – believe me, everyone does – what incentive would you have to stay together and work things out?"

"We love each other, that's what," he declared.

"Ah, my boy. Love ebbs and flows. When you're going through a rough patch it's easy to conclude you don't love each other anymore. You decide you're not right for each other. And someone else can look awfully good."

"The voice of experience, eh?"

Gramps nodded his head, laughing. "Believe me, Rob, it can happen to anyone. No matter how much you love each other now."

"I hate to think that would happen to us." He shook his head soberly. "So, what's your point?"

"It's this." Gramps looked at him intently. "Marriage is based on promises."

"I know, '*better or worse*' – right?"

"Yes, exactly. And those promises should be based on knowing each other. Being sure of each other. On trust." Rob put his fork down and listened. "Trust needs to come first. Then you can make your promises. Then your marriage has a greater chance of success. When you have problems, you have an incentive to work at it, to re-build your love. Rob –" he looked at him intently, "commitment, based on your promises – that's the glue that will hold you together, to help you get back that loving feeling and be stronger than ever. Rob – believe me, it's true."

"That's good," he shrugged, "but look at my parents. They weren't exactly poster children for marriage. It didn't take long for my mother to leave my father for another man. So much for promises."

Gramps shook his head. "No, no. A number of things were wrong with that situation. She was pregnant first, that's a strain. They were too young, just not ready, not mature. And," he smiled ruefully, "I bear some blame. I told Allen, '*If you love her, marry her.*' But how could they be sure? It was too fast. Better if I had told him to wait a while, get pre-marital counseling. That would have helped them make a good decision."

"Yes.... lots of issues there."

"One last thing, Rob. Breaking up is almost never easy. It leaves broken hearts, sometimes broken people. Maybe broken children, innocent children who didn't ask for this to happen. Cheated out of two parents who love each other."

"But Gramps, that happens in marriage. Look at me, I never even had a chance to meet my father."

"Yes, of course," he sighed. "Marriages do break up. People quit too soon." Rob nodded. "But statistically, you are ten times more likely to break up if you are living together than if you are married."

Rob thought for a minute. "Hmm. Would that be the commitment factor?"

"Yes. And maturity, preparedness. Don't you want to give yourselves the best possible chance? Both of you, and –" he chuckled, "your unborn children."

Rob sat and considered what he'd heard. "That's a lot to think about. The fact is, though, everybody seems to be living together. I want to! Nothing wrong with wanting to, is there? I'm just not ready for marriage."

"Nothing wrong with those desires. But watch where they take you." Patting Rob's hand, he smiled. "You can make it, you and Aimee. She's a fine young woman, you're lucky to have her. And she's lucky to have you. Listen to her."

"Gramps.....I'm lucky to have you! Thank you for....your love." Impulsively he threw his arms around the older man. "It means a lot."

They said their good-byes and he left.

Driving home Rob struggled with his thoughts. *Maybe they're right, Gramps and Aimee. Much as I hate to admit it. But....I don't want to get married. I'm not ready. Not yet.*

He turned his car towards the park by the Lake where he and Aimee had picnicked a couple of months earlier. *I'm not ready to go home yet,* he told himself. He drove around until he found the bench where they had sat and talked and kissed. He got out and sat on the bench. Night was coming on and a wind was rising but it felt good as he tried to think things through.

Have I been making it difficult for her? She's been clear from the beginning. If I really love her I will respect that. Of course I would never force her, he assured himself. *I'm not that kind of guy.*

But something kept nagging at him. Against his will he was having a conversation with Granny. '*You wouldn't force her, no, just set it up so she'd violate her beliefs, right*?' He twisted uncomfortably. What had Bryan said? '*They all give in eventually.' He must know. The rat! And would she hate me? Probably not. But wouldn't she hate herself?* He saw Granny nod.

I haven't been fair to her, he admitted reluctantly. *Why not? I don't have to agree with her to honor her wishes. So why haven't I? I want to – but my desires take over. That's selfish, isn't it? No, I'm not a selfish person. I just don't want to take 'no' for an answer. Ha! Like the 4-wheeler*. He laughed in spite of himself. *Oh, how I wanted that 4-wheeler! But Grandpa and Grandma wouldn't budge, no matter how much I argued.* '*You'll just have to wait,'* they said, *'eleven is too young. Rob, you'll just have to respect our 'no', even if you don't agree. We say 'no' because we love you and want what is best for you.'*

Okay, okay. I love Aimee enough to want the best for her. I love her enough to respect her and honor her wishes. He shook his head. *I don't want her to think I'm some eleven year old kid who can't take 'no' for an answer.*

"It's so good to be together again!" Aimee exclaimed as they brought food to their back booth. "The longest two weeks of my life."

"Mine too," he agreed. "So....you've thought, and I've thought too. Honey, I said I would respect you but.....I haven't. I haven't been fair to you."

Their eyes met. "Thank you, Rob. My sweet Rob. This hasn't been easy for me. It's so easy to have beliefs and convictions when they don't make a difference. It wasn't that hard, over the years. Not until….you." She took his hand. "I've gone back over my reasons, my beliefs, and they're still important. I still mean everything I said. The only thing that's changed…. is me. The feelings I have for you. So – I've concluded, it's our hormones. They're pulling us like magnets. I need to fight that, to keep to my convictions."

"Is it hormones? Or is it our love, drawing us together? Aren't you fighting our love?"

"No, no, that's not it." She sighed, shaking her head. "I didn't know it would be so difficult! Rob, I want to be sure. Very sure. Our emotions, our hormones, they get in the way. They could take us where I don't want to go."

He was bewildered, hurt. "You were so sure you were in love with me! You were so happy. Aren't you anymore?"

"Yes, yes, yes….I do love you. But, do you understand, I want to be sure it's really love and not hormones. I get confused. I want to be sure."

"Well, it sounds like you are and you aren't! How can you ever be sure?" he asked, exasperated.

She struggled to find the right words. Holding his hands tightly she took a deep breath. "This must seem so unfair to you. I want you to know….it's not easy for me either. But – I believe we have to wait. Get to know each other better. Do you remember how we felt when we met? That instant friendship…."

He smiled and kissed her fingertips. "We felt like we'd been friends all our lives."

"Oh, yes! Honey, we need to build on that friendship. Get to know each other in lots of ways. As we've been doing. Do you see how much closer we feel in just a couple of months? Without the distraction of sex."

"Hmph! That's a strange way to put it."

"What I mean is….this isn't the right time. We need to know each other first. Honey, I'm convinced this is the right thing to do." She studied his face anxiously.

"Well! How did you get so smart?" he asked smiling but with sarcasm.

"Rob, I think about things. I look around, at other couples who've been living together from Day One and – I believe we're closer, we know each other better, we trust each other.....you know, we have real intimacy. The intimacy that matters."

"We've grown closer. I'll agree with you there."

"Sweetheart, it's been good! I want to know you better, grow with you....then I'll know, I'll be sure what I feel for you is real. Not just emotion, or hormones."

"I know how I feel. I love you, Aimee! I know what I feel for you is real. I don't have any doubts," he said passionately.

"That makes me feel.....so wonderful," she replied warmly, caressing his hand. "So –will you continue to honor my request?"

He shook his head and laughed. "Honey, are you ready for a shock? Believe it or not, I'm beginning to agree with you. Your convictions."

She looked at him skeptically. "Are you sure?"

"I talked with Gramps. I hope you don't mind, you know, telling our business."

"No, I don't mind, I trust him. I'm glad you did."

"He gave me a lot to think about. He, uh....he said some of the same things you do," he admitted sheepishly. "But still – I'm not ready for marriage. So where does that leave us?"

"My dear Rob....thank you," she replied, beaming, and once again he fell under her spell. "It's a beginning. I'm willing to wait for you. You're worth waiting for. Now...." she took a deep breath, "what this means for me is, I've got to continue keeping limits on myself. I trust you to respect that. Even if you think I'm weird."

"I'll respect you, honey, from now on. You have my word." They smiled in agreement. "Yes. I just wonder....how do you decide on these limits? Not from your own experience."

"No, you know that. From someone else." He gave her a questioning look. "From my mother."

He frowned. "Oh, so your mother gets a play-by-play of everything that goes on between us?" he asked with a touch of irritation.

"No, of course not. Mom respects our privacy and so do I. She and I have talked a lot, over the years. She said if I was really serious about this, what she called a lifestyle decision, to wait until marriage, there were things I needed to know."

"Such as?"

"Like, what I do, how I act. Where to draw the line in what I do with a guy. Know when to stop."

His eyebrows shot up. "For instance?"

"Like, don't start anything romantically, sexually, that I don't intend to finish."

"That could have a couple of meanings," he replied deviously.

"But only one meaning for me," she retorted. "The right time, the right place, with the right person."

"The right person, of course," he nodded his head.

"Yes! My husband."

"Ha, ha! Yes….I know that."

She took his hands, looking deeply into his eyes. "Darling Rob….I want my first time, sexually, to be with the man I love." His eyes lit up. "Yes, within the security and protection of marriage." He was quiet a moment, then he smiled at her. "I will respect that. We'll help each other, honey. I promise." *Even though I'm not ready for marriage*, he told himself. *Not yet*.

"Suppose a guy wasn't as nice about it as I was? You know, you really put me off at first."

"Aha! That's when I make my own moves. Karate. My dad taught me. He's a black belt, you know."

"Honey, you amaze me. I guess I was lucky, huh? That I didn't land on the floor."

"Luck had nothing to do with it. You're a good guy," she told him warmly. "You respected me. I didn't have to use karate with you."

"Aimee –" he held her hands tightly, "I admit, I think you take weirdness to a new level," they laughed, "but I will respect you. I love you. We'll keep our limits, okay? Both of us. If I get out of line, just use a karate chop."

"You're crazy!" she told him. "Maybe that's why I love you." *Oh, my,* she thought, *I have to be careful. Karate's good to know. But....what if I didn't want to use it?*

"And I love you," he replied, kissing her hand.

"Honey....When you were talking with your grandpa – did you ask him about his album?"

He rolled his eyes helplessly. "One thing at a time," he explained. "With you gone....it was all I could do to keep my mind on school. The album – I had to put that on the back burner."

"But not anymore," she replied decisively. "If he doesn't bring it up, you do it. I know how important it is to you." She smiled at him. "It's important to me too."

He pulled her up, took her face in his hands and kissed her. "My darling Aimee. That's why I love you so."

A few days later she dropped in to see Gramps.

"Aimee, my dear! What a happy surprise you are!"

"Gramps, would you like to meet my parents? Dad says anyone who enjoys his history books is worth getting to know."

"Well, yes, I –"

"Okay, then, they'd like you to come to dinner. Is next Friday night all right? Rob will pick you up, he's done with the steak house now so he can come early, about 4:00." She knew he didn't like late evenings. "Are you okay being there on your own? Mom and Dad have been wanting to have you and this is the only opening in their schedule for weeks to come. But Rob and I have other obligations."

"I'll do fine. I'm sure we'll find lots to talk about. Thank you so much."

She sure is a fast worker, he thought. *And a fast talker!* But he was pleased, and they made arrangements.

"Now I have to go. See you soon."

Chapter 12

The following week Rob picked Gramps up to take him to the Loves' where he would trade him for Aimee, then come back later to take him home. They were going to Julie and Zach's wedding rehearsal.

Aimee and her father met the car when Rob and Gramps pulled into the drive. "Well, Allen, Roger Love," her father said, introducing himself, "at last." He and Rob lifted Gramps out of the car and into his wheelchair. "Glad we finally get to meet!" he said warmly as they shook hands. "I can't tell you how glad we are to have you here!" They had been exchanging notes with the books. "Aimee's talked a lot about you."

"I can't tell you how glad I am to be here! That's a wonderful daughter you have." He smiled at Aimee. "She's really brightened my life."

"Aimee has that gift," Roger replied, giving his daughter a wink.

Once inside, he was warmly welcomed by Aimee's mother Elaine and sixteen year old Jacquie and Jason, who she then sent to set the table. "Ah, the family dog," he observed, as an impressive white Siberian husky came over to sniff him.

"Aimee's dog," Roger corrected him, "Grendel."

"An interesting name."

"Aimee named him. She had her reasons."

Gramps reached over to shake Grendel's paw. "What a beautiful animal."

"Yes, he is. A wonderful creature. He doesn't bark, unless he has to. And then – watch out!" Elaine laughed. "Well, dinner's in the crockpot, so we can visit for a while."

"Ah, yes," Gramps replied. He sighed with pleasure. "You don't know what a treat it is to be here, to get to know Aimee's family. You know, I can't remember when I've had a home cooked meal. Years, really. I can't begin to thank you."

"We wanted to get to know Rob's family," Roger began.

"Yes," added Elaine, "We've enjoyed getting to know him. We think very highly of him. Rob's the first boy she's ever gone out with more than a few times –"

"Don't think she's ever been serious about any boy, has she?" Roger asked his wife.

"Aimee's very hard to get," she replied. "Single minded. She's kept her mind on her studies, all these years."

"Much better that way," declared Roger.

"But then she saw that article about you and Rob, and she said, '*I want to meet that guy,*'" continued Elaine, shaking her head. " '*I'm going to find him.*' Can you believe it?"

Roger laughed. *'Don't get your hopes up,'* I told her, *'You know how many thousands of students are on that campus?'* "

"Then she told us she'd met Rob," Elaine went on, "and she said, '*He's really a nice guy!*' I never heard her say that about any other fellow. Not like that."

"That's what I said too, when I met him," Gramps interjected, "*what a nice guy he is.*" He remembered Aimee saying she was going to marry him. *Well, her secret's safe with me.*

"Then, would you believe, she said she was going to marry him!" exclaimed Elaine.

Gramps remembered an old song about how a boy chases a girl, until she catches him. *Ah*, he mused, *I sure hope they catch each other.*

Elaine shook her head. "It wasn't, '*I want to marry him*', but '*I'm going to marry him.*'"

"That's Aimee," Roger nodded. "When she wants something she goes after it. But she's nobody's fool. If she hadn't liked what she found she wouldn't have stayed with him."

Gramps nodded with approval.

"I told her, '*Aimee, be careful*," her mother continued, shaking her head. "*You haven't had much experience with boys.*' I didn't want her to get hurt."

"Of course not," Gramps agreed.

"We'd never seen her react to anyone the way she did to Rob. Scared us a little," Roger said.

Gramps laughed, eager to hear more.

Elaine continued, "She told us, '*You'll love him!*' Her head was really in the clouds."

"*The clouds?*" Roger echoed. "Another planet was more like it. I said to her, '*Come here, honey, and tell me why I should like this guy.*' "

"Yes," Elaine mimicked, " '*Will he meet my impossibly high expectations?*' "

"I didn't say that, did I?" Roger asked.

"No," Elaine laughed, "but we knew what you meant, Aimee and I."

"Ever the protective parent, eh?" Gramps asked.

"No, not exactly. Aimee's an adult and we respect that. But I reserve the right to my opinion. Yes. She can take it or leave it, I won't interfere. Ha, Elaine wouldn't let me, would you?"

"You're right about that!" she shot back.

"So, what did Aimee say?" persisted Gramps, curious to know her thoughts about his grandson.

" '*Dad,*' she said to me, '*if you'd met him first you'd have brought him home to me.*' "

"I like that," laughed Gramps.

"Aimee's very shrewd," Elaine went on. "It takes a lot to impress her. But the way she went on about Rob –"

"Right," her dad continued, "We thought, he's either the real deal or a very smooth worker. We hadn't met him yet. In fact, we didn't meet him for weeks because we couldn't find a time to get together. It worried us a little. Finally we had him over for Saturday lunch."

"He's a very likeable young man," Elaine declared.

Roger rolled his eyes. "He knew how to charm the parents! He left Aimee and helped Elaine in the kitchen. Then he talked world events with us all –"

"You were impressed, you know you were," Elaine insisted. "He held his own. Then we put him to work. It was the day after that big storm and we all did yard work –"

"Well, Elaine, he volunteered."

"Yes, he did. Worked hard too."

"Even though he couldn't take his eyes off Aimee," Roger laughed. "Can't blame him for that. But...." he shook his head. "He certainly does want to please."

"You think too much?" Elaine asked. "Of course he wants us to like him. Because of Aimee."

"He goes right out to the kitchen to help you, every time. Doesn't seem normal."

Aha, Gramps thought with a sudden flash of insight, *he's probably had Rob checked out. I'll bet he knows more about him than I do! Well....maybe I'd do the same thing.*

"He likes to cook," Elaine answered her husband. "He comes out to see what I'm making so he can do it. Not for long, you know that. He manages to find his way back to Aimee. Oh, yes," she laughed. "I'm glad we're finally getting to know him. We took him to Sunday buffet –"

"That boy can eat!" Roger added. "Not that I'm complaining. I was the same at that age."

"Actually, we see more of him now, since he's started med school," Elaine explained. "It's working out well. We have him over for dinner on Fridays or Saturdays and they spend the evening with us, now that they don't have those restaurant jobs –"

"And I get them on Sunday afternoons," Gramps chimed in. "Rob is a good young man, and I'm proud of him," he declared. "Ha, ha, why should I say that? I had nothing to do with his upbringing."

"Good genes, that's what," Roger explained.

"You've got a pretty special daughter too."

"That's what we think. We're not prejudiced, are we?"

"Not much! Well, they seem to be good for each other," Gramps went on.

"We'll have to see how this works out," Roger replied. "See if he's the man for her."

"We'll have to see," Elaine concluded with a shake of her head. She turned to Gramps. "Allen, how wonderful it must have been for you and Rob to discover each other. Wasn't it bittersweet, though? Never having known him before?"

"Oh, no, no.... I had given up hope of ever meeting my only grandchild. Now, it's all good."

"We're glad for you. You're about his only relative, aren't you?" Elaine asked

"Just about, yes. His mother is in and out of his life. They're not close. I seem to be the only one who cares about him."

"He's lucky to have you. Now, I need to excuse myself and go get dinner on the table. Where are those kids?" as she called for Jason and Jacquie. "You two men can visit for a while."

Gramps and Roger made their way into the family room. "Ah, here's the source of all those good books!" Gramps exclaimed with delight.

"Yes. I'm glad to find someone who loves the same stuff I do." He led Gramps to his desk and opened a humidor redolent with cigars. "Would you like....?" offering him a cigar.

"No, but thanks anyway. I gave that up a while ago. You go ahead, though, you won't bother me."

"Oh, I'm fine," he replied, closing the box. He gestured to a side table where he had some new books laid out. "Anything you want to borrow?"

"Ah....a new World War II book. It looks interesting. Thank you."

They chatted a while, then Roger asked abruptly, "You a military man?"

Gramps looked puzzled. "Uh.....no. I guess my ignorance shows."

"No, no, not at all," Roger laughed. "I just wondered if you are a veteran."

"No....I never served."

"Something Aimee said made me think you were. A veteran, that is."

"No." He shook his head. "You are, I see." Gramps pointed to pictures and memorabilia on the wall.

"Right. Army, Retired. Major. Bosnia, Desert Storm."

"That's....good." He wasn't quite sure what to say. "I guess I should say, thank –"

Roger cut him off. "Don't. By the way, Aimee told us about your son. I don't want to bring up sad memories, but Elaine and I want you to know that...our hearts go out to you. Even though it was long ago. That kind of makes you one of us. Military, I mean." He patted Gramps on the arm.

"Thanks. Thank you." He didn't know what else to say.

Roger changed the subject. "You've got a good boy there, Allen. He'll go far. I think he'll make you very proud someday."

"He already has. He is who he seems to be, it's not an act," he asserted.

"I think so too. But –" Roger shook his head, "these young men are all the same."

"What's that?" asked Gramps, sensing disapproval in his tone.

"That shaggy look! Hair on the face....like a billy goat." He gave a half laugh. "I'm military, you know. The clean-shaven look."

"Oh," laughed Gramps, relieved. "I kind of like his goatee. He is clean shaven, except for that edge of beard. Look here," Gramps told him, "I'm from a different generation. We knew how to grow hair! And it wasn't always neat."

"Oh, I've got no complaints about the hair," Roger assured him with a smile. "I'm sure if Aimee didn't like it, it'd be off by now."

"Ha, ha, I'm sure you're right," Gramps agreed.

"Well, now, here's Elaine. Wants us to come eat. Sure does smell good, hon."

"I'm ready any time," Gramps replied.

Dinner was a blend of good food and fast-paced conversation. Jason and Jacquie entertained him with stories about living in Europe when their father was stationed there and they seemed genuinely interested in his accounts of hiking adventures with kids. After dinner the adults moved into the living room for dessert and coffee.

After thanking Roger and Elaine for an unforgettable dinner, Gramps added, "That's quite a wonderful daughter you have, Aimee. I can't get over the fact that she takes an interest in an old man like me. And not just when she's with Rob. She comes on her own."

"That's Aimee," replied Roger. "That's who she is."

"I think it has something to do with her grandmother. My mother," Elaine explained. "We called her Gram. Aimee really got to know her when we moved back here. I went back to work, nursing at the V.A., and Gram moved in with us, to be with the kids. She and Gram got close. I think she's quite comfortable with older people."

"Is she still with you?"

"No. She passed away.... a year and a half ago. Heart attack, very unexpected," Elaine said with a pained look. "We miss her."

"I'm very sorry. I'm sure you miss her a lot," Gramps replied.

"Thank you. Yes, we do."

"Aimee and Gram were two of a kind," Roger remarked dryly, "two strong minded women."

"Why, Roger, you always said Aimee was just like you," Elaine replied with a smile.

"And so she is," he said proudly. "But our Aimee isn't entirely a paragon. She can't cook at all."

"She works in a restaurant," objected Gramps.

"A fast food place. It's not the same," Roger corrected him. "She makes sandwiches. But when it comes to real cooking...."

"I just couldn't teach her," sighed Elaine. "Aimee says Rob is a pretty fair cook."

"Maybe he'll teach her," Roger suggested.

"I'm sure he wouldn't mind trying," Gramps replied with a laugh.

They were interrupted by Rob and Aimee coming in. "We can't stay," Aimee said, "we'll take Gramps back to Sunset Woods and then we're going to the rehearsal dinner. I hope you didn't tell too many stories about me," she warned her parents, laughing.

Her father shrugged his shoulders. "I'll bet your ears were burning."

"Good to see you two back together again," Gramps commented as they rode back together. They were eager to hear his account of the evening and he was happy to tell.... *though no need to tell everything,* he decided. *As for Roger, he's an enigma. Does he approve of Rob or doesn't he?*

Ah, well, they're a fine family. The apple didn't fall very far from that tree. Aimee and Rob, they deserve each other. Of course they would never agree to that. No, but that's as it should be.

Chapter 13

"So you're back with Aimee," Bryan said the next week. "Things any better with you two? I mean, has she loosened up any?"

"I don't know what you mean. I'm glad to be with her, and yes, thank you, we're doing fine," Rob replied with a grin.

"Hey, I wish you'd talked with me before you found yourself a girlfriend. I could have helped you. I think you've got yourself more than you can handle."

"Well, thank you very much," he replied coolly.

"No, this is not personal. When you're looking for a girl –"

"I wasn't looking," Rob reminded him.

"Anyway, you said '*yes*'. Now, listen to my words of wisdom, bro. You've got to learn to choose more carefully. You want a girl who's hot. You also want a girl with brains. Some guys don't care about that, but you and I would. Dumb girls can be tiresome, very one-sided, if you know what I mean. Okay, your Aimee's got both, beauty and brains."

"I'm glad you see that," he said sarcastically.

"Hear me out. You want a girl who wants you. One who'll do anything in the world for you."

"I don't get it," he shrugged. "I want her to want me, sure – but do anything in the world for me? Like a slave, huh?"

"No, no, Rob, it's because you don't want arguments, fights. She's got to be able to give in, I mean, because she loves you."

"You mean, she's needy."

"That's not what I mean."

"That's what it looks like. So, you want her to love you. And what are you giving her?"

"I give her what she wants, I give her love, and there's no fight. We're both happy. It's a win-win."

"Sounds like a power trip to me." *Something is wrong with this picture*, he thought. *But what?*

Bryan frowned. "Well, your Aimee, she's a little too strong-minded for me."

"But not for me," Rob replied.

"Then don't complain to me when she makes you miserable. Look here, I think she'll give you more grief before you're through with her."

" *'Through with her'?* What the hell do you mean by that? I don't intend to be *'through with her'*, ever!"

"Okay, Rob, back off! I didn't mean to offend you. You two can live happily ever after, that's fine with me."

"Well, thank you." He glared at Bryan. "Just watch what you say about Aimee, okay? Now, I'm out of here. See you next week."

Later, he puzzled over the conversation. *'Through with her?' Do I really know Bryan at all? He was there for me all the years of school, always a good friend. When Grandma and Grandpa….* He shook his head. *I owe him so much. But – he's changed. He's not the Bryan I always knew. Well…. we still have good times together. He's still a buddy.*

"Hello, Gramps! Good to hear from you. Everything okay?"

"I'm doing well. Say, Rob, I would like to have the two of you over for a special afternoon or evening. There's something I want to ask of you. A favor. I sure hate to take away from your time with each other…."

"Don't worry about that. Aimee and I are usually free on weekends. We love spending time with you. We'll arrange something. You've got me curious."

"You'll just have to wait," he replied with an air of mystery. "Now, I'll arrange for a meal."

"We'll plan on it. How about next Sunday?"

"I'm sorry Aimee couldn't make it," Gramps commented as Rob greeted him the following Sunday. "She's not sick, is she?"

"No, no.....she sends her regrets. We'll do the dinner next week. She's got news," he said mysteriously.

"Oh ho! I want to hear." He stopped and reflected. "You know, I look forward to seeing her as much as seeing you. You don't mind, do you?"

"Not a bit," he laughed. "Makes me feel good. Well, the story with Aimee is – it's pretty exciting!" Gramps nodded for him to go on. "She's starting an internship today."

"Today? Sunday? What, that research job?"

"No, I'm glad to say. She wasn't looking forward to it. Research isn't her thing. Her advisor knows that, and...." he nodded excitedly, "he managed to get this just for her."

Gramps looked on expectantly. "It's a brand new internship, at the Children's Museum in the city."

"Well!"

"They interviewed her the other day, they liked her of course, and they want her to start tomorrow. They've got something big going on tomorrow with children and she wanted to get oriented today so she could start right in. The museum is open seven days a week, so Sunday is okay with them." He shrugged his shoulders. "It's not so great with me. I didn't want to give up my day with her – though I'm really glad for her. "

"I'm sure you're disappointed. But I'm glad for her too," he said, nodding his head. "Well, now....what do you have there?"

Rob opened a bag and pulled out a chess set.

"Ah, Rob, it's been a long time. You'll have to teach me all over again."

"I don't think so," he replied with a shake of his head.

It took a while for Gramps to regain his confidence and skill but eventually they were playing a close game. As Rob was contemplating a move his mind wandered. *I feel like I've known him all my life,* he reflected. *Is it because he's family? Hmm, what better time to ask him about his album? As soon as the game is over.....*He moved his piece.

"Checkmate!" Rob paid dearly for his moment of distraction.

"I didn't see that coming," he laughed. "Well, may the best man win."

From then on it was a hard-fought game with Gramps finally emerging victorious. "I feel guilty about winning," Gramps said apologetically, "I'm sure your mind was on Aimee instead of the game." Rob laughed as Gramps went on, "I've been wondering, what's happening with you and Aimee?"

"Happening? What do you mean?"

"Where do things stand with you two? I know you love her."

"You know I do! I love her."

"Well, then, what are your intentions?"

"Gramps," he frowned, "that's old fashioned."

"Maybe. But it's still a good question."

He shrugged. "I don't see how we can be married, or even engaged, for a long time. Maybe a couple of years. I told you... .I'm just not ready."

"You know what I think of Aimee. She's a jewel. It's been wonderful for me to get to know a new granddaughter as well as a new grandson. Rob," he laughed, "tell her I missed her today. It's always a bit brighter when she's here."

"It sure is. I call her my firefly."

"Yes – she brightens a dark world."

"That's exactly what I tell her! I can't imagine my life without her."

"Rob, a girl like Aimee won't wait forever. Don't let her slip away."

"I don't know," he sighed. "We can't afford to get married, even if I thought I was ready. I still would like us to live together, but I respect her feelings. You know," he laughed, "I think you convinced me. I'm not pressuring her to change her mind, not anymore."

"I'm glad to hear that."

"So, I feel like we're in limbo. No plans, no hope –"

"If you could afford to live together, why couldn't you afford to get married?"

"I suppose we can't afford to live together. Neither of us has an income. Her internship is unpaid. Wedding costs – I don't even want to think about it. Aimee's folks will pay for some but most of it will be up to us. And –" he shrugged, "marriage is a big step."

"Not like living together, huh? Well, Rob, don't let her slip away…."

Rob shook his head in frustration. *What's a grandfather for, if not to give advice? Advice…but no answers. What am I to do?* He took leave of Gramps more confused than ever.

So, what are my intentions, he asked himself. *Why am I dragging my feet about marriage? I want to spend the rest of my life with her, now and forever, so it's not a matter of commitment. She's my world! But it's still a huge jump, going from zero involvement with girls, to marriage, almost overnight. Am I ready for it?*

Is living together any different from marriage? Well, that's a jump too. It would be easier to get out of if I found anybody else. After all, Aimee's the first girl I've ever been serious about….so am I sure she's right for me? She's had a lot more experience. Do I really need experience? No, no, I don't need experience to tell me she's right for me and I'm right for her! I want to spend the rest of my life with her. Only her. So no, it's not a matter of commitment.

But something is holding me back. What am I missing? I can't quite get hold of it.

What's the only marriage I know anything about? Grandma and Grandpa Ferguson. They weren't romantic but I know they loved each other. They were happy. I guess I didn't think about it until they celebrated their fortieth wedding anniversary a few years ago. They renewed their vows. '*Why?*' I asked Grandpa. '*Didn't you get it right the first time?*' I was a smart college kid.

'*As a matter of fact, we didn't,*' Rob remembered him saying. '*It took me a long time to learn to be a good husband and father. I was all about making money, giving us a lifestyle.*' He knew the rest of the story. Their first-born, his mother's older brother, had died in an alcohol-related accident in his teens. Grandpa said that had sobered him up even though he wasn't a drinker. '*I had to learn to put my family first, learn to give of myself. That's when we began to have a good marriage.*'

I remember when Granny died. She had left Grandpa a modest inheritance and I was ready to help him spend it. '*No, Rob, Grandma needs to help me decide.* '*Why?*' I asked him. '*It's your money.*'

'*No*', he replied, '*we share and share alike.*'

'*That's not right!*' I told him. But Grandma had a slightly different view. '*Well, we each have our own spending money, but Grandpa's right,*' she said, '*what's mine is his and what's his is mine.*'

Maybe that's what's bothering me, he concluded. *I'm not selfish, but I'm not ready for that! Aimee and I could live together very happily and not....uh, belong to each other, not like that. Why, Grandpa and Grandma used to call each other about every little thing.*

No. I love Aimee. But I like my independence!

He decided to talk it over with her. *She's the most independent person I know. I'm sure she'll understand.*

A few days later they met for lunch in their back booth.

"Aimee....would you say we belong to each other?" he began hesitantly.

"Hmm....I'll have to think about that....no, I'd say we don't. Not now, not until we're married, or when we're engaged. Until then, we're free to come and go. Date other people." She looked at him with concern. "Do you want to, Rob? Date other girls?"

"No, that's not it," he assured her. "I'm committed to you! With or without a ring. I've told you that already, I want to spend my life with you –"

She studied him curiously. "Then what's this about belonging to each other?"

"According to you – when we're married, then we belong to each other. I don't like that at all. I think it would be stifling."

"Stifling!" She drew back in surprise. "What's so stifling, anyway? I don't believe what I'm hearing!"

"Aimee, honey," he spoke reassuringly, "It's the whole idea of being answerable to someone else, of sharing everything, well, money, for example – I'm not ready for all that. Honey, I prize my independence! I worked hard for it. I'm just not ready to give it up."

"It's a good thing I'm finding this out now! That's exactly what marriage is, it's sharing everything! What do you think '*the two become one*' means?" she asked, her voice rising.

"Now, Aimee," he said evenly, "I believe we could be married, be committed, exclusive to each other, and still be independent. Not get into all this sharing business."

"I can't believe this! I thought I knew you." She shook her head in shock.

"Honey, honey, nothing's changed. I still love you!" he exclaimed. "I'm just being honest, that's all, about my ideas of marriage. Isn't that what you want?"

She stared at him, unable to speak. Then – "Well, Rob, I'm glad I found this out now!" She reached in her purse, drew out a bill and flung it on the table. "There! I wouldn't want you to have to pay for my meal!" She got up, grabbed her jacket and ran out.

She texted him. 'Let's cool it for a while. I need 2 think. So do U. A.'

What just happened? What's going on, he asked himself, trying to control his anger. *She wasn't even willing to discuss it! She just jumped to conclusions, didn't even give me a chance! And what's this 'A' ? Not 'LL', 'love, love' our code.*

He was so troubled that night he couldn't concentrate on his classwork. Finally he forced himself to put her out of his mind. He knew that trick well.

Later, he tried to sort things out. *I don't want to go running to Gramps. No, this is for me to figure out. I don't want to talk to him or anyone about this. Certainly not Bryan.*

But he'd promised to visit Gramps the next Sunday afternoon and there was no way he could keep it secret. He told him what had happened. "So that's what it's about," he concluded. "I finally figured out why I've been resisting the idea of marriage. I want to spend my life with her, but marriage seems smothering to me. As if we owned each other."

"That's too bad," he sighed. "It's best I not get involved between you two. I can't tell you what to do. Or take sides. All I can do is help you think things through."

"I worked hard for my independence! Why should I give it up?" he demanded. "Why should I be answerable to someone else?"

"Those are good questions. Very good questions. But there's one element that you're overlooking….."

He shook his head. "I don't know. What are you getting at?"

"Love, Rob. It's love. You give up some of your hard-won independence, though not all of it, because you're gaining something much better. You're willing to give yourself, even to sacrifice…..because you love."

Rob sighed. "I know you're right, because I feel that way about Aimee. I'm just not sure I'm ready for it, all my life. To give like that." He shook his head. "I remember a story I read in school about a newlywed couple who were very poor, and they sacrificed their most precious possessions to give to the other one. The girl sold her hair; I don't remember what the guy did. I don't remember the name of the story. Their sacrifices cancelled each other out. I thought it was very sad."

"Ah, yes. '*The Gift of the Magi*'. A wonderful story. But look, they weren't sad."

"They weren't? Why not?"

"They realized how much they were loved. How wonderful is that? Rob, how much do you love Aimee?"

"Oh – I'd do anything in the world for her! Anything she wanted. I'm like a jellyfish when I'm around her. So – I know it doesn't make sense, that I feel the way I do."

"You're closer than you think. Look, if you were married and had a paycheck, would you spend it on yourself or would you put it in the pot, so to speak, for both of you? Expecting her to do the same."

"I see your point, Gramps, but I don't know. I wouldn't want to give up everything. I'm not selfish, but I think you have to save something for yourself. That's what Grandma Ferguson said."

"Nothing wrong with that, as long as you both agree. As long as your priorities are each other. Your grandmother and I, we had to learn to share and share alike. By the way, we're all selfish, in our own way. I think we need marriage, to knock it out of us. Learn to care about the other person more than we care about ourself."

"I don't know about the selfish part. That's not us. I'll have to think about it."

"You do that. One last thought. Our little Allen needed very expensive medicine for a while, when we were young and poor. What do you think our priorities were?"

"Well, the baby, of course. I have no problem with that. But – as I said, I have my reservations." He shrugged helplessly. "I don't think I'm ready."

"Keep thinking about it, Rob."

"I will. Now....about Aimee. I don't know what got into her. She got mad all at once, and stormed out."

"She must have been hurt."

"I certainly didn't mean to hurt her. I can't figure it out." He shook his head. "I'm not going to crawl back to her. I think she needs to make the first move."

"I said I wouldn't tell you what to do. I'll only suggest.... don't let it go on too long."

"Gramps, thank you. I'm glad I came."

He left feeling no closer to an answer than before.

Then without warning their peaceful lives were disrupted by a voice from the past. Rob and Gramps were notified that Damien's case was coming to trial and they might be called as witnesses for the Prosecution.

Rob texted Aimee to tell her about it. *I know it's in the news but I want her to hear it from me*, he told himself. She texted back that she would try to arrange her hours at the museum and drive Gramps if he was called upon to testify. She knew Rob had classes. If he had to testify she would try to be there to support him.

"I hope we're called. I'm ready for it," Rob told Gramps.

"You've changed your tune. No more '*Mr. Nice Guy*', huh?"

"Not any more. What I saw of him earlier, wasn't the Damien I thought I knew."

"Of course, the media has him guilty already."

"Well, overlooking that, I still didn't like what I saw. He was defiant. That doesn't sound like an innocent man. I'm ready to testify."

"So am I! If I can help put him away, I will."

The Prosecutor's staff visited Gramps and took a deposition, then helped prepare his testimony. Rob's preparation took place at the Court House. The question was, would they be called? The trial began and went on for a week. They eagerly followed it on TV. The case against him seemed compelling and the Prosecutor thought they would not be needed.

Just when they thought it was over Gramps was called on to give his testimony. Aimee picked him up, expressing Rob's regrets at having to miss. "Nervous, Gramps?" she asked.

"Not one bit," he declared. "I've been ready for this for a long time!"

Aimee listened with pride as he testified in a voice that could be heard to the back of the Courtroom. First, that he had heard Damien declare his belief that old people had a responsibility to die and make way for younger people, and secondly, that Damien had personally threatened him.

'Threaten with what?"' the Defense Attorney was quick to ask. "That he'd get the *'same thing'?* And what exactly was that? As for old people getting an injection, he didn't say he would do it, did he?"

He could feel Damien's eyes boring through him as he spoke.

Gramps said nothing on the way home, ignoring Aimee's cheerful assurances that he had done well. Finally, as she took him to his room he looked at her and shook his head. "I don't think I did any good. No good at all."

Unexpectedly, Rob received a text from Aimee. '*I was hasty. Let's talk.*' They set it up for the next day.

Chapter 14

He arrived early and waited for her in the back booth. He was still trying to understand. *It's been almost three weeks since I've seen her – I miss her so much! But I still don't know why she was so angry. How did I hurt her? I'm not so mad any more. I need to give her a chance to talk.....I hope she'll give me a chance to talk....*

She came over and he got up to help her off with her jacket. "Rob, you're always a gentleman," she smiled. Suddenly they were in each other's arms, holding each other close, kissing. "Oh, Rob," she murmured, "I can't live without you!"

"And I can't live without you...." He kissed her again, then kissed tears in her eyes, not wanting to let her go.

A little girl in a nearby booth clapped her hands and smiled at them. Smiling back at her, they kissed again then broke away from each other and slid into their seats, holding hands across the table.

"Rob, it was the trial, when I was with Gramps," she said with feeling, "and all I could think was, you were there! You were there with me in spirit. I knew then, you are a part of me and I am a part of you. We love each other. Nothing can change that. We mustn't let anything change that."

"No more doubts, honey?" He patted her hand.

"My darling Rob." She shook her head. "No doubts. We belong together."

"Aimee…." he held her hand tightly and kissed it. "I know I hurt you and I'm not sure why. But we love each other and we will work this out." He gave a little laugh. "I made up my mind I wasn't going to talk to Gramps." She looked at him as if to ask, '*why not*'? "I knew what he'd say – '*Go back to Aimee*,' – and I didn't want to hear that. I was hurt too, and mad, I couldn't understand what had happened and I wanted to work it out myself."

"So what did you do?" She didn't tell him that her mother had scolded her. '*Aimee, he's a good man and you love him. Don't act like a spoiled princess, sit down and talk this over with him. It's an important issue. You need to talk about it.*' But she had waited, struggling with her feelings….then the trial intervened….and now here they were.

"Well, do you think I could keep it from him? I was over there on a Sunday and it all came out. And you know what? He said he wouldn't take sides. He wasn't going to tell me what to do. But he would help me think about it."

"I appreciate that. He's a wise man."

"He said I would be giving up some of my independence for something better, and that's love. He also has the idea that marriage can – as he put it – '*knock the selfishness out of us*'. Because we learn to put the other person first. I don't think I'm selfish, I think I'm pretty unselfish!" She nodded in agreement. "But I guess giving up some of my independence would be the test of that."

"Ah, your precious independence." She smiled. "I talked it over a little with Mom and Dad. I hope you don't mind…."

He shrugged his shoulders. "I guess not. I just don't want them to know all about us."

"I agree with you. But they were helpful. Mom said for her, the biggest difference between living together and being married was when they were living together she came and went as she pleased and spent her money as she pleased. I guess Dad did too. Then when they were married that caused a lot of fights."

"I don't understand that. Why would marriage make that difference? But honey, all of a sudden, my independence isn't so important any more. You are. Our life together."

''I'm so glad! I knew we could work it out. Now why don't I go order food?"

When she returned he had a question for her. "Honey, what do you know about independence? How can you understand what I'm struggling with when you've always lived with your parents? That's a fair question."

"See, there's still so much we don't know about each other! Actually, I did live on campus the second year I was here, my junior year, with my girlfriend Bridget – you've heard me talk about her. We shared a room in the new dorm. It's co-ed, of course. That took some getting used to. I learned a lot about life, fast. I worked part time. Yes, I was independent. Almost the whole year." She frowned.

" '*Almost*'? he repeated, puzzled. "Why didn't you continue?"

She answered slowly. "Some scary things happened, around me.....I didn't feel safe. I didn't tell my parents, I knew they'd pull me out of there and I didn't want that. But then – something bad did happen –" A shadow crossed her face and she looked away.

"Aimee, what?" he asked with concern.

She tried to answer but couldn't. Finally, with head lowered she managed the words. "I was almost raped. After a date –"

Rob seized her hands. "Oh, honey, honey. That's awful! That must have been terrifying. How did you get away?"

She took a deep breath, then haltingly told her story. "He forced his way into my room, after a date. It all happened so fast....he was so fast....holding me, hurting me....I screamed and Bridget came in from the bathroom." She stopped, squeezing Rob's hands. "He panicked and ran. Karate helped....a little....I was able to throw him off balance." Tears burned her eyes.

"Oh, honey….." He tried to take it in. "My sweet Aimee." He held her hands tightly. "Was that the guy who used a different name with each girl, he pretended to be a student…" She nodded. "They finally caught him, didn't they?"

"Yes…I'm so glad I didn't have to testify! They had DNA evidence, he pled guilty."

"Oh, baby….how are you now?"

She was still, trying to speak. "Well….I had nightmares, for a while. I saw the campus shrink and I think I'm over it now. But before then, my parents and I had some pretty heated discussions. I wanted to stay. I didn't want to give up and go home in defeat. Bridget and I would look out for each other. Hmph! Mom was not impressed!"

"So what happened?"

"They made me an offer I couldn't refuse. I could be independent at home. They would let me come and go as I pleased as long as I followed a few house rules, you know, not come home drunk, do some chores, pay a little rent when I'm working, they wouldn't question me -anyway, it's working out fine. I've had my '*street independence*', I call it, and I feel independent now. Oh, and Grendel was part of the deal. He protects me."

"Good old Grendel. But why do you need protection at home?"

"When I'm running. He always runs with me. Jacquie too, when she runs. I would never run alone. He's my guard dog at home and you're my guard dog in the city."

"Arf arf! I like that. Um, wasn't Grendel a monster? In mythology?"

"Yes. A man-eating monster."

" '*Man-eating' !* Should I be afraid?"

"Oh, he'll tear you from limb to limb! If you were going to hurt me. Mmm, he's such a sweet dog…..well," she assured him, "you and Grendel get along just fine. So far so good."

"Oh, Aimee." He thought about her story. "What a terrible thing to go through! Honey – were you worried about me? Do you feel safe with me? I remember you didn't want to come to my apartment for a long time."

"Rob....I always felt safe with you. And loved."

"But then – why wouldn't you -?" He didn't want to tell her that his motives weren't always pure. *Nothing wrong with that,* he thought, *I'm a normal guy! But I'd never have taken advantage of her.*

"Oh, honey, no, it was me, my feelings." He shook his head, not comprehending. "I didn't trust my feelings." *With good reason,* she thought, remembering their dinner together in his apartment.

"Oh....oh! Sweetheart." He took her hands. "You'll always be safe with me. I will always honor your feelings." *Yes, I will,* he promised himself. *She's worth it, she's one in a million. Even though I hadn't expected this when I met her.* He thought again of Bryan and Natasha, their comfortable life together.....

"And Rob, I'll always respect you. I love you....Now let's eat!"

The Damian case. It was now in the hands of the jury. They waited, anxiously. When the verdict was announced Rob sped over to see Gramps.

"I can't believe they let him off! *'Not Guilty'*! I know he's guilty!"

"Rob, remember, '*Not Guilty*' doesn't mean innocent. The problem was, they just couldn't prove their case. Not enough evidence. You and I know he's guilty, and I'll bet everyone in that Courtroom knew he was guilty."

"Including the Defense Attorney?"

"Especially the Defense Attorney. I'm sure of it. He's one clever weasel and he was able to get him off on '*Reasonable Doubt'*."

"Yes – of murder! That's disgusting. But –" he shook his head, "I don't get it. Aimee said your testimony was great. Very forceful."

"It was a desperate attempt to save a failing case. They just didn't have any firm evidence."

"There's a pattern, though. Those deaths in his last place.... and what about Sunset Gardens? He could have killed some people there. I think he did."

"The problem was, they couldn't bring up previous incidents. They had to stick with the present case." He frowned. "The arrogance of the man! It makes my blood boil."

"He'll walk free, and if I know Damien he'll be laughing all the way to his next job."

"He's not free yet. He may do a few years on drug charges – I hope so. They did convict him of that. But with credit for time served...."

"Oh yes, and he'll be out early on good behavior. I know Damien."

"I agree with you. I don't think he got what he deserved. I think people are safer when he's behind bars." He remembered Damien's look and shuddered.

Chapter 15

A few days later they were at Aimee's house, spending some time by themselves in the living room. The rest of the family was watching a movie in the family room. Grendel was curled protectively at her feet.

"I'm glad you got over your fear of men….after that awful incident," he said as he pulled her close to him.

She pulled back. "It wasn't just fear, Rob. It was hatred! I hated men."

"I can understand," he nodded sympathetically, stroking her hair.

"I know it could have been so much worse. But still, it was horrible." She shuddered. "I was lucky, I mean, he didn't actually – do it –" she couldn't bring herself to say the word – "but another minute and he would have." She broke into sobs and buried her head in his shoulder.

"Oh, baby, baby –" He kissed her hair and held her gently. "Go ahead and cry."

Between sobs, she went on with her story. "The campus shrink, she helped. But I still hated the sight of a man. What gives a man the right to think he can just take what he wants?"

"Some men are animals." He kissed her forehead. "How did you ever get over it?"

"Dad. It was Dad. He put me back together. He talked with me, helped me understand that sick thinking....he was kind, he was good. And angry!"

"Yes! I know what I'd like to do to that guy!"

She shook her head, remembering. "I told Mom to hide the key to the gun cabinet."

"Do you think he would have....?"

"I don't know. No....he didn't do anything when they finally apprehended the guy. That would have been his chance. But..... it was Dad. If it weren't for him, I'd be very bitter today, I'm sure of it."

"And I'm the beneficiary." He held her away and looked in her eyes. "Aimee, baby. That guy – what he did to you, it was ugly, it was frightening. I don't want it to scar you. I want to be the one to show you what love really is. Beautiful. Honey – I hope to have that privilege, some day. As your husband." He took her hands. "Someday soon."

"Yes, someday soon," she repeated.

"I'm glad your dad was there for you. Your mom, too, I'm sure she helped you."

She nodded agreement. "He's a good dad. That's what I want for my children. A good dad. A loving dad."

He kissed her face. "Aimee, I'm that man." He looked at her intently.

"Oh, Rob....I sure hope so."

"I will be," he declared fervently, "a good father....to our children."

She looked searchingly at him. "Rob – darling – are you saying what I think you're saying? Are you talking marriage? Really?"

He laughed sheepishly. "Yes – of course. Someday soon. There was never any doubt."

"What? You mean, you're ready for marriage? Rob," she laughed, not sure what to believe, "when did this happen?"

"Oh, Aimee, baby –" he took her by the chin – "The last few days, it just came over me, how much I love you. I want you to live with me – but I'm not ready for marriage? How crazy is that?" He gave her a resounding kiss. "There! Does that show you I mean business?"

"Wow….yes!"

He broke away, laughing. "I'm a blockhead, that's what! I've known since the day I met you, I've always known I would spend the rest of my life with you." Taking her face in his hands he kissed her face and then her lips. "I just had to get used to the idea of marriage," he explained. "I'm a dumb schmuck who never even had a girlfriend, and suddenly – I'm in love! It took some getting used to."

She laughed and held him close. "Don't apologize for not having girlfriends! I'm glad I was the first one. You've had friends who are girls, you know how to treat a girl. It's not like we're an alien race." She shuddered. "Honey, I was afraid I would lose you. In the beginning, that is. My weird principles – I was afraid you'd give up on me."

"Aimee, darling, I was never going to give up on you." He frowned and shook his head, looking away. "There I was, minding my own business in the food line when all at once the most beautiful girl in the world casts a spell on me. Before I knew what was happening," he grinned, "I knew I wanted to spend the rest of my life with her, making her happy," he kissed her, "and I wanted to protect her. Oops – I'm sorry, most girls don't want to hear that."

She nodded seriously. "That's love, honey. And remember, I'm not '*most girls*'. I'm proud that I can take care of myself – most of the time – but I know my limitations. You make me feel….." she snuggled up to him, "very loved. Loved and protected," she nodded, "I like that."

"Always, always…." He hugged her.

And he'll always be safe with me, she thought. "Talk about casting a spell! My boss was worried about me. I went to work that day, an hour late, and I told him I'd met the man I was going to marry. Level-headed Aimee Love!"

" '*The man you were going to marry'?* " he repeated with surprise. "You never told me that."

"Oh my goodness, I couldn't tell you that, I was afraid I'd scare you off. So I told you, '*the man of my dreams*.' Like some love-sick teenager."

"Either way, I like it," he laughed. "Anyway, now we have each other. And marriage – I'm not afraid of marriage. It wasn't a matter of commitment, or the lack of it.....I just had to get used to the idea. Giving up my independence. All that sharing business! Now I'm ready. To be a husband. A father too. But not too soon. Fatherhood, that would take some getting used to. I'm not ready for that."

"Aren't we smart, not making babies? I would not want that strain, not yet. But Rob, you will be a wonderful father, I know it."

"How would you know?" he shrugged. "When have you seen me around kids?"

She thought about it. "That's true, I haven't. But by now, I know you as a person. I know what's important to you," she looked at him, her eyes shining, "I know how you treat people. You'll be a good father."

He nodded. "It's important to me. I'm glad I had a good father, Grandpa Ferguson. Whatever I am today, as a man, it's because of him."

She smiled contentedly. "We've got so much to look forward to....So!" she exclaimed excitedly, "is this a proposal? I can't wait to tell my family!"

"No...no, not yet," he shook his head seriously, then suddenly he lifted her to her feet.

"Baby...." he whirled her around, laughing, "when I propose, you'll know it!"

"Well, that's something to look forward to!" She kissed him. "Nothing to my folks?"

"No, please, not yet. Not Gramps either. No one, okay?"

"Yes...oh, yes." They fell back onto the couch, stumbling over Grendel who didn't seem to mind. "Oh, Rob, I love you!

You and Dad. The two men in my life." A shadow crossed his face. "Don't worry, Rob – you're number one. You always will be." She reached down and stroked Grendel. "Ah....the other male in my life." She buried her face in his fur. "My sweet baby dog...."

"Your baby!" he patted Grendel. "Honey, he's ten years old."

"Don't tell him that. He'll always be my baby. My faithful guard dog," she said, nuzzling her face against his. "Mmm.....I have to add Gramps to that list. I've only known him a few months, but I do love him."

"I'm glad you do," he said warmly, "he's my family."

"He's a good man. His love, his gentlemanly ways....and he's a man of character. I'm so glad he's a part of my life." She laughed. "Our life."

"Honey, why don't we take Grendel with us when we visit him Sunday?"

"Hmm....that's a nice idea." She thought for a moment. "I don't take him anywhere, except when I'm running. Not in the car – ha, he'll think he's going to the vet! He may not want to go. Well....we could try it. We'll have to come straight back here because we can't leave him in the car while we go somewhere else."

"We can do it. Gramps would love to see him, I'm sure of it."

"Yes. They did okay when he was over here for dinner. Yes, let's do it. Now – we need to get back to the family." She shook her head. "I won't say a word." She gave a sly look. "Do you think they'll guess?"

"Of course not! We always act crazy."

I need to talk with Aimee's parents, he told himself later. A marriage proposal would come as no surprise to them, but could he count on their blessing? *'Blessing', that's a strange word to use....the question is, will they be pleased?*

He had long felt accepted into their family, but as a son in law? He wasn't so sure. The Loves lived a comfortable, even affluent lifestyle. Roger had bought a thriving security business upon his retirement from the military and he was a newly elected Councilman in their town. Suppose they wanted Aimee to '*marry well*'? What did he, Rob, have to offer? Ambition, resting on a commendable academic career. Not bad.

But family, now that was something else. Family meant everything to Roger, not lineage but stability, support, love. He had expounded on it one time and Rob had wanted to melt into the shadows. He had a wonderful grandfather, yes, but a mother who at best was an embarrassment. A subject best left unmentioned. His mother and the Loves, *may they never meet*.

I need to know where I stand, he told himself resolutely. *It shouldn't be so hard to find a time to talk with them alone, now that Aimee has these crazy hours with her internship. I just have to do it. But what if….?* He didn't want to think about it.

Now that the trial was out of the way Rob and Aimee were happy to be back to normal and get together with Gramps as they had planned weeks before. This time they brought a guest.

"Well, my goodness! This wonderful creature," he exclaimed with pleasure as he stroked the dog's head. "Grendel, isn't it? Thank you, thank you for bringing him! We'll have a nice time tonight, won't we, boy?" he asked Grendel, who settled himself comfortably at the side of the wheelchair.

"Would you look at that! He never leaves your feet, does he, hon?" Rob asked Aimee.

"Uh…no," she answered as she watched Grendel move closer to Gramps. "Looks like I have some competition."

They sat down to eat and Rob broached the question they'd been wondering about. "Okay, Gramps, what's the mystery?"

"Rob. I have a special favor to ask of you. I would like you to contact the local VFW –"

"VFW?" He looked puzzled. "I've heard of it –"

"Veterans of Foreign Wars. It's a lodge. I'd like you to arrange for me to speak at a meeting, to have the whole program. Can you do that? And I'd like you to be there. Aimee too, if she wants."

"I'll be there," Aimee promised. "I wouldn't miss it."

"Do you have a title for your program?"

He shrugged his shoulders. "No title. You can call me '*The Mystery Guest'*."

"Ha, ha," Rob laughed. "That ought to bring a crowd! Well, I'll be glad to arrange it. Might take a couple of weeks to schedule, though."

"That'll be okay. Would you arrange for the press to be there?"

"The press?" *That sure is strange,* he thought. *Gramps doesn't like the press*. He shrugged. "Sure, if you want."

"I do. Maybe you can get the person who did our article. She did a good job. Now, if you have to say more, at the lodge, you can tell them I'm the father of a veteran. But that's not for publication."

"Yes, yes! This will be wonderful!" he exclaimed, as understanding dawned. *This is about my father, oh, yes….!*

"And maybe we can smoke your mother out."

"My mother?" He shook his head, his happy mood broken. "Not her again."

"Just an idea of mine."

"You know how I feel about that. About her," he said grimly. "The less I have to do with her the better."

"Don't worry about it, Rob. She won't be there," Gramps assured him.

"That's a relief. Why spoil a good evening*?" But what is he getting at*, he wondered. He took Aimee's hand.

"I'm with Rob," she told Gramps. "I think he needs to keep his distance from her. She's hurt him enough already."

Gramps smiled serenely. "It will be all right."

Rob seemed lost in thought.

"C'mon, Rob," Aimee pulled him up. "Let's clear away the dishes."

As they were working he glanced over at Gramps. "Honey," he whispered, touching her arm. "Look." Grendel was leaning against him, his head on Gramps' feet.

"Now don't you disturb a sleeping dog!" Gramps admonished them.

Aimee sat down, laughing. "Gramps," she said, "he's never done that with anyone. Why would he do that to you?"

"He knows what he's doing. He obviously has a mind of his own."

"I see he hasn't given up on wanting to meet my mother," Rob grumbled as they were driving home. "What do you think about it?"

"Well, I'm the outsider looking in, you know. I see things differently. It makes sense to me. I can think of lots of reasons he'd like to."

"I guess so....but...." he shook his head, unable to go on.

"I agree." She patted his hand. "He should leave you out of it."

"Right about that."

He was silent a while, lost in his thoughts. "Another time with Gramps, and he still hasn't said anything about that album." He shrugged his shoulders. "I can't seem to make myself bring it up, either. What's wrong with me, honey?"

"Nothing is wrong with you," she told him. "Hmm.....is it because you're afraid of losing him?"

"No, we're past that. But it's been –what, six months, and he still hasn't shown it to me. I'm dying to see what's in it. That's my family, Aimee! I have a right to see it. He has to show it to me!"

"Well, he'll do what he wants. Why don't you just go ahead and ask him, again? Maybe he forgot."

He sighed with resignation. “I’m sure he didn’t forget.” He thought about it. “I won’t ask him for a while. Not while he has this VFW talk on his mind.”

“That’s very thoughtful,” she said kindly.

“No, I’m just putting it off. I’ll bring it up when that’s done. I will. Hmph, why is it so hard?”

“I don’t think there’s anything wrong with you, honey.” She patted his hand. “Of course you want to know. As for why he won‘t give it up – well, that’s anyone’s guess.”

“I think the reason is....there’s something about it that’s painful to him. I don’t want to cause him further pain, but – I have to know! After the VFW talk, when we take him home, I’ll ask him then.”

“Sounds good to me. As long as he’s not too tired.”

“Aimee....did you get a look at Grendel tonight? What he was doing?”

“Aside from the fact that he was using Gramps’ feet as his pillow....what are you getting at?”

“A couple of times he dropped something, his napkin, a spoon – and Grendel was right there, picking it up! It’s like he was trained to do it.”

“Well, I’ll be!” she exclaimed in amazement. “I could drop things all day long and Grendel would never pick up anything for me.” She shook her head and laughed. “It’s as if he knows –”

“Yes, he knows you’re not helpless,” he completed her thought. “But he knows that Gramps is.”

“Right.” She reached down and patted his head. “Good boy, Grendel.” She frowned. *I’m willing to share him,* she thought. *But I don’t want to lose him.*

Chapter 16

A smiling Rob wheeled Gramps into the VFW hall. It was crowded with veterans, mostly older men.

"Dad would be so proud!" he told Gramps, patting him on the shoulder.

Oh Lord, he thought with a groan, *I hope I don't disappoint him. Dear God, help me.*

Rob sat in the front row, smiling at Gramps to encourage him. Aimee made her way to the local news reporter, who didn't know why she was there. Rob had told her it would be worth her while but he didn't know either.

Gramps had been billed as '*The Mystery Guest*', topic unknown. Nothing more was said. A microphone was placed on his lapel. After a few opening formalities, he, Rob, and Aimee were introduced. It was noted that he was not a veteran but they welcomed him anyway. There were a few cheers. Speaking without notes, he began.

"Gentlemen, I come before you tonight to share something that is deep in my heart." He took a deep breath. "It will not be easy to talk about."

A voice from the audience called out, "Tell it, brother!"

"Gentlemen – I have the greatest admiration for you all," he began slowly. "For your service, your sacrifice. Some of you volunteered, some were drafted, but all of you went to foreign shores leaving behind your lives and loved ones. You watched as your buddies were killed. You were thankful to come home. You men who went to Vietnam – and I want to talk to you especially tonight – you left an enemy behind, and you came home to an enemy. Protesters who greeted you with ugly words, people throwing things at you, calling you names –" Some of the men shifted uncomfortably, remembering.

"Gentlemen –" he paused, gathering courage – "I was one of those protesters." A gasp went up from the audience. He saw the color drain from Rob's face. He dropped his head, unable to go on.

He felt a hand on his shoulder and he looked up to see one of the men from the audience.

"We're with you, brother."

Rob came over, sat beside him and took hold of his arm. He handed him a handkerchief which he used to wipe his eyes. Some of the men stared straight ahead. Old memories were being disturbed.

"My fiancee and I were college students, hippies. I won't deny the pot smoking and '*make love, not war*'. I'm not proud of that." There was some embarrassed laughter from the audience. "We were caught up in the anti-war movement, the protests and all that. We truly believed in what we were doing. We felt we were superior because, we hated war! But deep in my heart I knew it was not right to treat my fellow human beings the way I treated these men – as I treated you. I can't begin to tell you how sorry I am. So very sorry." Shaking his head, he took a sip of water.

"After a while we got married, dropped our hippie lifestyle and built a new life. But we were still anti-war, anti-military, even anti-government. We had a son, Allen. He knew all this. We hid nothing from him. We were proud of our beliefs. Allen, too, built a life. He was an outstanding young man. We planned college for him. Nothing but the best."

"Then, on his 18th birthday he came to us and said he had enlisted in the Marines! I felt betrayed! I never saw it coming.

My beliefs hadn't changed one bit. Where had he gotten his? Well, we fought. I said terrible things to him. He was so hurt, he didn't even try to defend himself. Yes, I broke his heart. He went off to boot camp the next day with my angry words ringing in his ears."

Rob held tightly to his arm. He blinked back tears.

"My wife said I should accept him because I loved him, said I didn't have to agree with him. She was right, but I wanted to do more. I wanted to understand him. So, I began reading books of his, researching the history of our country. I read of the struggles for freedom, the battles, the courage of men who hated war but took up weapons for the rights of others. My actions, years earlier, were now a source of shame for me. I felt – and I still feel – that I cannot look a veteran in the eye." He dropped his head and took a deep breath, then raised his head and with ringing voice went on.

"But I found that I was proud -so very proud – of my country. Of our military. Of you veterans. Proud of my son. I was able to tell him this, and we reconciled."

He took a sip of water. "There is just a bit more. A few years later, my son, Pfc Robert Allen Douglas, Jr., gave his life in the first Gulf War. I tell you this, not for sympathy, but to let you know that, as much as I miss him and the life he might have lived, I honor his sacrifice and all the sacrifices that have been made by his fallen brothers."

"Gentlemen, I thank you." He bowed his head.

Suddenly he was overwhelmed by sustained clapping. He looked up to find men crowded around him, some with tears streaming down their faces, shaking his hand, hugging him. "Thank you, brother, thank you." A few men remained in their seats, still struggling with their memories.

Rob put his arm around him. Aimee blew him a kiss, then came running over to hug him.

Exhausted, he was barely able to manage a little light refreshment and then Rob and Aimee took him back to Sunset Woods. They were prepared to wheel him back to his room when he stopped them. "There is a bit more I want to tell you. I've got my second wind now. I think a little snack could revive me some more." Aimee took the hint and went to get him something to eat.

When he had eaten a little, he went on. "Rob, your father came home before he was deployed overseas. We had a wonderful visit. His great sadness was that he could not locate you. His buddies had no idea where your mother was. Then he left and was shipped to Kuwait. Sometime later, two young Marines came up our walk. I thought, they must have something wonderful to tell about Allen. How ignorant I was! They were there to tell me that.....he had been killed in action."

"Oh," Aimee whispered, "how awful!"

"You already know that. I just wanted to give the details. His funeral was held here and we hoped your mother would show up. It was in all the news, she couldn't miss it. But no, she didn't come. Not long after, his mother, my Kate, died. A quick-acting cancer. I think she died of a broken heart. My heart was broken too. Everyone I loved was gone. It was the beginning of a very dark time for me." He shook his head. "I can't go into that now. I'm wiped out."

"Gramps", they hugged him tightly, "We're so proud of you. And we love you very much. Good night."

"Gramps! Rob glanced at a text he'd just received. "You've gone viral!"

"Whatever that means. I'm too tired to care."

He was soon to find out.

"Mr. Douglas!" shouted the aide who was helping him dress a couple of days later. "You're on TV!" She pointed to Howard's TV.

"Hey, buddy, looky here! Good gosh!" Howard exclaimed as he listened to a sound bite. He patted Gramps on the arm. "That took guts."

Gramps watched in disbelief, then realized it was not local TV he was watching. It was national.

"Howard, I'm going to skip breakfast," he decided instantly. "When you're done, would you bring me a roll and coffee?" He remembered the buzz after he and Rob had discovered their relationship. He knew intuitively that the attention would be far greater now and it could be negative. "I'll just stay here for a while. I'm not ready to face the questions."

"Sure thing."

The aide flipped to other channels and they watched as the story was told again and again in a few sensational sound bites.

Ten minutes later Howard was back with an aide who was carrying two meals on a tray.

"It's on the dining room TV," Howard told him. "Most of the residents don't care. The staff is all a-buzz. People have strong opinions. Both ways." He handed Gramps a plate and took the other for himself. "Couldn't eat down there."

"Thanks, Howard." He wasn't sure he could eat either.

"Max and Jerry are with you all the way. Jerry's a Korean War vet, you know."

"Thanks, Howard. That means a lot."

Just then an aide appeared at the door. "I'm here to take Mr. Douglas to see Mrs. Markowitz. Right away."

"Uh oh," Howard muttered ominously. "Principal's office."

Mrs. Markowitz waved him in. She had a harried look and she talked rapidly. "Come in, come in, Mr. Douglas. First of all, let me say I admire what you did. I'm sure it took a lot of courage. I saw the article in today's paper – that was a surprise! I need to see the video. But Mr. Douglas, we have a problem! Our phones are ringing off the hook. I have local news, cable news, even a Congressman wanting to talk with you. We have to prepare a statement for the press. Mr. Douglas, everyone wants to talk to you!"

"No, no. I don't want to talk to anybody," he replied, his jaw set.

"Mr. Douglas, you don't understand. It's bedlam here! I'm in on a Sunday – that's okay, I don't mind – but I have a health care facility to run. Now, what do you want to say to them?"

"I have nothing to say. Let the video speak for itself," he declared. "You know, I never expected any of this to –"

"Well, if I may say so, if you invite the press you have to expect this kind of reaction."

"I wanted the press," he insisted. "What I had to say was important."

There was a tap on the door and Rob was escorted in. "Hello, Mrs. Markowitz." Rob had worked under her administration at Sunset Gardens. "Gramps, first of all, how are you? Have you been sleeping well?"

"Best sleep I've had in years."

"Aimee texted me that you were on TV. I thought I'd better come over and give you some support. Howard told me I'd find you here."

"Rob, I remember your news a few months back. Now you're doing it to me again," Mrs. Markowitz said with a wry smile. "But this is a lot bigger. We've got to get it under control. I was just telling your grandfather that he has to prepare a statement for the media."

"Okay, let's get something together," Rob replied.

"No, no statement. I have nothing more to add," Gramps stated firmly. "Let the video speak for itself."

Rob knew better than to argue with him. "Well, then, let's say that." He turned to Mrs. Markowitz. "I can help you set up a dedicated phone line with that message, and we can put it online too. Gramps, you keep a low profile, watch out for roving reporters who may try to ambush you, get you to give details, try to embarrass you."

"I will stay in the shadows," he assured them with a nod.

"Our Security will be your protection," added Mrs. Markowitz.

"I'll say goodbye now, Gramps. I'll work this out with Mrs. Markowitz and then I have to get back to my place. I'm glad you're doing well."

"Doing great now! Thank you, Rob." They parted with a warm embrace. He headed back to his room. *I need to retreat for a while,* he thought. *Before I face the world.*

"Dad! Hello, how are you?"

"I've been better. Sorry to call you on your way to work. Honey, Mom and I are pretty upset. We just saw that video clip on TV –"

"Dad," she broke in, anticipating his reaction, "you need to see the whole thing."

"I've seen enough. I don't get it. Mr. Douglas –" he would not use his given name – "a war protester? You know what I think about war protesters! I have no time for people like that. I tell you, I'm pretty steamed."

"Dad – Gramps is really sorry –"

"Sorry? Well, I guess better late than never. Hmph, I'm going to have to re-think my friendship with him!"

"Oh, Dad....you don't mean that...."

"Yes I do. All that business – it affected my family, you know."

"Yes – your Uncle Dave?"

"Yes, Uncle Dave. For Heaven's sake, Aimee, do you know what it was like for him? He went through hell when he came back from 'Nam. Him and his buddies."

"No – I don't know. You never told the details."

"Well, there he was, coming off the plane, glad to be home, when the war protesters came at him, throwing rotten food, calling him names, '*baby killer*' – spitting on him!"

"That's terrible! I didn't know any of that. But I still say, Gramps is a different man today. Back then, he didn't know any better."

"I need to think about it."

"Dad, you have to see the whole thing. Get Mom to find it on YouTube."

"Right now, I'm more worried about your uncle. If he catches this on the news it may stir up everything he's tried to forget."

"Or it may have the opposite effect! It may help him."

"We can hope. Anyway, I thought I'd go and see him. He and Aunt Darla moved, you know. They're in Assisted Living at one of those Sunset places, Sunset Manor, or maybe the one where Mr. Douglas lives, I don't know, I'll have to check."

"Dad – be careful what you say, please?"

"Don't you worry about me. Hey, I'll see you tonight. Bye, love you."

"Bye, Dad. Love you too." She groaned. *Oh, Dad, Dad! He has to understand! He just has to!*

After a short while in his room Gramps was ready to return to everyday life. *By this time I'm used to notoriety,* he thought, *and besides, I asked for it*. To his surprise he found welcoming acceptance from staff and residents, those who had paid any attention to it. A few staff members, relatives of Vietnam vets, spoke to him and thanked him for his apology. Even a few visitors sought him out to thank him. There were a few negative opinions, mostly a cold shoulder, but nothing extreme.

The following Friday Aimee and Rob paid him a short visit. "We want to make sure you're doing all right," they said. They had barely gotten settled when she excused herself to take a phone call. "It's Dad. He'd like to speak to you," she said with trepidation as she handed the phone to Gramps.

He caught his breath. He'd been worried about Roger's reaction.

"Allen. Roger here. Saw your video. Just wanted to tell you that – um, we appreciate what you said. It took guts. Most people would just bury it in their past."

"Thank you, Roger. Your opinion means a lot to me."

"I'll admit, I didn't get it at first. But Elaine and I watched the video all the way through. Um, that was quite a story. Not easy to tell. Well, we're on the same side now. That's all that matters."

"Yes we are. Thanks so much, Roger."

They said their goodbyes, then he turned to Aimee. "That's a load off my mind. You have no idea."

"Oh, I think I do. Mine too." She hadn't told him of her father's reaction. *No need to say anything now.* The past week had been painful at home, the subject barely mentioned in the family. She had hoped her parents would eventually watch the video in its entirety.

"I wondered how people would react." He shook his head. "I hope I didn't embarrass you two."

"Not at all," Rob replied, taking his hand. Aimee nodded in agreement.

"I'll admit, we've talked of nothing else," she added. "Well, almost nothing else," she laughed. "It was a surprise, a shock to hear. But Gramps, we're very proud of you!"

"Yes, we are," Rob stated firmly. "Believe it! Now, I wonder, any regrets at having the press involved? The story seems to have died down a lot. You're not in the spotlight anymore."

"No, thankfully. And no regrets, none. I think it was the right thing to do."

"Even if you hadn't had the press, I got it all on my phone. But don't worry," she assured him, "I would have asked you first, before sending it out."

"I know how that goes," Rob interjected, "you propose, he accepts."

"Ha!" she laughed, "you're funny."

*Hmm....*thought Gramps, *must be a private joke.*

"Time for us to say goodbye," Rob said with disappointment, thinking of the album. "Wish we could stay. But we've got a big event tonight."

"Well, then, look happy," Gramps ordered with a smile. "Promise me you'll have a good time!"

"Oh, we will....we will," they assured him as they bade him goodbye.

Chapter 17

"Rob, it's unbelievable the change in Gramps since he moved here," Aimee marveled a few weeks later, pulling into the drive at Sunset Woods.

"I hate to admit it but....it was a good move. It's made all the difference in him, and with the two of us. Gotta thank you, huh?" He gave her a wink. "Much as I hate to admit it." As they wheeled him around they watched him greet staff and his fellow residents by name and with a smile, at times stopping to talk.

"This isn't the Gramps we used to know," Rob teased him, "it's great to see you socializing."

"This place has done wonders for you," said Aimee, as they stopped at a little alcove to talk.

"Yes, in some ways it has. I made some friends right away which helped a lot." He stopped to reflect. "But as a residence, it isn't much different from my old place. Either of them. Do you know the biggest difference? For me?"

"No...what is it?"

He took a deep breath. "Dealing with my guilt. Telling a story I thought I never could tell. Getting it off my chest."

Rob took his hand. "That must have been pretty rough for you. All those years."

"Yes, it was. When I was alone I could put it out of my mind, but once you came into my life, Rob, and then Aimee, I could no longer live with myself." They nodded understandingly.

"But my torment was....if I told it, would I lose you? Lose your respect? Finally I decided I had to take that risk. The funny thing was, having you with me, in my life, made it easier, even though I was afraid I could lose you. Doesn't make sense, does it?"

"It does make sense, Gramps. It's love. Our love for you and your love for us," she explained.

"Well, you two! Let's not get sentimental....Now, I invited you here for a reason. I have something to show you. Let's go to my room."

Once in his room he went to his dresser and pulled out a stack of letters, banded together with a rubber band. "Look! From all over. In the last couple of weeks." There were a dozen or more letters, most addressed simply to him with the name of the city. They were touching letters, thanking him, telling their stories. Aimee and Rob read them with amazement.

"Oh....this makes it all worthwhile!" exclaimed Aimee, wiping away tears.

"Yes, Gramps, this is what you wanted," Rob assured him. "Healing."

Gramps pulled out a couple of others. "Comic relief," he said. They were hate letters, filled with obscenities.

"Throw them out!" exclaimed Aimee, and they did.

"But in all of this, the one person I hoped we would hear from..." he shook his head, "we have not. Your mother." He looked at Rob, who shrugged.

"You know how I feel about that. If she contacts me I'll make the arrangements, but I don't want to get involved."

"I understand. You don't have to decide now. When the time comes you'll know what to do."

"Looks like the time isn't going to come."

"Looks like the time is never going to come for me to see that album," he complained on the way home.

"C'mon, Rob. I'm sure he's forgotten about it with all that's going on in his life. Now it's up to you."

"I know. I'll do it. Even if he says no."

"That's it, isn't it?" She squeezed his hand. "That's what's been holding you back!"

"I think you're right. Yes! It's like....then, I'll never see it. I can't see myself pushing him about it. I could never argue with him. I'd just never bring it up again." He thought about it, then concluded, "but.... '*no*' or not, I'm ready to ask. Right, honey?"

She smiled in reply. "You'll do fine."

The following Sunday Rob and Aimee joined Gramps in the little parlor. Rob was carrying a Scrabble set. *We'll play a game*, he decided, *then I'll bring it up when we're ready to leave. Better that way.*

"Like to play a game, Gramps?"

Gramps looked at him with surprise. "Yes....yes, I'd love to! Haven't played since I was in my other place, the first one...." He stopped, reminiscing. "Rob – you like to play, don't you?"

"Yes, I do. Used to play with my grandparents. But Aimee's the champ. She whips her family and it's all I can do to hold my own against her, when we're playing with her family."

"But you do, hon," Aimee replied. "It's a good competition, Gramps."

He smiled. "Rob, you're like your father. He was a Scrabble champ. We used to play, he and his mom and I, every now and then, sometimes with his best friend." He nodded, "Allen was good."

"I like to hear how I'm like my father! What other ways?"

"Hmm.....little things, mostly, an expression here and there, the way you move your hands, but also – your interests. Running, for instance. Your father took medals in track. Your interest in current events and history, just like your father. Remember that time at Sunset Gardens when we almost argued, and you looked stuff up online?"

"I remember that," he laughed, "That was something, wasn't it!"

"You debated just like your father would do."

"Wow, that makes me feel great."

"It works both ways. You remind me of your father, and that brings back happy memories." He smiled with satisfaction.

"Gramps," asked Aimee thoughtfully, "didn't you suspect? Back at Sunset Gardens....did you wonder about it? The similarity?"

"No....no, I didn't. Why should I? The only time was....Rob, do you remember when I'd just gotten my glasses, right after I moved there, and I was shocked to see you?"

"No. Can't say that I do."

"You startled me. For a minute, I thought I was seeing your father. It was uncanny, but," he shrugged, "I thought it was just coincidence."

"Didn't you look up Dad's picture in your album and compare us? I mean, we look so much alike," Rob asked.

"Didn't you suspect then, that Rob could be your grandson?" asked Aimee, incredulously.

He shook his head. "No, honestly, it never entered my mind." They looked at him with surprise. "Well, your name wasn't Douglas. I didn't know you'd been adopted. But more than that, I figured you were off somewhere across the country with your mother. I never dreamed you were in the area, raised right here, not fifty miles from me. Really, I never even considered that I would see you. Ever." He smiled as he shook his head.

"Rob, didn't you wonder at the name? Allen Douglas, the same as your father?" Aimee asked him.

"No. I wasn't thinking of my father at all. As far as the name Douglas is concerned, I don't even think of myself as Douglas, I've been Carlyle for so long."

"Don't forget," Gramps added, "I'm listed in the records as Robert A. Douglas. You wouldn't have known that I go by '*Allen*'."

"Okay....but that picture," he persisted, "sometime, when you looked at it during the year, didn't you wonder? About the resemblance?"

He sighed deeply. "The truth is, I never looked at your father's picture. I couldn't. I wouldn't even open the album because – because I couldn't bear to look at his picture," he replied vaguely, looking off into the distance.

"You never opened the album?" Rob asked, surprised.

"No...no....I couldn't. Not since – not for years."

"Because of his death?" he asked. "I don't know how you'd ever get over that."

"That's not it. I had come to terms with his death. That's a story I haven't told you yet. I will someday. But I – I hadn't made peace with myself. I hadn't forgiven myself for how I treated him. I told you we reconciled. Yes, he was so forgiving. He was glad to know his Dad understood."

He struggled to go on. "But – I couldn't let go of what I had done to him, and in a way, to your mother. If I hadn't fought with him, his mother and I would have been a part of their lives. We might even have helped them. So you see, I couldn't forgive myself, who I was, what I had done. All this time, I just buried it away. It was too painful to think about." He took out a handkerchief and blew his nose. "I carried the album with me because...." he stopped to think, "it was all I had of my past. It was my security."

"What a burden to carry!" exclaimed Aimee. "In more ways than one."

"Let me tell you, though....talking about it in public, admitting what I'd done, that helped me to let go. I never expected it. Now I'm able to forgive myself."

"Oh, Gramps." Aimee and Rob put their arms around him. "I love you, Gramps," he whispered in his ear.

"Rob." Gramps looked at him and sighed. "Rob, I've been putting you off. About that album. You deserve to see it. It's about time."

"Gramps!" he exclaimed, shaking his hand, "yes, thank you – I've been wanting to for so long!"

"As I said, I haven't looked at it in years. Except that day with you, when I pulled out your father's picture. It was a miracle I found it right away. Haven't opened it since. Well! We won't do it now, I have to get my mind ready for it. How about, the next time you come, both of you?" Aimee nodded, "we'll devote to the album."

"Gramps," Rob replied with excitement, "that sounds like a plan! Now," he opened the Scrabble box, "are you ready?

"Game on!"

Rob and Aimee arranged the board. They gave him the first turn. "Oh," he said jokingly, "I'm losing my touch. Only six." He placed six tiles on the board for a triple point word.

"Is that really a word?" Rob asked skeptically.

"Look it up!" Gramps retorted, handing him the pocket dictionary in the box. "It's perfectly good."

"Aimee," announced Rob, "you've met your match."

On the way home she held his hand tightly. "Honey, I'm as excited as you are! Well, almost as excited…"

"Aimee, do you know what's just as wonderful as knowing that I'm going to see the album?"

"No….?"

"It's sharing it with you. That's one reason I love you so."

"And I love you." She squeezed his hand. "Next week, the album. I can hardly wait! You and I….and Gramps."

The following Friday afternoon Gramps met them in the little parlor. On the table in front of him was the pillowcase with the album in it. "There's nothing mysterious here," he told them as he slowly pulled out the album, "don't get your hopes up. No dark secrets. Just a jumble of old pictures. I'll do my best to remember who and what and when."

Rob could hardly contain his excitement. "You don't know how much I've been wanting to see this," he seized Gramps' arm, "it's my father, my father! I want to know about him!"

"It's all here. His life. The album ends with him. His mother was the picture-taker, and after he died and she passed away, I hardly took any pictures." He shrugged. "No reason to."

It was a grand revelation as they began to sort them according to age and year, school pictures and family pictures. "He looks a lot like me," Rob observed with satisfaction. "I'll have to dig out my school pictures. Grandma and Grandpa left me a couple of albums."

Rob pulled out one picture and studied it carefully. "Gramps, look at this!" he called as he handed it to him.

"May I see, may I see it?" Aimee asked impatiently.

Gramps took hold of it with a smile of recognition. "Well, I'll be." Eyes glistening, he put it to his lips and held it there. Aimee looked on, willing herself not to speak.

"My goodness, Rob, I'm glad you found this!" Gramps started to give it back to him, then, "Aimee, here, take a look," he said as let go of it reluctantly.

"How beautiful!" she said in a whisper.

"Your family," Gramps told him with pride. Three people were standing in a yard on a brilliant autumn day, a handsome middle aged couple and between them, a tall young man with an engaging smile who looked remarkably like Rob. "We took that, or rather, a neighbor took it for us, the last time he was home, before he shipped out. I'm sure it's the only one of the three of us."

"You look very happy, all of you," Aimee remarked.

"Yes, I'm thankful that we parted in peace, with happy words instead of angry ones. I'm glad....so glad you found that," he said, his voice breaking. "All of us together."

"Gramps," said Rob with sudden inspiration, "let us take this and enlarge it, make copies. One for you and one for me." He looked at Aimee. "For us."

"Oh....I don't know," he shook his head as he took it back. "I don't want to let go of it." He thought about it. "You do have a right to your own copy. How long will it take?"

"We can have it back tomorrow." Gramps looked surprised. "We'll do it ourselves, at a store."

"In that case...." he tore out a page from the old album and wrapped the picture in it, then handed it to him. "Thank you."

Rob resumed his rummaging through the pile on the table. Suddenly he seized a picture and held it up, laughing, smiling knowingly at Gramps. "Who are these characters?" It was a young couple holding hands, he with shoulder-length dark hair and a beard, wearing tattered jeans, she with long blond hair and soulful brown eyes; both with tie-dyed shirts and wearing sandals, she with a long peasant skirt.

Gramps snorted. "I'll have you know I was very proud of that head of hair. Your grandmother, she was beautiful, wasn't she!"

"Yes, she was," answered Rob. He hadn't paid much attention to her in the family pictures, focusing mainly on his father. "Dad looks like her."

"Were you '*flower children*'?" asked Aimee.

"They called us that. '*Hippies*', too. We were just normal college kids."

"Gramps, what are these?" She took a rubber band off a group of pictures. "Are you in any of these?" They were group pictures, mainly; students crowding into and on top of a Volkswagen Beetle, students carrying signs praising drug use, students carrying anti-war and anti-police signs, campus protests, police arresting students. She unfolded newspaper articles about campus demonstrations and war protests.

"Oh, no!" he groaned, covering his face with his hand. "I forgot all about those! That's a time in my life I'd like to forget." He waved his hand over them. "Burn them all!" he ordered. "I told you before, I'm not proud of that."

"You must have believed in what you were doing. I'd like to understand you, you and my Grandma. Won't you please tell us?" Rob pleaded, holding on to the pictures.

"Yes, Aimee added, "we've read about it, but that's not like hearing it from you." She remembered telling him he was '*living history'* the first time they met, and his stubborn refusal to talk about his life. "We want to hear."

His lips tight, he shook his head, refusing their request. There was a long silence as with anger his eyes met theirs. At last he shrugged, "Why not? You're my family….and….I love you."

He sighed. "Rob, Aimee, we did believe in what we were doing. We cared. We cared about something greater than ourselves. Ha! Changing the world, for all the wrong reasons." He shook his head. "In all the wrong ways. I don't apologize for caring. But we were also very gullible. We listened to campus leaders who appealed to our emotions and we weren't willing to think things through. We wouldn't listen to our parents, who tried to reason with us. What did they know? They were over thirty –"

"What does that have to do with it?" asked Aimee, puzzled.

" *'Don't trust anyone over thirty'* was our motto." They laughed, shaking their heads. "We thought we were morally right, so that made us superior. Drugs didn't help either. They clouded our minds. So….we did a lot of stupid things. Harmful things; we hurt ourselves and others. I've already told you about that. But – and I'm not making excuses – we cared, we wanted to change the world. Today's young people, I don't see any passion." He shook his head. "Kids today are wrapped up in toys… technology….entertainment." He shook his head sadly.

"They're like drugs, wouldn't you say?" she asked.

"I think so," he nodded. "Now, let me say something to you both." He looked at them searchingly. "There's more to life than yourselves. You can't just live for yourselves, even for each other. You need to find something worth living for….and worth dying for." He took their hands. "Something….someone. What I was looking for back then, in all the wrong places. My dear Rob and Aimee, that someone is God. I know that now. He can use you to change the world. The right way."

"You lose me there," Rob replied. *God? Now where did that come from,* he wondered. "No offense," he patted him on the shoulder, "but that's a discussion I don't want right now. Maybe someday, huh?"

"Sorry, Gramps. That's not for us," Aimee added gently.

Rob moved his chair in front of his grandfather and wrapped his arms around him. "Gramps, thank you….thank you for giving me my father. And my grandmother, and you. I know it wasn't easy. I'll never be the same again."

Aimee joined Rob in hugging him. "But will you complete the story?" she asked. He gave her a questioning look. "How did you change from radical hippie to family man?"

"That's just it. Family. We got married, we lost interest in protesting, we were vagabonds across the country for a while…."

"How exciting!" cried Aimee.

"It was….and it wasn't. Enough said. We loved each other and our baby. We stopped our drug use because we saw what it was doing to our minds. But as I said before, we remained anti-establishment. We were successful but we rejected the country that made our success possible. Until…" he stopped and looked at Rob. "Until our son called us to account."

"What a wonderful ending!" exclaimed Aimee. "Really, it's a beginning. Rob, you have so much more to look forward to with this album! Now, we have to leave, we're meeting Bryan and Natasha for dinner."

"Thank you, Gramps." Rob took his hand. "Thank you. I love you." He kissed him on the cheek. "Good night."

What to do about the pictures, Rob wondered, *the 'protest pictures'*. Gramps had groaned when he used that term and he resolved not to say it again. He had called Gramps to talk about disposing of them. Now, a week later they lay, banded together, on the table along with the album.

"Burn them." Gramps waved his hand dismissively. "I don't even want to touch them."

"I don't want to. I don't want to burn them," Rob declared. "I want to keep them."

Gramps' jaw tightened and Rob wondered if his ears closed at the same time. "You what? What are you talking about? I want to forget that whole sorry time! So why won't you –"

"If you want them destroyed, why don't you do it yourself?"

Gramps squirmed in his chair and sighed heavily. "I don't want to – I can't – if I put them in the wastebasket someone might find them...."

Oh, Rob thought, *he can't do it himself and he wants me to.* "I don't want to," he repeated.

Gramps frowned. Rob went on, "I want to keep them, I want –"

Exasperated, Gramps cut him off. "Why, in the name of heaven! Rob," his voice rising, "those pictures are a violation of everything I hold dear today. Get rid of them!" he shouted. "Or I will now!" He reached out to take the pictures but Rob seized them first.

"No," he pleaded, "let me explain." He smiled at Gramps who looked at him in stony silence.

It was a face-off. Rob didn't trust himself to speak. For a long moment the two men looked at each other. Then Rob spoke. "I understand, I really do. You're not proud, you're ashamed of that part of your life." Gramps looked at him in silent agreement. "But – I'm proud of you. We're proud of you, Aimee and I. You stood up for what you believed. You were willing to go to jail –"

"Yes, I was and I did. Go to jail. And for what? The right to spit on someone else and the right to get high? To barricade a building? There's nothing noble about that, Rob. It wasn't even for civil rights. I'd be proud today, if I'd gone to jail for that. No, it was all selfish."

"But you wanted to make a better world. You told us that."

"No," he shook his head," when you come right down to it, it was just plain selfish."

"Even so....Gramps – I hope I would stand up for what I believe, if I had to."

What would I stand up for, he asked himself uneasily. He pondered, while Gramps shook his head, not speaking. *What do I believe in? I believe in Aimee. Aimee and I. Well, that's kind of selfish. I'm proud of Aimee, standing up for what she believes. That takes courage. What about me? I believe in helping people. I would stand up for someone who was being attacked, because I know what it's like to be the underdog.* He remembered his early school years and not fitting in. *Do I believe in anything else? Not really.*

"You haven't told me why you want those infernal pictures!"

"When Aimee and I are married –" Gramps' eyes lit up and he smiled in spite of himself.

"Married? Are you going to?" The atmosphere was warm again.

"Oh yes. There was never any doubt. I just had to think it through, understand what I was doing. We haven't told anybody yet."

"My dear boy. That makes me very happy. Now, will you please tell me what you want with those pictures?"

"Someday we will have children," Rob said with a warm glow in his heart, "and they will study this in history. We want them to know about their great-grandpa and grandma –"

Gramps' eyes shot fire and he shook his head menacingly.

"Know, and be proud," Rob went on. "Proud that you opposed war, even if you went about it the wrong way. Gramps, you were a fighter. You and my grandma. No halfway measures." He held out his hand, "We're proud of you. I only hope I could be as strong for what I believe."

Gramps was silent a moment, then he took Rob's hand and handed him the pictures. "Take them. I trust you. You're a dear grandson." They held each other for a moment. "But – I never want to see them again."

They visited for a while longer, then said their goodbyes and Rob left.

Re-living the conversation on his way home, he remembered telling Gramps, *'we're proud of you.' Not 'I'*, he thought, *but 'we'. I love it! But wait, am I speaking for Aimee? That wouldn't be right. No, not in this case. I know her, I know she would agree with me. We're one in our thinking. 'One'. I like that.*

A few nights later they had some time alone at Aimee's house and he told her about his encounter with Gramps. As he finished she shook her head. "For someone who said he could never argue with Gramps, you two sure went head-to-head," she laughed and patted his hand. "I'm proud of you! You parted on good terms."

"I'm proud of me, too," he agreed. "It never got ugly, even though we were both pretty steamed. I guess the love and respect won out." He pulled out the packet of pictures. "Now that I've got them, what do I do with them?" he asked.

"I don't want them. I don't even want to look at them again," she grimaced, "they're....they're ugly. It's a part of Gramps I don't want to think about."

"I know," he nodded understandingly, "but I feel I should keep them. Actually, they help me understand what went on between him and my father. I didn't tell you that after this was settled between us, I stayed a while longer and asked him questions. I wanted to clear some things up."

"Hmm, I'm interested. Like what?"

"Well, think about it. How did Dad and his parents grow so far apart in their beliefs, and Gramps never know it? Was Dad trying to get back at them by joining the military?"

"I wondered about that. It's kind of '*in your face*' to drop a bomb like that without any warning. And then leave the very next day."

"But it wasn't that way. Gramps said Dad had been very tactful, trying to explain his position. And Gramps just blew up. He felt betrayed. Dad tried to keep his cool, he told them he was a patriot, not a killer. He loved his country and he wanted to defend it so people like his dad could have the right to make money and complain and protest. He said there were bad guys who hated us and he was willing to fight to defend us."

"Rob, I like your father!"

He laughed and put his arm around her. "I do too."

"Grandma tried to come between them, even though she agreed with Gramps, but it didn't work. Finally Dad stormed out. He wasn't supposed to be inducted for a couple of weeks but he told them, '*you won't get to see it*'. Later they found out he had been staying with a friend close by but Gramps never tried to locate him."

"What a shame. It sounds like they were both pretty mad."

He nodded. "It must have broken my grandma's heart. She began writing Dad. Gramps wasn't ready to, he wanted to understand first. He went into Dad's room; he saw a side of Dad he never knew, or hadn't wanted to see. Dad was a Civil War fan, he had books and videos and memorabilia. A lot of patriotic writings. Gramps started reading them and that got him into U.S. history, just like he told in his VFW talk."

"My goodness, that is amazing!"

"When Dad came back home a year or so later, before he was deployed to the Gulf they talked about all this. It was a real meeting of the minds; they realized that now they were so alike –"

"And so are you! You fit right into your family, and you weren't even raised with them. How strange is that?"

"It makes me feel good. Except for being sad that I never knew my Dad."

"Oh, yes." She patted his hand. "Well, go on."

"How could Gramps and my grandma not have known this about Dad?" Aimee nodded in agreement. "How he felt about war and patriotism? They talked about it when he came back. Now – I didn't know that Dad had graduated from high school a few months after turning seventeen."

"So, that's where you get your brains."

"I guess so. Not from my mother, that's for sure."

"He stayed home and worked for a year –"

"Like you did –"

"Yes. Strange, isn't it? Anyway, he became his own person with his own beliefs. But even so, he couldn't tell his parents about his interests because he was sure they would mock him. He knew they held people who disagreed with them in contempt. He wanted his father's approval. He didn't want to risk losing it."

"Surely not his own son? He would respect –"

"Gramps said he and Grandma wouldn't have mocked him, not intentionally, but they would have told him where he was wrong, in no uncertain terms. It would have seemed like mocking. Dad didn't want to tell them ahead of time that he was interested in the Marines, he knew they would try to talk him out of it. He didn't want the battles. Well, he got a battle all right. More than he ever expected. He was very hurt."

"I'm sure he was. The important thing is, they talked about it. They did reconcile. So Gramps –" she said thoughtfully, "he did a one-eighty from campus radical to conservative? And what about your grandma?"

"Yes, and Grandma with him. They talked, they read, they thought, it was their own decision."

"You know, Rob, I'm thinking about my parents. They're on opposite sides of the political spectrum. They always say their votes cancel each other out, though that doesn't stop them from voting. But they respect each other. And others who are on the opposite side. I've always known I could be my own person, believe what I want to believe and Mom and Dad would not stand in my way."

"That's pretty neat. What's ironic to me, I never thought about it before, is that Gramps, the campus radical, the arch-liberal, should have been so....so closed-minded. So unwilling even to listen to other ideas."

"That doesn't surprise me. I see it all the time. Mom complains about it; some of her friends consider Dad to be *'the enemy'*, to be destroyed. What hypocrisy."

"What about your dad's friends? Are they the same way?"

"No – remember, they're the ones who will give their lives to protect people's right to be stupid. They're like, *'live and let live'*."

"I like that. I know how I want us to raise our kids," he said soberly. "Your parents are a good act to follow. Okay, now," he picked up the packet, "what do you think?"

"Well….." she thought about it, "I think we do need to keep those pictures. For our children….someday. There's a lot they need to hear about. But no, not me. I'm not ready to look at them again." She waved her hand. "You take them."

They could hardly wait to get back to the rest of the pictures, to study them at leisure and hear their stories. A few days later they were together with Gramps. "We don't have to twist your arm, do we? To tell us about the pictures?" He was perfectly willing to oblige. Their time together passed all too quickly.

Thus began a comfortable pattern, getting together on Friday evenings or Sunday afternoons in a little parlor or in Gramps' room. He would bring out the album and regale them with family stories, the good, the bad, and sometimes the ugly. There were medals and awards, newspaper photos and articles, letters of tribute, family pictures going back to Gramps' childhood, all stuffed in the old album, each one with a story. To Rob it was like *'going home'*.

The old album was too much for Aimee. She began to come in on her own, bringing in new scrapbooks and assorted materials for scrap-booking with him. Rob and Aimee began to learn about his father, his grandfather, and the grandmother he had never known. Sometimes they were joined by Howard who would entertain them with old stories and corny jokes, or they would join in a round of cards. Occasionally they would bring Grendel along, though not often enough for Gramps. Most of the time they had other plans after their visit which could not include a dog.

What Rob had longed for was finally happening.

It had been years since Gramps had celebrated Christmas. "I'm not Scrooge," he told Howard, "I remember it in my heart, that's all that matters." The noise and trappings didn't interest him. All that changed this year with an invitation to dinner with Aimee's family, he and Rob together. He ordered a special dessert to take along, and he wasn't surprised to have such a good time he hated to leave.

A week later Rob and Aimee took him out to dinner and afterwards to tour the Christmas lights. This time he could hardly wait to get back because he had a surprise. He had planned this for months, though not necessarily for Christmas: a special package for Rob. He waited anxiously for Rob's reaction as he opened it, to reveal a handsomely mounted picture of a stern-faced boy-turned-man in Marine uniform. It was his graduation photo.

Rob knew immediately who it was. After a moment of stunned silence he broke into tears and then sobs. Aimee held him and Gramps put his arm around him. He tried to stop but couldn't. The emotions of years came pouring out. "I've never cried like this before in my life," he finally said, apologetically.

"It's time you did," Gramps assured him. "You needed it." He was finally able to dry his eyes, and they marveled again at how much Rob looked like his father.

"But how did you get this? It wasn't in your album," asked Rob.

"The social worker here helped me contact the Marine Corps, and they located your father's picture. Then we took care of framing it." He smiled, pleased at the success of the secret he'd worked on for so long.

"Gramps," Aimee told him, "you need your own copy."

"Next time you're in my room, take a look around," he replied. "Now, Aimee, I didn't forget you." She opened a package to find a leather carrying case.

They too had a surprise, giving Gramps a wool coat sweater in soft blue. "Excellent! This will keep me warm when I'm sitting by the windows reading. Thank you! Hmm, it's easy to get on and off, too."

"What a wonderful Christmas this has been! Thank you," he told them, gratefully.

"The thanks are ours. You've given us so much," they said as they kissed him goodbye.

After they left he sat quietly, reflecting on the evening. *Celebrate Christmas 'in my heart' only? That's not possible. Christmas is giving and receiving. I can't do that 'in my heart'.*

Maybe I am Scrooge. I've been avoiding, that's what. I used to celebrate, even after Allen and Kate passed away and I was alone. I celebrated....because Christmas is celebration.

Why did I stop? I don't know when but I know why. It was when I entered Bright Horizons....seven or was it eight years ago? My dreams had crashed all around me, I didn't fit in, I was younger than the others, Christmas came barreling down on me and I wasn't in any mood to celebrate. I was angry....yes, I remember that. Well, I got over the anger and adjusted pretty well, but I lost Christmas and never got it back.

Now, here we are. 'Tis the season'–for all kinds of nonsense in the name of Christmas. It holds no interest for me. I'm interested in the heart of Christmas. Hmph, what was that announcement I saw up front? Christmas caroling and a worship service with people from a nearby church? Yes, I'll do it. I'll go!

He could hardly wait. Christmas would never be the same again.

"Honey, let's do our own surprise for Gramps," Aimee said as they were on their way home.

"What do you have in mind?"

"You know he doesn't have any separate picture of your grandmother...."

"Right, all the portraits were on his wall and got burned in the fire. That's too bad."

"We could take your copy of the picture of your father and your grandparents. We could make another copy, cut out your grandmother and enlarge it as much as possible and make a portrait for Gramps.

"His Kate.....he'd love it!" He pulled to the side of the road. "Honey, that is brilliant! Just brilliant."

"Why are you stopping?"

He reached over and kissed her. "Any excuse will do! Can't do this while driving."

"You are crazy!" she laughed, returning his kiss. "Now, if we get to it right away we can have it done by Christmas day."

"We could sneak into Sunset Woods while he's at breakfast and put it in his room, anonymously," he added.

"While he's at lunch," she corrected him. "We'll be with my family on Christmas morning, remember? But we can still slip out and play Santa."

"As long as we're back in time for Christmas dinner," he reminded her.

"A man's gotta eat, huh?" She hugged him. "I think we'll have as much fun with this as Gramps did with your surprise!"

But her mother didn't agree when they talked about it the next day. "Aimee, Rob, that cuts things too close. Dinner's at 1:00 and his place is half an hour away. You can't go and get back in time."

"Well, we've got to figure out something. What if Rob and I left right after dinner?"

"That could work. That's a good idea."

"What's a good idea?" asked her father, coming upon them.

They told him about their plan to surprise Gramps.

He shook his head. "No, no. How about this. We can all go after dinner, bring him a plate of food. Aimee, you can sneak down to his room and put it on his dresser while we're getting settled. He'll never miss you."

Rob shook his hand. "Roger, that sounds like a plan!"

"Yeah. I'll call and ask him to reserve one of those little rooms."

"Will Jason and Jacquie be going too?" asked Rob.

"Oh, yes. Christmas is family day at our house," Elaine explained. "They wouldn't be doing anything with their friends.

I think they'll want to go with us. They're getting rather attached to 'Grandpa Douglas', Rob."

"Oh, no!" Roger exclaimed, with a stricken look. "The game! I forgot all about the game. I never miss that."

"Well, now, Roger, this was your plan," admonished Elaine with a smile, putting her arm around him, "in the presence of witnesses."

"We should get back in time, if we leave early enough. I'll record it, just to be sure."

"The Christmas Day game is a tradition at our house," Elaine explained to Rob. "Roger and Jason, Uncle Dave. And now you, if you want."

"Sure! I'd love to."

"Do I get to watch with you?" asked Aimee, smiling at her father.

"Aimee, you mean you want to watch the game with your old Dad?" asked Roger, winking at Rob.

"Of course I do," she replied, linking her arm in his.

"Well, I don't know. This is a guy thing. We'll take a vote on it and let you know."

"That's a neat idea, your whole family going out to see Gramps," Rob said to Aimee later that day.

"They like him. They want to do it – but, I think Dad regrets making the suggestion. The Christmas day game is sacred to him. He won't go back on his word, but for him, Christmas is the presents, the dinner, and the game."

"I wouldn't want to spoil that. I hope it will work out for him."

Chapter 18

"I've always loved this park," Aimee told Rob as he turned the car into the park at the Lake a few days after Christmas. "Thanks for coming here!" She took his hand. "It's a beautiful afternoon for a drive-through. Do you remember our picnic here to celebrate the first month since we met?"

"Um...I'm not sure about the picnic," he replied off-handedly. "Those dates and anniversaries don't mean much to me."

Am I going to have to educate him! she thought, stung by his indifference. "Well, that whole afternoon was pretty special to me! I'm sorry it wasn't special to you." She stopped herself. *I don't want to be angry with him, not now, I don't want to ruin this day.* "Oh, Rob, just look at the lake, the ice glistening in the sun....we're going to have a beautiful sunset. How beautiful.... how romantic! Thank you for coming here."

He pulled the car up to a bench overlooking the lake. "There's a good sunny spot," he pointed out. "Would you go and brush the snow off the bench?" He lingered behind.

Now why can't he help, she wondered, trying not to be irritated. "Honey, I do believe this is the bench where we sat and talked –" She turned around to find him standing there, beaming, with a large parcel for her. Eagerly she opened it, and at once her arms were filled with a bouquet of deep red roses. With delight she buried her face in the blooms, drinking in their beauty. Deftly he seated her on the bench, then with sleight of hand reached into the blooms and pulled out a little velvet box. He dropped to one knee, slipped off her glove, opened the box and took out a beautiful diamond ring which he placed on her finger.

"By the way," he said with a grin, "this is the seventh month since we met. Did you think I would forget?" he laughed. "Just don't ask me the date."

She looked at him with astonishment.

"I thought about giving this to you at the place we met, in line –" she looked at him with horror – "but that's not you, or me either. Besides, we'd be all around the world in five minutes. I couldn't do that to you. Then I remembered our picnic place."

She was still too astonished to speak.

"I almost forgot!" he exclaimed, seating himself beside her and taking her in his arms. "Aimee, Aimee, I love you….. will you marry me?"

"Rob – darling! Yes, oh yes…" Tears filled her eyes. "You do like to surprise me." She held out her hand and gazed at the ring. "It's beautiful!"

She frowned and began to take it off her finger. "Honey….I can't accept this. It's too much. It will take you years to pay it off. We can't start marriage that way." She blinked back her tears. "I don't need a fancy ring. I'm just happy to have you."

He kissed her tears and took the ring. "My darling Aimee. I was looking at rings, wishing I could afford something beautiful for you. And then I remembered this. It's my grandmother's ring. It's mine to give." He put the ring back on her finger.

"Oh, darling!" She gazed at it, appreciatively. "In that case, yes….yes! with all my heart, I'll wear it. Proudly." She turned and kissed him. "Consider this a down payment," she said, kissing him again, "a small down payment. On our future."

He held her hand, displaying the ring. "Aimee, my grandma wore this proudly. Grandpa had given it to her on their 25th wedding anniversary. She said I could give it to my wife on our 25th, because she'd be gone by then. Well….we don't need to wait twenty five years."

“I could live with that. This is so beautiful!”

“I remembered the ring but I didn’t know where it was. I called the bank which had administered their estate and found out there was a safety deposit box in my name. So I went to it and found the ring. Some other interesting stuff too, a couple of coin collections, some old jewelry.... the coins are valuable, and they don’t have any sentimental value. So, we might sell some to help pay for our wedding.”

“Honey, how wonderful!” They held each other, laughing, kissing, speaking words of love.

“Darling, this ring is yours. It’s a promise.” He shook his head. “Look, we can’t set a date yet. We have to be able to support ourselves.”

“Rob, darling, when we met, I dreamed of a Christmas wedding. But you’re right, we can’t get married with no income. I’d marry you tomorrow if we had an income.”

“Look here, I want you to have a beautiful wedding. The most beautiful wedding in the world. You’ll regret it all your life if you don’t, and so will your family. You said your parents are putting their money into education, not weddings. That’s good, but we have to figure out how we can do it ourselves.”

“Yes.....I want a beautiful wedding. But it doesn’t have to cost a fortune. I don’t want a major production, I want a wedding! Something simple and beautiful. Rob, I know it will happen. I just do! I’m a romantic.”

“We’ll do it! Somehow. Soon, soon, I hope.”

“Honey, just look....what a beautiful sunset! But we can’t stay, we have to get these roses into the car and we have to be at my house for dinner, soon. Let’s not tell anyone.” She held out her hand. “See if anyone notices....”

“Notices you flashing that rock in their faces?”

As they drove away Rob thought back to his meeting with her parents.

Why am I so nervous, he had thought as he approached Roger and Elaine at a time when he did not have classes and Aimee was at the museum. *I want to know they think I'm good enough for their Aimee*.

"*I guess you know I love Aimee and would like to marry her*," he had stammered.

Elaine immediately set him at ease. "*Well, of course! Welcome to the family, Rob*." She hugged him warmly. "*We wish you great happiness*."

Roger sat expressionless as he fingered a wrapped cigar. He began interrogating him about his interests and accomplishments in sports, school, and employment, and then questioned him about what he wanted to do in the medical field.

The longer they talked the worse he felt. *This feels suspiciously like a job interview*, he thought. At long last Roger nodded his head and concluded, "*Well, Rob, you'll do. Good, good. Welcome to the family. Aimee could do a lot worse*," he added cryptically, with a wink at Rob. Then he smiled and extended his hand.

Rob didn't know what to think. "*Roger*," Elaine scolded, "*don't be so hard on him! Rob, that's his way of giving a compliment. Yes, yes, we do welcome you!*" Putting an arm around him she kissed his cheek. Roger shook his hand again.

"*Rob*," she looked at him intently, "*why do you want to marry Aimee*?"

"*Well – because I love her*," he answered. Looking at Elaine he realized that was not a sufficient answer. "*Because…*" He was at a sudden loss for words. "*She lights up my life….I love being with her…*" He thought for a minute. "*You know, I always thought that getting serious about someone now would mess me up. I had to keep focused on my studies. But –*" he shook his head, "*it's been the opposite! I'm working harder and smarter, since I met Aimee. She brings out the best in me. What can I say?*" he laughed helplessly, "*I can't live without her!*"

Elaine hugged him. "*I think you're good for her, too*."

Roger shook his hand. "*I would offer you a cigar but I know you don't smoke,*" he said with a laugh.

"*Good thing,*" he replied, "*I'd probably get sick.*" *That would be unforgettable*, he thought.

"*This calls for a toast*," Roger responded. In a minute he was back with a bottle of wine, then he poured glasses for them all. "*To Rob and Aimee.....may they enjoy a successful and happy life together,*" he said with a smile at Rob.

"*To Aimee and Rob,*" Elaine continued, "*a long and happy marriage. And to Rob, our new son.*"

Rob thanked them, not knowing whether he should make a toast or not. It didn't matter. They welcomed him with hugs and a happy sense of belonging.

"*So,*" he asked hopefully, "*Did you ask Aimee the same question? Why she loves me?*"

"*Of course,*" Roger replied, raising an eyebrow and giving an almost imperceptible shrug. "*She said you had hypnotized her. What chance did she have?*"

"*Roger!*" Elaine shook her head at Rob, smiling. "*Don't believe a word he says.*"

"*You'll have to ask her,*" he told Rob with a conniving look.

They laughed and finished their wine. *Well,* he thought with relief, *I guess I passed the test*. As he was taking his leave he asked them, "*Please don't say anything to Aimee. I'm planning a surprise.*"

Now, he was bursting with pride and satisfaction as he drove to Aimee's house. They *might not notice her ring*, he thought, *but they'll notice me, I'm ready to explode! Aimee looks pretty happy herself.* He held her hand tightly. "*Happy, honey*?" he couldn't help asking.

"Beyond words. Watch out, I'll be crying soon. What will my parents think, me walking in with tears?" she laughed. "Honey, you're getting to be a fixture in my family. Did you have a good time on Christmas Day?"

"Beyond words, honey. Better than last year, for sure – I was alone. But yes, it was a great day." He reflected. "I like the way your Dad handled the game situation."

"Right. He just bundled Gramps up and took him home with us. By the way, that was a neat two-man-carry you and Jason did."

"It was easy. We didn't have to bother with a wheel chair. Just carried him out, ha, ha – sneaked him past the nurses' station, into the car, got him in the house, settled him in the recliner and he was good for the evening. He and Grendel."

"He said this was the first time he'd sat in a recliner in years. Let's see to it that it's not his last. I think sometimes we don't realize how restricted he is."

"Yeah. The wheelchair is his world." He smiled at the memory. "He sure enjoyed watching the game with us. You know, honey, we did vote you in. You could have joined us."

"I know. But wouldn't you rather have had me help with the refreshments?" she asked playfully.

"The refreshments, definitely," he teased.

"I joined you at the end. Didn't you notice?"

Rob was walking across campus when his phone rang.

"Hello Robbie.

"Mom! I wasn't expecting to hear from you. I can't talk long. I'm on my way to the lab. What is it?"

"Lab? What do you mean? It's Christmas vacation."

"This is extra. So, what's this about?"

"Well, you hit the big time, Robbie. Even my small town newspaper had your picture. And his. Your grandfather! So he apologized! Big deal. Too bad he couldn't apologize for breaking your father's heart."

"Mom, not that again. It's getting old." *What took her so long?* he asked himself. *That article was months ago! The sooner I can hang up the better.*

"Well, it's the only apology that matters."

"You're the one who broke his heart when you ran off with another man." *Uh, oh*, he thought, *I shouldn't have said that.*

"You shouldn't have said that," she snapped. "That's my business."

"Okay, Mom. I shouldn't have said that." *Um....that was hard. But that's what Gramps would want me to do.*

"Well! That's something."

"Mom, I want to get together with you." *What am I saying?* he thought, shocked at his words. "Or, rather," he went on, "you get together with us. My fiancee and I."

Oh, he thought, *that sounds great! My fiancee. I proposed and she accepted. Ha! Just yesterday....I want her to meet Aimee....Mom's the first one I'm telling, not even Gramps. But won't he be happy to hear....*

"Rob," said his mother sharply, breaking into his thoughts, "you're not listening to me. I thought you were in a hurry. I said yes, I'd be happy to meet your fiancee."

"Good, great! Now, he'll be there too. My grandfather. Mr. Douglas."

"Oh, no, Robbie, not him. No way."

"You sure are hateful. How can you hate somebody you've never met?"

"Hmph! Hating's easy, when you've done it a long time."

"Look, I'm not going to beg. He wants to meet you. We'll set a date, I can pick you up and we'll have dinner together." The last was a sudden inspiration. He knew Gramps liked to serve food when they were meeting together.

"Well....you'd have to pick me up. I don't have a car anymore. But I didn't say I would."

It may have been because he didn't argue, just expected she would come; he didn't know, but she did agree and gave her address, a town about an hour away. They decided on a day and time a week later.

"Why are we leaving so early? We'll get there in the middle of the afternoon."

"It will give us a chance to talk. And Mom, no alcohol, please?"

"Don't you worry about me. Now, good bye. Before I change my mind."

He hung up, unable to believe what he had done. *I'm the one who didn't want to have anything to do with her! What could have come over me? Well....I want her to meet Aimee. Show her off, you know. Nothing wrong with that! And Aimee has to meet Mom sometime. Actually, it makes sense. I'm sure she would never meet with Gramps unless I was there.*

Quickly he texted Aimee, then the next day told her the full story.

"I can't believe what I've committed myself to. Not only that, I said I'd pick her up! I'm counting on you being with me," he pleaded. "An hour alone with her would drive me crazy. I'd be sure to tick her off."

"I can't go with you," she said quietly, patting his hand. "You need to go alone."

"What? Why not?" he asked, surprised and hurt. "I thought we'd go together. C'mon, honey, I need to have you with me! I know how you feel about her, but –"

"Rob, that's not it. I know what I said before, but I've thought it over and....I don't hate her. How can I hate someone I don't even know? I don't want her to hurt you ....but, I don't know, I'm willing to give her a chance."

"Then you're a better person than I am. I'm just doing this for Gramps. So, why won't you go with me?"

"If I went along with you she and I would be competing for your attention. That would get us off on the wrong foot. You go alone. It's better that way."

"I never thought of that. Still, I'd rather not go alone...." He held out his hand to her.

"Look, try to forget who she is. Just be polite. If she insults you, ignore it."

"All right, all right, I'll do it, I'll go. For Gramps." *That's the only reason,* he told himself.

Gramps, for his part, was pleased with the arrangements Rob had made. "I'll take care of the room and the food," he offered.

He was very pleased to hear of their engagement. "I had great confidence in you," he told Rob, taking his arm. "Aimee, what a beautiful ring! It's far too beautiful to stay in a safety deposit box," he said approvingly. "But not as beautiful as the one wearing it." He took her hand and kissed it. "It deserves to be worn with joy and gladness. My blessings on you both."

"By the way," he said with a shake of his head, "I thought I was too old to believe in Santa Claus." They looked puzzled. "It seems that Santa visited me anyway. Left me a gift from the past." His eyes met theirs. "I'll treasure it always."

They looked at him and shrugged.

Chapter 19

Mustering his courage, Rob drove out to get his mother as they had agreed. She was ready when he arrived and seemed to be sober. The ride back went smoothly. She had nothing to say and Rob said very little. *Better that way*, he thought, *so we don't get off on the wrong foot. Why do I always let her get under my skin?*

She entered the little parlor warily, looking around. He made introductions. "Mom, this is my fiancee, Aimee Love." It still gave him a thrill to call her his fiancee. Aimee welcomed her warmly. "My mother, Lenore…." *What was her last name*? It had changed many times.

"Lenore Gallagher," she broke in, guessing the reason for his hesitation, "but Lenore is okay."

"And my grandfather, Allen Douglas…"

"Lenore, I'm so glad to meet you, at last," he said, reaching for her hand. She gave a little shake and mumbled a quick hello. "I'm sorry I can't stand up to greet you," he said, graciously. She ignored him.

After a few minutes getting settled, Gramps came to the point. "Lenore, I'm glad you came. I've wanted to meet you. You were the wife of my only son, the mother of my dear grandson. Now, Rob told me what you told him, that I broke his father's heart. You are right. I did break his heart. We had a terrible argument the night before he left for boot camp. I said some terrible things to him. I've had to live with that memory. I can't tell you how sorry I am –" he sighed, shaking his head.

"Oh, you're sorry, are you!" She had been waiting for her moment. "Well, let me tell you what it was like for Allen! I met him halfway through boot camp. He was in a terrible state. He was so down. He was going to drop out or be kicked out, he couldn't keep his mind on his training, he was so broken up – because of you. Well, I was all he had. I put him back together. I gave him something to live for!"

Gramps broke in. "Lenore, thank you. Thank you for helping my son." He reached for her hand but she pulled it back. She went on, ignoring him.

" '*Forget about your father*!' I told him. That's what he needed to hear. Then – you had to call him. Oh, now he was up, up, up. '*My father and mother are coming to my graduation!'* he said. He was so excited. *'Allen,'* I told him, *'don't get your hopes up. Maybe they will, maybe they won't.'* And guess what – I was right, wasn't I?" she smirked. "Oh, what that did to him! So, now I had to put him back together again. '*Something must have happened,'* he said. *'I know they'd have come if they could.'* But no, no word from his parents. Just like I said," she declared triumphantly.

"Lenore." Gramps broke in again, emphatically. "Lenore, something did happen." He waited until he had her attention, then he told her about his wife's stroke and his failed attempts to reach Allen. "Lenore – we had our tickets. We were planning to be there. We were so disappointed. His mother was still in the hospital."

Their eyes met. His look was piercing but kind. She dropped her head and put her hands to her mouth, unable to speak. There was an uncomfortable silence.

"Mom, it looks like you broke Dad's heart! Not Gramps," Rob said accusingly.

"Rob, don't!" cried Aimee.

He went on, relentlessly. "You might have put Dad back together, as you say. But then you dropped him for another man."

"Rob, you don't understand! I never intended to," she said defensively. "Your dad was shipped out to California and – I'm afraid of flying. I couldn't go with him. It looked like I didn't have any future with him – even though I loved him. I was pregnant with you and I – I can't stand to be alone. I needed someone. I needed someone to love me. You don't know what it's like! I never felt loved at home –"

"Don't give me that!" he exclaimed with disgust. "Grandma and Grandpa weren't like that."

"I'm sure they weren't, with you," she retorted. "They did a wonderful job with you. But they learned on me! I was never good enough for them. And Dad! He was never there."

"I don't know whether that's true or not. I don't care. All I know is, we can't blame our parents for our problems. And they're not here to defend themselves, are they!"

Aimee didn't like the way things were going. "Lenore," she broke in, "do you know there are people here who love you?"

Lenore looked at her skeptically.

"Gramps has enough love for all of us. And I love you, or rather, I want to love you, if you'll give me a chance. Rob – he'd love you in a heartbeat if he didn't think you were going to throw him to the curb." She smiled at Lenore. Rob frowned and looked away.

Gramps decided the time had come for him to speak. "Lenore," he smiled, "I would like to add something that may help at this time. It's part of my story that I wasn't able to tell before, when I was talking with Rob and Aimee. Is that all right with you?"

"Well....I guess so." The others agreed, and he began.

"It was not quite twenty years ago. Allen, my only child, was dead and his mother, my wife Kate had just died. I had a grandchild that I never expected to see. Everyone who was important to me was gone. I felt that my life was over. I had nothing more to live for. I entered a deep, dark pit. Alcohol became my friend

– my only friend." His eyes met Lenore's. She looked away, nervously.

"One day, cold sober, I reached a point of no return. Life or death. I could see no reason to go on. No reason to live. I was ready to take my life. And then, amidst the darkness I saw, or felt, a pinpoint of light. It was drawing me back, back to my childhood faith. I had turned away from God when I was in my teens and never looked back. I knew that back there, in that faith, was life." He paused, looking intently at her. "I gave myself to Christ, and I found a reason to live. I found hope, and love, and forgiveness. He, Christ, was my reason to live." He smiled warmly. "Life now had meaning. And happiness."

"Wow," Rob exclaimed thoughtfully, "that's....quite a story."

Aimee looked puzzled and shook her head slightly but said nothing.

Lenore looked down. She sighed deeply, shaking her head. "I...I guess I've made a mess of things." Her eyes welled with tears as she covered her face with her hands, sobbing quietly.

"Now, Lenore," Gramps went on, "I don't know whether you have a childhood faith. But I want you to know that what I am telling you is real. There is hope for you. There is forgiveness. A new life. In Christ."

Looking up she shook her head, puzzled. "I don't know what you're talking about. It sounds....hopeful. I want to know more. But not now....I'm not ready. I've had too much today." She blew her nose and wiped her eyes.

"Lenore, it is hopeful," he replied.

No one knew what to say. Then with a quiet voice Lenore spoke up. "Rob." She kept her eyes averted but she gained strength as she went on. "Rob, I hated that you were taken away from me. So I thought, *Okay, I'm a bad mother. I'll act like one*. I took my anger out on you." Aimee gave her a questioning look. "Yes, it's true. Alcohol made it worse." She took a deep breath. "I don't know whether you believe me or not, but – I want to do better. I want to be a good mother. I want to love you again – so that you might – maybe – be able to love me."

Rob glanced at her. "Well...." he said cautiously, "I don't know. We can try."

"Aimee." She looked at her but didn't quite make eye contact. "I think Rob has found himself a good wife. Or wife-to-be. Aimee – I hope you're smarter than I was. I....I thought I was helping my man...but, I guess I wasn't. I was trying to run his life." Aimee smiled warmly at her.

She took a deep breath. Looking down, she spoke softly. "Mr. Douglas, it's hard to say it but – it looks like I was wrong about you. I hope you can, uh, overlook the way I treated you."

"Yes, Lenore. Of course I can. I forgive you. And call me Gramps, please."

"No, I – I can't. It wouldn't be right. But – thank you." She stopped and shook her head. "I don't get it! It's the strangest thing."

"What do you mean?" Gramps asked.

"It's strange," she repeated. "I don't have any desire to drink – none at all." They looked puzzled. "Usually by now I start to feel desperate."

"Thank God," Gramps replied, quietly.

There was a knock at the door and an aide stepped in. "Are you ready to eat?" he asked.

Gramps answered yes. He brought in a large round table and set it up, whisked a cloth on to it, then brought in a cart with food.

"I'll serve," offered Rob.

"I will too," said Aimee.

As they got up Rob nudged Aimee and whispered darkly, "I don't know about '*love you in a heartbeat*'. Why should I do that?"

"Because she's your mother," she whispered back, with a nudge.

"Not a good reason. That doesn't entitle her."

"Don't worry about it now," she replied with a smile.

They sat awkwardly in two groups, Rob and Aimee, Gramps and Lenore. Conversation did not flow easily. Rob and Aimee made a few attempts to talk with her. She didn't respond. Before long they were engrossed in one another, oblivious to everyone else. Gramps remembered the long-ago days when he only had eyes for Kate. *Ah, young love.*

He too had tried to engage Lenore in casual conversation but to no avail. Now he tried again. "So, Lenore, what do you think of your son?"

She frowned and the words poured out, impassioned but quietly so he would not hear. "Look at him! I don't deserve him! Look at what he's done….look at who he is, what a good person he is. And I had nothing to do with it!" Tears spilled from her eyes. "I can't even look at him because I've failed him so much. He must hate me! He has every reason to."

"Lenore," Gramps began. He didn't know what to say. *Dear God, I'm not a counselor, or a priest – what do I do now?*

The words came. "Lenore, you can't go back and change the past. But you can make a new beginning. You can make a better future. For you, and for Rob."

She shook her head in confusion, struggling to find words. "Mr. Douglas….I don't know how to be loving to Rob. It was easy to have an attitude with him, put him in his place…. like I said, I was taking my anger out on him. Now – I don't know where to begin."

"Well….think about how you'd like someone to treat you. Maybe that will help. We've had a long day. Rob will be taking you home pretty soon. Just try to say something nice to him."

Lenore dried her eyes. "I'll try."

"When you get back, why don't you look up A.A.? It helped me."

"I will," she nodded.

Before they left, Gramps took Rob aside. Without telling him what his mother had said, he asked him to be gentle with her. "Just ask her a friendly question about her life," he suggested.

"Yeah, okay. If that's what you want."

What to do about Mom, Rob asked himself for the hundredth time. It was a lot easier when they were barely speaking. He never gave her a thought until she would break into his life with some odd request or complaint. He would do his best to keep his cool with her but usually not succeed, then he would feel bad for days afterward. Now, she said she loved him and wanted to be a better mother. *Well, fine*. Gramps had asked him to be kind to her when driving her home. And he had, he'd asked her, very nicely, if she liked her new home, and she had replied, "*No, I don't,*" and clammed up.

'I'm sorry to hear that,' he had replied but that was as far as it went. The next thing he knew she was asleep. Or was she trying to avoid talking to him? *How should I know*, he asked himself bitterly.

He dumped on Aimee. "It's been three weeks and she hasn't tried to contact me," he grumbled. "I can't say I'm surprised. She wanted to be a better mother, did she?"

"You're disappointed, aren't you...."

He looked away, unable to answer.

"Oh, Rob," she sighed. "Why don't you do something? You could send her a '*thinking of you*' card."

"Not me. Besides, guys don't do things like that."

"So, when is her birthday?"

"I have no idea," he shrugged.

"Honey, what do you know about your mother? Is she living with anyone? Does she work, does she have any skill or job history?"

"How should I know? I hardly know anything about her." He spit out the words. "My grandparents used to try to get her to come around and see me. When she did, sometimes she was drunk, then they would fight." He stopped as snatches of memory came back to him, scenes he had tried to forget. "In fact," he continued painfully, "I think that's why she stopped coming around.... It broke my grandparents' hearts. They kept waiting for her to '*clean up her act*'. Ha, it never happened!"

"Well, now, somebody needs to make the first move. Looks like it's not going to be her. So…." She looked at him.

"No!" he interrupted angrily. "I won't do it! Why bother? I don't want to get my hopes up."

"Because, Rob, because!" she almost shouted. "Because of what happened with Gramps! She was a different person walking out than she was coming in." He looked at her skeptically. "She shook your grandpa's hand. And she smiled, well, a half-smile, at me…." She shook her head. "I don't think she's used to smiling."

"Yeah, well, she doesn't know how to smile."

Aimee sighed, shaking her head. "I shouldn't criticize you for not making an effort." She thought about it. "I understand what you've been through with her. Maybe you're not the one, not yet. Maybe, woman to woman, I could. Yes, maybe I –"

"No, no, no!"

She drew back, startled by the vehemence of his tone. "Rob, Rob…" She held his hands tightly.

"Honey, that's good of you…." he frowned, squeezing her hand, "but I don't want you to get involved. I don't want you to get hurt! Besides….ha! you were the one who told me not to have any more to do with her."

"That was then, this is now. And thank you, I can take care of myself."

"I'm finding that out." He struggled with his feelings. "Okay, okay….do what you think is right. I don't want to stand in your way. But – don't move her back here!" He gave her an anguished look. "I don't think I could stand it."

She smiled. "Oh, honey, I wouldn't do that again. Never, unless you wanted it." She thought about it. "Let's see." She opened her planner. "Oh, look….I'll be at a school next Thursday, not far from her town. I could call her and set up a dinner date. My treat, and maybe we'll go to a buffet."

"I'm sure she couldn't resist that," he replied coldly.

"I'll do it," she smiled warmly.

"Just….be careful, okay?"

"Of course." *Maybe I can be a catalyst again*, she thought with a thrill of hope. *It worked before....look how well Rob and Gramps are doing! Yes, yes! But he's right, I would never move her back here.*

She texted him after she got back, just enough to whet his curiosity. The next day they were spending some time alone after dinner at Aimee's house.

"Rob, your mother is really a sad case."

"I can't say I feel sorry for her," he replied with a shrug.

She ignored him. "I picked her up and took her to a buffet. We ate, then talked for a couple of hours. First of all, her housing is pretty bad. She lives with a man she doesn't like. He took her in when she was homeless –"

"Did you say homeless? Mom was homeless?"

"On the verge. She'd been living here, in the city, working as cook in a bar and grille. She got a DUI, lost her license, lost her job, spent a few days in jail and had to sell her car to pay her fines. She was mandated to go to A.A. but she didn't go. The man she was living with didn't want her anymore because she had no income. So he gave her a week to get out. Then, out of the goodness of his heart, she says, he sent her to live with Carl, his buddy, in exchange for housework... and other, shall we say, '*favors*'."

"Oh, Aimee – the guy's a bum! They both are."

"Yeah, really. Well, that got her away from the Court order to go to A.A., she's in another county, but she doesn't like Carl. He doesn't abuse her, at least not physically, but she feels trapped. She can't afford to live on her own because she has no income."

"What an awful story. My own mother. You wouldn't know any of that to listen to her."

"She didn't want you to know. I violated her confidence to tell you this. Please don't let on that you know. Actually, I'm surprised she told me. She was surprised she told me. She's very ashamed."

He was quiet, trying to digest it all. "I can see why she didn't like my question. About her new house."

"You could say that. But she seemed really happy to see me. I think we hit it off. One good thing, amazing really, is that she's not drinking anymore."

"Or any less?"

"You're too cynical! She's been attending A.A. It's been good for her. She said she'd tried it before but didn't like it. This time seems to be different. Somebody picks her up for meetings. But she doesn't have a sponsor yet."

"A sponsor? What's that about?"

"Rob, you really don't know anything!"

"Not that," he snapped. He was ashamed of his reaction. "Why should I?"

"I'm sorry," she apologized. "What I mean is, you're sheltered. A sponsor is like a mentor. Somebody who has been sober for a long time. The sponsor takes this person under her wing and helps her learn to live without alcohol."

"Hmm," he replied thoughtfully. "No, I didn't know. So how did you learn all this?"

"It was my Gram. I told you, she had been an alcoholic when Mom was growing up, but when I got to know her she'd been sober for a long time. She never stopped attending A.A. meetings, which is probably why she remained sober. She sponsored many women. She used to tell me about it, though she always had to be private, she couldn't reveal any names. So – your mother needs to find a sponsor, to help her stay on the path."

"Well, that's interesting and I'm glad for her. But I want to stay out of it. I'm not sure we'll ever get off the ground." He looked at her and shook his head. "I don't want to see you dragged into my family's problems, either. I don't want to see you get hurt."

"Honey, look at it this way. We're on the road to getting married. Then your family will be my family and my family yours.

I care about your mother, because she is your mother. I feel like….I have to get to know her."

He shrugged as he held her hand tightly. "I hadn't thought about it that way. Thank you, honey. I can't stop you, I wouldn't. Just….don't get emotionally involved, okay?"

"My eyes are wide open. Oh, Rob, I won't let her hurt me! I'm getting to know her because I want to! There's something about her….I can't explain it but….I like her. Maybe I can help her. Honey," she looked at him hopefully, "she loves you. She does. She just doesn't know how to act around you."

"Well, that makes two of us. Aimee, I'm torn." He shook his head, struggling with his thoughts. "I don't hate her. I don't know how I feel about her. What do you say we talk to Gramps? He's the one who started this! He needs to help us now. Or help me."

"Yes, yes. I was thinking the same thing."

"Nothing you've told me surprises me," said Gramps when Aimee had completed her story. "Rob, your mother has hit rock bottom, and yes –" noting his expression – "it's her own doing. This could be a good thing because it looks like she wants out. So why don't we help her if we can?"

"Well, that's fine. I'm glad for her. But I have such mixed feelings about her!" He shook his head, frowning. "You can't blame me for wanting to keep my distance. I'm skeptical too. Who knows what will come next?" He got up and began to pace. Gramps could sense his anger. "I don't want her to hurt Aimee!"

"Rob, sit down for a few minutes. Let me tell you and Aimee a story." He waved his hand at Rob who stopped his pacing and came and sat by Aimee.

"There was a young man in a wealthy family," Gramps began. "He didn't want to wait around for his father to die, so he talked his father into giving him his inheritance now. The boy took the money and lived the high life for quite a while, gambling, call girls, you name it, and he lavished it on his friends. But eventually the money ran out, his friends deserted him and he ended up in a homeless shelter. He thought long and hard, and decided to go home. '*My father's employees are better off than I am*', he thought. But he was ashamed. He couldn't face his father."

"Now, his father never gave up on him. He kept hoping his son would return. One day his chief of staff said to him, '*Sir, you need to come down to the servants' quarters*.' He did, and there his son was being hired to work in the kitchen. His father threw his arms around him. '*My son has returned! Let's throw a party!*' The son was in tears, he felt so ashamed, but he accepted his father's love. Now, there was an older brother who threw a fit, thought his kid brother should suffer some more – but that's another story."

"What a lovely story!" Aimee exclaimed. "Where did you hear it?"

"Hmm…." replied Gramps, "I read it in a book."

"Gramps, you old joker," Rob gave him a nudge, "that's in the Bible, isn't it?"

"Could be. Well, that story is about a renegade son, or call him a prodigal son if you want. Your situation is, you have a prodigal mother."

"I never thought of it that way." He shook his head skeptically.

"She had a wonderful inheritance. A wonderful husband, a son, opportunities – and she squandered it all. She's lived her life selfishly, and now she has nothing left to show for it. She's trying to find her way home. Her Father in heaven hasn't stopped loving her. She needs someone to accept her, as that father did his son."

"I'm more the older brother type," he said dismissively.

Gramps looked intently at him. "Rob. '*He's a human being! Treat him like one!*' Do you remember those words?"

"No – should I?"

"Those are your words. When I was being admitted to Sunset Gardens, Damien was being rough. You said those words in my defense. As far as you knew, I was senile. You didn't know I could hear you."

Rob shook his head, contemplating what Gramps had said. "Did I say that? I don't remember."

"Yes, you did. I wasn't senile but I was disoriented. Frightened. I didn't know what was happening to me or where I was. Your words...." Tears filled his eyes as he re-lived that moment. "Your words offered hope. Somebody cared. I was ready to give up, but your words....they made me want to live again. I've always loved you for that." He took Rob's hand and held it tightly.

Aimee looked on wonderingly. She put her arm around Rob.

"Rob, that's who you are. That kind-hearted young man. Let go of your bitterness towards your mother. That's what's holding you back. Just accept her. As she is, not as you wish her to be. She knows she's made a mess of her life. Don't expect anything in return. She'll give what she can give."

"I don't know." He thought about it. "Yeah. I suppose you're right. I guess I could give her a chance –" Gramps started to shake his head, "No, no. That's not what you mean, is it? I'll do what you're asking. I won't expect anything from her."

"Right. Now, how about this? You're extremely busy right now with school. Too busy to visit her. So maybe Aimee can keep visiting her. Is that okay, Aimee?"

"Yes, yes, I can do it! I want to get to know her. I'll be glad to," she responded enthusiastically.

Rob rolled his eyes and shook his head. "Honey, be careful." He put his arm around her.

"I'm always careful." She smiled. "You don't have to worry about me."

"Okay," Gramps told Aimee, "see where that goes. Rob, you fit in where you can, when you can."

"I like her," she added. "I do! I want to visit her again. I think we get along very well."

"Thank you, Aimee," Gramps smiled as he took her hand. "Thank you for doing this." He looked at Rob.

"Okay...." he said warily. "I'll try to accept her. As she is."

"Good. I have faith in you. Now, you two have the evening ahead of you. I'll tell you goodnight." He took their hands. "I love you both."

Chapter 20

Gramps wheeled himself in front of the mirror. "Not bad," he remarked as he slicked back his hair.

"Not bad for an old geezer," agreed Howard.

"Look who talks," snorted Gramps. "Say, it might be cold in that theater. I'm taking my sweater." He put on the sweater Rob and Aimee had given him. "Just the occasion," he said admiringly. He and Howard were ready to go. This was a rare outing for him, an afternoon matinee of a Broadway musical performed by a local little theater group. He never took part in the usual outings, the shopping and restaurant trips, but he was looking forward to this.

A while later he was with his fellow residents in the crowded lobby of the theater, waiting for Howard to return from the men's room. All at once he was aware of fingers at the back of his neck, pulling away his sweater and thrusting something down his back. Reflexively he leaned back and he felt a crunch, then the stench of sulfur began to fill the air. He choked at the smell. Pandemonium broke out as people jostled one another to get away from it. At that moment Howard returned. "Good grief, what's going on here?"

"Quick, Howard, get me into the men's room! Somebody gave me a stink bomb!" An aide, seeing the commotion, hurried over. He too drew back but then he commandeered the wheelchair and rushed it into the men's room. There, he and Howard discovered the remains of broken, rotten eggs. Most of it was still caught in his sweater, the smell with it.

Howard took over. "Look, I'll clean him up. You go out and see if anybody saw anything," he said to the aide.

"Yes, but I'll see you both in five minutes," he replied. "I need to stay with Mr. Douglas from now on."

It became clear that he could not be cleaned up to any presentable level, so just as he was he and Howard rejoined the aide who deposited them in the back of the theater where they could hear, but not see a thing. He then left to investigate what happened. Even here the smell caused complaints. "It's no good," Gramps said with disgust to Howard. "I'm leaving. You stay here. I'll not have you miss this performance because of me." Howard protested but finally let him go.

He sat out in the lobby alone, stewing in his distress. He felt like a third-grader humiliated in front of his peers. An aide rushed out the door. "I'm supposed to stay with you," she announced.

"I'm not a child! Leave me be," he snapped. In a calm moment he realized she was only doing her job but he didn't have many calm moments. She went back inside but every so often popped out to see if he was still there. He was so angry he could hardly think. *What? Why? Who?* It was incomprehensible.

He dreaded the trip back in the crowded van but with a stiff upper lip and gallows humor he made it. "Now, back to my room and a shower," he told the aide who accompanied him.

"Oh, no, we've got to see Mrs. Markowitz. She's waiting for us."

Uh, oh, Principal's office, he thought.

Mrs. Markowitz had already gotten word of what had happened. "I thought I'd smelled everything," she said sympathetically as Gramps and the aide entered her office, "but this is the worst." She wrinkled her nose. "So very sorry, Mr. Douglas. Now, do you have any idea who did this to –"

"No, I don't! I don't have eyes in the back of my head. They didn't leave a calling card."

"No one saw anything, no one knows anything," agreed the aide.

"Well, my goodness, I don't want to think it was one of the staff –"

"And why not!" Gramps broke in. "Have you forgotten Damien? So you think it was a resident? Why couldn't it be staff?"

"Well – it may have been an outsider," she replied, weakly.

Furious, he wheeled himself out of the room.

Once he had cleaned up he felt slightly better. He looked with dismay at his new sweater. He wanted to throw everything out and the memory with it, but finally decided to send the sweater to the dry cleaner and the rest to the laundry. As for dinner, he had neither the heart nor stomach for it.

He would not call Rob and Aimee. It was too painful to talk about. *I'll wait until they come to see me,* he decided, putting it off. He retired early, turning the matter over and over in his mind. *Why me? Was it a random act?* His sleep, at last, was fitful.

Rob and Aimee were in their back booth enjoying a rare meal together in the middle of the week. She had texted him about an encouraging visit with his mother the day before. That was all she said.

"I hardly know where to begin," she declared enthusiastically. "The first thing is that she's staying sober, it's been four weeks now, and she's got a sponsor, a woman named Rose. Your mom wants me to meet her. Rose has her going to a counselor at a local mental health center. I think that's just what she needs. Another thing. She looks better."

"Well, that's a start."

"Yes, she's beginning to care about herself."

"I always thought she looked like a drowned rat, older than her years."

"That was my impression too, when I first met her, that she was much older. Now hear this! She's involved in a program that provides apartments for women who are trying to gain independence. It's run by a church organization. They have an apartment for her. She just has to break away from Carl. That can be harder than it sounds. He doesn't want her to leave. She feels she owes him –"

"Did you meet at her house?" he interrupted. "Is it safe – for you?"

"Yes, I did. She was embarrassed to have me at her house, but don't worry about me. I was safe. Carl left us alone."

"Well, okay....but I still worry about you," he said protectively.

She shook her head. "Back to your mom. She's kind of a dependent person, so independence is scary."

"What do you mean?" he asked, puzzled.

"To her, independence is like being out on a tightrope without a net. She feels helpless."

"Wow. I never realized. Maybe that's why she drinks? But, doesn't it help her to know that other people are supporting her, I mean as friends? I was thinking of you and Rose."

"That's a wonderful question. The answer is, yes. We can be like a safety net. Now, there's one thing I'm uneasy about. She's started attending a church."

"Uneasy? Why is that?"

"Two reasons. At this point I think A.A. and counseling are plenty. Why confuse her with church? And that's the second point. My mother had some bad experiences with the '*institutional church*', as she calls it. She says you can be religious without going to church; she is. Who knows what could happen to her? Why jeopardize her recovery with the risk of being hurt?"

"I think you should let her decide for herself."

She shrugged, unconvinced. "I guess. So far it seems okay. She loves it and it seems to be helping her. She says the people accept her as she is."

"Gramps would approve of that."

"Rob, she talked about the Bible until I wanted to scream. It was just too much!"

"That can get under your skin. But if it helps her, who are we to say?"

"Yes, yes, I know. It just makes me....uncomfortable. Overall, I'd say she's doing very well."

"So, does she have a deadline to move into this new apartment?"

"Yes, a couple of weeks. Rob, I think the time is right to bring her here. The three of us can do something together. Not a meal, we'd just sit and stare at each other. I was thinking about a fun thing, an old 60's play or something like that. I happen to know she likes stuff like that."

"I could do that. I'm actually looking forward to seeing her. You've got me curious."

"I'll see what I can book for us. Now – I've got to leave, I've got lots to prepare for tomorrow." Rob helped her on with her coat. "But first....a good night kiss...." as they told each other goodnight.

Brimming with excitement, Aimee burst into Gramps' room a few days later, Rob alongside her. She planted a kiss on Gramps' cheek. "It came through! My grant!"

"Ah, the one to develop a re-enactment program for school kids?" he asked.

"So, you're going to have them fight the battle of Gettysburg?" Rob asked innocently.

"Yes, of course," she replied archly. "We've already got the blue and gray uniforms and the little toy rifles." Looking around dramatically, she went on, "Well, as I was saying – before I was so rudely interrupted –" she smiled at Rob, "I've developed research modules for the kids to use in their classrooms. Then they come to the museum and act them out, things like a day on a pioneer farm or a Native American village, or a one-room schoolhouse –"

"My, that sounds like fun," commented Gramps, wistfully. "Makes me wish I were back in school. At your museum."

"Yes, but you haven't heard the best part – the museum has offered me a job! As soon as my internship is over. With a very nice salary. How lucky is that? My dream job! I'm working with kids, and I can advance as far as I want," she announced breathlessly.

"That's wonderful!" exclaimed Gramps. "I'm not surprised, though."

"I'm proud of you, sweetheart. But it wasn't luck. You did it yourself." He caught her by the waist. "Gramps, this is what she talked about last summer, and now she'll be doing it!" He kissed her on the cheek.

"Can you believe it? I never imagined that I could make it work so soon! I've even going to have costumes for the kids, simple ones." She whirled away from him and faced him, giving him a peck on the lips. "Do you know what's most exciting about this?"

"Um....you tell me," he whispered in her ear, "my little firefly."

"We could get married!" She threw her arms around him. Gramps chuckled with delight.

"We could. Yes, yes, we could!" He held her close. "We'll have to talk about it."

"We can do it, Rob! Get married! My salary will begin about the time I graduate, and we could get married shortly after that...."

"We need to think it through.....you know we won't have medical insurance –"

"Not a problem! You'll have it, as a student. I'll have it pretty soon –"

He gave her a loud smooch. "Okay! You've convinced me!"

"Ohh...." She shook her head excitedly, "We have to pick a wedding date! Let's see, graduation is three months away....."

"Well then, how about the day after graduation?" She made a face and he backed away. "Okay, the week after, then."

She burst into laughter. "And you're the man who didn't want to get married!"

"You've convinced me, see –" he grinned.

Gramps shook his head, laughing.

"Rob, Rob – it takes time to plan a wedding.....at least four months –"

"That long?" He shook his head. "Why so long?"

"Oh, Rob, four months is barely enough, believe me – these things take time, even a simple wedding – but we'll do it! Mom and I."

"Yes, yes....we'll do it." He kissed her cheek. "Darling, I want you to have a beautiful wedding. Don't cut corners."

"It will be beautiful! We can do it. Let's set a date right now." They opened their planners and chose a date in late June.

Laughing, he picked her up and swept her around the room in his arms. "Happy, darling?"

"You're crazy!" she shrieked, "Put me down! Do you want to break your back? Get married in a wheelchair?"

"One wheelchair is enough!" Gramps agreed, laughing.

"Relax, honey, don't struggle," he told her, holding her tight, "or we'll both fall!"

"Mmm...." She settled into his arms. "I could like this....but put me down anyway!"

"Only if you kiss me...."

"How's this?" she asked, kissing him as he put her down.

"It'll do for now."

"We did it, Gramps, we did it!" he exclaimed, taking hold of her waist. "We set a date!"

"Come here, you two," Gramps said with a smile as he opened his arms to them. "Thank you for letting me share in your joy!" He wrapped them in a hug, then putting their hands together he declared solemnly, "My blessings on you both. I love you."

"And we love you....."

He said nothing about his misadventure at the theater. He didn't want to rain on their parade.

Chapter 21

"Well, Rob, it's good to get together with you." Roger guided him to a table in the dining room of his lodge as they sat down to a meal together. "Been wanting to, ever since you and Aimee announced your engagement – that was some ring you gave her! That's a good heritage," he added. "Well, I got too busy. Now that you've a date set it's time to get to know my new son in law, man to man. Uh, son in law to be."

"I've enjoyed getting to know your family," Rob replied as he took a chair. "You've made me feel at home, I feel just like part of your family."

"Ah, so that's the reason you're marrying Aimee," he said with a sly smile.

Rob smiled. "There are....other reasons."

"I hope so!" Roger exclaimed gruffly. But his manner was friendly as he went on. "You know, parents always think no man is good enough for their daughter, or woman for their son – that is, we always did, but I have to say, I think you and Aimee are a good match. We're glad for her." He extended his hand to Rob. "You're a fine young man. That's the most important thing. I think you've a great future ahead of you. You're a go-getter, and I like that."

"Uh, thank you, Roger." Embarrassed, he wasn't sure how to answer. "It's good of you to say that."

"Ah, medicine. A good field. Maybe not as good as it used to be, but you can still make a good life for Aimee."

What, is that why he invited me here? he thought uneasily. *He wants to make sure I will support her in the manner to which she's accustomed? Does he think Aimee's marrying down? I may be a poor student now but I haven't always been poor*. "Well, Roger," he paused and gave him a cool look, "I hope I can live up to your expectations."

"Don't worry about that. You're fine, just be yourself." As they settled in to eat he poured a couple of mugs of beer from the pitcher on the table, giving one to Rob. "Actually, I didn't invite you here to talk about you." Rob smiled, relieved.

"You and Aimee. Your relationship is your own business. I don't ask Aimee questions. But Elaine and I appreciate that you're not living together. Playing house isn't marriage. I don't think it helps."

"How do you mean?" asked Rob. *What is he getting at*, he wondered.

"It isn't that I'm old fashioned. I'm not." He paused and looked piercingly at Rob. "It's the voice of experience. Living together, it's not the real thing. You're holding back. You're roommates, that's all. Then when you get married, it's a whole different relationship. It's permanent. Everything changes. That's what we found out."

"Ah....I'm trying to figure it all out," he replied, beginning to relax.

"Aimee, she has some pretty strong convictions about this. There aren't many men who would honor that."

"We've talked a lot about it. I admit I don't always understand, but I respect her."

"Thank you for that. Mind you, I'm not asking you your business." He poured himself a second mug. "That's enough, I've got to drive home," he said, pushing the pitcher away. "Unless you want another?"

"No, I've had my fill," he nodded. "Thank you for inviting me."

"That's okay. I wanted to help you understand Aimee." He sipped his drink slowly and looked away, contemplating what to say. "You and Aimee remind me of Elaine and me. She turned my world upside down – as I believe Aimee has done with you – though in different ways than you and Aimee."

"She sure has," he smiled.

"Elaine and I met in college. I fell for her, hard. But, I couldn't score with her." He laughed, shaking his head. "Why not? I couldn't understand because I knew she had been around, so to speak. I knew the guys she'd been with. Well, she told me that she'd decided, a while earlier, that she was sick of being cheap, of going from one guy to the next as she'd done for years. She hated being used and she hated using men. So, now she wasn't going to be with any man until she met the man she was going to marry, and then she hoped not until marriage because she wanted to be sure."

Ah, déjà vu, thought Rob. *Almost.*

"Aimee's told you some of this, right?" Rob nodded. "That was a wake-up call to me. It made me think. I saw myself in what she had experienced. See, from the time I discovered girls, in junior high school I was Roger Love, the lover. I had to live up to my name, you know. Rob, I'm not proud of this at all." He lowered his head. "I became very good at getting what I wanted. I knew just what to say – and once I got what I wanted, I was gone. Love 'em and leave 'em."

Rob struggled to conceal his surprise as Roger went on. "Except it wasn't love. It was total selfishness. I didn't think much about it until I met Elaine. And you know what? I loved her so much I was willing to do what she wanted. To wait. Until marriage. Remember, she wanted to be sure." He laughed. "It had to be love because I cared more about her, making her happy, than I cared about myself. And that was not Roger Love!"

In a sudden shamefaced moment Rob wondered whether he loved Aimee as much as he said he did.

"So I told her, okay, let's set a wedding date as soon as we can. And we did. As soon as she graduated from nursing school. '*We've got a lot to look forward to,*' I told her."

Rob nodded agreement. *Déjà vu.*

"Well – it worked for a few months. But we didn't have much self control. After a while I was staying at her apartment. Then, she was pregnant. We got married, a nice little wedding. You know, it wasn't about me. I wanted to make her happy. Love makes the difference. Like I said, I cared more about her than I did about myself."

"She wanted to make you happy too."

"Amazing, isn't it. What did she see in me? I'm still trying to figure it out."

"That's how I feel," he said with a nod of his head. "Roger, that's a beautiful story. Thank you... for taking me into your confidence."

"Oh, that's just the beginning. You think we lived happily ever after? I wish. We just weren't ready for marriage." He reached for the pitcher and poured himself a third mug. "I need it to get through this," he explained. He pulled out his keys and tossed them to Rob. "Here, you drive us home tonight."

"Glad to," he nodded.

"Well, going on. The good part was the baby. We hoped it would be a girl because we wanted to name her Aimee. Because of our love. She's told you this, hasn't she?"

"Partly. I guess she was your private joke."

" '*Private joke' ?* Hey, I like that. Yes, she was our private joke. The bad part, we didn't know how to get along. I was irresponsible. We fought a lot, even though we loved each other. We didn't know how to settle anything. We could make whoopee but that didn't solve our problems. And the baby, she complicated things. My advice, Rob, don't have a baby too soon. If you can help it. There's too much to get used to all at once. But we never thought of giving up. Oh, I didn't tell you, when we got married we used the old vows, you know, '*better or worse, as long as we both shall live, etc., etc.*' A good idea, you know....not like some of our friends, '*as long as we both shall love.*' "

"I like that. I'll mention it to Aimee."

"People think you can erase the past, just like that. Well, I'll tell you...." he sighed deeply, "it doesn't happen that way. Our pasts came back to haunt us, and we fought a lot. One night we were going at it, and there was little Aimee, hands over her ears. I'll never forget the look on her face – she was so scared. She was about a year old. Elaine and I, we decided then and there, we had to stop screaming at each other."

Rob nodded sympathetically. "That must have hurt, seeing her like that."

"Oh, yes. We knew we had to change. It wasn't about us any more, it was about our baby. We got help – we men don't like to do that, do we," he laughed. "Actually, Aimee saved our marriage. Not directly, but if we hadn't had our baby I don't know if we could have stuck it out. Elaine always said she didn't want to raise a child the way she was raised, in an unstable home without a father."

"That's a good motivation to work things out."

"It was hard. Things went from bad to worse. I couldn't keep a job, I had dropped out of school, Elaine was trying to juggle her job and the baby....Then one day she said, '*Roger, why don't you join the Army? They'll pay for your education. And we're not at war.*' Ha! Not then. I thought, why not? Well, Rob, that was the second-best decision I ever made. The Army and I got along very well together. Really, it made a man of me."

"So things got better for you and Elaine?"

"Slowly. My parents, they're good people, they helped us. Helped me. Now, we weren't going to have any more children. Aimee was enough! Very strong willed."

"I'll have to tell her that," Rob laughed.

"We were still trying to work out our own problems. We didn't think we could handle any more. Of all things, we had twins! But they were the light of our life. You might think Aimee is my favorite. No, no, I try not to play favorites. Each one is special. And that kinda brings up the other thing I wanted to tell you."

He swirled the drink in his mug, pondering how to say it. "Having children – it changes you. It changed me. When I looked at my little Aimee I realized how I'd treated women all my life. What a jerk I was! Why – if some guy took advantage of my girls the way I used to – I'd kill him." He turned his face away. "*I should have*," he muttered, "*I wish I had*." Seeing Rob's startled look he added, "Don't get me wrong, I never forced myself on a girl. Um, I don't think so. I just knew how to say what I had to say, to get what I wanted to get, and pretty soon I'd be gone. I broke a lot of hearts. Then, because of Elaine, I began to realize, that's serious business." He sighed, "I live with a lot of guilt. I wish I could go back…."

"Maybe you need to talk to a priest, or a pastor," Rob offered helpfully.

"Nah, that's not for me. What would a priest do? Actually," he took the last swallow of his drink, "it helps, telling you. Unburdening myself. No….I deal with my guilt by trying to do better with my kids. And….uh, I get drunk now and then. But not in public. Look here, Rob," he spoke confidentially, "not even the kids know that. Only Elaine. Don't tell Aimee, I'm asking you."

"Of course not," he assured Roger.

He paused and looked directly at Rob. "I've never told Aimee what I told you. About myself. I know Aimee's told you about her mother, she told us that – but, I've never told her about me." He looked away "I've been afraid to. I don't want her to…. to hate me. Or look down on me."

"Roger….I know she wouldn't hate you. But I won't say anything."

"No. That's not fair to you. Having secrets. Tell her the whole story. The ugly with the good, except, what I asked you not to. In a way, I'd rather she hear it from you. I don't think I could tell her, or Jacquie, any of this. I've told Jason. I'm glad I did."

"Yes, I can see why you would. You know, I was brought up to respect girls, women – but that might not have lasted once I got to college. I know what I wanted to do. If I hadn't been so shy with girls, I might have been stupid. That's what Aimee says."

"Well, once you start you don't want to stop. If I hadn't met Elaine I would have gone through life being stupid. As Aimee would say, strange are the mysteries of the universe."

"Roger, you, that is you and Elaine, have done a great job with Aimee. She's her own person."

He sighed. "We try. To tell the truth, I leave most of that up to Elaine. But I back her up." He seemed lost in thought. "Elaine and I, we don't want our girls to fall into the arms of a Roger Love. We want our girls to be strong, not sell themselves cheap. Not tease a guy, that's just as bad. And Jason, I want him to be a better man than his father."

"Better than his father was," Rob corrected him. "But now, I'd say you've given him a lot to look up to."

"I hope so." He poured the last of the beer from the pitcher into his glass. "Like I said, having kids changes you. Ha, ha, that's a good thing."

"Roger, thank you. I think I understand Aimee a lot more. Why she's the person she is. You can be very proud of her."

"We are," Roger agreed, "but it has to come from the heart. Aimee, or Jason or Jacquie, they can't make decisions because it's what their old man, or their mom, want them to do. It has to be their own free choice. I think Aimee is making some pretty good decisions. That makes us proud. Mighty proud."

He looked at his watch. "How did it get so late? I'm glad you're driving, not me." He started to rise, then settled back in his chair. "Listen, Rob. I've got one thing to say to you." He looked at him intently. "When you stand before the preacher and say your vows, I hope you mean them with all your heart."

"Yes, sir," Rob answered, suppressing the urge to salute him.

"One other thing," he growled, "love my daughter!"

"Yes, sir!"

Rob had invited Aimee to dinner at his apartment to celebrate their setting a marriage date, or so he told her, but he also was eager to tell her what Roger had told him. The effect on him had been profound. *She's worth it*, he thought, *she's worth waiting for. I don't regret what we've done. Or not done! Look how close we've become, how we're getting to know each other, in a lot of different ways…..*

"Honey, I'm impressed! It looks so special," she told him as she entered the apartment, greeting him with a kiss, taking in the carefully set table and plates of food.

"Thanks, honey," he responded, taking her coat and helping her into her chair. "Half is take-out, half is my own cooking. I leave it to you to figure it out."

"I have no idea," she said, "it all looks delicious."

They were almost finished their meal when she stopped eating. "I want to talk with you about something." She studied him for a moment. *Do I want to go through with this,* she asked herself. *Yes, I do!* "Rob…..I've been thinking and re-thinking my convictions. I know this has been difficult for you. Well, it has been for me too."

If I waver at all, she thought, *we'll both give in. Is this what I want? Yes, yes, let's end this struggle! I'm tired of fighting my feelings. It's too much, for both of us*. She took a deep breath, "Here we are, only a few months from our wedding day. A lot of my objections don't make sense anymore. Except, and this is really important, I don't want to get pregnant." *There*, she thought, *I've said it! Am I doing the right thing?*

"Oh, Aimee!" His pulse quickened and he seized her hand. "Are you saying what I think you're saying?"

"Rob….darling…" She looked at him with eyes full of love.

He withdrew his hand and got up and walked around. "Honey – before we talk about this I want to tell you what your dad and I talked about the other night."

"Oh, Dad! He's quite a talker, isn't he? I hope he didn't bore you."

"Oh, no, not at all." He sat back down and gently, briefly, told her what her father had said. By the time he had finished she was in tears.

"Dad, Dad. That's quite a shock….his past." She shook her head, contemplating what she'd heard. "I'll have to digest it. But Dad…." she spoke almost to herself, "I love him so much…. and Mom too…." *So that's the rest of Mom's story*, she thought.

"The important thing is –"

"Yes. He turned his back on that. He's not the same man today. He's quite a man, isn't he? And Rob, so are you." She took his hands, held them tight, then kissed him lightly. "Darling…. forget what I said. We can do it. We can do what Mom and Dad weren't able to do. What a gift they gave me!" She shook her head in amazement. "Their love. Their commitment."

He nodded his head. "Baby, I'm with you. I'm committed, I mean it. Let's give ourselves something wonderful to look forward to! We've come this far, we'll help each other…..Oh…by the way, I didn't tell you what he told me at the end."

"What was that?"

"He ordered me to love you."

"He what?" she laughed. "Well….you be sure to do that, Rob."

"Oh, yes," he replied, seriously. "I have to. He's got a black belt, you know."

"Rob!" she shrieked as she cuffed him.

Chapter 22

It was a quick lunch in a quiet corner of a busy restaurant. Aimee and Julie were glad to be back together.

"I'm sorry it's a family emergency that brings you back to town," Aimee began, "but it sure is good to be with you. Thanks for making time for me."

"I'm glad I could. Facebook is fine but face-to-face is better. Well….you look smashing, as usual," Julie observed after they had placed their orders. "Not for me, I'm sure."

"Ha, ha, I'm seeing Rob tonight, after I do some shopping."

"Nothing wrong with looking good for your man, right?"

"And I like him to look good for me. We please each other that way."

"A lot of women don't see it that way," Julie said.

"I'm used to that! So what else is new?"

After a few minutes of chit-chat their talk turned serious. Looking directly at Julie, Aimee began. "Is it worth it? What we've committed ourselves to? Waiting until we're married to become one, to have sex?" Julie began to laugh as Aimee went on. "Our wedding date is less than four months away. Why not give in, end all this frustration for both of us?" She frowned. "What's so funny?"

"Been there, thought that," Julie told her. "But why not ask Zach? That is, if he were here."

"Zach! What would he say? He didn't always agree with you."

"That's true. But the important thing is, he honored my wishes." She smiled. "It made me love him all the more."

"Rob has been good about that. Though maybe not at first. I do love him more and I respect him, because he respects me. But c'mon, what's this about Zach?"

"Aimee….after we were married, he thanked me." Aimee's eyebrows shot up in surprise.

"Yes, really. He'd lived with a couple of girls – though not as many as some guys – and he said our relationship was so different, the trust level, the depth of our love, we were sure of each other, committed, it was so different from the casual stuff before. He was glad we had waited, to be sure of each other and get to know each other first."

"Wow. That's quite a revelation….and gratifying, too…."

"But there's more. He felt bad….that he couldn't give me what I gave him, virginity, the only one, no baggage, no comparisons…." Aimee nodded. "He said this is what we'll have to teach our children someday."

"It certainly worked with me. I've told you about my mother…." Julie nodded, "and the impact she had on me. So! What you say about Zach is pretty amazing. I should tell Rob." She shook her head, frowning. "It bothered me that I had to be the one who set the limits, in the beginning. Do the '*heavy lifting*', you know."

"But of course. It was your idea, not his."

"Yes…." she thought about it, "I guess you're right. It's easier than it used to be, Rob agrees with me now. But I'm still wondering….now that we're engaged, why not?"

"I can't tell you what to do. You make your own decision. I'll tell you this, I had those same thoughts, and what I finally decided, and I told Zach, was that I didn't want to run the risk of pregnancy. I didn't want to be pregnant and preparing for a wedding at the same time."

"I'm sure you're right."

"I don't know about you, but for me, abortion wasn't an option. Anybody who says that's not a baby is in denial, and I'm not going to kill a baby."

"I agree with you," she nodded.

"Now that we've been married seven months I'm so glad we don't have a baby, not yet."

"Why is that?"

"Let me prepare you, girlfriend. No matter how compatible you two are, you will have adjustments. Be prepared for it. You don't just '*live happily ever after.*' Marriage takes work, and it would be harder with a baby, or struggling through pregnancy."

"I hear you. As a matter of fact, my mother said the same thing. She and dad started their marriage with me. Pregnant, that is. It was rough going."

"I'll bet. But you know, Aimee, pregnancy isn't the main reason. Not really." Aimee looked puzzled. "It's the anticipation factor. Like waiting for Christmas to open your presents," she laughed, "times ten, as I told Zach. It meant a lot, to know we had that self-control. Maybe later, down the road, we'll be glad for it. Actually," she reflected, "I think it made us both grow up. Our time together, we focused on getting to know each other."

"Oh, yes, that's been amazing," Aimee agreed. "We're even learning how to settle disagreements. Well, we're starting to. Ha, ha, I don't storm out of the room anymore." Julie laughed understandingly.

Aimee stopped and reflected. "The self-control aspect – I've thought about that too. What if we're separated for a while after we're married? I'd like to know I could trust Rob, and myself, to have self-control."

"I think that's very important. Well, Aimee, all this talk about Rob makes me want to see him again. Do you think you two could stop over to my folks' house for a little while tonight? For dessert?" Aimee quickly texted Rob, and she and Julie began making plans.

"By the way," Julie concluded, "Zach lets me know he values me very highly."

"Oh?" asked Aimee. "What do you mean?"

"He waited for me, he worked for me...."

"And you give him lots to appreciate, don't you!"

"Oh....yes." Julie nodded and smiled. "This may sound sexist," Julie continued, "but I think it's a guy thing, that sense of conquest. I wasn't easy to get."

"Oh, Julie, that is sexist. We all value more what we have to work for...." She thought about it, "though I do agree, women tend to give in much too fast. They don't respect themselves and then they're not respected. So men treat them badly."

"My point exactly." She and Aimee got up to leave. "I'll look forward to seeing you two tonight – and then, your wedding!"

"Did you have a good time tonight?" Elaine asked Aimee as she joined her in the kitchen a few nights later.

"Umm, always," she replied dreamily. "We went to a new restaurant at the Waterfront with Rob's friend from school, Joel Greenberg and his wife Marta. Good food and they had a local band."

"You're home early."

"The guys have a test tomorrow, they wanted to study. They were quizzing each other at dinner. Ugh! Everything you never wanted to know about infectious diseases – at dinner!"

"I can believe it," Mom laughed. "I'm a nurse, I've heard it all."

"Ha, ha. That's when I got Rob up dancing. Well, almost dancing," she laughed, "he's awkward, self-conscious."

"You'll have to teach him."

"I hope so. I love to dance! Mom, where is everybody? Are the kids out?"

"They won't be '*kids*' forever, honey," her mother admonished. "They're seventeen, in fact, seventeen and a half."

"I know, I know. It's a habit," she replied impatiently.

"Jason's delivering pizzas, Dad's at the lodge and Jacquie is asleep in bed." Aimee looked surprised. "She has a big track meet tomorrow, out of town," she explained.

"That's right. I'd forgotten. Well, I wish her luck. She's getting pretty good, huh?"

"Yes, she is. We're very proud of her."

"Then.....since it's just the two of us, I'd like some private time with you." Smiling, she put her arm around her mother.

"Anything wrong?" Mom asked with concern.

"No, nothing's wrong. I've been wanting to ask you some questions, without Dad. Look, it's an excuse for some of your wonderful chocolate cake!" She cut pieces of cake as she prepared tea for them. "Ah....I'll miss this when I'm married. Do you think you can make us a cake now and then? Just for us?"

"I have a better idea!" Mom replied, "I'll teach you how, then you can make your own."

"I was afraid you'd say that." She rolled her eyes. "That's so intimidating. But...."

"Honey," Mom interrupted, "we don't have much time if you want to talk without Dad. He's coming back early from his lodge meeting. We're going with Jacquie tomorrow."

"I didn't know. Okay...." she took a deep breath, "let's get to it. Mom, I'm trying to digest what Dad told Rob about himself–" Mom's eyebrows shot up – "No, I don't hold anything against him," she added quickly. "That's not it. I respect him for the changes he made in his life. Please believe me," she patted her mother's hand, "I love him all the more. For who he is today."

Mom frowned, shaking her head. "I told him he should tell you himself! You and Jacquie, together. Certainly not leave it for Rob to tell you. But –" she sighed, "he's ashamed. And he said he couldn't bear to see the look on your faces if he did tell you. He was afraid you would think he was a hypocrite, considering the way we've brought you up."

"No, I never would! But....this raises more questions than it answers." Elaine looked puzzled. "Mom, what attracted you to Dad? He was everything you had turned away from!" She shook her head. "Why would you want to have anything to do with him?"

"Oh....I knew all about him!" she exclaimed hotly. "Especially from my girlfriend Patty, the one I made my pact with. She hated him!" She stopped, wondering how much to tell her daughter. "He had hurt her deeply. So when he became interested in me – of course, it was the old Elaine he was interested in – I told him I didn't want anything to do with him. And I told him why, in no uncertain terms! That was the end. So I thought."

"But....Dad says you reformed him."

"I don't like him saying that, because that's not what happened. I would never go with a man to reform him, believe me! What happened is, a while later he looked me up, told me he had changed. I didn't believe him. *He may think he's being clever*, I thought, but I never wanted to see him again."

"I guess no girl had told him off before. So that would make him more interested in you."

"Maybe, I don't know," she shrugged. "For some reason, I listened to him....and I heard a different Roger Love. I – I don't know why – I gave him a chance. He showed me how he had changed. We began to see each other, casually, just as friends. Before I knew it, I was falling in love with him, though I didn't tell him that."

"Yes....you'd want to be sure he really had changed. And to see if he loved you too."

"I knew he loved me. Or thought he did. But yes, I had to be sure about him. I wasn't going to throw my love away on someone who could hurt me, or wasn't worthy of me."

"Mom, you were strong!" she said approvingly.

"Ha, for a while." She shook her head.

"But....you haven't answered my question. What did you see in him?" she frowned. "He's always felt indebted to you, he's made that clear. I can see why he would be attracted to you. You were strong, you knew where you were going. And beautiful, I know that," she said with a laugh. "But he was selfish and undisciplined. You wouldn't want me going with someone like that!" She rolled her eyes. "What did you see in him?"

"Oh....Aimee," she began, a faraway look in her eyes, "underneath all of that, he was a good man. He wanted to be different, a better man. He had goals, like I did. A moral code, strange as it may seem. He went out of his way to help people.... and, we began to realize that we were very good for each other. We helped each other."

"That sounds like the Dad I know," Aimee replied with a nod.

"And yet," she laughed, "we were still '*just friends*'. We did a lot of things together, had a lot of fun. I was keeping control of my emotions – ha, ha, I thought I was. Eventually, we admitted we loved each other." She smiled as she remembered. "You ask me what I saw in him? It's not everything, but it's the most important thing. Something I had never thought about before."

"What was that?" Aimee asked, intrigued.

"His love. Unconditional love." Aimee looked puzzled. "Ah, that doesn't mean anything to you, because –" she shook her head, trying to explain, "you've always known it. You take it for granted." Aimee looked at her intently. "Darling Aimee....I had never known that. Growing up, I loved my mother, I knew she loved me. But I also knew....she loved alcohol," she said sadly. "That was her first love. It....it changed her. I was never sure what to expect from her. She could be loving or she could be harsh.... even rejecting."

"Oh, Mom. How awful for you! That must have been so painful." She took her mother's hand.

"Yes it was. But I just accepted it, I didn't know any better. Until –" she smiled, "your Dad. His love was different. It was constant, unchanging. I needed that." She laughed. "His parents, too."

"Grandma and Grandpa Love. They're like that."

"Your Dad took me home to meet his parents. He told them I was the girl he wanted to marry. Honey, they were so welcoming –" tears filled her eyes, "your grandma came over, put her arms around me, told me that if I wanted to I could call her Mama

Love. Papa Love too. They taught me about unconditional love. About forgiveness too."

"I guess I do take it for granted," Aimee agreed. "But it's true...." She thought about it. "Rob is like that. I know his love is unconditional. I guess he learned that from his grandparents. It makes such a difference in a relationship."

"Yes. But I had a lot to learn. We were both so young, too young to get married....but you know that story already." Their eyes met. "We fought a lot, and it was mostly my fault. I couldn't '*let go*'. We asked your grandparents for help. They taught me about forgiveness." She shrugged. "It was new to me. I remember Papa Love saying, '*Your love is more important than what you're fighting about. You've got to work it out, then forgive each other.*'" She smiled at Aimee. "Good advice to remember."

"I will remember that," she nodded.

"Years later it helped me when we came back to the States and I had to get re-acquainted with my mother. A sober mother. She'd been sober for a number of years, she'd '*worked the program*' in A.A. and she wanted to make things right with me. But oh –" she grimaced – "I wasn't ready. I had to learn to forgive her. Your grandparents helped me."

"Hmm, I never knew that. It makes me appreciate them in a new way. And Gram. Kind of like Rob and his mother. Though she hasn't been sober that long."

"Yes....it brings back a flood of memories. Well, Rob's lucky. He has you to help him, thanks to Gram. Now –" she took Aimee's hand, "does that answer your questions?"

"Not quite. She smiled disarmingly. "Mom, hearing about Gram, the way she was....you were looking for love. If you don't mind my saying this....I can understand why you got into – um, promiscuity. I'm sorry to put it that way –"

"Ha, ha. That's a kind way to put it. That's okay, honey. I've heard a lot worse, believe me. And you're right. I never thought about it until I began getting my life together, then I realized I had been looking for love in all the wrong places." She took

Aimee's hand. "I wanted better for the children I would someday have. I knew I had to change." Aimee nodded in agreement. "By the way," Mom frowned, "your grandparents don't know anything about my past. They never will."

"Not from me," Aimee assured her. "But....what about Dad? I don't understand, why did he become....the way he was? He wasn't brought up that way."

"You're right about that. We've talked about it. I think – after the first girl, there was no turning back. And he was only twelve or thirteen. He dropped out of church, turned away from God. Ha, he had been an altar boy, very sincere. The sad thing is, living that way changed him. He began treating girls like objects, not persons, individuals. He became very selfish."

"Mom, I'm glad he found you. You helped him change. I know you did."

"Oh, honey....I had been the same," she said in a pained voice. "I knew what it was to use men, for conquest, for my own gratification. I was just as selfish."

Aimee seized her hand, holding it tightly. "That's hard to talk about, I'm sure."

"That moment of shame, that I told you about....when I wanted something better?" She shook her head. "To this day, I wonder that I was strong enough to act on it, to follow through. It helped that I talked with Patty and found out she felt the same way. We helped each other. I had counseling, too. I got strong enough so that when I did meet this Roger Love character, I could tell him off." She laughed warmly. "It was funny. Oh, it was fun!"

"Mom, that's a wicked laugh," Aimee said approvingly, patting her hand.

"I was doing it for Patty! Even though –" she stopped, unable to go on.

"Mom, what is it?"

"I.... lost her friendship."

"Oh, no! Mom –that's sad. What happened?"

"Yes," she sighed. "When I started going with him she saw it as a betrayal. She couldn't believe he had changed. She never gave him a chance, or me either." She shook her head as the memories came back. "But he wanted to change. Who would have believed it? Get back to who he used to be."

"Are you saying he changed, just like that? How can that be?"

"Oh, no. It took time, and he had help." She shrugged. "I'll tell you the whole story some day...."

"Mom, yes, I want to hear. I'll ask you later. So," she reflected, "he got back to his roots."

"Yes, Except, he never went back to his church. It wasn't for him. That was fine with me, I didn't like church."

"And now.... he's an atheist."

"That came later, you know. Back then, he still believed in God, though he didn't want organized religion. Like me. But I've developed my own religion and it's worked out very well. Everyone should have a religion," she said pointedly.

"It works for you," she shrugged. "About Dad – did Grandma and Grandpa ever find out? About his past?"

"Oh, no," replied Mom, shaking her head. "Hard to believe, isn't it? Between you and me, I think he was a bit spoiled by his parents, his older sisters. Maybe they looked the other way. The youngest child, he could do no wrong. Well, that didn't work around me."

"I'm sure it didn't." She reached over and hugged her. "Mom, thank you. Thank you so much. I know this wasn't easy....but it's been helpful to me."

"This is just a bare outline, you know. It's all we have time for. Let me know when you want to hear '*the rest of the story*.' "

"Oh, yes, I will. And – I admire you and Dad. Not many people would accomplish what you've accomplished, a good marriage and family, good lives – but that raises one more question." Mom raised her eyebrows. "Why marriage? That puzzles me." She studied her mother. "With your background, I think you'd run away from marriage, you'd be afraid of making the commitment –"

"That will have to wait," Mom interrupted. "I heard the garage door open, your Dad will be coming in." They began clearing dishes away.

"Well, well," Roger remarked a few minutes later as he entered the kitchen. "Two of my favorite girls." He gave each a kiss. "Time for bed, but first – a piece of cake." He looked at his wife. "Are you ready to go up? Morning will come early. I hope Jacquie's in bed." Elaine nodded.

Aimee got up and put her arms around her father, kissing him on the cheek. "Dad....I love you very much! I just wanted you to know that," she said, then turning to her mother she kissed her. "Mom, I love you very much!" she told her as she quickly ran out of the kitchen.

"What brought that about?" Roger asked Elaine, shaking his head.

"Just appreciate it," she smiled, taking him by the arm. "Come on....time to go up."

Chapter 23

"Rob, hello."

"Hi, Gramps! It's good to hear from you. How are you?"

"Oh, I'm fine. Say, there's someone who wants to meet you. Can you make it on Friday this week? Early evening? The little parlor?"

"Yeah – Friday's fine. Somebody wants to meet me? Anybody I know?"

"Wait and see. Come and be surprised."

"Surprised, huh? You've got me curious. I can't stay late though. Aimee too?"

"No, just you. See you about 6:00 – okay?"

"I'll be there." He hung up wondering what it was all about. *Not to include Aimee….? Well, I won't lose any sleep over it…. but, who could it be?*

As he entered the room that Friday night he saw an ordinary looking man of middle years with a warm, open face, talking with Gramps. "Rob," said Gramps, "this gentleman came to me because he didn't know whether you were working or in school –"

"I didn't want to just walk in on you," the stranger added. "Rob, do you know who I am?"

"No…" he shook his head, puzzled, "No, I don't."

"I'm Scott Carlyle. Your father."

His jaw dropped. Long-forgotten memories flooded in.... wrestling on the floor, being carried in his arms, playing ball in the yard. Smells....shaving lotion, sweat, newly cut grass....

Scott strode over and put out his hand. "Rob, it's so good to see you! I didn't know where you were." Their eyes met. "I've always loved you."

He remembered the love. He reached for Scott and the men held each other in a bear hug. "Dad, Dad – I remember you. I made myself forget, but.....I remember you."

They sat down and Scott began, "Rob....let me look at you. It's so good to see you – at last." There were tears in his eyes as he blew his nose. "What a fine young man you are."

Rob's mouth opened but he couldn't reply. Tears filled his eyes.

"Ah, Rob," he smiled, "I was present when you were born. You were my son. I always felt that way." He stopped a moment. "Let me back up. Your mother and I met in college. She was pregnant, she had left your father. I didn't take her away from him. I never met him. He was clear across the country." He stopped to remember. "I loved her, I wanted to take care of her. We had some good years. And another child, your brother Mark."

"Mark?" He tried to remember. "My brother?"

"Yes, Mark. Your brother. Well, things got bad when he was born. Your mother couldn't seem to handle two children. I think she was depressed, but I didn't realize it then. She started drinking. Then your father was killed...." he sighed, "and she went to pieces. Even so, we went ahead and got married. We couldn't before because she wasn't divorced. I thought it would help her but it didn't. She...." he shrugged his shoulders. "She couldn't handle things."

"This is unbelievable!" He felt he would burst with happiness. "When did you adopt me?"

"When we were married. I loved you as my own, and I wanted you to have my name. I'd always been your Dad. Now I was, legally."

"Ah....yes. So – Dad – what about Mark? I'd almost forgotten about him."

"You were two when he was born. We were together as a family, though not always a happy family, for the next two years. Then your mother met someone else, a drinking buddy. She took you and left. I think her boyfriend didn't want two children. Your mom felt she couldn't handle two kids and manage her life...."

Rob frowned and shook his head. "That sounds like Mom."

"She moved out of town. I put her out of my mind, I was scrambling to take care of Mark. Then I heard you were taken from her – ha, it didn't surprise me because I was sure she was drinking, neglecting you. Her parents fought to get you. So did I, but I didn't stand a chance. They had a good attorney, they could give you a better life....so I signed you over." He shook his head. "I've always regretted that."

"You mustn't," Rob said warmly. "You did what you thought was best. So, what happened to Mark?"

"Oh, he's with me! He's a great kid. Young man. By the way, how is your mother now? Your grandfather said you're in touch."

He shrugged. "It's hard to say. I think she's trying to straighten herself out."

"Tell her I wish her well. I don't need to see her. I'm happily married now."

"I will....Dad." It felt strange to call this man '*Dad*'. *Strange but....I like it.*

"Your mother loved you. I loved her. She was easy to love. A bit unstable though. I could have been a better husband, more understanding. Rob, you were my son. You still are."

"Dad – Dad, I know that." He was blinking back tears. "I'm remembering things now." He shook his head, puzzled. "How did you find me?"

"It was that video! Mark found it on YouTube, by accident. He called to me, '*Dad*,' he said, '*you'd better come here!*' When I saw you introduced at the meeting along with that lovely young lady, I wondered. Then I heard your grandpa's story and I knew immediately it was you. My kids said, '*find him on Facebook*', but we couldn't."

"Ha! Believe it or not, I'm the only person in the world not on Facebook. Too busy."

"That's okay, I didn't need it. I arranged to come here with my job so I could see you in person. I figured I could locate you through your grandpa." He laughed. "It was hard, I wanted to see you right away, talk with you! But I had to wait a month."

"Oh, Dad," replied Rob, trying to take it in. "What do your kids think about me? Do they mind? Knowing you have a son – an adopted son?"

"First of all, forget the '*adopted*' part. You really are my son, if you'll have me as your father."

"Yes, yes, I will," he replied with a laugh, still trying to believe what was happening. "Of course I will!" He reached for Scott's hand and shook it.

"Remember, Rob, I was with you from birth. As for my kids, they've always known. And when we all saw the video, well, they couldn't stop watching it. Looking for you – for their brother. We prayed as a family that I could find you."

"What's that?" he asked, puzzled.

"Yeah, we're like that. Your grandpa wasn't hard to find. I called and asked him about you. So here I am."

Overwhelmed, Rob had no words. He shook his head. It was still too much.

Scott took his hands. "Your grandpa told me about how you two found each other. God is good, huh? I bet you thought you were an orphan."

"I did, I really did. My grandparents, uh, they passed away. They didn't have much family left, and I felt alone in the world. It was hard at first, but I got used to it. I like it. I'm very independent. My grandparents, the Fergusons, I have good memories of them. And now –" he shook his head in amazement. "This is going to take some getting used to." They hugged again.

"Rob, would you like to come around to my motel for a while? I won't keep you late, you probably have lots of studying to do. I brought some baby pictures, family pictures...."

"I sure will!" He didn't need to think about it. "I can't say no to that...Dad." *Oh, well, what's another all-nighter when I get home? This doesn't happen every day!*

Gramps gave them a warm goodbye. *This is not the time to tell my problems*, he thought.

I'll wait till I see them again.

"Rob, you are full of incredible stories!" Aimee exclaimed the next evening when they were at her house. "Wonderful things keep happening to you. First your grandpa, now Scott –"

"Don't forget a girl named Aimee...." he interrupted.

"I'm happy for you! I'd love to meet him," she said enthusiastically.

"You can. He's invited us for a weekend visit with his family. He lives about four hours from here. There's his wife, Marie, and Mark, my brother....my brother! Imagine that. Man, I'd love to see him," he exclaimed excitedly. He shook his head. "I still can hardly believe it! Also two younger girls, I don't remember their names. I guess I'd call them my sisters."

"Probably. See how they feel about it. But I don't know whether I should go. I'd feel like an interloper, going out there to stay with strangers. Much as I'd like to meet him," she added.

"Don't, Aimee. You'll like him! He's genuine. I'm sure the rest of the family is too." He stopped and caught his breath. "Honey, I had such a fantastic time with him at his motel! He told me about my past. You want to know when I really felt like an orphan? When I went to live with my grandparents. I had nothing. I brought nothing with me, no toys, no pictures.... only bad memories. I felt so alone. Well, would you believe, Scott had my good memories. Of me, Mark, my Mom, himself. It brought back my childhood! It's just....amazing." He shook his head in disbelief.

"Oh, honey, I'm so happy for you! You deserve this." She nodded her head. "Okay, you've convinced me – I'll go. I want to see those pictures! Let's plan a trip as soon as we can, before I get too close to graduation."

"It will be soon, I promise. As soon as we can fix a date. I can't wait to see him again. And meet my brother!" He shook his head. "My brother."

Gramps and Howard were on their way to breakfast, the smell of bacon drawing them on. "D'ya think we're finally back to normal?" Howard asked. "It's been almost two weeks since.... you know." He stopped himself, not wanting to say more.

"I sure hope so. I never want to go through that again," Gramps replied.

"A prankster, huh?"

"So Mrs. Markowitz told me; that's what Security decided. Somebody from the outside. It looks like I was a random target." He shook his head skeptically.

"Too bad it was you," Howard said sympathetically. "Guess we'll never know why."

"Hmph!" Gramps replied as he shifted his position in his chair. All at once another smell, the putrid smell of rotten eggs contended with the sweet smell of bacon. At the same time he felt a cold, clammy wetness on his thigh. He cried out in anger. The hall, crowded with residents on their way to the dining room and staff going about their duties moved away from him as the smell assaulted their nostrils. Howard alone remained with him and once again he felt like a child humiliated in front of his peers. A nurse appeared and quickly turned the chair around, back to his room.

"We'll get you cleaned up, Mr. Douglas, and you can get breakfast. Then we'll go see Mrs. Markowitz. She'll want to know about this."

"Forget breakfast," he snapped, "I've lost my appetite. I'll get cleaned up and then see Mrs. Markowitz. Let's get it over with. Hmph, what a start to her day! And mine."

Back in his room they discovered that two rotten eggs had been placed in the folds of a blanket on his chair. "Ah, this is deliberate and well-planned. Somebody must hate me very much." He shook his head, perplexed.

He calmed himself enough to discuss the incidents with Mrs. Markowitz, first apologizing for his outburst the previous time. She accepted it with understanding. "Now, we have to discover our culprit and put an end to your misery and embarrassment," she told him kindly. "Do you agree we should not involve the police?"

"Yes, yes – I mean no, I don't want the police either."

"These are '*Unusual Incidents*' and we should handle them in-house," she concluded. That was as far as they got. Staff would watch the halls at night, but he knew it was futile to expect them to find anything. They had better things to do. And – was it a staff member or a resident who was responsible? The meeting ended with mutual frustration but on better terms than before.

In the days that followed some of the residents were sympathetic and some avoided him, as if afraid of it happening again. He was used to avoiding the tittle-tattlers who made a story out of everything. The loyalty of his card-playing buddies, led by Howard, was a comfort, but mostly he preferred to keep to himself. He couldn't bring himself to call Aimee or Rob. It was just too distressing to talk about on the phone. *I'll tell them when I see them*, he decided.

His sleep was troubled with questions of who and why. *Could it be someone in the Assisted Living section who bears me a grudge, someone I might have offended, perhaps at mealtime? We eat together and they have easy access to this section. They could walk undetected at night, if they're careful.*

It could be Damien. He could be out of prison by now, it was just a short sentence. He wouldn't attack Rob, but I'm vulnerable. He can get to me. No...he wouldn't dare show his face around here. But wait, he isn't known here at Sunset Woods. And he's smart enough to know how to by-pass security and get in.

Is he still in prison? I must find out. He turned it over and over in his mind. Sleep eluded him.

Because of his sleeplessness he had been prescribed a sleeping pill. He had always tried to avoid sleep and pain medications, but reluctantly he now began using it.

Howard, ever helpful, remarked that it improved his mood considerably. '*Who said my mood needs improving?*' he grumbled.

I don't want to burden Rob and Aimee with my problems, he thought, *but I need to unburden myself.*

Chapter 24

Instead of taking Lenore to a play, Aimee and Rob decided on an early Spring festival at a park in Lenore's town. There would be entertainment, games of chance and skill, music, and of course, all kinds of food. "*I've never done anything like this before*," she had told Aimee excitedly. "*I'm looking forward to it! Thank you!*"

They picked her up at her house. Rob noticed what he hadn't paid attention to before, that it was a shabby house made over into apartments in a run-down neighborhood. "Don't say anything about her house," Aimee told him. "She's aware of it. She feels ashamed."

A tense, nervous Lenore met them at the car. She managed a faint smile of greeting and said very little on the way despite Aimee and Rob's attempts to strike up conversation.

At the park she continued unsure of herself and could not relax. They were hardly talking with each other. In the late morning when she excused herself for a cigarette and bathroom break Aimee and Rob discussed the situation.

"It's not working, Aimee," he stated flatly. "She's not having fun. She's just not ready for this. It's miserable for us all. We should end it now."

"I agree she's not having fun. But she was looking forward to it! Do you think she's been drinking?"

"I don't think so. I can usually tell."

"Well, it hasn't been miserable for us. You and I, we're having a great time." She thought about it. "Maybe that's part of the problem....remember when I said she and I would be competing for your attention? Today, I've had your attention. She's left out."

"We gave her a chance," he objected. "In the car, we both tried to talk with her and we didn't get anywhere."

"I think she doesn't know how to talk to you. What to say."

"She never used to have any trouble. She could put me in my place, fast."

"She doesn't want to do that anymore. Now she doesn't know what to say."

"I don't know about that. She can talk to you just fine. Why not me?" He frowned. "I don't know what to say to her."

"All that history between you gets in the way. With both of you. Just forget she's your mother." He frowned and shook his head. "Rob, you have a wonderful way with people. Gramps told me how you were at the nursing home. I've seen you with my family, and strangers....it's a gift."

"I don't know about that," he said dubiously.

"Oh, you big lump. It's because you care. People sense that. Why not with your mother?"

"I care about her....I think I do....but I just don't know what to say to her. And don't tell me to forget the stuff between us! It's not that easy."

"Okay, okay. But now, you and I should forget about us and concentrate on her."

"Now that would scare her off, if we give her too much attention! But – we're here, so we probably should give her another chance. I don't know – maybe we have left her out. '*Two's company, three's a crowd*', right?"

"Exactly right. But listen, we could pay attention to her, we could ask her what she wants to do....instead of us trying to give her a good time. And let's kind of....uh, ignore each other."

"Ha! Not even a wink?" he asked with a wink.

"Especially not! It makes her feel left out. We can even let her come between us. Walk between us, that is."

"All right! Just this once. Now, if I'm going to ignore you later I'll make the most of right now!" He grabbed hold of her and kissed her. "*Carpe diem!*"

A few minutes later Lenore rejoined them. They began to give her attention and they could see her begin to relax. They let her lead the way.

"What do you know, we like the same music," Rob whispered to Aimee. She had led them to a rock band.

"It's classic rock to us," she replied, "but this is her music. I'm glad we can enjoy it together."

A while later they came upon a jazz ensemble. Aimee dragged Rob out on to the grass where couples were dancing. "Hey, I can't dance!" he told her. "You know that."

"I haven't given up yet!" she replied, but it didn't take her long to agree with him. "You win," she said as he sat down. She pulled Lenore over and they danced a few numbers together.

Lenore then drew them to a comedy act, bypassing a group that was doing historical re-enactments to the disappointment of Aimee and Rob, but suddenly they were laughing together. By this time they were ready to eat. They found the food vendors and picked out their lunch, then found a table in a sunny spot.

"Are we having fun yet?" he joked.

"I can't believe it – this really is fun!" Lenore nodded happily "You know," she reflected, "I'd forgotten what it's like to have fun."

"That's strange, Mom," Rob replied. "What do you mean?"

"Not like this," she explained. "The only kind of fun I've had for years has come out of a bottle or a can. And that's not fun. Not like – today."

"This is what we want for you, Mom. Real happiness," he said earnestly.

"I guess I have to learn all over again. I hope it's not too late for me," she sighed.

"You mustn't think that," Aimee admonished gently.

Lenore shrugged and shook her head.

They relaxed after their meal, enjoying the beauty of a Spring day. Then Aimee asked, "Lenore, have you decided about the apartment?"

"I want to do it. I really do. But Carl, he's doing everything he can to get me to stay. He tells me I can't make it without him. I think he's right." She shook her head. "I'm not used to being alone."

"Mom....you'll have lots of support. You can make it."

"Then he tells me how much he's done for me. So I start feeling guilty for even thinking about leaving him."

"Ha! You've given him plenty. You don't owe him a thing. Lenore, nobody has to live this way. You don't have to."

"Mom –" he wanted to encourage her. "Somebody was asking about you, and wished you well."

"And who might that be?" she asked suspiciously.

"Scott Carlyle. He looked me up. He sent you his best wishes." He decided not to say anything about Mark.

"Scott!" She was quiet for a moment. "Scott Carlyle. He's a good man. He always was." Her tone grew cold. "That's two good men I lost. Scott and your father. Now I'm left with the bottom of the barrel."

His heart melted. "Oh, no, Mom. You deserve better." He put his arm around her shoulder.

She pulled away, not meeting their eyes. "I told Carl we deserved each other. We're two of a kind. Losers, both of us," she said with a bitter laugh.

"But you're not," Aimee insisted. "You're not a loser. You mustn't even think that! You've decided on a better life. Has he?"

"Um....no." She shrugged. "Rose tells me the same thing."

"Mom –" Rob took her hand. "For the sake of Dad, and Scott – leave this man. That's what they would want." She pulled her hand away.

"Lenore, Carl will pull you down. He's a threat to your sobriety."

"Oh, Aimee," she gave a little laugh, "you know the A.A. language! But you're right. My sobriety is the most important thing to me now."

"Aimee and I will do whatever we can to help you get out."

"If you think he'll try to stop you, we'll see to a police escort. Has he threatened you?"

"He threatens to kill himself. But not me. And he doesn't have any weapons that I know of. He just yells a lot."

"Is it okay if I talk this over with Rose? She might be able to talk to your counselor, and – don't you have a case manager? They could help. If you're going to keep that apartment you'll have to be in it by the middle of next week. You have no time to lose."

"I'll do it," she took a deep breath, "I will! Yes, you can talk with Rose, any time. I'll give you her number."

"Great, Mom! Now, let's go have some more fun."

"Yes," agreed Aimee, "we still have an hour or so. What would you like to do?"

She got up and took Aimee's hand. "Let's go find out!"

Before they left to take her home Lenore thanked them for the happiest day she'd had in years, then announced she had something to tell them.

"You're right. I don't have to live this way. With God's help, and the people from my church, I'm going to move. They've offered to help me."

"They're complete strangers. You mean they'll do that?" Aimee asked, surprised.

"They said so. I guess I'll find out. And something else. I want you to know that I made a commitment at church. I'm not ever going to drink again. Not ever, ever."

"Lenore, I'm glad. Just remember, though, one day at a time."

Rob put his arm around Aimee. "Who would have believed this?" he whispered in her ear.

On the way back home Rob asked, "Honey, why are you doing this? Giving up so much of your time for my mother? She's not exactly the easiest person to know."

She looked at him with surprise. "It's because she's your mother. My future mother in law." She took his hand and held it tightly. "Besides, I want to help her! I think I'm the one who can! Didn't Gramps ask me to work with her?"

"Sweetheart, you're pretty wonderful, you know." Aimee laughed and shook her head.

They stopped to eat at a little restaurant. While they were waiting for their food to be served, Rob took her hands. "Aimee, I could marry you tomorrow!" he exclaimed excitedly. "I should marry you tomorrow. Mrs. Aimee Carlyle – or Aimee Love-Carlyle, if you want. I like that."

"Rob, what brought this on?" she asked, puzzled.

"You and I are such a partnership. We're one. I love you more than ever. I want the world to know!" He kissed her fingertips.

"You're happy about your mother...." she began.

"It's more than that. I've been thinking about it. Marriage is a commitment, for the rest of our lives! It's a contract, it tells the world of our commitment to each other."

"That's it! That's what I've been trying to figure out," she stated with satisfaction. "Why marriage is different. It's a statement – to the world."

"Yes, that we're committed to each other!" he went on enthusiastically. "For life."

"Oh, darling, it all makes sense. And I love you so much. But we need to quiet down, the whole restaurant will hear us."

"I don't care. I want the world to know!"

When they went to pay their bill the cashier told them their meal had been paid for. "An old couple sitting near you," she told them, "they said to tell that young man '*he's got it right.*' They've been married fifty years so they must know. They were in a hurry so they didn't tell you themselves. They wanted to pay for your meal."

Speechless, Rob and Aimee did the only intelligent thing to do in that situation. They kissed, much to the delight of the cashier.

"Oh, Rob! What a day this has been!"

On their next visit to Gramps, their happy mood seemed a rebuke to his gloomy feelings. But he made an effort to share their happiness about the good day with Lenore, and he felt deep joy at hearing Rob's revelation about marriage. "Ah, Rob, I couldn't have said it better myself. I had great faith in you. I knew that sooner or later, you'd see things clearly."

"But Gramps," Aimee told him anxiously, "my parents are upset about our marriage. Seriously. The wedding, that is." Rob already knew but she wanted the comfort of Gramps' listening ear. He looked puzzled. "No, no, it's not Rob," she explained. "Mom's really upset. She said, *'I wish you two had consulted me when you set your date. It's just not possible to get it all together in four months! Six months, possibly, but four months, never.'* Poor Mom. I hadn't realized. Especially because she's organizing it all."

"I hadn't either," Gramps replied sympathetically. "To my mind, you just get married." Rob nodded in agreement. "There's obviously a lot more involved."

"They say there's no way they can book a hall for the reception," she explained. "And a wedding chapel. These places get booked a year in advance. I didn't know that. Dad's trying to pull strings to get his lodge, which I don't even like. But I don't want to change the date."

"We told her we would help every way we can," said Rob.

"Oh, Aimee, Rob –" Gramps said, comfortingly, "This is so important to you both. I will be remembering you in my prayers. I do believe things will work out for you. Now, don't you fret. I want you to be happy." He sighed heavily, a far-off look on his face.

Rob looked at him with concern. "Gramps, you're not yourself. Is something wrong? I've felt it all evening."

"Yes....yes. It's hard to talk about." Their concern encouraged him to continue. Slowly, painfully he related the two rotten egg incidents and the humiliation he felt.

They were shocked, silent. Finally, "Oh, Gramps," said Rob, taking his hand, "I wish you'd told us."

"Why? What could you do?" he asked irritably.

"It's not what we could do," explained Aimee, "it's that, we care. We can share it with you. But who would do a terrible thing like that? And why?"

"You don't think it's a member of the staff, do you?" asked Rob.

"And why not?" he snapped. "Have you forgotten Damien? Has everyone forgotten Damien?"

"Well, Damien was a special case," Rob argued. "Something must be wrong with him mentally. I just find it hard to believe that somebody who's dedicated himself to caring for others could do something bad. Like this."

"Oh, really," he retorted. "Rob, we all have it within us to do bad things. To hurt people. Deliberately, even."

"I'm sorry, but I can't believe that," Aimee replied heatedly. "Good people don't do bad things. There has to be something wrong with them mentally. Most people are good and they'd never do anything to hurt someone else."

"We all can be pretty bad if we want to be. There's wickedness in all of us. You'll find that out someday," Gramps said with a warning nod.

"Wickedness? In me, or Rob? Or you? I can't believe that. But.....oh, I'm sorry, Gramps, I don't want to argue with you. This is such a terrible thing, I know you're on edge about it."

"Listen, you two. I'm sorry I'm in such a foul mood. I've got to excuse myself, take one of those sleeping pills. Hate taking those things, they knock me right out. But maybe that's what I need tonight. Good night to you both, and....I love you."

They hugged each other goodbye.

Tomorrow morning I'll call the Prosecutor's office, he thought. *I've got to find out if Damien is out of prison.*

"My heart aches for him," sighed Aimee as they were driving back to pick up her car. "He's such a good man, he wouldn't harm a soul, he's never done anything to harm anyone – Oh, stop!" she seized his arm. "We have to turn around. We have to go back."

"What? Why? Did you leave something there?" He slowed the car and moved to the edge of the road.

"Oh, no. Rob, I know why somebody is doing this to him."

He stopped the car. "You do? Why?"

"It's because he was a war protester! I'm sure of it. It all makes sense. Somebody's doing to him what he did to them."

"But – I don't think he ever threw anything, rotten eggs, you know – oh, that wouldn't make any difference. He was there. Hmm, you may be right. But why go back now?"

"I want to tell him," she pleaded. "It may set his mind at rest."

"We can't, they'll be putting him to bed now. But I agree, you should tell him about this. You may be right. Do you think you could call him tomorrow morning? I can't, I'll be in class."

"Oh, I will. You're right....he may already be in bed by now. But I'll call him tomorrow, from work. Yes, I'll do that."

Driving home, having taken leave of Rob, she kept thinking about Gramps as her eyes filled with tears. *I feel so helpless*, she thought. *He doesn't deserve to have this happen to him, not now.* She found herself praying. "Oh, God....I don't even know if you exist. But Gramps believes in you. He loves you. He's such a good man....will you help him? Keep him safe – help him to get a good sleep tonight, without those sleeping pills. And help us to figure out who's doing this. Thank you. Good night." She didn't know if her words went past the car roof, but she felt better.

Gramps took the sleeping pill offered by the nurse but decided not to use it right away. *Only if I need it*, he thought. He was comforted by Aimee and Rob's concern but he felt no calmer. *I've got to find an answer.*

He knew he had to think things through, again. *Is it Damien.... or someone else? Damien....he views us all with contempt, we older people. That was evident at the trial. I dared to stand up to him. His eyes – they bored right through me as I was testifying. If looks could kill I would have been dead on the floor, then and there. Yes, he's getting back at me. Not himself, he's in prison – I've got to find out for sure – but even if he is, I'm sure he has somebody here who would do his dirty work for him. Yes, that's it,* he concluded with satisfaction, *it's Damien. It must be Damien.*

Yet something kept nagging at him. Sleep would not come. Against his will he was re-living his hurt and embarrassment. He could feel anger bubbling up within him. *Why me? What a terrible thing to do to another person!*

He stopped. Eyes wide open, he was dreaming. Or remembering. Coming off a plane were rows of young men in uniform, dazed and bewildered at the sight that greeted them. An angry crowd, shouting obscenities, calling names, throwing things.... rotten eggs, rotten vegetables and worse....at these young men. *And where was I? I was among the angry crowd, hurling insults. Was I throwing things? I don't know, I can't remember. But it doesn't matter. I was there.*

He felt overwhelmed by shame, followed by an immense feeling of relief that washed over him. *Now I know. This is the reason, I'm sure of it. There is a justice to it. I needed to know what it was like for these young men. They didn't deserve it. But I....I do.* He lay there remembering, re-living the emotions, asking God for forgiveness. *Now at last I can sleep.* He began to doze off, with a prayer in his heart for the person who was doing this to him.

In the morning, confirming his revelation of the night before the nurse found a note taped to his blanket. In neat block letters it read, *'Now you know what it feels like.'*

Tucked in his chair she found two rotten eggs. Despite her care in handling them they broke in her hands, to the distress of them all. *Oh, my*, thought Gramps, *I must call Aimee and Rob. Right after breakfast. This will set their minds at rest.*

Right after breakfast Howard took him aside. "Looky here, this stuff has gotta stop. If we don't do something about it nobody else will. Now, I've got some ideas." Gramps agreed. Together they hatched a plan.

Chapter 25

"Hello, Gramps. I'm so glad I reached you! How are you today?"

"Aimee, I'm fine. It's always good to hear from you! Is anything wrong?"

"I have something to tell you! I know, at least I think I know, why these things are happening to you!" She paused, then said gently, "I think it's because you were a war protester."

"Oh, my goodness. Well, Aimee, I arrived at that same conclusion last night. Lying in bed, thinking about it. I was going to call you and Rob but you got me first."

She gasped. "Oh – I'm so thankful!" Tears filled her eyes.

"I purposely didn't take a sleeping pill so I could stay awake and think. And it all came back to me. I know that's why. There's a justice to it. I slept very well. Please tell Rob."

"This is unbelievable! I'm so thankful, so thankful! I was worried about you."

"Thank you, I'm fine. Howard and I have a plan to catch this character."

"Gramps, be careful. You don't know who you're dealing with."

"My dear, thank you for your concern. I'll be all right, I assure you. Good bye now."

Gramps and Howard had decided they could stay awake all night if they had to, sitting up in bed. Gramps would stay awake until about 2:00 AM when Howard got up to go to the bathroom, then he would sleep while Howard stayed awake. If anyone came into the room to do mischief, they knew what to do.

It took about a week. Gramps woke suddenly at hearing Howard shout. His bedside clock read 4:10 AM. Howard's lights were at their brightest so Gramps turned his on too. Howard was making his way to the door which he closed. He pulled up a chair in front of it and sat down. Standing by Gramps' wheel chair was a small older woman, a nursing assistant who they recognized as Vivian. Her arm was over her eyes to shield them. She was holding something in her other hand which she threw defiantly to the floor and as she did, the rank odor of sulfur filled the air making them cough and choke.

"Fine! You had it coming!" She gave a feeble spit in his direction.

"Vivian," asked Gramps, "what is this all about?"

Howard interrupted, "Vivian, take this chair and sit down." He brandished his cane at her and gestured to a chair near him. Cowering, she moved the chair to the center of the room and slumped into it.

"What's going on here?" Gramps demanded.

"You know!" growled Vivian. "Said you was sorry, did you? Well, words are cheap. Too late to help my Joe. All that nasty stuff he got when he came home."

"And who is Joe?" asked Gramps.

"He was my husband. Drank himself to death, he did, never got over what you did to him when he came home from Vietnam."

"You're not old enough to've had a husband in Vietnam," Gramps observed.

"That's what you think. I was his second wife. He told me plenty."

"What made you decide to do this?" asked Howard.

"Hmph! I found a nest of rotten eggs and I thought, *this was meant to be,*" she exclaimed triumphantly. "You all were going to that theater and I went along as a volunteer, 'cause I don't work days. It was so easy to put it down your back, it worked just perfect! Nobody even noticed me." She gave a sardonic laugh. "Joe should've lived long enough to see it. Me and Joe, we had a chicken farm and he always made me get the eggs. Said he didn't want to get a rotten one. It reminded him of when he got rotten eggs all over his uniform."

Gramps and Howard remarked at how clever she was.

"You bet I am! I even got the head nurse to give you sleeping pills. So I could come in here and not wake you up. '*He lies awake all night,*' I told her. After that you slept like a rock. Until tonight. Hmph!"

"But, why did you keep doing it?" asked Gramps. "You made your point."

"I had more eggs. I had to use them. Like I told you, it was meant to be. Besides, you had it coming," she snarled.

"Yes," Gramps replied softly, looking away. He turned back to her. "You certainly thought this out very carefully."

"Oh, yeah. You got yours. It was worth it." She started to get up. "Well, I've got a shift to complete. I'm getting out of here."

"You ain't goin' nowhere!" ordered Howard with a wave of his cane, "so get back down."

"We should call the police, but we're not," added Gramps.

"Am I supposed to thank you?" She remained standing, defiantly.

"Vivian," he said sternly, waiting until he had her attention. "I have my call light on. When someone comes in we'll call Security. You aren't going anywhere except with them. Understand?" She glared at him but said nothing. "Now, I'm going to call my grandson. He used to work here and he will contact Mrs. Markowitz."

Slowly she sat down.

He punched in Rob's number. "Hello, Rob."

"Gramps, are you okay? It's 4:30 in the morning!"

"Ha, I know that. Say, Howard and I have caught the chicken who laid the rotten eggs. We need your help."

"You what? Be careful, he could be dangerous."

"Well, the he is a she and she's here in our room. A night nurse. We're waiting for Security to come get her. Rob, could you contact Mrs. Markowitz? You probably still know how to reach her. Ask her to call me."

"I'll get right to it. Wow, what do you know....Be careful, now. Bye, Gramps. I'll talk to you tomorrow."

A nurse appeared at the door and drew back, repulsed by the foul odor which Gramps and Howard had gotten used to by now. She rushed in to open their window. At their request she called Security but then wanted Vivian to complete her shift. Gramps explained that they were waiting for instructions from Mrs. Markowitz, and Howard clinched it with, "She stinks to high heaven. You can't send her out to people's rooms smelling like that."

Mrs. Markowitz was on the line. "Mrs. Markowitz, I wanted you to know the mystery is solved," Gramps told her with satisfaction. "Yup, her name's Vivian. Don't know her last name..... Oh, she was caught in the act," he explained. "Admitted the whole thing." Mrs. Markowitz agreed that Vivian should wait for Security. She promised to meet them shortly, then asked to speak to the nurse.

When they were done Gramps resumed the call. "I want to ask you not to press charges," he went on. "She's not remorseful, but she's ready to retire. You could just let her go."

Mrs. Markowitz considered it a moment, then thanked him. "Mr. Douglas, we definitely must press charges. This is patient abuse and we cannot afford to treat it lightly. Between you and me, I think she'll get Probation and a fine, no jail time. Our attorney will recommend counseling. She certainly needs it. Mr. Douglas – I can't thank you enough. You have taken a huge worry off my shoulders. I have learned not to underestimate you."

"And Howard Grayson, don't forget Howard," added Gramps firmly. "This was his idea."

With that, they ended the call. A Security officer came in and took Vivian away.

"Howard, aren't you hungry for breakfast?"

"You bet. We put in a night's work." He looked at the clock and sighed. "Two more hours to go."

"You fancy some eggs?" Gramps asked with a chuckle.

Rob and Aimee laughed themselves silly when they visited Gramps and Howard the next evening. "I can't believe it," Rob said between laughs, "I'm surprised you didn't swing her up by her ankles and hang her from the ceiling!"

"We thought about it," replied Howard.

"People who come in our room better mind their manners," Gramps declared ominously.

"You should have seen me leap out of bed," Howard bragged.

"Howard, your leaping days are long past...."

"Yeah, you got that right," he admitted. "Well, we surprised her. She could have been out that door in a flash, but she didn't know what was going on."

"Well, brother Howard, we cracked that case, wouldn't you say?"

"Ha, ha. What's our next one going to be?"

"You never know what might hatch around here," Gramps replied dryly. "Wait and see."

Later, when they were alone Gramps asked Aimee how wedding plans were going.

"They're not," she said despairingly. "Mom is almost in a panic, and we're arguing, something we haven't done for a long time. She can't find a wedding chapel and we can't get a hall at this late date. Dad's trying hard. It holds up the invitations."

"This is serious," he agreed.

"Mom found a gazebo in a park across town, not the nicest place. I call it the graffiti gazebo, for obvious reasons. I thought we could cover the graffiti with garlands and flowers –"

"I volunteered to sneak down in the middle of the night and paint it," Rob added.

"Mom says she doesn't want her daughter's wedding there. I don't either. I guess we will if we have to. If nothing else is available."

"People get married in strange places....the zoo, or....a museum?" Gramps offered helpfully. "Or the garden here?"

"No, that's not me. I'm a traditionalist. And I'm a private person. I don't want our wedding out in public."

"I'm with Aimee," agreed Rob.

"How about a church?" Gramps asked.

"No, I don't go to church. That wouldn't be right for me."

"Well," he took her hand and kissed her fingertips. "I wish I could help you. You are in my thoughts and prayers."

"I know. We love you, Gramps."

On the way home Aimee made an observation. "You and Gramps are two of a kind. You're both gallant. You kiss my hand, or my fingers, and so does he. I love it."

"Well, we're the same family. But I never saw him do it before."

"Yes, that proves it! Better than DNA."

Gramps and Howard found themselves instant celebrities at Sunset Woods. Many of the staff thanked them for solving the mystery that had baffled and embarrassed them. They had sympathized with Gramps and feared that what happened to him would happen to other residents. To the staff they were heroes.

But to fellow residents they were near sainthood. They had accomplished what staff, who held their lives in their hands, could not. "Power to the people!" some said, and hoped the two men would become their problem-solvers.

Gramps and Howard loved every minute of it.

Chapter 26

Rob and Aimee were on the way to their visit with Scott and his family. They left on a Friday afternoon and expected to arrive in time for a late dinner.

"Aimee, I don't know what to call him," Rob said, shaking his head. "Dad, or Scott? It's all so new."

"Maybe you'll call him both, for a while. If he's like you say he is, he won't mind."

"And Marie. What should I call her? I can't call her 'Mom'."

"Marie, of course." She patted his hand. "Rob...you're really tense. What are you so nervous about?"

"You know how to read me." He sighed. "It's Mark. I'm worried about meeting him."

"Mark? Why?"

"I lay awake half the night thinking about it. You know, Mom took me with her and left Mark. What does that do to a kid? Talk about sibling rivalry. '*Mom loved you more than she loved me*.' What do I say to him?"

"Hmm. I see what you mean. Well, I'm not a fount of wisdom. Just....try not to worry about it. Remember, you're not responsible for what your mother did." She clasped his hand tightly. "You'll be fine."

"Thanks hon. That helps."

The sun was just setting when they pulled into the drive of a large, comfortable looking house. As they got out of the car they were immediately surrounded by the family. Scott made introductions. "This is my wife, Marie." She wrapped him in a warm hug. Scott quickly made it a three-some.

"Rob, welcome to our family," Marie told him warmly. "Welcome home."

Rob, overwhelmed, murmured, "thank you.... thank you."

"And this is – ?" Marie smiled at Aimee.

"My fiancee, Aimee Love," he announced proudly as she was included in the hug.

Scott went on, "...our daughters Heather, she's thirteen, and Holly, eleven. Girls, this is your brother Rob." They welcomed him with shy hugs. "They've waited a long time to meet their other big brother."

"But where's Mark?" Rob asked.

"He works late on Fridays. You'll get to visit with him in a while," answered Marie. *Oh, no,* thought Rob, *I'll have to wait longer*.

The initial awkwardness of meeting new people disappeared as they relaxed over a good meal and the laughter and banter of a loving family. To Aimee it was like home; to Rob it was what he enjoyed most about her family. The girls vied for Aimee's attention but seemed a little shy around Rob. After dinner they took Aimee upstairs to see their bedrooms and have her choose which girl she would room with, then they decided the three of them could sleep together. "Can we stay up all night and talk?" they asked her.

"Yes, if you're awake when I come back up," she promised.

Rob, Scott, and Marie relaxed in the family room. "There's so much catching up to do," Scott said, "but we should wait for Aimee. We can't leave her out."

Rob offered to check with her. He was down in a few minutes. "She says to go ahead, she shouldn't be too long."

He wanted to know about Scott and Marie, their lives. They told of meeting and marrying when Mark was quite young.

"Mark took to Marie right away. She's always been Mom to him." They told of putting each other through college and then the births of their daughters, of some religious experiences which seemed strange to Rob, but he didn't question them.

"We've been through some rough times," said Marie, "with a bad house fire ten years ago, but we found that we had God and our family. And now God has brought another person into our family," she smiled at Rob, "or should I say two persons?"

"I'm still getting used to it," he laughed. "Aimee too. Now, what about Mark?"

"Ah, Mark. He did very well until he hit his teens," explained Scott. "Then he began to wonder why his mother had walked out on him. After hardly thinking about her for ten years, this was hard for us to understand. He was depressed, miserable, and.... he took it out on us. But with the help of God and a good counselor he began to put that behind him and be a normal kid. Now, my finding you and knowing you were coming here seems to have opened old wounds. He wants to know about his mother. I think maybe he wonders why she took you and left him."

"I've wondered about that too. I don't have any answer. I'm nervous about meeting him. Talking with him."

"Oh, don't be," they insisted.

"I don't know what to say to him, because I'm still trying to get along with her myself. When I was growing up I'd hardly ever see her, and when I did we fought. So I just wrote her off. I lived my life without her. Now, thanks to Gramps and his involvement, she's changing. I'm glad for her. I want her to do well. But for me, it's hard. I'm trying to love her. But I never did, and I don't know how."

"You did love her, very much," Scott told him. "That's why she's able to hurt you."

Rob looked at him with surprise, trying to understand. "I don't remember the love. I'll have to think about it. But....it makes sense. Why she can hurt me."

"Sure. If you didn't love her, deep down, you wouldn't care. Mark, now, he was pretty young when she left. He missed her at the time, but I don't think he remembers anything."

"So what now? Do I talk to him, or what? I can guess how he must feel about me."

"Nothing bad, I assure you. Son, don't look so worried. Just see what happens."

Hearing Scott call him *'son'* had a calming effect. He liked that. He wasn't used to being called *'son'*. But yes, he was apprehensive. "I miss Aimee," he admitted, "she's good at these personal things. Runs interference for me."

"I don't see any sign of her. You're on your own. You'll do fine."

They visited a while longer, then a voice called out, "Hey, I'm home! Anything to eat? I'm starving!" Rob got up to greet him and came face to face with – a younger edition of himself.

"Hey, Marie, didn't I tell you they look alike?" asked Scott.

"You might even think they're brothers," she observed with a smile.

Mark clapped a hand on Rob's shoulder and then gave him a bear hug. "Hey, my brother!" Rob liked him immediately.

"You go ahead and eat first, then get acquainted," suggested Marie. "Rob, could I persuade you to eat a bit more?" She filled his plate, with no protest from him.

They devoted themselves to eating and then took seats in the family room. "Hey, Rob, how's our mother?" Mark asked.

He swallowed hard. *What do I say?* "Well, I hardly ever see her. She's trying to get her life back together after twenty years of, well, bad stuff. Drinking and all that."

"That's good. I really don't care." Rob remembered that he used to say that too, though he did care. "I've got my Mom – hi Mom –" he waved his hand at Marie – "and that's the most important thing. When I was younger I was dumb. Like, why didn't she love me?" He shrugged. "It's not up to me."

"You're right," Rob assured him.

"But – when I heard you were coming I started thinking about it again. Man, that's dumb. Waste of time. It's not your fault. I've got Marie. She's my real Mom." He smiled at her.

"Right," Rob said with relief. *Piece of cake*, he thought. *Why did I worry?*

"Mark, do you want to meet her?" his father asked.

"No! No, I don't!" Rob was surprised at his intensity.

Looking around at everybody, he went on. "I've got my family – I've got my home. I don't want her coming 'round here and messing up our lives!"

"Well –" Rob assured him, "She wouldn't come here. She doesn't even have a car."

"No! I don't want to see her! I don't want her in my life."

His words echoed in the silence. Then Marie asked, "Mark, if you could see her, what would you say to her?"

He clenched and unclenched his fists. "I'd ask her why? Why did you leave your own kid? What kind of mother walks out on her own kid?" Elbows on his knees, he buried his face in his hands.

Rob quickly got up and sat beside him on the couch. He put his arm around his shoulder. "Mark – I don't know why. But look, buddy – I do know, it wasn't your fault."

Mark looked up. His face was streaked with tears. He shook his head in agreement. "I know. I know. It wasn't me. And it wasn't you either. It was her."

Rob took his hand and shook it. "Just remember that, Mark." He nodded his head. "We'll get through it. You and I." They held each other, awkwardly, for a moment.

Rob went back to his chair on the other side of the room.

Mark looked at Rob. He took a deep breath. "So, man! Now I've got a brother. 'Bout time," he laughed. "Somebody to look up to."

"Mark, that's pretty cool. You don't know how it feels to me. I never had a brother. Or sisters. You and I are gonna make up for lost time."

Rob asked Mark about himself. He told of graduating from tech school with a degree but not able to find a good job, of his thoughts of going back to school, maybe for an engineering degree....

"Hello, everybody! Say, are you the long-lost brother?" Aimee asked Mark as she entered the room. "I could tell."

He shook her hand, unable to say anything, then made room for both of them on the couch. She apologized for being so long. "The girls – they talked until they had nothing more to say. They finally fell asleep and I fell asleep with them!"

The adults talked until they were too tired to go on, though with much left to say. As they said goodnight Scott patted Rob on the shoulder. "Good job, son."

The next morning Rob awoke early and followed the aroma of freshly brewed coffee to the kitchen where he poured himself a cup. He took it out to the patio to join Scott, who was reading.

"Ah, Rob, what a beautiful morning! Come join me. I'm enjoying the beauty of God's creation." He waved his arm. "Breathtaking, isn't it?"

"Thanks, Dad, I'd love to. Uh – excuse me – I don't want to be rude, but – do you really believe that? I mean, '*God's creation*'? I don't know anybody who does."

"I'm glad you asked. Yes, yes, I do."

"But you're a man of science. How can you?" Rob knew that Scott was a chemist in a pharmaceutical firm.

"Do you know there's not a single simple thing in nature? Every little thing just explodes with complexity."

"Uh....so?"

"And order. Can anyone explain how randomness can produce such beautiful order? What I see in my laboratory and under my microscope compels me to believe in a designer. In God! And Rob.....that God I worship."

"Ah, Dad. That's....that's....out of my frame of reference. It's contrary to everything I was taught."

"Look around you, Rob. Look within you, at everything you've learned about the human body. Then make your case for '*chance*'."

"Dad." He nodded at him. "Well. You've given me something to think about."

"I've got a couple of things you might like to read, Rob, by scientists. Nothing too weighty because I know you're very busy right now. I could give them to you before you leave. For Aimee too."

"Yes…I would like that. Thanks." He looked around, as if seeing the world for the first time. "You're right. It really is a beautiful day….oh, and here comes Marie." He welcomed her to join them.

On the way back home they were strangely quiet, Rob pondering the troubling new thoughts introduced by Scott and Aimee the warmth and acceptance of people who a month ago had not known either of them. Then Aimee spoke.

"Rob, you were right. They are unbelievable people. I felt so at home with them."

"I'm glad! Me too, it's great to have a new family," he laughed. "I still can't quite believe it."

"Except–" she struggled to find the words.

"What, honey?" he asked with surprise.

"I felt uncomfortable when they asked us to go to church." She shook her head.

"Yeah. I forgot about you and church. I was okay with it, even though I'm not on very good terms with God. But when I saw the look on your face I thought I should back you up and stay home."

"That was good of you. I didn't want to be rude, but –" she shrugged, "I wouldn't know what to do at a church. I would have felt uncomfortable." She reached over and patted his hand.

"That might have made it difficult for them. I've never been to a church before."

"Nothing to fear. You would have done fine. Well, it worked out, Heather stayed home sick. At first I thought she just wanted to be with you, honey, but she actually was running a fever."

"Yes, and you got extra time to study. Just one other thing." She frowned. "Not to be critical, they're such nice people, but don't you think they could have skipped church once? Especially because you're so important to them."

"Maybe they had obligations. I wouldn't take it personally. Church is like a habit thing. People don't want to break the habit."

"Ugh!" she groaned.

"I saw that with my grandparents. After I stopped going they didn't stay home, they went anyway." He started to laugh. "Changing the subject –"

"Please, let's do."

"Honey, I was sure you had hypnotized Mark the same way you hypnotized me! With your eyes."

"Oh, Rob," she purred, looking over at him, "I only have eyes for you."

"You'd better have eyes for the road," he laughed as he squeezed her hand.

"By the way, how did your talk go, with Mark? We've been so busy I didn't get a chance to ask you."

"Better than I'd expected! He's not upset with me. He doesn't blame himself, or me. He just asks '*why*'. How could she do it to him?" He shrugged helplessly. "How can I answer that? I don't know if anyone can." He told her what Mark said and how they had talked together.

"Honey, I'm so proud of you!" She squeezed his hand. "When the time came you had the words. I knew you would. I'm sure you helped him."

"I don't know. I hope so. Can you imagine it, she walked out on him. A two year old boy! He must have missed her so much."

"Well, he wouldn't remember it. But I'm sure it hurt him at the time. And now, the idea of it, the rejection." She pondered it. "How can he ever get over it? How can anyone?"

"I wish I knew."

"So what about you? She wasn't so great with you."

"It was different for me. She didn't walk out on me. She just neglected me. Sometimes it was scary but I never blamed her." He shrugged. "Then I was taken from her, and I blamed the people who took her from me. Not her."

"That makes no sense at all. But –" she thought about it. "From a little kid's perspective, I guess it makes sense. She was all you had."

"Right. That's it. It was hard for me to adjust to my grandparents – even though I wanted the safety of their home. But, do you know who I cried for at night?"

"No...."

"I cried for '*Daddy*'. My grandparents told me that. I'll have to tell Scott. See, I didn't miss my mother all that much. She might have been all I had but I wasn't close to her."

"It's confusing but it makes sense, in a way."

"I remember crying for '*Daddy*' back when I was with my mother."

"Sure. He was the one you were close to. And now you've got him back! Rob, that's so unbelievable....it's amazing! It could be the beginning of something wonderful." She patted his hand. "I hope so."

"Yes....like you and Gramps. I don't know how much more '*amazing*' I can take!" he said with a wry laugh, then he took out a book. "Hey, I've got to quit talking and start studying. We've got three hours ahead of us."

"If you don't sleep all the while."

"Don't worry, I won't."

A few minutes later he was asleep. She tried to rouse him but with no success. *I'll try later,* she decided, *I'm sure he needs it. He must be emotionally drained.*

Over the next few days Rob struggled with conflicting feelings about his mother. If he supported her in her progress was he being disloyal to Mark? Or should he just let her go to the devil and be what she always had been?

Aimee, who knew nothing of his internal struggles suggested a drive to see Lenore in her new apartment. "She's made such progress, we owe it to her to back her up, don't you think?" He shrugged his shoulders, not certain what to think. She then suggested a housewarming gift but insisted he buy it. "She's your mom, you buy," she declared. "We're going to start this marriage off on the right foot."

As he shopped, reluctantly at first, he remembered their outing together. *If she's really trying to make a new life, why shouldn't I try to help? Maybe, in the long run, it would benefit Mark.* The act of choosing a gift stirred in him a desire to do something good for her. He was pleased with his purchase.

They made arrangements to see her and a few days later they made the trip. Lenore was surprised and happy at her gift. Rob had chosen a beautiful lap robe and pillow set. "It gets chilly in here at night. I can really use this!" She proudly showed them around the apartment. They were impressed by how well it was furnished, "Down to the last detail," she told them, "by my church family."

"Now, that's a new term to me," Aimee said.

"They're like that to me. Like family. They did a lot, and Rose and I did the rest. We made good use of Goodwill too. Oh, Aimee, Rob, my church has helped me so much!" she exclaimed happily. "You need to find a church home."

Aimee wasn't sure what a church home was but she knew she didn't need to find a church.

Rob didn't like to be lectured on religion by his mother, of all people. Each started to change the subject.

"Lenore, what did Carl say about your leaving?"

"Did he give you a hard time?" asked Rob.

Her face clouded over. "Oh, he carried on about how he couldn't live without me. Wouldn't lift a finger to help me. Said his life was over. I felt so guilty I almost gave in. If Rose hadn't called me when she did, I would have stayed."

"It sure is a good thing she called when she did," he remarked.

"Yes – and what do you think?" she asked bitterly. "The very next day, he moved somebody else in! I know her too, she's a tramp."

"Why that no-good, low-down, scum-bag, pile of dirt –" Aimee convulsed in laughter.

"Well, it wasn't funny to me," Lenore responded with a hurt voice. "I felt bad. What did he think about me?"

"Mom, that tells you who he is. A real jerk. You are better off without him. You don't want to go back to him, do you?"

"I couldn't anyway because I signed a lease to stay a year. I have to get a job or job training....but it's lonely, already."

"Lenore, I wasn't laughing at you," Aimee explained, still laughing. "I was laughing at him, for being such a jerk. He didn't deserve you. And I'm sure you do get lonely here, sometimes."

She nodded. "You have no idea." Then, hesitantly she asked, "Rob, you said you saw Scott Carlyle. Did he...did he say anything about Mark?"

"Actually, we saw Mark ourselves." They told briefly of their trip, though nothing of his intense feelings. "He's doing well."

She was silent, reflecting. "Dumb, stupid, alcoholic decision! The stupidest thing I ever did in my life! Give up my own baby. I regret it every day of my life."

"Oh, Lenore...." Aimee took her hand in hers.

"Is Scott's wife good to him?"

"Yes, she is," answered Rob. Aimee nodded agreement. "Mom, it might be possible for you to see him someday." *Now why did I say that?* he wondered. *That could spell disaster.*

"Oh, no, no. I could never do that. I could never face him. After what I did to him, I could never face him. He must hate me."

"Mark doesn't hate you, Mom. But he does have questions. That's only natural. And you're facing me. I don't hate you."

Lenore stared off into space, not hearing him. "I think about Mark....wonder about him." Tears filled her eyes and slipped down her cheeks. She cried silently without sobs. "It's comforting to know that he's loved. I always knew Scott would care for him...."

She spoke of comfort but Aimee could feel her mood becoming more morose.

Remembering stories her Gram had told of women she had sponsored, she feared Lenore would relapse after they were gone. She thought she should try to lift her spirits by changing the subject. She handed her a tissue which she used to dry her eyes. "Lenore, Mark doesn't hate you. I know that. Now, I want to tell you something special...."

Lenore blinked and looked at her, coming back to the present. "Lenore, do you remember about my graduation? It's six weeks from now. I was able to get extra tickets, and I want you to come. Rob will pick you up, won't you, honey?"

"Uh – okay – but we have to leave here early, so we can get parking."

"Aimee, that's nice," Lenore replied. "Are you sure....?"

"Of course! Lenore, I want you to meet my parents –"

"I know Gramps would like to see you again," added Rob.

"My grandparents are coming up from Florida. You'll enjoy meeting them. So, will you plan on it?"

"Yes.... If you're sure you want me." She gave a weak smile. "Thank you ....thank you very much."

"Say, honey, you put me on the spot back there. About driving Mom to your graduation."

"Oh. You're right, but it was spur of the moment. I guess I could have told her we'd have to work out transportation. I didn't have to offer you."

"That would have been better. The problem is, I'd rather not do it. I remember my own graduation. The parking lots around that arena fill up so fast. We'll have to get there pretty early so we don't have to park blocks away."

"I could call her and change it."

"No, don't do that. I told her I would, so I will. All I can say, is, she'd better be ready on time."

"She's good about that."

"I sure hope so."

Chapter 27

"Gramps, something is bothering me and I'd like to talk with you about it." Rob was unable to concentrate on his studies and decided to drop in on Gramps. Aimee had an errand to do for her mother. It was an early Sunday afternoon a couple of weeks after their visit to Carlyles.

"Certainly, if I can help...."

"I hope so. Something came up when we were visiting Scott. About creation. He's the first intelligent person I've met who believes in creation, and I'm confused."

"I'll pretend I didn't hear that."

"Oh, Gramps!" Ashamed, he tried to backtrack. "I wasn't thinking. I do respect your intelligence. I know you believe in God. But – creation, too? Really?"

"Hmph," he grunted, "what does that make me, ground meat? As you kids say."

"Chopped liver. But I guess I take you for granted."

"It's my fault too. I don't talk about my faith very much, so you might not be aware of it. I stand corrected. So, how are you confused?"

"Well.....I've been taught that no thinking person believes in God, that religion is the enemy of science....and of course, I didn't think anybody believed in creation. No intelligent person. Then, along comes Scott. And you, you believe in creation?"

"Yes, I do," he said firmly. "I've given it a lot of study and thought. But Rob, let me say this about God." He looked deeply into Rob's eyes. "This attack on God, it's nothing new. Every young generation for hundreds of years has tried to do away with God. It gives them freedom to do what they want, because then they're not answerable to a higher authority. Today, though, the whole scientific establishment has taken that position, young and old. They're pretty ruthless in attacking anybody who believes in God."

"I've seen that," he nodded. "It can get ugly."

"Have you discussed this with Aimee?"

"Well....no, I gave her some articles Scott gave me and I guess she's reading them. I've thought about getting her point of view but something else always seems to come up. Maybe I'm, uh....scared of what she'd think....about me," he admitted.

"My dear Rob. This is the most important conversation you'll ever have in your life, with Aimee or me –" Rob looked skeptical – "Yes, about your relationship with Almighty God. You need to talk with her – but we'll go ahead without her for now."

"Thanks for taking time with me. I'm pretty good at putting things out of my mind, on a shelf, so to speak – but this is too much. I feel like I have to sort it out before I can do anything else."

"Good! It's that important. You know, true science isn't afraid of questions." Rob nodded in agreement. "But there's nothing scientific about stomping out opposition. Some of the greatest scientists who ever lived, past and present, have been believers in God. Einstein, for example, saw an order in nature that he said could never have occurred by chance. Many scientists say their faith in God makes them better scientists. If religion were harmful, don't you think it would hold them back? It wouldn't help them."

"I never thought about that, but....you're right. My real issue is this creation business. It's unscientific. At least I always thought so. But what I was reading, by scientists, makes sense.

It makes a pretty good case for design. So if there's design, who did the designing?"

"Exactly. Who but God? But if you're determined to do away with God, you have to reject creation. So you start out with a bias against creation."

"I guess so," he said thoughtfully. "That's not scientific."

"No, of course not. Evolution becomes a philosophy to be defended at all costs. Yet if evolution were true, the evidence should be all around us. We should be able to observe it taking place. The fact is, it's not there. There's not a shred of evidence of change ever taking place between species –"

"What about the fossil record?"

"Fossils don't *'prove'* anything. They show that everything existed at one time or other and often alongside of each other. Rob, evolution is counter-intuitive. Everything around us displays *'design'* – magnificent design, yet we're asked to believe it all happened by chance. Random acts."

"Or maybe God, if we concede He exists, used evolution?"

"So God used *'chance'* to create design? It's a contradiction in terms. When you think it through, you just can't have it both ways...."

They talked at length, a good intellectual debate, until at last Gramps called a halt. "I think we both need a break. Can I talk you into getting us something to drink? Something cold and refreshing."

Rob agreed gladly. When he left the room Gramps dropped his head in his hands with a sigh of frustration and a sense of failure. *Oh, Lord. This is the most important matter in the world and I can't get anywhere with him.*

A thought pierced his mind, clear and direct. *'It's not up to you. You've given a good defense, now simply tell what you know. Don't worry about the results.'* Gramps smiled with relief. *Oh....thank you.*

They drank from glasses of iced tea Rob brought and he re-opened their conversation. "These are good arguments, Gramps, but does it matter? I can respect you and Scott for believing in God, even going against the flow. So what? I mean, God is not relevant to me. I've lived twenty-some years without him. Him. He doesn't bother me and I don't bother Him."

"Ah, Rob. The difference is this: the same God who created the universe loves you and me. Because He created us He has a claim on our lives. He wants to do his work through us. He has a plan for your life. A wonderful plan, Rob."

"What if I don't want that? I'm happy the way I am."

Gramps thought a minute. "Remember when I told you how God brought me back from despair to life? I asked Him to give me something to live for and a purpose to life. He did."

"Yes. That was quite a story."

"Then again years later the fire destroyed everything I had. I was ready to give up, die. He rescued me again. I, a useless old man in a nursing home."

"Oh, yes. That was almost...." he shook his head, "almost the end for you, wasn't it?"

"Yes it was. Ah, that was God's wonderful love! He had more in store for me....much more." He smiled warmly at Rob. "When I discovered that you were my grandson I began to pray for you –"

"Pardon me, Gramps. '*Pray*'? What do you mean by that? I've never known what it is. Are you wishing, or begging, or talking to yourself? I don't know."

"I'll let you decide for yourself. Rob, I began to ask God, in other words, pray, that He would help you....that He would send good people into your life....and most of all, that He would help you come to know Him."

"Um....some of that has happened. I'm thinking of Aimee, and Scott and his family....But don't you think that would have happened anyway?"

"Maybe....maybe not. Then I began to have the insistent idea that I should pray for your mother. So I began to. I don't know why," he said with a shrug, "but I had the strong idea that I should meet her, get to know her. It seemed impossible, didn't it?"

Rob was silent as he considered the implication of Gramps' words. "Gramps....that really shakes me up! The rest could be coincidence. But if you hadn't prayed....my mother would still be drinking....she'd still be with that man, who knows, maybe drinking herself to death....I can't believe how she's changed! She says it's God." He paused, deep in thought. "If you hadn't prayed – for yourself – you'd be dead."

Gramps nodded his head vigorously. "Yes, but it's more than that! If there wasn't a God, if that God hadn't answered my prayer, I would have just been talking to the air! And I would be dead. Killed myself."

Rob pondered this. "Scott told about when he and Marie first met, they turned their lives over to God, only he said, '*to the Lord*', he said God '*turned their lives around*', '*transformed them*, he said, gave them happiness, a purpose in life. They endured a terrible house fire...."

Gramps smiled. "That's God. Rob, God not only created the universe. He created you, and He loves you. I know He's calling you to come to Him – or we wouldn't be having this conversation."

He was silent for a long while, head in his hands, struggling with his thoughts. Finally, "I don't understand it, but I know what you are saying is true. I can't just....shake it off. Scott, and you, and now my mother...How do people come to know God, anyway?"

"You come to him on his terms. Humbly, through Christ."

"Jesus....hmm, I learned about him in Sunday School. A little, not much."

"What you need to know, is that Jesus is the Son of God. He is the bridge, the doorway to God. Oh –" he looked around the little parlor – "let me get the Bible I keep here." He wheeled over to an end table and pulled a Bible from a drawer. "Rob, let me show you how to know God, personally."

"Gramps....maybe I'm crazy, but I know this is the right thing to do," he said with feelings of nervous anticipation. "I know it, I feel it, strongly." Together they began to read from the Bible in Gramps' lap.

Aimee and her family had a long-established custom of going out for Sunday brunch. Today after the meal her mother wasn't feeling well and wanted to go straight home. She asked Aimee if she would do an errand for her at a discount house near where Lenore lived.

"Oh, Mom," she replied impatiently, "Rob and I planned to spend the afternoon together! Now that I'm not working Sundays anymore –" her dad gave her a look – "but okay," she agreed reluctantly, "I will."

"Aimee, remember, it's for your wedding. I can't do it. You can still see him afterward," she replied sharply.

"I'll work it out." *Annoyance, annoyance,* she thought, swearing under her breath. *What a day this is turning out to be. Rob skipped brunch to study so we could spend the afternoon together. We were looking forward to it – and now this!* She texted Rob of her change of plans. He replied that he needed to keep on studying but maybe they could get together for dinner at his place. '*Maybe!' Oh, well*, she thought grudgingly, *Mom is right, this is for me. But I don't have to like it.*

Hmm, I could drop in on Lenore. Or I could see Gramps for an hour or so. We haven't seen him for a while. A friend of hers had remarked how wonderful it was that she and Rob visited an old man in a nursing home every week. Aimee corrected her*; no, we love being with him. I miss him when we don't go. We owe him so much. If he hadn't been friendly with Rob he never would have discovered Rob was his grandson. Rob and I would never have met. Yes, that's it, I'll drop in on Gramps.*

But after she had completed her errand a detour took her in the direction of Lenore's apartment. Waiting for traffic to begin moving she texted her and asked if she could visit. Her answer came back quickly, *'come on, love 2 see U.'*

A while later the two women were sitting together in Lenore's living room. Aimee gave her a kitchen appliance she'd bought earlier in the day. "I planned to give it to you some time later; I didn't know I'd get a chance today," she explained.

Lenore accepted it with thanks but some internal misgivings. *Aimee does so much for me,* she thought. *I'm thankful, but.... sometimes it's too much.*

After some chitchat and an impromptu lunch she invited Aimee to stay a while longer. "My Bible study group is meeting at 5:00. I'd love for you to come!" she exclaimed breathlessly.

Aimee politely declined. She could think of nothing she'd rather do less than Bible study. Before meeting Lenore, she'd never known anyone who read the Bible. She felt it was beneath her, though she would not be rude enough to say it.

"Aimee," Lenore went on, "there are some younger women in it, your age. I know you'd enjoy it!"

Aimee decided it was time to discourage any further invitations. "Lenore, thank you, but I'm just not interested. It's fine for you, but it's not for me."

With innocent zeal Lenore plunged ahead, "Oh, Aimee, Bible study has helped me so much. It would help you too. We all need it, you know. We need to know the Lord!"

Aimee was decidedly uncomfortable. *Do I look like I need any such thing,* she wondered with annoyance. "Lenore, thank you, but no. Some people need it, that's okay, but I don't. So –"

"Aimee, you think you don't, but yes you do! You're not any better than I am, you just act like you are!"

"Lenore, I didn't mean that at all!"

"Well, that's what it sounded like. You think you don't need God because you're so special, but I do because I'm a loser," she replied with a hurt voice.

"Oh, no, Lenore – I mean, you say you need God, but you're not a loser."

"Well, we all need God. You're a sinner too. We all are."

"Me – a sinner? No, I'm not!" she said indignantly. "I've never done anything bad –"

"Of course you have. We all have. I'm a sinner but you are too."

Aimee stared at Lenore. She shook her head in disbelief, shocked as much by her words as by her reproachful manner. "Lenore, no! I'm not a sinner! You don't mean that, I am not!"

"Aimee...." Lenore was fighting back tears, "you really hurt me. I think you should leave." She got up and walked towards the door, surprised at her boldness.

Half in a daze, Aimee got up. "Goodbye, Lenore...."

Lenore said nothing.

Aimee stumbled to her car, tears burning her eyes. She started towards home. *How could this have happened,* she agonized. *Lenore and I had such a good friendship. What now? How can I make it right? Should I even try?*

It's not right! Why should she turn on me that way? Hurt her? She said I hurt her. Yes, she was really hurt. What did I do, anyway? I never meant to hurt her. But....is she right? Do I think I'm better than she is? Maybe....maybe I do. That would hurt. Did we really have the friendship I thought we did, or was I just trying to help her, to feel good about myself? That would hurt. How can she call me a sinner? Her of all people! I've never done anything illegal or even bad. I'm a good person. A sinner? No, I'm not! But I hurt her, badly. Does that make me a sinner?

Aimee turned her car off the road and texted Lenore. *'I'm confused. I need 2 see* U.' Lenore texted back, *'Come right away.'*

Rob had received a text from Aimee saying something *'wonderful but scary'* had happened and she was coming with dinner. *Now, is that confusing or what*? he thought. It would be a late dinner, they had planned to meet earlier than this. Suddenly she was at the door, almost dancing in.

"Aimee, you look like you swallowed a light bulb!"

"Oh, Rob!" She dropped the food containers on the kitchen table, held him and kissed him, then took his hands. "Come in the living room with me. I have something to tell you."

Holding his hands, she began to tell what had transpired at Lenore's.

"Ohh...that must have hurt," he said sympathetically.

"Yes, I did hurt her."

"No, I meant you, it hurt you –"

"Well, yes, it did. I thought she was so unfair. Then I began to see through her eyes and I realized she had a point. I looked at myself....and," she dropped her head, "I didn't like what I saw. I didn't like the word *'sinner'*. Not me. But she said anything bad was sin. I felt I had to go back. I hoped she wouldn't be too mad."

"And was she?"

"She greeted me with a hug! She apologized, she said, *'If I'm trying to show the love of Christ'* – she explained that He's God – *'how can I let my feelings get hurt like that?'* She apologized because she hadn't told me that Christ loves me. Well, as we talked – I had this burning feeling inside of me – I can't explain it, but I wanted to know God the way she does."

She looked cautiously at Rob. "And....it's not only her. Gramps too, he's really shaken up my thinking. I could feel the love of God coming from her, just like Gramps. I know that sounds silly but I could. I thought, she's teaching me, and I'm the one who's supposed to be helping her. That...." she shook her head, "that was an eye-opener."

Tears filled her eyes. "Rob, I humbled myself. Me, Aimee – I gave myself to Christ." She was getting nervous. She stroked his face. "Darling – this is the scary part – I don't know how you'll feel about this. Oh, Rob – I hope it's not a deal-breaker. I know you're not religious. I don't know what this will do to our relationship."

"Oh, Aimee – baby, darling –" holding her hands tightly – "Oh, no, it's good, good." He cradled her face in his hands and kissed her tenderly on the lips. "Now.....I have something to tell you."

"Wait a minute, honey –" *What is he doing?* she asked herself. *Don't change the subject, this is important, we have to talk about it –*

"You aren't going to believe what I have to tell you." He paused for a long moment, keeping her in suspense.

"Well....go ahead, then," she said unwillingly.

"You aren't going to believe this –" grinning, he kissed her on the nose – "but I met God today too. I mean, I gave my life to Christ, to God –"

"What? You're right, I don't believe it –" she looked at him with astonishment – "but I do. That's unbelievable! Honey, is it really true?"

"Yes, yes....." They held each other, laughing with delight.

"So tell me already!"

He took her hand. "You know, I had all this material to learn about brain function. Honey, the brain is so amazing! How could it possibly have evolved?" He shook his head. "I studied for a long time, four or five hours, and all the time I kept having these nagging doubts, questions, things I'd read that Scott gave me –" she raised an eyebrow, "so finally I took a break, and while I was eating I looked at one of Scott's books and I was more confused than ever. I wanted to talk to him but then I thought I would go see Gramps. I thought he might be able to answer my questions. He lives so close, I could spend an hour or so; I knew I'd still have time for studying and you and I would get together later."

"Anyway –" He told how Gramps had introduced him to Christ. "I'd always dismissed God as irrelevant. But Gramps and Scott, they made a good case for God the Creator. If God created everything, then He was relevant whether I liked it or not. It was all very logical."

"So that was your pathway to God," Aimee smiled, taking his hand.

"No, no. I was still saying *'so what?'* Then...." he shook his head wonderingly, "I realized that Gramps and Mom both owed their lives to God. Their lives, Aimee! Talk about relevant, that brought it home to me. After that, it was like a magnet drawing me to God. That's when I realized.....I did need God."

"Oh, honey, I am so happy! What is happening to us?"

He laughed and shook his head. "I was worried about you, what would you think of me? But I knew I had to do this. It was the right thing to do, no matter what you thought."

She nodded agreement. "Me too. Rob – what have we done? Is this real?"

"Aimee, it's the most real thing in the world," he said with conviction. "I feel peace inside. And love....I can't describe it. For the first time since....since Grandma and Grandpa died." There were tears in his eyes. "I can't explain it. It's the light Gramps talked about."

"Oh, my goodness!" She looked at the time. "I told Mom and Dad I would be home by now! I have to prepare for tomorrow." She started to text them.

"Darling, wait." She stopped texting. "Wait a minute –" She looked at him expectantly. "I want to do something. Honey, this is bigger than both of us. I think we should talk to God about it," he explained, hesitantly. "This is all new to me. I want to do it right."

"It's new to me, too! Okay, Rob. You lead." They held each other's hands, tightly.

"Dear God, Jesus," he began, "we don't know what's happened to us, but....we want to do what's right. We want to give ourselves to you, as a couple –"

"Yes," Aimee breathed, "yes, we do."

"Show us what to do next. Thank you."

Aimee closed with, "Thank you, God, good night." Putting her arms around Rob she gave him a quick kiss then jumped up, texting as she did.

"Aren't you going to eat?" he asked.

"No, I'm not hungry! Who can eat at a time like this?" She kissed the top of his head and ran out.

Rob wasn't ready to eat, not yet. He quickly texted Scott and in a few minutes he and Marie were on the phone with him. They laughed, Marie cried, Scott said a short prayer and they promised to keep in touch. Rob hung up, feeling light-headed and more light-hearted than he could ever remember feeling, even when he first met Aimee.

He went to the kitchen and ate both meals, cold.

The next morning Aimee could hardly wait to speak with Gramps. He didn't answer so she left a message. She couldn't concentrate on her job and hoped no one would come into her office. At last they connected.

She told Gramps what had happened to her. "Gramps, did you ever hear of such a coincidence?"

"Oh, my dear. With God, there's no such thing as *'coincidence'*." He chuckled as he shared her joy. "I think God is laughing with delight, just as I am."

"He is? I never thought of God laughing."

"You have a lot to discover. Now – I wonder if you and Rob could come over here this week, Wednesday night. If I can arrange things, that is." *She's not the only fast worker*, he thought.

"I can. I'll have to see about Rob."

"Oh, and Aimee, could you and Rob bring a meal for four? Unless you'd rather have some of our world-famous institutional food. I'll reimburse you."

"Sure! What do you want? For four? Tell you what, I'll surprise you."

Chapter 28

Wednesday afternoon Aimee and Rob entered the little parlor and found Gramps with an older man, somewhat younger than Gramps who he introduced as Dr. Bruce Buchanan.

"This is such a beautiful Spring day, let's see if we can find a table in the garden and eat there," Gramps suggested. Shortly after, they were seated in the garden and enjoying dinner together in the warm sunshine.

Gramps asked Dr. Buchanan to tell about himself. "I'm not a medical doctor," he explained. "My doctorate is in Biblical languages, and I'm pastor of a nearby church, Christ Community Chapel. We hold services here on Wednesday afternoons which your grandpa attends. I've come to know him pretty well. You can call me Pastor Bruce if you want." Rob and Aimee nodded. "He asked me here today because we have an outreach to the university community. We'd like to help you grow in your Christian life and meet other young adults who are Christians."

"Ah – this is very new to us," Rob replied. "That would be helpful." Aimee smiled in agreement, taking Rob's hand.

"We have a college and young adult Bible study on Friday nights at 6:00. It's led by our assistant pastors Peter O'Connor and his wife Ming. Then, we have worship services on Sunday."

"Well," Aimee demurred, "I'm interested, but we usually visit Gramps on Friday evenings. And Sunday morning my family always gets together for brunch."

"Friday shouldn't be a problem," Gramps interjected. "You can come earlier and have a meal with me. Or come another day."

"We're interested, if we can work it out," said Rob as Aimee nodded in agreement. "Not this week though, we have something else. Now, what's this about church?"

"Pastor Bruce, church is brand new to me. I've never been to church in my life. I mean never," Aimee told him.

"That's not unusual, Aimee," he reassured her. "That's true of many young adults today. I wonder," he paused, "do you have an hour or so now? We could go over to the church and I'll show you around."

"We can do it," she replied. "I am so curious. There's something exciting about this!"

"Honey, you sure have done a one-eighty," Rob marveled. She laughed in agreement.

"Aimee, I've been wondering," Gramps asked, "what did your folks say when they found out you'd become a Christian?"

"Oh, it was funny," she laughed. "Mom and Dad were in the kitchen when I came in. Mom asked me what had happened to me. She said I'd always been her *'sparkly Aimee'* but now I was *'sparkly on steroids'*. Imagine that!"

"I can imagine it," he replied with a smile. Rob nodded.

"I told them the whole story. Mom was totally shocked. Said she had never expected anything like that from me. She was okay with it, I think, but she was worried about me getting involved with a church. She doesn't like the *'institutional church'* as she puts it. I think she had a bad experience in church, as a child. Says she has her own private beliefs and that's all that matters."

"A lot of people feel that way," replied Pastor Bruce. "They've been burned, and they never get over it. They miss out on being part of a church family."

" *'Church family'?* " Rob asked. "That's the second time I've heard that term. I have no idea what it means."

"Ah....Christians the world over are the church family, and our own little gathering here, Christ Community, we are a part of the church family too," Pastor Bruce answered. "I hope you two will soon find out, in a wonderful way." Aimee and Rob nodded with interest.

"Aimee, what about your father?" asked Gramps. "What did Roger think?"

"Dad's a live-and-let-live kind of guy. He trusts me. He just doesn't want me to become a religious extremist."

"You need to know that Jesus was an extremist," Pastor Bruce told them.

"He was?" they asked.

"He was not a half-way person. He asks for our whole devotion, our whole heart. No half-way measures."

"That is pretty extreme," Rob agreed. "It's like, '*all or nothing*'."

"He has the right, because he's God," Pastor Bruce exclaimed with passion. "He's the creator of the universe, He holds all things together, and He loves you. He's changed your lives – you may not realize it yet, but you have the very life of God within you and you will never be the same. What He asks in return is for you to give your life back to Him, give Him your heart."

"Um, that's a tough one," Rob replied. "Aimee has my heart." He put his arm around her and kissed her forehead.

"Didn't you both say you came to Christ in spite of what the other person might think?" asked Pastor Bruce.

"Yes....yes, we did."

"Then I would say you're on the right track. Now, are we ready? You can follow me in your car."

The church was a large, newer building, *Christ Community Chapel. How beautiful it is*, Aimee thought, observing the garden setting.

Pastor Bruce invited them to sit for a few minutes on a nearby bench. "I'd like to tell you a story," he said, "it will only take a few minutes." They agreed.

"I was a freshman in college," he began, "and I got a student deferment from the draft, so I didn't go to Vietnam. My best friend who I grew up with went, and – he was killed there. Jack." He paused as memories flooded back. "Well, the student protesters on campus made a mockery of Jack's death and all the others. They didn't care. All they wanted to do was protest."

"Fast forward to the present. Someone told me about your grandpa's story, so I watched it online. I hadn't realized that I still carried some bitterness from that time on campus. Hearing your grandpa, and I already knew him, you see, it was wonderful. It healed the hurt." He smiled warmly, tears in his eyes.

Aimee and Rob looked at each other. "It goes on and on, doesn't it?" said Aimee.

"I wanted you two to know that. I thought I might not have a better chance to tell you. Do you realize that you are the reason he told his story?"

"He told us that, but I wondered," replied Rob. "I mean, he lived with it for forty years. Why now?"

"He said he'd never gotten that close to anyone before, since his wife died. He just kept it buried, figured he would never tell it. But then he felt he couldn't keep it from you, and God began to speak to him about making it public. For a private man, it must have been incredibly difficult."

"I can imagine," said Rob.

"God speaks to people, even now?" Aimee asked.

"Honey, I'll have to tell you what Gramps told me. About my mother. It's pretty amazing. And about my grandparents, too. But later, not now."

"Yes, I want to hear." She smiled and took his hand. "Soon."

"Well! Let's go in," said Pastor Bruce. He led them to the entrance to the sanctuary. Aimee paused, hesitant to go in. "It feels kind of….holy. And it's so beautiful." The late afternoon sun streamed in the windows casting a soft glow over everything. She observed a large wooden cross in the front and beside it, a smaller one with Jesus on it. "Oh, yes. It's about Jesus, isn't it? she asked, almost in a whisper.

"Yes, Aimee."

"That one "- she pointed to the crucifix – "He died for us, didn't He. I never knew what that meant. Until now."

"Yes. We like to have the cross with Jesus on it to remind us of what He went through for us. Then, the empty cross reminds us that He is alive."

"I'm learning."

He took a few minutes to tell them about the meaning of worship and why it was important to meet for group worship. "We have two services on Sunday, one at 8:30 and the other at 11:00, each one an hour or so. Take your pick. Both services are what we call blended in their worship styles and both have a mix of ages. I like it that way." He saw their confused looks. "I'm sure this doesn't mean anything to you." They laughed in agreement. "Don't worry about that now. You'll understand as you go along."

Aimee told him about her family's brunch tradition. "We could do the early service and then get together with my family."

"Honey, I don't know!" Rob protested. "That's an ungodly hour on a Sunday morning. When I think of when I'd have to get up…."

"That's okay," she replied sweetly. "You can meet us after brunch when your service is over." She looked around. "Pastor Bruce! Pastor Bruce, this is beautiful! Do you ever have weddings here?"

"We've had a few," he replied with a smile.

"I wonder if it would be possible for us to have our wedding here?" she asked, her excitement mounting. She gave him the date.

As the pastor checked his planner Rob told him about her unhappiness with the gazebo.

"It is available," Pastor Bruce announced with satisfaction. "It's yours."

"Honey, this is it, this is perfect!" she exclaimed, throwing her arms around him. "This is just what I've been waiting for," she sighed happily.

"It is beautiful," he nodded, hugging her. "You're right, it's perfect! I like it."

"I'm happy for both of you," smiled Pastor Bruce. "There's something very special about a church wedding. It's a time to consecrate yourselves to God. Now, do you also want me to perform your wedding?"

"Yes, definitely," answered Rob.

"No, I'm sorry, we can't," Aimee objected. "Mom has somebody she knows. I have no idea who. I'd rather have you, Pastor Bruce. I'll see if she can get out of it. And we'll cancel the gazebo!" She texted her mother, *'Mom, I've found a heavenly place, cancel the gazebo.'*

"Pastor Bruce," Rob asked, "do you have banquet facilities? I know Aimee is pretty unhappy with the lodge her father rented."

"Rob, thank you but no, I couldn't do that to my father. He pulled a lot of strings to get it for me. I don't like it but we're stuck with it." At that point her phone rang and she chatted happily with her mother.

"Let me show you something else," the pastor said as he took them around to a courtyard, fragrant with ornamental trees and flowering bushes. "We often have weddings here." He pointed out a room with sliding doors which could hold an overflow of guests. He checked his planner. "It's available. At the moment."

Aimee swept around the courtyard taking in all the details. "It's beautiful, beautiful.....I love it!"

Rob watched her with pleasure. "My beautiful firefly," he remarked to no one in particular.

"Yes, the fireflies are beautiful here," Pastor Bruce said, coming up to him. "But it's not dark enough for them, not yet. Aimee, what do you think?" he asked as she came up to them.

"I'm too overwhelmed to decide! I will let you know. Tomorrow. Oh – I almost didn't tell you! Dad was at the computer working on the invitations. He would have run them off tomorrow. So I'll have to decide by then. Oh," she turned to Pastor Bruce, "you can do our wedding! Mom says it's my wedding, not hers."

"Honey," Rob observed thoughtfully, "do you realize that if we hadn't come here tonight the invitations would have been in the mail tomorrow? With the other location? It would have been too late for us to have the wedding here." He shook his head. "Amazing. Do you think that's coincidence?"

She laughed. "Strange are the mysteries of the universe. Hmm. Do you think God had something to do with it? Maybe we should give God credit, d'ya think?"

"Aimee," replied Pastor Bruce, "you've got that right. Absolutely right. And on that happy note I'd like to offer you a blessing." Putting his hands on their shoulders he spoke a short prayer.

Very strange, Rob thought. He could feel love emanating from this man, and yet they had just met. He didn't even know them. He couldn't remember feeling that kind of love from anyone except family….yes, and Gramps, even when he was simply Mr. Douglas, resident. He asked Pastor Bruce about it while Aimee was in the rest room.

"Rob, love is supposed to characterize us as Christians. Jesus told us, that's how people will know we are His disciples, if we love one another. Even if we don't know them. Of course, we don't always let it happen."

Rob gave him a puzzled look.

"You'll find out, Rob. I don't want to give you too much tonight."

Aimee rejoined them and they said goodnight. "Here, let me give you my card," he said. "Feel free to call me if you need me."

Rob was driving Aimee to her car when her phone rang. "It's Dad." Rob heard strange, garbled noises from her, nothing intelligible, and then a low moan.

He pulled off the road. "Are you all right?"

"Rob – Dad said, I only get married once, he hopes, and he wants me to be happy. He said, *'Forget about the lodge rental. Find out if that church has a banquet hall and rent it if you can.'* I can't believe it – I've got to text Pastor Bruce right away!" She did, and a few minutes later she squealed, "They do, and it's available. It's ours!" She collapsed in his arms with a happy sigh.

"Honey, you didn't just swallow a light bulb. You swallowed helium!"

"So, honey, what did you think about church?" Rob asked the following Sunday as they headed to the restaurant for brunch with Aimee's family.

"First of all, I'm glad you were able to roll your body out of bed and go with me. I think you were even awake!"

"Well, I wanted us to be together our first time at church. But I don't guarantee it every week. Not that early, anyway."

"In answer to your question....I didn't expect the music. Of course I've seen old movies with church services in them, people singing hymns, but this was different."

"Churches can be different, you know. This church wasn't anything like the one I used to attend. That was very formal, traditional, I guess you'd call it. This....there was something about this church...."

"The music, Rob – it blew me away.....*'Open the eyes of my heart, Lord,'*" she sang softly, '*open the eyes of my heart, I want to see You....*' What a thought! That's awesome!"

"Yeah. I know. It hit me too. You were crying. I was worried about you, at first."

"I know. I couldn't stop. I didn't want to stop. I wasn't sad. It was something else. I felt – cleansed, deep down inside. It was a beautiful feeling."

"I'm happy for you, honey. I felt it too. I think it's the love of God." He squeezed her hand.

"What I liked best, though, was when Pastor Bruce talked."

"It's called a sermon, Aimee."

"Smarty! You think I didn't know that? Well, I liked it. It will give me something to think about all week. Do you know what impressed me the most?"

"What was that?"

"It was love. People treated us with kindness and love. Total strangers. It was almost overwhelming. The same love I feel from Pastor Bruce, and Gramps too."

"I know. I felt it too. – So, what will you tell your folks? If they ask you?"

"Oh, my! I don't think I can talk about the music. It was too… too personal. Let me see…I'd tell them it was all about love, a different kind of love. And that sermon."

"I'm with you. Honey, are you prepared to go back? Every week? Is this right for us?"

"Every week? I don't know about that." She thought about it. "Even if I don't feel like it? No, then it would just be a habit, and that doesn't seem right."

"I'm thinking about this. You know, Pastor Bruce told us we should go every week because we needed it. *Make a commitment*, he said. You go to brunch every week with your family –"

"Sure, we like to eat."

"Yes, and that's an important tradition for you. Isn't it also a commitment?"

She raised an eyebrow. "What are you trying to say?"

"I was thinking about keeping fit. You run every day and I work out. Even when we don't feel like it. Why is that?"

"I know if I miss a day or two it's harder to get back to it. Hmm," she reflected, "I guess you're saying, that's what church will be like, harder to get back to if we miss a week or two –"

"That's what commitment is."

"Well….that's true. But if I went to church every week it would be an early morning instead of sleeping in. Or else miss brunch, which I don't want to do. Today was okay but…. every week?"

"I'm thinking about this. We've already made a commitment. This is part of that commitment. No halfway measures, right?" he asked.

"Yes….but let's not get locked into something. We've got to see if this is right for us."

"Right. We don't want to be too hasty. Why don't we try it out for a few months, maybe until we're married? We can see how we feel then."

"That's a good idea." She took his hand. "I can do it. I just have to get used to 8:30 every Sunday. What about you?"

"I can do it if I make up my mind to it." He pulled the car off the road and into a parking lot.

"What's wrong?"

"Nothing's wrong. I wanted to talk for a few minutes." He took her hands. "A year ago I was just another college student. I wasn't sad, I wasn't happy. I was just kind of existing. If you had asked me what was important to me I would have said..." he thought for a moment, '*helping people*'. That's always made me feel good. Then, Gramps and I found each other. Now I had someone who loved me, and I loved him. But I was still just.... existing."

"Go on," she said encouragingly.

"Then one day a girl named Aimee smiled at me and I smiled at her. She wasn't the first pretty girl who smiled at me, but she was the first one I wanted to smile back at. Just like that, my world was changed! I've been smiling ever since," he said warmly. "I knew I wanted to spend the rest of my life getting to know her and making her happy. Is it so crazy that my life could change just like that? In a heartbeat?"

"Oh, no, Rob, not at all! I felt the same....."

"I thought, my life is full and complete. I have Aimee, I have everything in the world. She is my world! Now I know real happiness."

"Well," she smiled, "this is nice to hear. But where are you going with it?"

"A week ago, God came into my life. God, Christ. It was '*Aimee*' all over again! Just like that. My life is turned upside down! Just like that, in a heartbeat." He put his arm around her. "It's so life-shaking, honey. I thought I knew love before, but.... this is different."

"Yes....yes, I know."

He stopped to reflect. "Gramps talked to me about Jesus forgiving my sins. I didn't even know I had sins to forgive. What I'm struggling with now, is why? Why? There's more to it than just forgiving my sins. What does God want to do with me? What does He want me to do?" He gave her a worried look. "It's not just me, anymore. It's us. What does He want to do with us? And – are you with me, in this?"

"Rob, darling. I'm with you. You're so right, there has to be a reason Christ came into our lives. We're in this together. I feel like.... life will never be the same again."

"Yes, yes, that's it!" He shook his head. "I'm not ready to say all this to your folks. I'll wait and see. But I had to talk to you, see if we're together in this."

"Yes, honey. We are." She put her arms around him. "We are."

They found Aimee's family strangely uninterested in their church experience. "Hope you had a good time in church," her mother said off-handedly, then went on to other matters. Her attention was centered on graduation which was fast approaching and for the time took her mind off wedding plans.

Afterwards she asked Rob to drive over to see Gramps, "Just for a few minutes. I can't wait to tell him about my experience with church."

"Honey, I can't believe you were never in a church," he commented as they were on their way.

"Oh, a couple of times for weddings. That doesn't count. Never to a meeting or service. Mom, she discouraged us from going with friends. Not in a hateful way; she just didn't want us to start going to church because she didn't like church and she didn't want us to get hurt, as she'd been hurt. So I had quite a negative impression of church and church people. The Bible, too. She thinks the Bible is too dogmatic. Mom's beliefs are more – well, she says '*a little bit of everything*'."

"And now here's her daughter hooked up with a church and Bible study."

"That's another strange thing. Now I want to read the Bible! Actually want to. I'm glad Pastor Bruce gave us our own Bibles. That was good of him."

"Your dad – did you say he doesn't believe in God?"

"Dad's an odd duck. He says he's an atheist but sometimes I wonder. He doesn't talk about it. You know how people say there are no atheists in foxholes? Mom says it was war that made him an atheist. Like, if there's a God why is there the horror of war?" She shook her head and shrugged. "He doesn't argue it. He always taught us to respect other people's beliefs. Not to hurt anybody. He even taught us not to swear, because it can offend people. Though he sure can swear when he's around his buddies."

"Well, he figures he's not offending them. That's one thing I liked about you, Aimee, you're not a swearing person. Not much, anyway. I was brought up that way too. It didn't stop me from swearing, though, a lot."

"You hardly do now."

"I couldn't swear at the nursing home. Or DeGeorgio's. So I had to stop. Most of the time."

"Now, what about you and church?"

"My grandparents took me to Sunday School. They wanted me to learn the Bible stories, and learn to be good, I guess. When I got older I'd stay in church with them. I found it very boring. And Sunday School got irrelevant so I just stopped going. It went against what I was learning in school. If I asked questions nobody had any answers. It was like they never had thought about it. I was told, *believe it because the Bible says it.*"

"That would turn me off in a hurry. I notice Pastor Bruce isn't like that. His sermon made me think."

"That's what I notice about Scott. And Gramps too."

Gramps was happy to hear their experiences and impressions, and he noticed that Aimee, along with her usual sparkle had a new serenity. "It's a funny feeling," she told him. "It's such a change for me. When I think how I resisted Lenore trying to interest me in Bible study – and now, this is what I want! I feel as if I've come home, this is so right, that I've found the key to the universe. Oh,

I'm mixing things up. Gramps," she shook her head with surprise, "would you believe we now have a place for our wedding and reception?"

"Not that old graffiti gazebo," added Rob.

"I'm not surprised," he said, to her surprise. "I've been praying about it. I felt quite sure that God was going to do something. I didn't know what, of course. But I'm not surprised."

"Neither am I. Not after what you told me last week," Rob added.

"So where is the wedding going to be?"

"The church. Imagine that! Actually, the courtyard of the church." Gramps smiled to hear it. "I made my decision and the invitations are out. Look for yours. The church is so beautiful! Have you ever been there?"

"No, I haven't. But I will be there for your wedding. Nothing would keep me away."

"First of all, Aimee's graduation," Rob told him. Just four weeks!"

"Right! I'll be there. Rob," he chuckled, "What a year has brought forth! Last year, your graduation. This year, Aimee's. And everything in between. Who would have believed it?"

Chapter 29

A week later they met with Pastor Bruce at the church to discuss wedding plans and begin pre-marital counseling. "Before we leave," Aimee told Rob, "let's take another look at the Courtyard. I can't wait to see it again! I need to see it in the light of day." She wasn't sure what she remembered from that memorable first sight when the sun was setting.

"Right. Too bad it was raining last week when we were here for church. We couldn't get a good idea of it."

"Beautiful, beautiful, beautiful!" she exclaimed as they stepped into the garden. "It's everything I thought it was – it's perfect!" They sat on a bench beneath a trellis. "See, this bench is moveable, we'll stand here and the pastor will stand in front of us."

"Looks like it was designed that way," he observed. "I'll bet there have been lots of weddings here."

"In a couple of months all the flowers will be in bloom and the wisteria will cover the trellis – I can hardly wait!" she sighed with pleasure.

"For the wisteria? Or the wedding?" he asked.

She gave him a convincing non-verbal answer.

"So, what did you think of Pastor Bruce's little talk?" she asked playfully.

"Is this a test?"

"Of course not! It means a lot to me, to know what you think." She squeezed his hand.

"Well...." He thought about it. "I never knew God had anything to do with marriage. When he started talking I thought, *okay, what does God have to do with this?"*

"That was a surprise to me too," she agreed. "But imagine, God actually planned it, for our pleasure. That's great! Rob – wasn't that wonderful, about ancient Israelite soldiers? God told them to stay home the first year of their marriage to give happiness to their wives! I would love that...." she said wistfully.

"And so would I! Well, it tells me what God wants marriage to be. It's for our mutual pleasure."

"Unbelievable, isn't it? And people think God spoils their fun."

"Yes....and here I was, afraid of marriage. I didn't understand it. Actually, we're a gift to each other. I like that! But marital intimacy, as he put it, is so much more than sex. It's knowing each other, how did he put it? '*in the deepest possible way*'."

"Yes, yes, I caught that too. It blows my mind. I guess that's what it is to '*be one*'. Be a part of each other. Belong to each other. Rob..." she looked at him carefully, "does that still bother you?"

"Not any more. Actually – I've done a one-eighty on that. Why didn't I see it before? That's the whole idea of marriage, that we belong to each other, we are one. I'm happy to belong to you."

"By what lucky accident did we happen to learn this now?" she laughed. "Before we messed up our lives with....with substitutes. Counterfeits."

"Your mom, hon. Her words to you. It was pretty hard for me to accept, at first. But that's what made you strong. And I'm the lucky guy who benefits." He laughed at himself. "You, on the other hand, get a guy who was just too dumb or scared to get into the usual selfish relationships."

"Look here, Mr. Rob Carlyle." She took his chin and looked in his eyes. "Don't sell yourself short. You kept your eyes on your goals. You worked hard. You didn't let yourself get all messed up and crazy like most of the guys around here. Now, you've got a lot to give. And I'm the one who benefits."

"Mmm.....all for you." He stopped and reflected. "If people only knew how they're cheating themselves, and the other person, when their focus is on taking instead of giving...what can I get, how can I score...."

"According to Pastor Bruce, it's a life-long battle, against our selfishness."

"That's what Gramps says. I didn't believe it. I never thought of myself as selfish. But I guess I do have a selfish streak..... much as I hate to admit it."

"I guess the real test will be to sacrifice some of your independence, do y' think?"

"Ha, ha. I guess you're right."

"I'm not worried about you. Well, not anymore."

"All this confirms what your mom told you about marriage."

"Yes, isn't that amazing? Mom and Dad stumbled on to God's plan and didn't even know it, and God blessed them with happiness. That's how Pastor Bruce put it."

"Yes..." he reflected, "God's laws make sense, they actually make things better for us. But I can't agree with him about '*joy and happiness when we do it God's way*'. It hasn't been easy for me. For you either, honey. Sometimes it's been torment."

"I know. But, I think you were fighting God."

"You're probably right. Because it's easier now."

"Yes....yes. God is helping us. He's certainly helping me to hold to my convictions. We didn't have that before. I think –" she stopped to think about it, "someday we'll look back and be glad we did things the way we did."

"Right. It's been worth it, I can see it now," he admitted, laughing. "My Grandpa used to say, anything worth having is worth working for. And waiting."

"Yes, like our education. Look how far we've both come. It hasn't always been easy, has it? Some of it's been a struggle."

"I get the point. Ah, my new education will be you," he smiled suggestively.

"Don't you ever forget that," she warned him, laughing.

"Not a chance! Honey." He took her by the chin. "The other thing that impressed me was....that God wants us to create a new generation, the product of our love....a new generation to love God. Now that's something to look forward to."

"Oh, yes, yes...that's exciting! Something to look forward to. But....when he said that God's purpose for marriage is to create a new generation, that '*it's not about us*'....that's almost a contradiction, don't you think?"

"I noticed that." He thought about it, shaking his head. "We're a gift to each other, for each other's happiness....yet it's not about us."

"It does make sense, now that I think about it. We're beginning to learn that Christ is first and foremost. Not us."

"That's true."

She stopped and thought. "God has it right," she nodded, "children need marriage. A good marriage, parents who love each other. That's their security. I've always known that, from my mom and dad."

He put his arm around her, kissing her hair. "I'm beginning to understand what you told me, way back when.....about doing what is best for the baby. You were right."

"Mom was right. Rob...." she stopped, a new thought occurring to her. "Do you remember when I told you that I had a terminally boring life but yours was absolutely fascinating?"

"Yes....back when we were getting to know each other."

"You said you'd gladly trade my life for yours. Well, I was thinking about what Pastor Bruce said, about babies and families, and I realize that I'm the one who had the wonderful, fascinating life. It wasn't perfect, but it was good. Yours was sad, and sorry, until you were rescued, and even then it was a struggle." She sighed. "Oh, Rob. No child should ever go through what you went through, neglect, too many fathers, alcohol – I'll never again call my life boring."

"That's okay, I understand. I'm glad I was rescued."

"But honey, that could have been my life! I see it now." Rob looked puzzled. "Yes, if Mom hadn't made that '*life-style decision*' – I call it a '*life-changing decision*' – not to be cheap, if she'd met my dad, and got pregnant with me, then he would have been out the door, she would have been a single mom –" She stopped, a stricken look on her face. "Oh, my goodness." She clutched his hand. She could hardly speak. "What could have happened to me…." Tears filled her eyes. "Oh my goodness." She buried her face in his shoulder.

"Honey – what is it?" he asked, holding her close.

"Rob…." She looked up, struggling with her thoughts. "Rob, Mom had other children. Two children." He looked at her with surprise. "She called it, babies that she gave up. Gave up to get ahead."

"Gave up? Like, for adoption?"

She dried her eyes on his sleeve, regaining her composure. "No, she called it '*termination*'. Abortion. The first time, she was in high school and it seemed like the smartest thing for her to do. She was determined to go to college and make something of herself. A baby would have ruined all that. She was three or four months' pregnant. She said it was easy, she was glad she had done it."

"I agree with her. At three months the baby's pretty small. I can't agree with aborting a baby that's viable, but at three or four months, why not?"

"That's what she said. And again, in college. It was not a big deal. Then, when she gave birth to me….it hit her, what she had done, she had killed her babies." She shuddered. "It was terrible for her. She says she'll never have peace of mind about it. The only way she can deal with it is to block it out of her mind. We only talked about it once, when I was in high school and she didn't want me to go down that road. I've never heard her mention it since."

"Gosh, that's pretty…..upsetting. I didn't think abortion would affect a woman that way. It must have been very hard on your mom and dad, with everything else they were going through, trying to adjust –" He stopped as her words suddenly registered with him. "Oh….now I know what you're saying."

He held her hands, shaking his head. "Since it didn't bother her before....she might have aborted you! Because you were inconvenient.

"Yes, that's it." She dropped her head. "But it's all '*if, if.*' In fact," she pondered, "It makes me wonder why she didn't.... didn't abort me."

"Oh, baby, baby," he crooned, holding her close. "I'm so glad your parents made the decisions they did....with each other. Because you are the result."

"Yes, oh, yes! Rob, don't ever say anything to her, please."

"You know I wouldn't."

"That's really a big reason why I said no, why I wanted to save myself for marriage. I never wanted to have to choose between having a baby and getting an education. I didn't want to juggle both, either, even though many girls do. I wanted to grow up, get an education, and then get married, make babies. In that order. Honey, I have no regrets."

"You never told me." He shook his head.

"I couldn't. It was my mother's secret. But now that we're becoming one, I think it's okay. Anyway, after that talk with my mom I went to my dad and asked him if he'd had any other children that I didn't know about. I was pretty smart-mouthed."

"You were curious – but I wonder he didn't give you a swat!"

"Ha, ha. He said he didn't think so. I thought that was the dumbest answer! I didn't know any better. Now I do, of course."

"I hope so," he nodded jokingly.

"I think the important thing is, who my parents are today. They're great people and I admire them. They're willing to admit they made mistakes. Yes, and they want me to do better."

"We are....but they laid the foundation. Now it's up to us. And God." He kissed her. "This is a promise," he said, "of more to come. By the way, did I pass the test?"

"I think so," she teased. "But it wasn't a test. Just a little.... um, discussion after our counseling. With more to come."

"Do you really think we need more? More counseling? Don't get me wrong, I enjoyed it today and I got a lot out of it, but I think we're as well-suited for marriage as any couple and better than most."

"Well, he won't marry us without it. So....keep an open mind. Who knows, you might even learn something."

"I might. We'll have to see."

"Are you meeting your friends again tonight, for Bible study?" Gramps asked as they prepared to say goodbye after a Friday afternoon visit.

"Bryan and Natasha? No, I don't think they're ready for it," Rob answered. "But the main reason is, they've split up."

"Oh?" he replied with a lift of his eyebrows.

"He's graduating, going to Harvard Law School and he said he's '*cutting her loose*' so she can find someone to marry, since that's what she wants," he explained.

"They had a big fight," Aimee continued.

"It seems he'd planned all along to drop her when he graduated. He thought he had everything under control. He didn't expect a nasty breakup, and he blames us because Natasha didn't handle it well."

"He blames you?" Gramps asked.

"Yes," replied Aimee, "she saw that we really love each other, not in a starry-eyed way, I think we're beyond that –"

"Oh?" Gramps interjected, smiling.

"She saw that we care about each other, we try to please each other – and their relationship is nothing like that. So she took it out on Bryan."

"I'd say that breakup is a good thing," Gramps concluded. "Although I hate to see anyone hurt."

After Bible study Rob and Aimee were enjoying a restaurant meal together.

"That was good of you to share the blame, when we were talking to Gramps," Aimee told Rob. "Bryan didn't blame us. Natasha said he blamed me."

"That's okay," he shrugged. "That's Bryan being stupid. He didn't want to blame Natasha so he blamed you. He didn't want to blame me because we're old friends."

"Well, that is stupid. Sounds like he's done that before, hey? But why would he break up with Natasha? She never expected it." Aimee and Natasha had had lunch together a couple of days earlier. "She fully expected to go to Boston with him and transfer her credits."

"She shouldn't have. Bryan never promised her anything. He says he never led her on. He never told her he loved her." *Hmm*, he thought.... *he told me he 'gave her love'. Is there a difference?*

"But they were crazy about each other! You told me that. Of course...." she reflected, "what I saw is that he's crazy about himself, but she kept hoping he would fall in love with her. I think that's why she felt bad when she got to know us. Did you know he was her first love?"

"Uh, no. She never said, not to me. Her first boyfriend?"

"No, she'd had other boyfriends. But she loved Bryan. She gave herself to him, I mean, she gave her virginity to him. I think that's why she's so hurt now."

"I can see why. She'd be really disappointed. Listen, I don't want to see her hurt. But I don't blame him."

She frowned. "Well, I sure do. Why are you sticking up for him?"

"He never promised her anything. No, honey, he didn't," he argued. "He told me he '*gave her love*', but he never told her he loved her." He thought about it. "I think it wasn't love that he gave her. It was....mutual convenience."

"That's all it was! But Rob, she gave up a lot. Her friends, because she devoted herself to him. And that old story, she gave up a baby. He insisted."

"Gave up? You mean terminated?"

"Don't be shocked. It happens all the time. I said a terrible thing to her. I said, '*at least you're not a single mother*.' I should have known better, me, of all people! I was sorry the moment I said it. She broke down, she said she'd rather have had her baby, even though Bryan would have been a terrible father, he's so selfish –"

"Oh, Aimee. That's too bad...." He stopped and considered what he was hearing. "Honey, I thought I knew Bryan. Now I'm not so sure. But I still say, she went into it with her eyes wide open. He never said he loved her, he never promised her anything. Why did she expect him to love her?"

"You don't understand. Women want love. They'll do anything to get it, sad to say."

"Except wait for it! As you did." He nodded with satisfaction.

"Yes, yes, that's right. I feel so vindicated! I know I did the right thing. I got you," she smiled possessively.

"I'm glad you did! It takes a strong woman, to wait, stick with your convictions. In spite of me," he laughed. "That's the only kind I want." He looked at her with love. "My sweet Aimee." He frowned. "Honey...." For a moment he was silent, then he spoke resolutely.

"I'm thinking about Bryan. I can't have him as my best man." He shook his head. "No. Not after the way he talked about you."

"No, Rob, thank you, but I'm a big girl. I can handle it. He's your friend."

"Is he? I don't think so. Not anymore. He disrespected you. And....I think he was using Natasha. I see that now. He and I –" he struggled with the words – "well, this is the end."

"Oh, honey!" She took his hand sympathetically. "Are you really sure?" He nodded as she kissed his hand. "I'm sad for you. That's got to be rough. But....as for best man, what can you do about it now? It's too late to find another best man. Oh, maybe when he sees what real love is, he'll change...."

"No, honey, I don't want him. I've made up my mind. I don't know how to handle it, though. Call him, go see him, or what?"

"I don't know. It's got to be handled very carefully. You don't want to make a bad situation worse. Whatever, it's got to be soon."

"I know. I'll think about it. Your support," he told her, "it helps a lot. Now – how about happier things?" He reached across the table and took her by the chin. "Are you all ready for graduation? Just two weeks away! It's your special day. Your family is pretty excited. So am I!"

"Well.....it's going to be a long day for everyone but me. All I have to do is walk across the stage, that's it! For you – it'll be a long day, getting your mom so early, taking her back home and then coming to my house, four hours of driving...." She shook her head. "Hurry back, Mom has quite a party planned! Grandma and Grandpa Love can't wait to meet '*Aimee's young man*'. They're coming up from Florida later this week. And I can't wait for you to meet them! They're wonderful people."

"I can handle it. A long day, it's nothing. I'm looking forward to meeting your grandparents."

"You'll love them and they'll love you, I promise! Oh, I'm so glad your mother is coming to my graduation. Not just for me, but because she's your mother. That's important. She's your family and soon she'll be part of my family too."

"I'm still getting used to that," he replied with a shake of his head. "Getting along with her."

"Are you worried about her meeting my parents, honey?" He shrugged his shoulders. "Don't be. They'll do fine together, I'm sure of it. Now, look here, this is your day too! Enjoy, get to know my family! You'll be the center of attention. Not me."

" '*The center of attention? Enjoy?*' I don't know about that," he replied as he thought of meeting her extended family which thankfully for him, was not large. "Is anybody good enough for their Aimee?"

"No. Not just anybody. But you are! Just remember that. Mom and Dad approve of you, and that's what matters. Though it took Mom a little longer – oh, I shouldn't have said that! Rob, don't look so alarmed!"

Hurt, he replied, "Here I thought your Mom and I hit it off right away."

"Of course you did. Rob, everybody loves you. You're easy to love –"

"So, what was it?" he persisted.

She replied kindly, "Mom thought you were an angry young man. She was afraid I might get hurt by your anger….but honestly, I told her I'd never seen you lose your temper. So I don't know why she thought that –"

"Why would she think I would hurt you? I never would! And I'll tell her that!" he replied indignantly. He shook his head. "Never, Aimee. I would never hurt you."

"She says a man who is angry at his mother will be angry at his wife."

"I don't know about that. I suppose she has psychology to back her up?"

"Of course. You know Mom."

"Honey, I would never hurt you. No." He thought about it. "Well…she's right about one thing. I was angry, you know that. Angry at my mother. Angry at God, because the people in the world who loved me most were taken from me. I didn't know it until suddenly I realized….I wasn't angry any more. Now...I'm not."

"I can tell. That is amazing." She smiled warmly. "What made the change?"

"Hmm….I'm at peace with my mom. That's the biggest thing. I still have my moments, but I'm not angry any more. It used to be like an undercurrent, all the time."

"But why? Why are you at peace? Is it because you're a Christian?"

"I think it started with Gramps. He forced me to think. His love, it kind of rubbed off on me –"

"He's like that."

"You know what else? It was you."

"Me? How is that?"

"Yes. You….you helped me to heal. Grandma and Grandpa Ferguson," he explained. "I didn't realize how hurt I was. But –"

he shook his head, "I couldn't talk about them. Not to Gramps, not to anyone. I was afraid – if I did, I'd get mad. Or cry. So I kept it all locked up." He took her hand. "You made me unlock all those doors and go in all those rooms I didn't want to go into, and you didn't pity me."

"Rob, I'm so glad!" she replied gratefully, patting his hand. "I didn't know, I hoped I was doing the right thing."

He kissed her hand. "My darling Aimee. Thank you!"

"Do you think we got them all?" she asked tentatively. *What about his music?*

"Well – if there are any more –"

"We'll do it together," she replied. "Remember, I do love. Not pity."

"Ha, I remember. Oh, baby. I hope I can give you some of what you've given to me."

"Rob, you already have! You complete me. I am so much more because of you. I feel like I can do anything, anything, and you'll back me up."

"Absolutely. You could be President! I'd support you all the way."

"You're sweet. I just might do that," she smiled. "Well, I know, whatever my need, you'll always be there for me. That's what matters."

"Always, honey. But you're right, becoming a Christian, that made a difference. I felt peace. Do you remember that night in my apartment, when we broke our news to each other?"

She laughed. "I'll never forget it! That was so funny." She thought about it. "Yes, you said you were at peace about your grandparents' deaths. In fact," she reflected, "you used the word '*died*'. You never could before."

"You're right, I couldn't. I told you about what else happened that night after you left...."

"Yes, you wished you could tell your Grandma and Grandpa what had happened. You wanted to know that they were Christians, you didn't know."

"It was incredible," he laughed as he remembered. "Suddenly there was a voice inside me that said, *'Rob, they're with me. They're happy for you.'* That was neat."

"That's a good story. I'm just beginning to learn about God talking to us." She shook her head. "It still seems strange that He would bother with us, insignificant as we are and our insignificant little problems."

"Yeah. It's pretty amazing. I conclude that we're not insignificant to Him. He's God, and if every snowflake is different, I guess He can handle knowing each of us individually. Because He loves us."

She gave him a penetrating look. "You know, Rob, you are different. "Yes. I've seen a difference, you've begun to mellow out. You're.....light-hearted. And deeper."

He shook his head. "Whatever that means! Well, it's a good feeling. Honey, do you remember one of those old black and white movies we watched at your folks' house – they were singing about *'old time religion'*?"

"Mmm....I'm not sure." They enjoyed the old movies, a *'slice of history'*, she called them.

"Something about, *'that old time religion, makes me love everybody'*, he went on. "When I heard that I thought, that's crazy, how can that be?"

"Oh, I remember! There was a line about *'it was good for Grandma and Grandpa'*, wasn't there?"

"Yes, there was. Well, now, I understand. It really is true."

"Yes, it is. So, Rob – do you love your mom?"

"I think I do. But I'm not ready to forgive her."

"If you love her, why can't you forgive her?"

"She's going to have to prove herself a lot more before I can forgive her."

"I see your point. But at least, you're not angry at her anymore."

"No....I'm past that. It's a good feeling. By the way, you can tell your mom she doesn't have to worry about me."

"Oh, honey, she knows that by now."

Chapter 30

Lenore looked over at the clock and forced herself to wake up. *7:45.... I've got to call Rob before he leaves to come here*, she thought. *I don't want to make him turn around on the road. I have to call him! I can't go to Aimee's graduation. I can't do it*. She put his number in her phone.

"Hello, Rob."

"Mom! Are you all right? Will you be ready? I'll be there in a little over an hour."

"Well....that's why I'm calling," she said nervously. "I can't make it. I mean, I'm not going."

"What's wrong?" he asked with concern. "Are you sick?"

"No, no. It's hard to explain, but...I....I can't do it."

"You what?"

"I....I....I just can't face all those people. Strangers."

"Mom, no! You can't do that!" he replied, disbelieving. "Aimee is looking forward to you being there. It means a lot to her! And to me, too, I might add."

"I know, I know. Rob, I just can't do it. You'll have to tell her how sorry I am. I'd better go now," she said hurriedly. "Goodbye." *There*, she thought as she hung up, *I did it. My counselor said if I really couldn't do it I should stay home, though I know she wanted me to go. Well, I failed her and I failed Aimee.*

And Rob. Oh….telling Rob was almost as hard as going. But I didn't even tell him the real reason!

Slowly she started to move around and fix herself a cup of coffee. Her phone rang. "Rose? Oh, hello –"

"Lenore, what is going on? I got a very distressed call from Aimee. She doesn't know what's going on. Lenore, you can't let that girl down."

"Oh…Rose, we talked about it. You know how I feel about meeting strangers. Rose – I'm not good enough for them. Not Aimee's people."

"Lenore, Lenore. Everybody feels that way sometime," she said consolingly. "But just remember one thing, it's not about you. And, you can do everything through Christ who gives you strength. Well, that's two things. Lenore, you can give Rob a call right now. I'll bet he could still get there in time for the graduation. He won't have any time to spare but you could ask him. And you'll have an hour to get yourself ready."

"No, no, I told you, I can't," she insisted.

"Now listen, Lenore," she replied firmly. "You're saying that to the wrong person. I don't accept that. I've been down that road myself. Forget about yourself and concentrate on Aimee. And Rob. Think of what they've done for you."

"Oh, oh, oh…." She struggled within herself. "Well….I don't know. I know it's not about me – but it's hard….."

"I didn't say it would be easy. But you can do it. Listen, Lenore, if they like you, fine. I think they will. Remember, you don't have to tell your life story. You know what to say. If they don't like you, so what? You won't die. It's not about you."

"I guess so…. that helps." She took a deep breath. "Okay… .I'll do it. I'll call Rob."

"Good! Do it. He sounds like such a nice young man – and he's your son! Go ahead, call him. Do it now, before you change your mind."

"All right."

"I'm sure he'll be glad to come pick you up. I'll be praying for you."

"Thanks, Rose." She hung up the phone and sighed deeply.

What's going on with Mom, Rob wondered with irritation. *I'm glad I don't have to drive all the way out there and back but – she let Aimee down! Didn't she know it's an honor to be invited to her graduation? Aimee went out of her way to get her ticket! 'Can't face people'? How did she manage to go to church?*

His phone rang. It was Mom.

"Rob," she spoke rapidly, "listen, do you think you can still come and get me?"

"Mom – do you know what time it is?" He struggled to control his anger.

"Of course I do. It's almost 8:30. We can make it."

"Well, I had planned for us to get to the arena by 10:00. Now it will be 10:30 or later! We won't find any parking nearby. We'll barely make it." *I should just tell her no!* he thought angrily. *But....Aimee wants her there*. He sighed, "Yeah, I'll leave right away. Just be ready when I get there, okay? I'll beep for you."

"Oh, thank you! I'll be ready. I promise –"

He hung up feeling disgusted and angry at the whole situation. *First she can't go, now she can. I hated to call Aimee and tell her....Did Aimee call Mom, or did she get Rose to call her? I don't know and I don't care*. He started up the car. To put himself in a better mood he put on his favorite music and by the time he arrived his mood had softened a little.

Even so, there was an edge to his voice when he greeted his mother. "Just get in, Mom, quickly! We've no time to lose."

A thought, a voice inside him said, '*Cool it, Rob, she's doing the best she can.*' It had the force of a whack on his behind. *No, no, no,* he resisted. Again, '*Cool it*'. *Oh....all right,* he agreed reluctantly. Making an effort, he turned to Lenore. "Sorry I snapped at you, Mom. I'm glad you changed your mind." He could hardly believe what he had said, and that he meant it. He managed a slight smile.

"Honestly, Rob, I'm very sorry to do this to you," she responded in a contrite tone. She was quiet for a minute, then, "I'll try to explain what happened this morning."

"Okay." *Might as well give her a chance.*

"Rob, it's hard, I mean really hard, for me to meet new people. The only way I've been able to is with my, uh, liquid courage. If you know what I mean."

"Okay. I get it. But how did you manage to go to church and meet strangers?"

"I had Rose beside me. She was my courage. And the funny thing is, after the first couple of weeks I felt so comfortable there I didn't need Rose at all."

"I know what you're talking about, I do. I'll tell you later. But...." he shook his head, perplexed. "I don't understand, wasn't it hard for you to meet Gramps? Of all people! I didn't smell any alcohol that day."

"Little did you know," she said with an embarrassed laugh, "I was well reinforced. And I had a lot of breath mints. But.... look Rob, I'm trying to be honest here." She took a deep breath. "I have to tell you the whole story, about today."

"There's more?" He looked at her, raising an eyebrow.

"Yes," she sighed. "When you have a past, like I do, I mean, I've done things I shouldn't have done – I feel like it's written on my forehead, everyone knows it. Nice people, like Aimee's family will look down on me. So, rather than have them reject me, I reject them first."

"I've heard of that." *Psych 101*, he thought.

"Then I don't get hurt. Of course, if I have something to drink, that loosens me up and I don't obsess over it so much. I can face people a lot better. But I don't want to do that anymore."

"That makes sense." He thought about it. "Maybe I don't have *'a past',*" he told her, "but I know what it's like to worry about what other people think of me. Worry they'll reject me."

Hadn't I always felt that way about girls? Until Aimee, that is. "Believe it or not, lots of people feel like you do. I've had to learn to forget it, tell myself I won't die. That helps."

She laughed at that, and he was glad to see her relax. "Mom, I honestly don't think they'll reject you. But if it helps, I'll stay with you as much as I can."

"You would? I wanted to ask you, but I was afraid. So – would you stay with me?"

"Sure, as much as I can." *If this isn't the strangest thing*, he thought. *I feel like I'm the parent here! Maybe that's the way it has to be. I guess she doesn't have a clue how to be a mother…. or how to be an adult*. He felt ashamed of that last thought. *That doesn't help. I shouldn't expect anything of her. Didn't Gramps say to take her as she is?* He pondered…*As far as a 'real mom' is concerned, in one visit with Marie I felt she was a real honest-to-goodness mom to me! Now, what's a 'real mom', anyway?*

"Mom, Aimee and I have some good news to tell you."

"I'll bet I know. Aimee told me that you had become a Christian too. I'm so glad!"

"Well, you certainly helped her. I'm glad for that." This opened a new door of conversation to them and the time went by quickly. But as they approached the arena it was just as Rob had feared. Parking lots were full. They finally secured a spot about three blocks away. Laughing about it they made a mad dash to the arena, locating their seats with Aimee's family in the upper decks just as the ceremony was getting underway. He was amazed that it didn't bother him.

After a tedious ceremony brightened only by Rob catching a glimpse of Aimee as she walked across the stage, they all made their way downstairs to wait for her. Rob had introduced Lenore to Roger and Elaine and the grandparents, who he'd met the day before. They welcomed her warmly but suddenly they were preoccupied with one another. He winked at his mother and shrugged his shoulders.

"I'm fine," she told him.

Then Aimee danced over to them, throwing her arms around her family, Lenore, and lastly, Rob, who didn't want to let her go.

"You're the first one with the advanced degree! I have to live up to that…." He kissed her. "I'm so proud of you, baby…."

he whispered in her ear. “Now, Mom and I are going to get Gramps.” He had declined Aimee’s invitation to attend the graduation. That and the restaurant meal would be too much and the meal won out. He gave Aimee one last kiss. “See you at the restaurant.”

As he and his mother were heading towards the exit to go to his car he spotted Bryan in his cap and gown walking alone in his direction.

Uh, oh, he thought. *This is not a good time to talk with him.... but I might not get another chance.*

“Hey, Bry,” he said, extending his hand. Quietly he asked his mother to wait for him outside at the nearby exit.

They shook hands. “Congratulations! You came out on top, man.”

“Thanks, Rob.” He smiled with pleasure. “I had to live up to your example, you know.”

“Thanks.” *I wonder if I can go through with this*, he thought uneasily. “Hey – you got five minutes?”

“Just barely. It’s graduation, you know.”

“So I noticed. Bryan, I want to talk to you about Aimee.”

He frowned. “What’s going on with her?”

“Look....I know you were pretty upset at her. You thought she caused you to break up with Natasha. You said some pretty rude things. I want to stick up for her. She never intended to interfere with you two, she would never do that, I know her –”

“Then she sure did a good job without intending to!” His tone was cold. “And you got it wrong, Rob. I had already intended to break up with Natasha. A nice clean break. A few tears, a goodbye kiss, and it’s all over. Now, thanks to Aimee, I’ve got drama and a spittin’ female on my hands. She wants to know why I‘m not taking her with me, why I don‘t love her – it’s crazy!”

“I’m sorry to hear that. But why do you think Aimee is responsible?”

“Everything was fine until Aimee came along. She put ideas in her head. Natasha was a happy little chick –”

“If she was so happy, why did you want to break up with her?”

"Look, Rob, I never intended it to last. She was fine for the duration, but could you see her as a lawyer's wife? No, no way. I was going to cut her loose as a favor to her, so she could find somebody else."

"Sounds like a favor to you. It seems to me, if you love her you take her with you."

"Who said anything about love? I never did. Giving her love isn't like being in love with her."

"No....I guess not. But it sure builds up an expectation."

"C'mon, Rob. This is stupid, a waste of time. The fact is, my graduation is ruined, thank you Aimee. Natasha made a scene with my mom and dad, they don't understand, and it's none of their business anyway. I can't wait to get on a plane and get to Boston and start a new life. But hey...." he shrugged, "I'm not blaming you. It's not your fault. I'll be back for your wedding."

"The least you can do is take back what you said about Aimee."

"Excuse me?" he frowned. "What was that?"

"I'm giving you a chance. She's not to blame. Listen, when you disrespect her you disrespect me. She's the woman I love."

"Rob, that's crap. You know how I feel about Aimee. She hasn't helped you any."

"If you feel that way, I can't have you as my best man. Not if you're going to disrespect my wife."

"What! You mean you would break up our friendship over a female? How petty is that?" He looked at Rob, disbelieving. "Fine! That's fine with me. Now I don't have to fly back."

"Bryan – we can still be friends –" He held out his hand.

"Have a nice life, Rob." He spat on the ground. "You and Aimee. You deserve each other." He turned and walked away.

Rob stood there, frozen, Bryan's words echoing in his head. '*Break up our friendship over a female*?' *That's not just any female, that's Aimee he's talking about!* He wanted to punch Bryan, he wanted to punch the wall; instead, swearing, he punched his hand again and again.

Okay, okay, he thought. *I've got to move on. I've got to get Gramps.*

In a daze he made his way to the exit where he found his mother finishing her cigarette. He couldn't speak.

"Rob, are you all right?" She shook her head. "You don't look so good."

"Let's just go." They started walking towards the car.

He signaled her that he didn't want to talk. In the half hour drive to Sunset Woods he was thankful she didn't annoy him with questions as he tried to think things through. *I had wanted to disinvite Bryan – did I think it would turn out well? Why should I? Bryan has been pretty cold lately. Even so – it hurts. It hurts.*

Gramps was waiting on the portico, his face beaming. "It's a great day, isn't it?" Rob didn't answer. "Rob, what is it? What's wrong? You look like you lost your last friend!"

"Not my last friend. My best friend. Bryan." His lips tightened. "I just disinvited him as my best man." He shook his head. "It didn't go well."

"Come over here," he gestured to a bench, "tell me about it."

"My mom's in the car –"

"She won't mind waiting. Now – what happened?" Rob signaled to his mother to wait.

"Bryan – he's been nasty about Aimee. All along. Never to her face, but to me. I gave him a chance to take it back, he wouldn't, so I told him I didn't want him as my best man."

"You did the right thing. You want a best man who will support both of you. You were right to stick up for Aimee," he said approvingly.

"I know. It's still –" He couldn't go on.

"Oh, my boy, my boy." He seized Rob's hands. "I am so sorry."

Rob, seeing tears in Gramps' eyes, was comforted.

"Now, you can't rain on Aimee's parade." Rob nodded his head. "It won't be easy, but don't say anything to her. There will be plenty of time tomorrow to tell her. I wouldn't do it today. You've got to put on a happy face."

"I can do it. I've done it before. Though it might be a little harder with Aimee...."

"Good boy. You'll be in my prayers. Now – let's go join the others."

Gramps and Lenore greeted each other warmly. It was the first they had seen each other since their momentous introduction months ago. Rob forced himself to talk with them and he began to feel a little better.

Aimee placed Lenore beside her mother and father, then she and Rob joined her grandparents, with Gramps between them. "They're kindred spirits, I want them to get to know each other," she told Rob.

A couple of hours later Gramps was ready to go back and Rob was ready to take his mother home. It had already been a long day. He would then join Aimee and her family at the family party.

Although thoughts of his encounter with Bryan lingered, he managed a light-hearted manner as he dropped Gramps off and then drove his mother home.

"Mom, you and Elaine Love sure seemed to hit it off. The two of you were laughing it up!"

"You know, I don't think I needed you at all. But thanks for being willing. And you know what? I really like Aimee's mother. Let me tell you what happened."

Rob hadn't expected any problems but he was interested in hearing his mother's account.

"I thought she knew all about me, from Aimee. So I expected the worst. But I guess she didn't know much. She asked me how I was doing in my new place. I almost panicked! If I told her the real reason I was there, I was sure she'd look down on me. But I couldn't tell her just half the story. Then I remembered what Rose told me. I said, '*This is a special apartment for women who are trying to get back on their feet. I used to have a problem with alcohol but now I'm getting my life back together.*' That was all I said."

"Wow, that's really blunt."

"As Rose says, you learn right away where you stand. If they can't handle it, that's their problem, it won't kill me. Elaine was just fine. She said Aimee had told her a little bit. Then she told me about her mother. She'd had a drinking problem, did you know that? After that we got along like we'd always known each other. I liked her."

"You amaze me. That's really great. You know, I'd like to meet Rose someday. She sounds like quite a lady."

"You probably will. Someday." With that she settled back and went to sleep for the rest of the trip.

"Where are you taking me?" Rob asked as Aimee seized him by the arm. "Oh, ho! A nice private living room!" The graduation party was in full swing in the back of the house and the yard. "I've been waiting for this all day!" he exclaimed, taking her in his arms.

"Mmm….so have I…." she replied as she returned his affection, then, extricating herself from his embrace she gave him a good-faith kiss. "No more," she said. "This is about you," she said with concern. "Honey, what happened? What's wrong? I've felt it all day." She seated him beside her on the couch and took his hands.

He shook his head and gave a little laugh. "Nothing. Nothing's wrong. I'm fine."

" '*Fine?*' You can't fool me. What happened with your mother? Something must have gone terribly wrong! Cancelling you this morning – why did she have to mess with you that way? I'm glad she made it, but honey, it's tearing you apart!"

"Oh, baby. I feel better already, just being with you. It's not Mom. That went really great, I can't wait to tell you, but I'll do it tomorrow. It's –" he heaved a sigh. "It's Bryan. I saw him, after graduation. I disinvited him." Aimee looked at him sharply. "It was ugly." He told her of their encounter.

"Ohh….he doesn't deserve you! But darling, I feel so bad for you. Losing your friend." She held him close.

"It was overdue."

"Yes, I guess so. But, the final break – it's hard. It hurts." She took his face in her hands. "Thank you for sticking up for me. It means a lot. Not everyone would do that."

"Well, of course," he replied, kissing her.

"Rob, if I'm wrong I'll admit it. But I don't think I did anything. I think he's a user. He used Natasha. He didn't want to take responsibility for the consequences. So – who will you have as your best man?"

"I haven't thought that far ahead."

"Well! What about..."

"No, this is my problem. I can see the wheels going around in your head! I'll deal with it, I'll let you know."

"You're right. Now – are you feeling better? We need to get back."

"Another kiss should do it."

The next day they were driving from church to join her family for brunch.

"Rob, I've been dying to ask what happened yesterday with your mother."

"Well, I had a very strange experience when I went to pick her up." She gave him a curious look. "You were asking how God speaks to people today."

"Yes. I mean, it's still hard to grasp."

"By the time I got there I was pretty steamed. I knew we were cutting it close and we'd probably be late. You know how I hate being late. And she didn't seem to understand, or even care." Aimee nodded in agreement. "Then, out of nowhere a thought popped into my head. Tell me what you think." He told about the message to '*cool it*' and how he had struggled to obey it. "It sure had an impact on me! It totally changed my day. And my mother's too, I'm sure." He told about their conversations in the car.

"I hate to say it but I know it didn't come from you," she said with a laugh. "It had to be God!" She shook her head, wonderingly. "That is so amazing. God getting involved with us…..I'll have to think about it."

"I know. It amazes me too." He squeezed her hand.

"Rob, do you think God would say '*cool it'?"*

"Why not? I think He would do whatever it takes. Anyway, it worked."

"It got your attention! I'll have to remember that," she said with a sly smile.

Chapter 31

"Honey, look!" Aimee showed Rob what she had been researching online. "Scholarship information, for sons and daughters of Marines killed in the line of duty. A new program. I didn't think you qualified for anything since your Dad died so long ago, but it looks like you are eligible."

"Let me see...." He skimmed through the material. "Wow.... that's fantastic! I should apply. Let's see what else I can find. I wonder if there are grants for med students who work in impoverished settings....wait wait.....look, I'm finding stuff. We'll have to check it out. You know what this means? If this comes through....."

"Yeah, you could stretch out your inheritance a little longer. I know you don't want a mountain of debt. I'm going to find the application for the Marine scholarship."

"No, I meant, are you willing to locate somewhere else? Anywhere in the world?"

"Um, I don't know. You know me, I'm always ready for adventure, but I wouldn't want to be too far from my family."

He frowned. "Is this going to be a problem in our marriage?"

"No, no," she laughed, "I'm independent, you know that. I'm my own person. Those apron strings are cut...."

"Then what are you talking about?"

"I'm close to my family. You know that. I'm willing to move out of town but I wouldn't want to move halfway around the world. Even though my parents did," she reflected. "I just – I don't think I could do it. What about you?"

"It's complicated. I always thought I could go anywhere, you know, *Doctors without Borders* or something like that, but now that I've got Gramps, well, he means so much to me, it would be hard to leave him." He stopped and thought for a moment. "I'd have to be really sure God was leading. Missionary work, maybe, or some special program. If I was sure of that, I'd go. I know that's what Gramps would want." He looked at her and laughed, "What am I saying? It's not 'I' anymore. It's us. We're in this together."

"Honey, I'm not quite there yet. Be patient with me."

"I'm not worried about you," he assured her.

"Maybe you should be. What if I didn't want to leave my dog?"

On a bright afternoon the following Friday Rob and Aimee picked up Gramps for a picnic in the park. Rob lifted him out of the car and into one of the camp chairs they had brought from Aimee's house. Grendel sprang out of the car and began running in circles. "Thank you!" Gramps exclaimed with pleasure. "It sure is good to be away from that contraption for a while." He gestured to the wheel chair.

"But wheels help," Rob replied. "I promise we won't go off and leave you."

"Glad to hear it," he joked. "Say, Aimee – will you hand me that stick over there?"

As she handed him a stick he wound up his throwing arm, then sent the stick sailing out over the grass. Grendel went flying after it and in a moment was back, dropping it in his lap.

"Gramps, that's quite a throw. Bet you played a little baseball back in the day, huh?" Rob asked.

"Yes – guess I haven't lost my touch. Okay, boy, here's another!" Thus ensued a non-stop game of fetch that ended only when Aimee and Rob pleaded with Gramps to stop and eat.

"Gramps, I think you look ten years younger!" marveled Aimee as they were eating their meal. "We need to do this again."

"Well, if I come four or five more times, with Grendel, of course," he nodded with satisfaction, "I'd be back in my childhood for sure. I say, let's do it."

"We'll see to it," promised Rob. "It may not be until we're married...."

"But we will," Aimee hugged him. "As soon as we can." She turned to Rob, "Honey, what does this park mean to you?"

"Oh – is this a test?" he asked innocently.

"My boy," remarked Gramps, "women like to remember things. It helps if you remember the same things."

"Hmm, I don't know," he answered with a puzzled tone. "Let me think. Um....I guess it's where the most beautiful and wonderful girl on the planet said '*yes*' to me –"

Aimee smiled and hugged him.

"You passed the test," Gramps said with a wink.

"Okay, Aimee. Your turn. What does this park mean to you?" Rob asked.

"Oh, Gramps – would you believe red roses blooming in the snow? And a diamond hiding in the blooms?"

He laughed. He had heard the story before.

"So it's the diamond, is it?" Rob teased. "I guess I know where I stand."

"But – what I remember best is the guy who put the diamond on my finger."

"Mmm....good answer...." He reached over and kissed her.

"Touche!" concluded Gramps. "I guess you both passed the test. You know," he reflected, "this is the perfect time to tell you a story. If you'd like."

Their interest was piqued. "A personal story?" asked Rob.

"A story about your father." They drew their chairs closer to him. "I've been wanting to tell you, we just haven't had time."

"Go ahead," invited Rob.

"You'll like this one. It's a good story. I think you're ready for it." He stopped to collect his thoughts. "I guess I'll begin when your father came back from California for a couple of weeks before he was deployed. He sat us down, his mother and I, and told us his feelings when he decided to join the Marines." He stopped, a faraway look in his eyes. Finally Rob tapped him on the shoulder.

"So, what did he say?"

"Oh? Oh, yes. He realized he might give his life. He had thought seriously about life and death, and he was scared. He had taken a Bible with him. My parents had given it to him. He read it some, but it didn't mean anything until he started attending church out in California. He told us he had given his life to Christ," Gramps said with a smile. "He said it was the most important thing he had ever done."

"Wow, my father.....a Christian!" He took hold of Gramps' hand. "That's...." he struggled for words, "that's unbelievable – I had no idea. It's wonderful!"

"I didn't see it that way," Gramps said with a frown. "Just like his decision to join the Marines, this religious decision went against everything I believed. Your grandma and I were, you might say, professional doubters. We doubted everything people believed in, especially organized religion."

"Oh," sighed Aimee. "What happened then?"

"I'm happy to say I'd learned my lesson! This time I realized he didn't have to agree with me. Our relationship was more important. I mean, I still disagreed with everything he said, especially when he started quoting the Bible. But I kept quiet, I let him talk, I didn't argue with him – your grandma was proud of me! I told him, '*Allen, I might not agree with you but I love you. That's all that matters.*' "

Aimee and Rob listened attentively. She took Rob's hand.

"He was still very concerned about you, Rob. Actually – did I tell you this? He didn't even know your name! All he knew, through the grapevine, was that your mother had given birth to a son. And she was with some man. He was angry at that, and he said he was praying that he would find you. He was convinced God would bring you two together. *Don't get your hopes up,* I thought. He said he prayed for you every day. He prayed for your life, and the kind of person you would grow up to be."

"Oh," Rob buried his face in his hands. "My dad, my dad! Praying for me. I never knew...."

"He also said he was praying for us, his parents. I thought, *what the heck? It doesn't mean anything*."

"What a wonderful story," marveled Aimee. "His prayers echoed down through the years. They've been answered in such wonderful ways! But...." she gave him a quizzical look, "it didn't happen right away, did it?"

"No." He shook his head. "It wasn't a smooth road. It got bad very quickly. He was killed! This God he loved, took him away from us! And his prayer to find you? It was never answered. I was angry at God, so angry!" He shook his head, re-living it. "Then Kate was diagnosed with ovarian cancer. I demanded that God heal her. Kate made it worse – she gave her life to Christ! '*All right*', I said bitterly, '*I suppose you're going to take her too*.' Which is exactly what happened."

Rob and Aimee listened through their tears. Gramps was smiling. "Yes, you know the rest of the story. I dropped out of life. Almost overnight I became an alcoholic. It got so bad, I was ready to take my life. I had it all planned. But then –" he smiled through his tears – "in desperation I called out to God. To Christ, who I had known as a child. Christ, who had come into Allen's life."

"And my father's prayers were answered! Gramps.....that is so amazing."

"I wonder...." Aimee stopped to consider. "I wonder if that's why you and Rob found each other," she asked Gramps. "Because of his father's prayers."

"I think prayer is responsible for more good things than we ever dream of," Gramps replied, smiling.

Joyfully, tearfully, they contemplated Gramps' words. Then spontaneously they put their hands together and joined in praise and prayer to the God who had brought all this about.

"Wow," Rob whispered, "This is awesome."

"God is," said Gramps. "God is awesome."

'*The Bryan situation.*' Thoughts of him kept intruding, haunting his happiness. *Why can't I just put him out of my mind, once and for all?* He couldn't get past it. There was a knife in his heart. Aimee said he was grieving. *I don't want to grieve*, he thought, *I want to be happy, my wedding is only weeks away.*

He remembered Bryan's prediction, that Aimee would bring him misery. *No,* he thought, *that's not what happened. The misery is Bryan's. But I don't feel good about it.*

What hurts most, besides losing a friendship of almost twelve years, is that Bryan didn't think it was any big deal to blame Aimee, rather than look in the mirror and take responsibility for his actions. Then, he expected us to still be best friends! Is that the Bryan I always knew? I didn't notice any change in him until Aimee came along, but she didn't do a thing. It was his reaction to her. Aimee says I was in denial. She knows about those things; that's what comes from having a mother who's a psychiatric nurse. The apple didn't fall very far from that tree.

So now – who will replace him? I'm not one of those guys with tons of friends – though I need to be more friendly. I guess I just dropped out of life after Grandma and Grandpa died, and now I've been focused on Aimee. There are guys at the church and at school I'd like to know better, but now I don't know who to turn to. We had decided on close friends and family for our wedding party, that was all. It was easy, Bryan, first and always. Then Jason, my soon-to-be brother in law. And Matt Brannigan from next door. He was like a big brother. Gosh, it'll be good to see him again, he'll be driving in with his wife and kids. I can't wait for them to get to know Aimee. So now – who else?

No other old buddies left. Kyle and Ben? Ha, I don't even know where they are.

Matt. Why not Matt? Well....he lives so far away and I need someone close at hand to help me. That's what a best man is for. We're not close anymore.... though I know we'd pick right back up when we see each other again. I just don't think he's the one. But who is?

Am I missing something? It seems that way. I'll talk it over with Aimee tomorrow. Sometimes she has too many ideas! I want this to be my decision – but I need her perspective.

Oh, and I mustn't forget to tell her about Mark.

"Well, now, honey! Your text said you'd made your decision. Are you going to let me in on the secret?" They had just completed a Saturday morning run in the park.

"I guess I'd better. Your mother is getting worried."

"That too. So -?"

"Joel. Joel Greenberg."

"Joel? Oh, that's wonderful!" She nodded her head. "He's a perfect choice. In fact, I was sorry he wasn't in the wedding party. You two have become good friends over the past year at school."

"Yes, I spend more time studying with him than I ever spent with Bryan."

She stopped to reflect. "I thought you might choose Peter. We haven't known him and Ming very long but –"

"Remember, they're going to be away the weekend of our wedding. Actually, I thought of him first. We've gotten close, Peter and I. It's surprising because we've only know each other for a couple of months, but we have a lot in common. And they're doing this mentoring thing with us...."

She nodded her head. "I'm sorry they'll miss. That's disappointing."

"We can't exactly ask them to stay! Anyway, he was pleased I asked him. I told him about Joel. I thought he might not want to be in a Christian wedding because he's Jewish but Peter said, invite him anyway. He wouldn't be offended."

"So what happened?"

"Joel said he'd be honored."

"I'm so glad! I think he'll be a very loyal and helpful best man. And I'll be glad to see Marta again."

"Remember when you met them?"

"Oh, yes. It was at the faculty reception last Fall. I had a great time with them. And you too," she said, warmly.

"Well, I'll never forget that night. I'd never seen you all dressed up before – wow!"

"Now, Rob. I'll have you know I'm more than a pretty face," she said sternly.

"I'll say. You were drop-dead gorgeous!" He would never forget the admiration of the other guys who envied him his '*hot date*'. '*Oh, she's more than that*,' he had replied, smugly.

"I'm glad you noticed." She snuggled up to him.

"Aimee, I take you seriously, you know that. I want an equal partner. But I sure appreciate the packaging," he said with a provocative look.

"Rob!" she laughed. "I can admire too." She looked appreciatively at him.

"You're embarrassing me," he joked. "Well, getting back to Joel – We've had good times together – remember that night at their house? The four of us got along so well –"

"And with little Noah – yes, I've always felt very comfortable with him. And with Marta. Joel – I think he's the perfect choice. When we're married and have a place of our own –"

"Sounds wonderful, doesn't it..."

"...then we can have them over. Something else to look forward to. That is, as long as I'm not doing the cooking."

"Oh, we won't worry about that. Now, honey – I totally, completely forgot to tell you something." He looked worried.

"Is this serious?"

"I'm afraid so. Your mother might freak out." She looked at him with concern. "Honey, I was talking to Mark on Facebook a couple of weeks ago and I invited him to be in the wedding. As a groomsman. He said yes. He was real happy about it."

"Oh, Rob, Rob. Another groomsman." She thought for a minute, shaking her head. "I wish you'd told me....but...." she shook her head. "Let me deal with Mom. Right now any change is too much for her."

"I don't know how I forgot – well, yes I do. Your graduation, my Mom, Bryan, just wiped it out of my memory."

She was hardly listening. "We can take care of the tux and the flowers – but who will we pair him with?"

He looked puzzled. "We need a bridesmaid to pair him with," she explained. "Oh, of course – Heather! He can walk with his sister. We can do it!" She ignored him, thinking and talking to herself. Rob looked on, bemused.

"I must text Marie...."she said as she began texting, "I think she'll be pleased, and Heather will be so excited!" She stopped texting as a new thought struck her. "What will we do with Holly? I don't want to leave her out. Oh, I know, she can be in charge of those little bird seed packets they'll throw at us..."

"What? I didn't know a wedding could be dangerous!" he said with mock horror.

"Now, Rob, just don't open your mouth and you'll be okay." She smiled sweetly as she proceeded to text Marie. "You're not supposed to swallow the bird seed."

Moments later she was talking with Marie. "Oh, yes, yes! So the girls can do it? That's wonderful! The dresses are open stock, she can get one online...the girls will look so pretty, pastel dresses, fluttery sleeves....Thank you Marie...."

"Rob, don't worry about Mom, I can handle her....I'm glad you asked Mark. He's your brother! Ha, Marie didn't even know. He hadn't told her." She shook her head. "You men are all alike. Ah....he and Heather and Holly, this will be just perfect. Those girls will look so pretty."

"Well, I know the only girl I'll be looking at. She'll be all in white. Drop-dead gorgeous. I hope I don't miss her," he said with a worried look.

Aimee shook her head seriously. "You be sure to look."

"Rob was able to get out early today," Aimee told Gramps as they sat down together at a table in the garden the next week. "This gives us more time to visit, before Bible study tonight."

"That's fine with me," he replied. "I'm glad to have you." He looked at them and smiled. "What do you think about Bible study? It's been almost two months ...."

"It's strange," Aimee reflected. "I used to resist Rob's mom whenever she talked to me about the Bible. I was beginning to be insulted. Now, do you know I'm almost through reading the New Testament? There's a lot I don't understand, but what I do understand is....I don't know how to put it. Life-shaking."

He nodded in agreement. "That's a good way to put it. Keep it up."

"I'm with Aimee," Rob added, "though she's a little ahead of me in the reading. I like our Friday night studies. They stimulate my thinking."

"Peter and Ming O'Connor teach it," Aimee explained. "You haven't met them. I wish you could. We get along well, and Pastor Bruce linked them up with us as mentors."

"My goodness, I wish I'd had something like that when I became a Christian," Gramps reflected. "I'm only now beginning to understand the Bible, meeting with Pastor Bruce's class each week."

"Mom doesn't get it. I tried explaining it to her and she said, '*Why do you need someone to tell you what to believe?*' " I told her, *that's not it, what they do is help us learn how to live out our beliefs. They have a lot more experience than we do, of course."*

"I wonder if she's afraid you'll be indoctrinated," he suggested. "That's a legitimate fear."

"Gramps, we're smart enough not to get ourselves in some weird cult," Rob protested. "We know how to think for ourselves."

"I know that. But, this could be your mother's thinking," he nodded at Aimee. "This is all very new to her –"

"So, you're saying I should cut her some slack," Aimee concluded.

"Give her time."

"But that's not all. Mom said again that she's afraid I'm going to get hurt. The more I get involved, you know, attending every Sunday, it seems to worry her."

"Aimee, "he replied with a shake of his head, "you had better not get married."

"Well, you got my attention! What's the connection here?"

"You're bound to hurt each other, you and Rob. Maybe a little, maybe a lot. So then what? What do you do? Do you call it quits, give up on each other?"

"No, of course not," she replied thoughtfully. "We would face it. Work it out." Rob nodded and took her hand.

"Why would you? Many people don't."

"Because we love each other and we're committed to each other. Hmm. I see….." she nodded her head, "like church."

"You're trying to tell us that church is a relationship, and relationships take work," concluded Rob.

"Pretty good, Rob," said Gramps.

"This from the guy who told Pastor Bruce we didn't need pre-marital counseling because we have a perfect relationship!"

"That's not what I said," Rob corrected her. "I told him we're perfectly compatible, so I didn't think we needed pre-marital counseling."

"There's a difference?" asked Gramps with a laugh.

"He said he wouldn't marry us without it," continued Aimee. "And I backed down. So we've had a couple of sessions already."

"With an open mind, of course. Who knows, you might even learn something."

"That's a possibility," he replied with a laugh.

"Aimee," said Gramps, "I think your mother must have gotten really burned because of church."

"Yes, when she was growing up. It was something about the church turning against her, I think because of her mother."

"How tragic. What a chance those people missed, to show love! Your mom, being a child, wasn't going to stay around and be hurt. So, she's lived with that bad impression. The truth is, Aimee and Rob, you might meet up with hurtful people within the church, which is the last place it should happen. So –"

"We should stay with it, work it through?" asked Aimee.

"If you can. Sometimes all you can do is forgive," he answered.

"Ah, the '*church family*'," observed Rob. "Just like marriage, huh?" he rolled his eyes.

"Well, speaking of family, when will you be visiting Scott Carlyle and his family?"

"Next weekend, and I'm so looking forward to it!" she exclaimed. "They made me feel like part of their family."

"We wanted to go before Aimee gets all caught up with wedding preparations," explained Rob. "We're only five weeks away."

"It's on my calendar."

"You'd better not forget it," she teased. "It will be our first year anniversary, since we met."

"What a great year it's been for you, and me too. Getting to know you both. No – I wouldn't miss your wedding for the world." He stopped, deep in thought. "But, speaking of Scott, would you tell him something for me, Rob?"

"Sure."

"Well, since my son wasn't able to be a dad to you, I'm glad Scott was there in the beginning. When it was most important. He gave you a good start."

"I will. But you can tell him yourself, at the wedding."

"Oh, yes. I look forward to getting to know him."

"Gramps, look at the time. We need to be leaving." They hugged goodbye.

"Something puzzles me," Aimee asked Gramps when they were together a few days later. "You and Pastor Bruce have such a good relationship, yet you've never been to his church. Why is that? I hope you don't mind my asking," she added apologetically.

"Ah...." He shook his head. "I should, I want to, but I never got started. I guess I don't want anyone coming out here and having to bother with my chair. As far as I know, nobody in the church lives near me, so I content myself with the Bible study each week. I don't set a very good example, do I?"

"You don't know what you're missing," Rob told him.

"Rob's right," she agreed enthusiastically. "It's such a loving group of people! We had no idea when we started, but now, I look forward all week to going to church. The people, and the worship, the sermon –"

"Honey, I'm still surprised to hear you say that!" Rob laughed, putting his arm around her. "Gramps, maybe we would be able to pick you up. After we're married, that is."

"Well......we'll see what we can work out, after you're married. I'd like to get started, though I don't want to tie you down. You both are so busy, and soon Rob will be even busier –"

"Gramps, it's settled," Rob told him, taking his hand.

Chapter 32

"Gramps was right," Aimee told Rob as they were on the way to Carlyles' the next Friday afternoon. "This has been a great year. Incredible! Look at all the new people in your life. People who love you. Gramps, of course, the Carlyles, my family, and your mother –"

"Don't forget yourself! You still take my breath away," he said ardently. "I hope that never changes." He squeezed her hand. "We won't let it change! Now – I'm looking forward to talking with Scott and Marie, getting some of their thoughts about marriage…."

"Oh, yes," she agreed, "they're pretty romantic, for an older couple."

"Right. Hey, I'll be glad to see Mark again."

"Yes, aren't you glad you're communicating on Facebook? Now that you've entered the 21st century."

"Not much, I don't have time. "But –" he shook his head, "he doesn't want to talk about Mom. That's off limits. So it's just casual stuff."

"That's too bad. I think he needs some words of wisdom from his big brother."

"Oh, no, no. Not this time."

The weekend with Carlyles seemed to pass even more quickly than their previous visit. There was so much more to talk about. Scott and Marie were pleased to hear about the changes in Lenore's life. "I'd like to get acquainted with her at the wedding," Marie said. Scott shot her a look.

"To encourage her," she explained.

"That could be sticky," answered Rob. "She's still feeling very bad about giving up Mark. But she's glad to know you love him. That comforts her, she says."

"Well....at least she's not jealous of me," said Marie.

"No, it didn't seem that way at all," Aimee assured her.

Rob couldn't bring himself to talk with Mark directly about their mother, so he and Aimee brought the matter up to Marie when they were alone.

"He says he has to work it out himself. He's asked us to leave him alone," she explained, "so we have," she said with a sigh.

"Does it worry you?" asked Aimee with concern.

"It does worry me. I'll admit it. I'm afraid of losing him."

"Losing him?" exclaimed Rob. "You could never lose him! I know how he feels about you."

"Oh, yes. We're very close. I'm the only mother he's ever known."

"So why are you worried?" asked Aimee, puzzled. "Rob said he's so angry at his mother."

"We could still lose him," she nodded. "I've seen it happen. The birth mother waltzes into a person's life and wants to make up for lost time. It's kind of thrilling! And then....he turns his back on the person who was there for him all along."

"Oh, Marie," said Aimee, "I never realized. But yes....that happened with a friend of mine who was adopted. It was sad. Do you think it could happen with Mark?"

"Scott says not to worry. He thinks it's better if I don't talk with her. He's got a point; if I talked with her alone I might say something I'd be sorry for." She sighed, "I try not to worry. But I do. Rob," she looked at him earnestly, "I don't hold anything against your mother. I'm glad she's getting her life back together; I'd be glad to encourage her. Though....I agree with Mark, I don't want her coming here, messing up our lives. But when she gave up her son – that was it! That was the end." She shook her head. "I hope she realizes it."

"And now he's your son," Rob stated, emphatically.

"Yes," she nodded, "my wonderful son."

"Yes, truly he is," affirmed Aimee. "I hope he sees that."

"I hope so," she said wistfully.

They hugged Marie and promised to pray for her. "And for Mark too," she added.

Scott and Marie kept them busy with sightseeing, family talk and sharing, so that Rob and Aimee increasingly felt a part of their family. Aimee helped Rob get to know Heather and Holly, who still felt shy with their new brother. Rob discovered in Mark a brother he could relate to, man to man. They enjoyed hanging out together. "Ah," laughed Marie, "it helps that you two missed all the years of sibling rivalry!"

Aimee was particularly happy to look at Scott's old pictures of Rob as a baby, two little boys together and a young, beautiful Lenore. There hadn't been time in their first visit. She took time to get them copied so she could get them in a scrapbook.

The two couples talked about marriage. In their previous visit Scott and Marie had been surprised and pleased to learn that Rob and Aimee weren't living together. "You'll be glad later on," Marie had said. Privately, Rob hoped so. *Better late than never.*

"I didn't see it as a Christian viewpoint," Aimee told Scott and Marie. "My mom learned it, from her own experience. Dad too, because he's backed me up all the way."

"It just goes to show, you don't have to be a Christian to understand what you gain by waiting until marriage," observed Marie.

"Most people don't, though," said Rob. "I didn't. Now I've come around to Aimee's point of view."

"I'm glad you have," she told him. "Now it's easier for me."

"I agree, it's been worth it. Never thought you'd hear me say it, huh?" he laughed self- consciously. "We've gotten to know each other, become best friends," he told Scott and Marie. "I loved Aimee a year ago. But if we'd moved in together then – it would have been all about me." He looked at Aimee. "It was all about what I wanted. I wanted you. I was pretty selfish," he admitted.

"And now?" she asked.

"Now….it's not just about me. It's about you too. Making you happy."

"Well, hon," she agreed, "it would have been the same with me. Those hormones I was talking about. I wanted you! Now I want to make you happy."

"There is a difference," said Marie. "Though the more you make the other one happy, the happier you'll be."

"I'm sure," Rob agreed. "So….we have a lot to look forward to, don't we?" he asked with a suggestive smile.

"Oh yes….I'm counting the days!"

"There's something more," added Scott, "when we do something God's way, he blesses us."

"So our pastor said," Aimee agreed.

"That was our experience," said Marie. "Do you want to hear it?"

"We'd love to! Go ahead."

Scott put his arm around Marie as she began the story. "It began when we met. We started getting high on the weekends –"

"You!" interrupted Rob. "I'm….surprised."

"You shouldn't be," replied Scott. "It's an old story. It was an escape, we were trying to find meaning and excitement…. it seemed like the thing to do. '*It's only pot,*' we said. We liked the feeling, we were sure we could control it. Fortunately, we stopped when we became Christians. Before we went too far."

"We told you about this on your first visit," replied Marie, "though not all the details."

"I wasn't ready to hear it," explained Rob. "Aimee hasn't heard any of this. She was upstairs." Aimee nodded in agreement.

"Yes, that's right," replied Scott.

"Well, going on," Marie continued, "we were already living together."

"Then," Scott continued, "we happened to go to a Christian concert at a park. We decided, then and there, both of us, to give our lives to Christ. We knew our lives would never be the same."

"It was all or nothing," Marie added. "We never looked back."

"We wanted our lives to honor God," Scott continued. "We were fortunate to get some good counsel right away, through a good church. About sexual purity before marriage, among other things. We thought, '*we're too late for that!*' But we talked about it with our minister and he told us that we could still honor God. He challenged us to move apart. Until we could get married."

"What was that?" exclaimed Rob, shaking his head in disbelief. "What did you say?"

"Yes, move apart. Our minister said, in addition to honoring God it was a good way to find out if we were really right for each other," Scott explained. "He said some couples realize the only thing holding them together is the physical aspect, and that's not enough. Better to find out sooner rather than later."

"Hmm." Rob considered what Scott had said. "That's a good point. I never thought of that."

"Ha, ha, Rob," said Aimee, "that's what I was trying to tell you! Way back when. About our hormones."

"Okay, I get it," Rob agreed, laughing. "So, Marie...."

"Well, at first we thought it was a crazy idea, but we talked about it and decided to do it. Like we said, we wanted our lives to honor God. So....I moved back with my mother. It wasn't easy, giving up the closeness we were used to. It was hard to go back to an earlier level, if you know what I mean."

"I believe it," Rob agreed.

"Another thing," Marie went on, "I was very close to Mark, and I didn't want him to be hurt. So every morning before I went to work I'd go over to Scott's apartment and get Mark up, have breakfast, then we'd take him to day care. I'd stop back at night and put him to bed, then go back home. For a couple of months. My mother thought I was crazy!"

"And people think I'm weird," Aimee shook her head.

"Wait a minute!" Rob interrupted, "Why didn't you just get married?"

"Oh, ho, ho," laughed Marie. "Scott was still married to Lenore. But also....it took us a while to make sure we were really committed to each other –"

"That's a story for another day," Scott broke in. "But as for your mother, I never got around to divorcing her. I put her out of my mind, except," he sighed, "I wanted you back. Then I found out how she was living. I didn't want her back and besides, Marie and I were together by that time. That's when I should have divorced her. But I just put it out of my mind. Until Marie and I –"

"He moved pretty fast, but it still took a few months," Marie continued. "We had a beautiful wedding. Our vows meant so much to us."

Aimee and Rob looked at them with surprise. "Marie," said Aimee, "That is amazing! You are, both of you."

"It sounds worse than it was," Marie replied. "Thinking about it, I believe what we did, years ago, blesses us to this day. Yes, definitely."

"How is that?" Rob asked.

"It gave us a foundation of trust and respect that we've built on through the years. Trust and respect, that's basic. Without trust and respect, love is hollow."

"It strengthened our love," Scott added. "Marie tried to make it easier for me, and I did the same for her. That's what love is all about. It drew us together."

"I'm taking note," Aimee laughed, drawing closer to Rob.

"We prayed together, too," Scott went on. "That made us closer, more than anything. Have you found that out?"

"It's a funny thing," Rob replied. "We started talking to God the night we came to Christ. We did after that, too. But we didn't know we were praying –"

"Yes, we thought praying was more formal," Aimee explained. "Not just conversation. Well, we found out quickly enough. We felt a little foolish –"

"But we've kept it up, praying together. I agree with you, yes, it's brought us closer," Rob stated, taking her hand. "Helped us in our commitment."

"I'm glad to hear it!" Marie smiled, "We found that too. God gave us strength, all the way. Friends were supportive, too."

"They'd been down the same road. That meant a lot," added Scott.

"I know how helpful that is," agreed Aimee.

"Did you ever wonder whether it was worth it?" asked Rob with a shake of his head. "Your story is so incredible, I'm still trying to comprehend it."

"Sure, now and then. But it was, absolutely," declared Scott, giving Marie a quick kiss on the cheek. "That blessing I was talking about? Oh, yes!"

"I'd do it again, if I had to," declared Marie. "I knew we were honoring God, even if I didn't always understand why. When we finally did come together, as man and wife, it was so different from before...." They exchanged glances.

"I saw that!" exclaimed Rob, teasing them. "Honey," he asked, looking at Aimee, "do you think we'll still feel this way about each other twenty years from now?"

"I think even more so. Am I right?" She looked at Scott and Marie.

"Oh yes. Much more!" Scott told them, hugging Marie who nodded in agreement.

Aimee jumped up and hugged them both. "I hope you'll let me consider you my in-laws."

"Well, of course! We'd love that," Scott replied. "Now, don't leave yet, we've got something to talk over with you. Something very special."

Rob and Aimee looked at them expectantly.

"You said you weren't planning to go on a honeymoon," Marie began.

"Ha, no, we can't afford it," Rob said. "Aimee would have to take off work without pay and I'm not even started in a summer job. Not to mention the cost of it. No, we'll have to wait till we have more money."

"You'll have a long wait, if you're like any med student I've ever heard of," Scott told him. "So, Marie and I would like to offer you a honeymoon cottage for a week.

Aimee and Rob were speechless.

"It's a cabin in the woods," Marie explained. "It's attractive and private, though not fancy. It belongs to friends of ours. We've stayed there ourselves."

"We've made arrangements for you to stay there....if you'd like," Scott continued.

Aimee and Rob looked at each other with surprise. "I don't know what to say," Aimee finally said, trying to take it in. "It's – it's incredible."

"But – why?" Rob asked them. "Why do this for us?"

"Because we love you," said Scott.

"We think a honeymoon is important," Marie went on. "Gives you time to get acquainted. Become one, before you have to go back to the real world. It's a good foundation."

"I guess we could manage financially," Aimee finally managed to say. "You think so, Rob?"

"I think so.....it sounds too good to be true..." He shook his head.

"Rob, I think this is part of that blessing Scott was talking about."

"...but I'm sure we could manage!" Rob decided, laughing, putting his arm around Aimee.

They looked at each other with delight. "How can we say thank you?"

"Then it's settled," declared Scott.

"We've arranged to stay there the weekend before so we can get it ready for you," added Marie.

"We're overwhelmed.....we're so grateful....thank you!" Aimee and Rob hugged them and tried to express their thanks.

"Now, one other thing," Scott said. "When you're on your honeymoon we want you to read a book of the Bible, *Song of Solomon*. But not until then."

"We'll have Bibles with us," Aimee replied. "But why this book?"

"It's a love poem. God smiles on marriage," Marie said with a smile.

"That's what Pastor Bruce told us," said Rob. "Sure, we'll do it." They thanked and hugged Scott and Marie again and then hugged each other. Conversation then turned to plans for the wedding, just four weeks away.

Chapter 33

"Hello, family!" Aimee exclaimed brightly as she and Rob joined them for brunch the following Sunday. "We have exciting news for you!"

"A summer job?" Roger asked Rob.

"You found an apartment..." her mother suggested hopefully.

"Wait, she's got a new shade of nail polish for the wedding," Jason said with a smirk.

"No –" Aimee replied, a bit deflated. "Rob and I are going to be baptized, when we get back from our honeymoon. We'd like you all to come."

An uncomfortable silence filled the air. Her mother and father looked away, not meeting her gaze. Jason and Jacquie looked at her with a blank stare. Then Aimee and her mother spoke together.

"I hoped you would –" Aimee began.

"Well, Aimee and Rob," her mother sighed, "I don't know what I expected, but not this."

"We understand," he said, patting Elaine's shoulder, "it might not mean much to you –"

"Sprinkled or dunked?" Roger asked.

"Immersed, Dad. We're going to be immersed."

"Sorry. I didn't know the word."

"Oh...." said Jacquie with a sly look, "you're going to come up out of the water, hands in the air, and shout hal-le-lu-jah!" She waved her arms in the air.

"Watch it, Jacquie, that's not respectful," chided her father.

"Okay, okay," she retorted, "but I'm going to take plenty of pictures."

"To turn up all over the internet?" asked Aimee. "I don't think so!"

"You two are really serious, aren't you?" asked Elaine with a worried look.

"Yes, we are," replied Rob, putting his arm around Aimee. "Elaine, don't worry about us getting hurt. It could happen anywhere. If it does, we'll deal with it," he assured her.

"No....no....that's not it," she admitted, tears in her eyes. "It's not that. I just – I don't want to lose you. It's like – church is taking over your lives. It's like a brainwashing, you're not yourselves any more. And now, baptism –"

"So what is baptism, anyway?" asked Jason.

"It's a kind of initiation," his mother replied.

"Actually, Mom, it's not. It's a statement to the world, an illustration –"

"We call it a testimony," continued Rob, "of what God has done in our lives."

"And all your sins are washed away," Jacquie interjected. "What sins are you hiding, sister dear?"

"Honey, it's not that at all," Aimee answered. "If you come – all of you –" she waved her hand – "you'll find out what it's all about."

"I think we could do that," her father replied.

"I should warn you, it's the early service," added Rob.

"We'll do it," Roger decided. He looked over at Elaine, who slowly nodded her head.

Aimee got up and put her arm around her mother, kissing her cheek. "Mom, please don't think you are losing me, or losing us. I love you more than ever. Because I love God."

"Hon, I wouldn't worry about brainwashing," Roger assured his wife. "I've seen kids in cults. This is nothing like that."

"Well...." Elaine considered, "I trust you, Aimee, and you too, Rob. But...please take my advice, and don't go off the deep end with the Bible. I've seen that happen. Now, let's change the subject and enjoy our breakfast."

Aimee was driving Rob back to his apartment. "That was disappointing. I was hoping they'd share in our joy –"

He shook his head. "Why would they? Look, how would you have felt, a few months back, if Julie had told you she was going to be baptized? And you didn't know what it was all about?"

"I know, I know. I would have been worried – like, '*what is she getting into?*' " She gave a little laugh. "Or your mother, I would have freaked out, '*oh, no, she's going off the deep end –*' "

"So, hon, you can't expect them to understand. Give them time."

"Yes," she sighed, "but I thought by now they'd have accepted our church- going and could understand a little bit."

"It's only been a couple of months. I'm sure your mom thought it was a passing fad. But, I think she has other objections, not just fear that we'll be hurt. I think we struck a nerve."

"I had that feeling too. It's funny that Dad, an atheist, was more understanding –"

"Just wait till they actually see the baptism. It may freak them out, maybe in a good way. I remember my feelings a couple of weeks ago when I saw my first baptism, it was all new, it took getting used to, but I thought, this is right, this is for me. I need to do it." He smiled at her. "I'm glad you felt that way too."

"See, we really are one."

"Don't forget, we'll be taking Gramps. It will mean so much to him."

"I can hardly wait..."

"Well, now. Don't forget, we've got a wedding first," he laughed. "And a honeymoon."

"Hmm! We don't want to forget that, do we?" she laughed as she pulled into his parking lot.

"Do you have a few minutes to talk?" he asked her.

"Sure." She stopped the car. "What is it?"

"Getting serious now...." he took her hand, "do you remember when I told Pastor Bruce, '*Aimee has my heart'?*" She nodded. "Well, now....God has my heart." He took her face in his hands. "My sweet Aimee, I love you more than ever.... but I love God more."

"Okay...." she nodded slowly.

"It's been a struggle...." he shook his head, "but finally I saw that if I love you more than God, then I've made you an idol. That's not fair to you, and I'm cheating God. According to Pastor Bruce, it could even ruin our relationship."

It hadn't been easy. *I won't take time to tell her now.* He had been reading the New Testament and had read the *Gospel of John* twice, each time getting stuck where Jesus asked Peter if he loved him most of all. *Do I? No, I don't, I can't, Aimee fills my heart – but I'm torn!* Finally, late at night he texted Pastor Bruce asking if they could talk the next morning. Immediately he called back saying he could talk now. So they had talked at length. After they hung up Rob at last made the decision that was so difficult but so satisfying, a decision that enveloped him with peace he had never known before.

"You're the most wonderful gift in the world to me, but I need to love God who gave you to me, more than I love the gift. I hope that makes sense to you," he asked hopefully.

"Rob, honey....I've been having that same struggle!" she told him, tears in her eyes. "I've been wanting to talk with you. I knew you'd understand."

"Oh, baby, we really are one." Reaching across the console, he put his arm around her.

"Let me explain," she began, looking deeply into his eyes. "It always meant so much to me that we belong to each other –"

"Me too, now that I know what it means –"

"But how could I give you up? If I gave you to God then you wouldn't belong to me. And I was sure God would do something terrible, take you away from me." She shook her head, smiling. "It sounds silly now, but it's true."

"Why is it so hard to let go?" He shook his head, reflecting. "We want the last word. We want control."

"Yes, that's it.... Well, then it struck me. What do I have control of, anyway? Not the air I breathe, not my life....oh, I can be stupid and throw away my life, but really, God has the last word. About everything." He nodded in agreement. "So...." She spoke carefully, thoughtfully, "can I give you back to God? You belong to Him, not me. Can I love Him more than I love you? I want to love God more than I love you. There! I said it," she laughed. "I hope I mean it."

"Oh, baby, baby...." He kissed her cheek, then her lips. "What did I ever do to deserve you?"

"God gave us to each other," she replied with a smile. "You know, it's not about us anymore."

"Yes," he agreed. "We've given each other back to God. It's the strangest thing," he reflected.... "I love you more than ever."

"Now that you've given me up?"

"Yes, how funny is that?"

Rob's classes had ended and he and Aimee decided on an impromptu picnic to celebrate. She was able to get off work a few hours early. They picked up some fast-food and went to a nearby park where they talked and enjoyed each other's company.

"Honey," she said suddenly, "let's go get Gramps. Get him away from there. He's only a few minutes from here."

"Umm....I don't know....not today, I don't want to share you...." He pulled her close.

"I know, I feel that way too....but....I think he'd enjoy getting out, a beautiful day like today....we could get Grendel too, don't you think? He loves being with Grendel."

"We did promise him." He struggled with his thoughts. "We could pick him up, then drive out to your house for Grendel. It's a bit out of the way but we could do it. Then we'll just see where the car takes us...."

Gramps, surprised and pleased, didn't need any persuading to join them. After picking up Grendel and a meal for Gramps they drove around and found a little park.

"This has to be a taste of heaven," Gramps reflected as he resumed his fetch game with Grendel. "Four good friends. What is better than that?"

"Well, Aimee and I have a special friendship...." he winked at her.

"We've got a problem with Grendel," she sighed. "We've been looking for an apartment that will let us have a dog, without paying too much extra. We can't find anything we like."

"What happens if you don't find one?"

"Then he stays with my family. Nothing against my sister and brother, but Grendel is my dog! I'm not ready to give him away. Besides, I'd miss him terribly," she replied, morosely. "Even Rob couldn't take his place," she said with a sly grin.

"And here I thought I was your guard dog!" She laughed and patted his head. "What will you do with him on our honeymoon? Do you want to take him with us?"

"Rob – that's up to you."

"Oh, baby, we could go around in circles on this. Do you want to take him? If you do, that's okay." *I hope she says no*, he thought, *I'd rather not have him along....*

"No." She smiled at him. "No distractions. Just the two of us. I've been away from him before. I'll manage, so will he. I'll tell him he has to. It's not that long."

"So that's settled," Gramps declared. "Now, what about a permanent home for him? You know, he could move in with me," he announced with satisfaction. "He would be closer to you than if he were with your family." He reached down and patted Grendel.

"Really....are you serious?" she asked, not quite believing him.

"I'd have to check it out," he nodded, smiling. "Some residents have pets. I'd have to certify that I can take care of him. And maybe pay extra too, I don't know."

"Oh, Gramps, I didn't finish my story. We did take an apartment. But we're not happy with it."

"No," Rob explained. "It's in student housing. Typical concrete block apartment. Fourth floor. We'd have to take Grendel down the elevator twice a day...."

"Ah, that could be a problem," Gramps said with a nod.

"And pay extra for him," Aimee sighed.

"Money we don't have," Rob added with a frown.

"We've been arguing about it," Aimee went on. Gramps raised his eyebrows in surprise.

"Not fighting," Rob explained. "Just a....difference of opinion. About the apartment. It's not settled yet. We sign papers Monday morning."

"Have you two prayed about it?"

They looked at each other. "Uh, no," Rob replied. "I guess we should have."

"We're still getting used to the idea of....well, involving God in all these little things...." Aimee explained.

"I know. I'm still learning too. But, honestly, I'm finding out that God really does care about '*all these little things*'," Gramps replied. "So, pray about it. Ask God's help."

"You're right," Rob replied.

"You two need to agree on this, whatever the problem is. And then....maybe that's not the right apartment after all."

"Yes," Aimee agreed. "You're right. We should pray."

"Of course. We should have done this before," Rob told him, taking his hand.

"Let's do it." Quietly, Gramps offered a prayer, to which Aimee and Rob added a few words of their own.

"Another thing," Gramps went on, "you could bring it up at your Bible study tonight. Mention it Sunday morning too, in church. Somebody may know something."

"We'll do it," Rob declared, taking Aimee's hand. "It can't hurt."

"Now," Gramps went on, "moving on to other things. Like I said before, a taste of heaven." He looked at them and smiled. "Allow me to be thankful for a few minutes. A year ago....well, a little over a year ago, I was a lonely old man. A self-centered old man, I'll have to admit. I literally didn't have a friend in the world and it was my own fault. I didn't dare call Rob a friend; after all, he was paid to take care of me."

"Gramps, you were never self-centered," Rob objected. "I never thought so."

"Well....the fact is, I was in my own world. That's pretty selfish."

"And then...." suggested Aimee.

"Ah, yes," he chuckled, "sometimes I still can hardly believe it." He smiled at Rob. "Now, a year later, I am the richest of men. I have more friends than I can keep track of!"

He stopped as a new thought occurred to him. "And that's not all! I'm not an old man. Not anymore!" He laughed, shaking his head. "No! I'm not an old man. I'm not seventy yet. Hmph, sixty-eight isn't old."

"No, it's not," Aimee agreed.

"I don't think of you as old," Rob assured him.

"But I was," he insisted. "Back then." He shook his head. "Back at Sunset Gardens, I was older than those ninety year olds. Yes...." he reflected, "I had given up on life. I didn't want to try to make friends. Thank you, Rob, for changing that. Even before I knew who you were." He laughed. "I want to stand up and shout!"

"Gramps, that's great," Rob exclaimed. "Well, now we're family. That's a special bond."

"Yes, yes," Gramps replied. "You both are family," he smiled at Aimee, "yes, my new granddaughter, not only family, but friends as well."

Aimee squeezed his hand. "You mean so much to me...." She put her arm around him.

"Yes," Rob agreed, patting his hand. "And look at the friends you have. You've got Howard...."

"Howard, yes. He's a true friend. We're so different, but we're good buddies. It means a lot to have a compatible roommate. Ha, ha, even though we might not always admit it." They knew Gramps and Howard liked to trade good-natured insults. "Then, Max and Jerry. They're my friends."

"I've seen you tool around in that wheelchair. I think everybody's your friend," Aimee added.

"It's been easier at Sunset Gardens to make friends. And Pastor Bruce is my friend. We seemed to hit it off right away." He smiled, remembering the Christmas worship service when they had met. "Aimee, I'm proud to call your father my friend. Your mother, too."

"What about my grandparents?" Aimee asked. "You got along very well at my graduation lunch."

"Ah, Frank and Magda, they're good people. Yes, I felt we were kindred spirits! I look forward to seeing them at your wedding. But your dad –" he frowned, "I was afraid I'd lost his friendship, after my talk. After all, it was a week before I heard from him."

"I was worried too," Aimee agreed. She decided not to tell him the whole story.

"Did you know, he was one reason I held back from doing it? You too, of course. I kept worrying, what will he think of me? With his background in the military I didn't think he'd understand. I hated to risk losing his regard, his friendship. Finally I decided I had to do it. It was the right thing to do, no matter the cost. You'll never know how I agonized over it," he sighed, remembering the struggle. "But – when Damien's trial intervened, I almost gave it up. If you hadn't called and reminded me of my invitation, I might never have done it."

"Really?" asked Aimee, incredulously. "It almost didn't happen?" She shook her head. "Strange are the mysteries.....of God, d'ya think?"

Gramps nodded in agreement. "You are right."

"Gramps, Rob began, earnestly, "I told you before how proud I was of you for trying to change the world –"

"Even though it was the wrong way?"

"Yes. But I'm even prouder now. Did you ever realize what came of what you did? Telling your story?"

"Well....many old wounds were healed. I'll always be thankful for that."

"But that's not all! What about my mother, all that's happened to her, and Scott and his family – they're in my life -and ours –" he waved at Aimee – "just because of you, telling your story! How amazing is that? If you hadn't told your story – none of this would have happened." He shook his head in disbelief.

"How true," Aimee reflected thoughtfully. "I never realized. Look at all that's come of that, in our lives!"

"I hadn't thought of that," Gramps said soberly. "It's a fact," he concluded, "I almost didn't go through with it." He smiled at Aimee. "Yes....strange are the mysteries of God."

"All because of you, Gramps," she continued.

"We'll thank God for that," he corrected her. "I'm as surprised as you are."

"Gramps," Rob added, "I hope you can get to know Scott. And the whole family."

"I'm sure I will, at the wedding. He was an easy man to meet. We hit it off right away, brief as our meeting was. Now....I think it's time for Grendel to get a little more exercise," he announced as he threw out a tennis ball.

And the game was on, until at last Grendel had worn Gramps out.

They were driving back after taking Gramps home.

"Rob," Aimee asked, "why are you fighting my father? About Grendel. He made us a very kind offer."

"Fighting him? Honey, I'm not fighting him. I love and respect him, you know that. I just don't want to have him pay the extra charge for the dog. I feel that's my responsibility."

"I love you for that. But the fact is, we can't pay the extra, and he's very willing to do it for us."

"It's a manhood thing. I'm responsible for my family. That's you, I, and Grendel."

"Does it bother you that I'm the one whose job will be paying our bills? Once you're back in school, that is."

"No, it doesn't, honey, because we're together in supporting ourselves."

"Well, that's not consistent. But it doesn't bother me. I'm glad I can do it."

"I'm glad too." He reached for her hand. "I appreciate your father's offer, I do. I just don't want to depend on his help."

"It sounds to me like a bit of stubborn pride."

"Look, honey, he's helped us already, buying my car. I'm okay with that, but that's enough."

"He wasn't doing us a favor, you could have sold it to anyone."

"Maybe, but he made it easy for me and gave a very good price."

"Oh, yes. Jacquie will be very happy to have that car. And we have money for our appliances."

"I love your dad, Aimee. He means well –"

"Ha, you'll probably do the same thing someday! Help our children."

"Someday, huh?" he smiled at her. "But I still want to pay for Grendel ourselves."

"Something else to pray about, right?" She was quiet with her thoughts, then asked, hesitantly, "Rob....what do you think of Gramps' offer? To keep Grendel?"

"It took me by surprise, but it makes sense. It could work out well. I'm sure you would see more of him that way." He glanced at her. "Is something wrong?"

"Of course there is!" she exclaimed, surprised and hurt. "You should know that. I don't want to lose Grendel. To Gramps, or Jacquie, or anyone."

He squeezed her hand. "I'm sorry, honey. I should have realized. You won't lose him, I'm sure you won't." *But I'm not so sure*, he thought.

Chapter 34

"My goodness, this is exciting! I'm glad you've got yourselves an apartment, at last," Elaine began as Aimee and Rob joined them for Sunday brunch. "We want to hear all about it."

"Yes. I'm glad you were able to get campus housing. It's more convenient," Roger added. "But is everything okay? Your text said you'd be a little late, but look, we're almost done."

They apologized, then Aimee added, "We got a different apartment. We just got back from looking at it. It's the ugliest thing I've ever seen. But it's perfect, just perfect! It's an answer to prayer."

"Remind me not to get married," Jason announced. "It's making Aimee crazy."

"That wouldn't be much of a job," added Jacquie, smirking.

Aimee raised her eyebrows at her. "Little Sister, if you're not nice to me you won't get my bedroom..."

"That's not for you to say!" Jacquie shot back.

"So tell us the story, already," demanded Elaine.

"We weren't happy with the fourth floor apartment, elevator or no elevator. It's just not a good place for a dog. But we didn't see any alternative," Rob began.

"We were talking with Gramps, and he said we should pray about it. Because we hadn't signed papers yet. And he suggested we ask about it at Bible study and church."

"Aimee, I don't like to burst your bubble, but if I had a dollar for every prayer I prayed that God ignored, I'd be a rich woman," Elaine declared, frowning.

"Oh, Mom....prayer's not like that –"

"Well, that sure has been my experience."

"Pastor Bruce told us that prayer isn't about us," Rob said. "It's trying to get on the same page with God. He sees the big picture, and we can't. So we ask, but we leave it up to him."

"Okay, okay, let's get on with it," Roger interrupted. "You've got a perfectly ugly apartment."

"No, it's ugly. And it's perfect." He threw up his hands and shook his head.

"Here's what happened," Rob explained. "We announced in church that we were looking for an apartment where we could keep a dog, in the campus area. We asked for prayer."

"After church a woman came up who we didn't know, a Mrs. Santiago," Aimee went on. "She has an apartment, a duplex, next door to her. She's kept it vacant for a month looking for the right people. She's had bad experiences renting before. This time she prayed to find a Christian couple she could depend on."

"Would you believe it, her house is just a short walk from my main building!"

"It's perfect, really," Aimee concluded. "There's a long, fenced-in back yard, perfect for Grendel! Nice kitchen, two bedrooms, we can use one for a study –"

"Or a nursery?" asked her mother.

"No, a study. For us both," Aimee corrected her.

"So where does ugly come in?" asked her father.

"It desperately needs decorating."

"Hey, I thought it was fine," said Rob, "but I want Aimee to be happy."

"Mrs. Santiago said she'd waive the security deposit if we do the painting and wallpapering. I can do that. And she'll pay for supplies."

"I'll be glad to help," her mother offered. "Probably your sister and brother too...."

"That's not all," Aimee went on, "the rent is less than the other apartment! She said she'll cut back on what she charges for an animal. We can afford it –"

"She's never had an animal there," Rob broke in. "But she'll take a chance on us –"

"- if she sees that we're responsible with him," Aimee continued excitedly. "Really, I think this could work out! Isn't it wonderful? But there is one problem."

"Yeah, the problem is your breakfast is cold," her father said.

"Who can eat at a time like this?" she replied. Jason took the opportunity to lift a muffin from her plate.

"Oh, you'll miss me when I'm on my honeymoon!"

"I'll miss having you to pick on!"

"The problem is, Gramps," she went on. "Getting him into the house. It has a front porch with several steps, though the back door has only two –"

"Dad, we can build a ramp in the back –" Jason began, excitedly.

"Not a problem. I've seen it done," Roger stated. "Just extend it into the yard...."

"That's what I thought," Rob added. "I'll work with you. Well, we'll have to take you there. Maybe after we eat."

"Oh, I'd love to, I can't wait to see it!" Elaine agreed. "Now, not to be disagreeable, Aimee, but why would you call this an answer to prayer? It sounds to me like a coincidence, a lovely coincidence. Nothing more."

"Well, Mom. This woman never comes to the early service, we've never even met her. Why would she come today? She said that something came up with her family at the last minute and she decided to come to the early service. Also, she'd been praying for some time to find the right couple. Holding that place vacant. So, I'll say, thank you God."

"That's very nice, honey." Her mom put her arm around her, drawing her to herself. "I'm happy for you."

"And I'm happy about Grendel," Aimee replied tearfully. "So happy!"

"We've been pretty silly about that apartment, haven't we?" Aimee asked as they were driving from the apartment to Aimee's house to spend the afternoon.

"What do you mean?"

"I've been silly. Wasting so much time and emotion on that apartment and Grendel, how to pay for him, when God had the answer all along. All we had to do was ask."

"You're right. It's humbling –"

"Discouraging is more like it," she corrected him. "We have so much to learn," she sighed. "If we hadn't prayed and asked at church we'd be moving into that high rise apartment – and still wrangling about it. That's scary."

"Don't be hard on yourself," he said, taking her hand. "We need to learn from it." *I could have prayed for her,* he thought, *I know how she feels about Grendel.* "Here's another thought. What if we hadn't gotten Gramps that day? Talked with him?"

"Right. But you don't know the half of it," she laughed. "The idea popped in my head, to get him, but to be honest….I didn't want to do it. To share you. So I mentioned it to see what you would think. If you'd opposed me," she shrugged, "I'd have backed off."

"Wow. We sure have a lot to learn. Listening to each other, listening to God….and now we have a good home for Grendel. And for ourselves."

"That's a lot to take in."

"Glad, honey?"

"So glad! He has his own special place. I still can hardly believe it."

"You didn't want to give him up, did you –" he patted her hand.

"No, I sure didn't."

"Maybe you need to give him up," he squeezed her hand, "like you gave me up."

"Rob, he's a dog, for goodness sake!"

"I'm just saying."

A few nights later they were shopping for Aimee's mother and found themselves in the direction of Lenore's town. They decided to pay her a visit.

"What do you think, should we say anything about Mark?" Aimee asked as she began to text her.

"I wouldn't know what to say. I don't think we should tell her how he feels about her. It would make her feel worse than she already does."

"Well, I think she needs to know about Marie, that she's afraid your Mom will take him away from his family. But – I sure don't want to be the one to tell her."

"Honey, that's too much for either of us. I'm not going to say a word about any of this. I'd be walking on eggshells."

"I know how you feel. But if she brings the subject up–"

"-then we'll do the best we can."

"Yes, honey. It worked out with you and Mark, remember that."

Lenore greeted them with pleasure and hugs. "We haven't seen each other since your graduation, Aimee, and now you're so close to your wedding and taking time to visit me! It's good of you."

"Just a short visit, Lenore. We weren't far away. Wedding shopping."

She seemed more relaxed and serene than they had ever seen her. "I'm doing really great," she told them. "I'm keeping up with A.A. and I'm finally over Carl."

"Carl? I didn't know you even thought about him," Aimee replied, raising her eyebrows.

" '*Over him*?' " Rob exclaimed with surprise. "I don't get it. You should be glad to be rid of him. He wasn't good to you."

"Oh...." she answered with a vague look. "He was and he wasn't. He took me in. I'm grateful for that."

"Mom," he replied sympathetically. "He got plenty from you. He didn't do you any favors."

"He gave me what I needed. I'm lonely without him. Maybe I didn't like him, but I miss him. Or I did. I told you, though, I'm over him."

Rob and Aimee looked puzzled.

"It's the loneliness. I never learned to deal with it. I'll settle for anything and call it good. I always did. Now....I have to learn I don't have to."

"Of course you don't have to, Lenore," Aimee told her.

"I know you don't understand." She sighed, shaking her head. "Look, you two are starry-eyed and in love. I remember how it was with me and your father, Rob. Like you. But – I don't think I was ready to be a wife and mother. Actually, I reversed the order, didn't I? Mother first. The fact is, I wasn't ready. I see it now, it's like I was rushing things." She shuddered. "It's been downhill ever since. Going from man to man...."

"But Mom. That was then. This is now. You're moving on, and there doesn't ever have to be another Carl. Right?" he smiled encouragingly.

She hesitated, then, "Right," she agreed. "Now, it's a matter of learning to be alone. I'm doing that."

"A day at a time?" asked Aimee.

"Yes, yes. I'm working on that." She sighed. "The biggest thing is, making myself believe I don't have to have a man to be happy. As a Christian, I should know that, but – it's still a struggle. Aimee, I think you got it right. I thought that the first time I met you."

"What do you mean?" she asked, curious.

"I'm not sure...." she pondered. "You seemed....sure of yourself. Independent. I thought, she'll be good for Rob." He laughed and took Aimee's hand. "I was right, wasn't I? I can't tell you how happy I am for you both," she told them. "I believe you'll succeed, where I.....I didn't."

"Lenore – we believe in you," Aimee told her. "And we believe you will succeed, now." Rob nodded agreement. "You know that, don't you?"

"Yes....yes, I do. Though sometimes I wonder why." She took a deep breath. "Now, I guess I won't see you until the wedding, and I want –"

"No, the rehearsal," Aimee reminded her. "You'll be there. We'll make arrangements to pick you up. We're putting you up at a motel that night."

"Are you sure?" She laughed nervously. "I don't know how to thank you. That sounds....so wonderful. All right," she smiled and took their hands, "I want to wish you God's blessing. I know He will bless you. You're getting a much better start than I did."

With hugs and kisses they said goodbye. "Thank you again for coming!" she exclaimed. "You've made my day."

Rob and Aimee left feeling uplifted and relieved. She had made their day.

But on the way back Aimee had some misgivings. "Rob, I'm relieved that she's doing so well. I just wish I'd said something to her about Marie and her worries."

"What would you have said?"

"That's just it, I don't know. But now that she doing so well, getting strong, what will happen when she sees Mark at the wedding? Will she unload her guilt on him and try to make it up to him? It could happen," she asked with a worried sigh.

"You mean, try to be a mother to him?"

"Yes, exactly. It worries me. I feel we missed a chance to say something."

"Well.....I don't know what we could have said. Let's just leave it alone."

"I've been thinking about Bryan," he said as they talked another day.

"Oh, honey. Does it still hurt so much?"

"When I think of him, yes....but I'm better. I'm beginning to see that people change. I wasn't willing to see it in Bryan. Ha! He had it all planned out, how he would use Natasha."

"It was mutual convenience. In a way, she was using him, too."

"Like my mother and Carl."

"Oh, no, Bryan and Natasha were crazy about each other, you told me that. Not like your mother and Carl."

"It's not too different. See how hard it is for her to break away from him?"

"Yes....but it isn't love....it's neediness." She shook her head. "It's very sad."

"Bryan wanted someone to meet his needs and take care of him. Very calculating, I would say. He never intended it to last."

"Ah, Rob, now I know why you wanted me to move in with you. To take care of you," she said, only half joking.

"No way!" replied Rob, "I wouldn't know how to have someone take care of me. I'm independent, to a fault. The all-around bachelor. I'm used to doing things for myself. My way." Her eyebrows flew up. "Oh, I know I have to change," he assured her. "We talked about that with Pastor Bruce, remember?"

"Yes we did. Now, I suggest we learn to take care of each other."

"I could be talked into that," he said, reaching for her. "Yes, you're right."

"Rob." She grew serious. "I just had a sobering thought."

"Baby, I'm not interested in sobering thoughts, not now." He kissed her.

"Internship. Residency," she went on.

"So? What are you getting at?" He kissed her again.

"We have to take care of our marriage. Above all. When things start to get crazy."

"You're right, that is sobering. Even though I may not want to hear it now...." He nodded. "We want to keep our promises to each other."

The days passed quickly. Rob had decided not to go back to DeGeorgio's. He would have to work nights while Aimee worked days. *"That's no way to start a marriage!"* he insisted, but for a while he could not find a day job. Then one of the men at church helped him find a construction job on a per diem basis with excellent pay. He could take off for the honeymoon with no penalty. Aimee had recently taken a job cleaning a couple of houses to make up for her lost pay, with Jacquie to take over while she was gone.

In her few spare hours she wanted to work at the new apartment but her family kept her away. This was their gift to her, they told her. If all went well she would view the final result before the wedding. With difficulty, she made herself stay away.

Chapter 35

Gramps looked around his room and smiled. The old album was gone, relegated to the dumpster. In its place were four bright new scrapbooks which took pride of place on his wall shelf. He took great pleasure in leafing through them and re-living past experiences.

But it had not begun well. He had welcomed Aimee's offer many months ago to arrange things in a new scrapbook but he quickly learned there was more to it than he expected. He watched her begin to sort pictures in piles, then to his horror she took scissors and began to clip and trim a picture. *"Oh, no, no, you can't do that!"* he exclaimed. She tried to explain, tried to communicate her vision of what his scrapbook could look like but her words fell on deaf ears. This was not what he had in mind.

He hadn't wanted to argue, so he suggested they set it aside.

"Maybe this isn't a good idea after all," he said with a smile but leaving no doubt as to his meaning.

"Okay, but let's not give up on it yet," she replied with her most winning smile.

"I don't think so, Aimee."
It was an impasse.

The following week she brought two scrapbooks which she had crafted in earlier years, one that portrayed her family's vacations and another her experiences as a student in Germany. As he looked them over, viewing her artful arrangement of pictures and the stories they told, he was won over.

"Um....Aimee," he said meekly but with a twinkle in his eye, *"do you think you can do that for me? As long as I have executive privilege, you understand."*

"Of course. I won't do a thing without your approval. Thank you, thank you!"

She explained her ideas and they began to work together. From then on he looked forward to their times together. He was extremely proud of the finished products. And so was Rob.

"Aimee, you did a great job!" he told her gratefully. *"This makes it so easy to get into! See, Gramps, your life is a book....a lot of books. And my father- now I have the story of his life!"*

Gramps told Roger about it later as he was showing off an album.

"Ah, yes, Aimee is very determined," Roger declared. *"A force to be reckoned with."*

"Well, determination can be a good thing," Gramps replied. *"If she hadn't been determined, I wouldn't be over here at Sunset Woods, and I would hardly ever see Rob and Aimee."*

"You've got a point. It was her determination that led her to Rob. We can't fault that, can we?"

"Right! She knows how to get what she wants."

Now, on a Saturday afternoon a couple of weeks before the wedding she and Jacquie stopped in to see him, Grendel by Aimee's side.

"A triple pleasure!" he exclaimed, taking their hands, then patting Grendel. "What do you have here? Another scrapbook? But we're all finished."

Aimee had a bag in her hand which she set on the table. "Gramps, you know how Rob and I like to take pictures?"

"I know you're always doing things with your – what are they – smart phones? but those pictures are too small to be any good."

"Not anymore! Take a look!" She opened the bag and out tumbled packets of photos, grouped in chronological order. "This is our last year, in pictures. Rob and I picked out the best ones and I printed them up. Jacquie and I will try to get them all set up in a scrapbook today. I figured if I didn't do it before the wedding I might not get a chance later. See, you can remember us while we're away." She put her arm around him. "What do you think?"

"Oh, my," he said as he pulled pictures out and looked at them. "You do believe in candid shots….." he muttered, "you sneaked up on me quite a few times."

"Here you are at our house, at Christmas…." Jacquie pointed out.

"Ah, that's a nice memory. Some good pictures here."

"Look, here you are at the VFW hall, and here are some of you and Howard….and our picnic at the lake….Rob and I and Lenore, my graduation, and Rob and I last summer…."

"Well, Aimee, who is this stunning young woman?" he asked, giving a low whistle.

"Now, Gramps, men aren't supposed to whistle at girls," she chided him with a laugh.

"Dad does, to Mom, and she likes it," Jacquie pointed out.

"That's different," Gramps said, "they're husband and wife. Aimee's right. I shouldn't have."

"Gramps, you can whistle at me any time you want. You tell Rob he can whistle at me any time he wants to," she told him, patting his arm. "But only you two."

"You certainly look lovely here, as you always do.....and very glamorous."

"That was at the faculty reception last Fall," Aimee explained. "See, here's one of the two of us. Joel Greenburg, our new best man took it. I told Rob he was my Adonis. He acted embarrassed – but he was flattered!" She smiled at the memory.

"Very good of both of you. Well now." He surveyed the pictures. "It looks like you have a pretty good summary of this whole past year. Let's get started. Maybe we can finish today. Ah, ha," he exclaimed as he pulled out another photo, "another glamour shot."

"Yes, we were at the symphony. That was my surprise for Rob. I got tickets because I know he likes music but it turned out, I had a surprise too! I'd never been to a live concert before, I mean, not the classical stuff. I'd heard it on TV and liked it – but live – oh, wow. I was on another planet – and Rob with me!" She nodded. "It was a neat experience."

"Was Rob pleased? Was he surprised?"

"He was thrilled! He had played some of that music himself. He wanted to play his air trumpet, ha, ha!" Gramps laughed, envisioning it. "Instead, I let him hold my hand."

"That was nice of you." He looked at her quizzically. "What was that? Did you say Rob plays the trumpet? I never knew that."

"Oh, yes! Didn't you know? He played in high school and college and he was in the marching band. Orchestra too. First chair, that's lead trumpet, you know."

"Yes.....my goodness! That's quite an achievement."

"Now he says he'll never play again." Gramps looked surprised. "He told me that, when we first met. He didn't want to discuss it."

"Oh, my," he shook his head, "that's too bad. I wonder why? Music would bring such pleasure to him as well as to others."

He sighed. "The longer he waits the harder it will be for him. He'll lose confidence."

"I know. But I still hope."

"Yes, yes. Hope and pray." He glanced at Jacquie. "I think we're boring you, honey."

"Oh, I'm used to that," she replied off-handedly. "Aimee, you're the one who said we had to keep our minds on our job, not get side-tracked. Well, I don't see any work getting done...."

"Now, Little Sister," Aimee began.

"Jacquie," Gramps broke in diplomatically, "you're absolutely right, we'll work as we talk. Aimee," he smiled with pleasure, remembering, "you must tell Rob that his grandmother was quite a musician. Did I tell you she was a music teacher in the schools? She had a lovely voice, she sang folk songs, she sang with a band when we were in college...." he stopped, lost in thought. "She could play anything she tried, the mandolin, the guitar...and she played piano as a child..." He stopped and smiled at Jacquie. "Back to work!"

"You told us some, but it's exciting to hear more details," Aimee replied as she resumed her work. "Rob always loves to hear how he's like his family. It gives him his roots."

"Well, his father didn't have a musical bone in his body. And neither do I, although I love music. Aimee, I'm puzzled. In all our talks, Rob and I, he never said he played an instrument. I knew he loved music because we talked about it. But he never said a word about playing in the band, and orchestra..."

"I can tell you why. It was too painful. It was a door he couldn't open. I understand that now. He had to drop out when his grandparents died. But I don't understand why he can't talk about it now, won't talk with me," she said sadly. "I think he really misses playing. Although he can't play now, of course, he's too busy.

"Maybe someday, Aimee. Maybe someday."

"Yes....I sure hope so."

When they were finished Gramps surveyed their work. "Thank you, more than I can say! Now I have something else to treasure," he told them as they were saying goodbye. "Aimee, that wedding isn't very far away." She laughed in agreement. "You be careful not to overdo."

"I promise! I'll just dump everything on Jacquie," she said as she nudged her sister.

"And what does Jacquie say about that?" Gramps asked Jacquie.

"Oh, I'm used to it," she replied with a roll of her eyes.

"We miss having Rob with us this morning. After all these months," Elaine remarked to Aimee as she joined her family for brunch the next day.

"Not as much as I do! Do you know, since he started work last Monday I haven't seen him once, not even once? His job site is across town and he's working dawn to dusk. I miss him so much," she said with a mournful look.

"He won't get to church at all, will he?" asked Roger.

"Probably not. And that's one thing I will miss so much. Worshiping together with him. I know you probably don't understand it," she glanced at her parents, "but that adds a whole new dimension to our relationship."

"No, frankly, I don't," replied Elaine, "but that's all right," she smiled.

"I'll see him tomorrow night. Our good friends Peter and Ming, you've heard me talk about them, they have Bible study and worship at their apartment especially for those who can't get to church on Sunday. It doesn't start until eight, so Rob will get most of it."

"Rob's busy enough right now, it won't kill him to miss church for a while," Elaine declared.

"C'mon, Elaine," Roger explained, "you know he's going so he can be with Aimee."

"No, Dad, that's not it." Aimee took out her phone and showed him a text. '*Don't try 2 come, u need yr sleep. LLL*'

"That's good," replied her father. "I'm glad he's thoughtful about you. He's a committed young man, and balanced. I admire that. But I'm sure he won't mind seeing you tomorrow night," he said with a wink.

"Yes, he is committed," Aimee replied. "When he became a Christian it was all or nothing, '*no halfway measures*', he said. Because it was such a radical change for him. He really means it. And I do too – though to be honest, I hope I see him! But I'm also going for the worship, because that means a lot to me."

" '*Radical change'?*" Elaine echoed in a worried tone. "Aimee, what are you talking about? How is he changing? Rob is one of the nicest people I know. Why does he have to change?"

"Mom, Mom," Aimee answered reassuringly, "Don't worry about him. Rob is still Rob. My sweet Rob. If anything, he's nicer."

"Well, then, what kind of '*radical change'* is this? I don't want to see him go off the deep end," she declared. "Or you either."

"Mom.....that's not happening." She thought for a moment. "I see it, because I know him so well. It may not be evident to others." Her mother looked puzzled. "He's more sure of himself. More confident. I'd say he's more of a leader now."

"I can see it," her dad reflected with a nod. "He's more relaxed, at peace. He's happier. Of course," he added, "you might have something to do with it."

"He always seemed happy," Elaine argued.

"Yes, on the surface. But I knew him better. I think I was his happiness."

"That's not good," Elaine said with a frown.

"That's what Pastor Bruce says," Aimee replied. Elaine rolled her eyes and shook her head. "Now, it's like – he's free. Free to be himself. And I think he loves me even more. Mom, I'll ask him to talk with you. He can explain it better than I."

"Well....that makes me feel a little better. You're adults, so what can I say?"

"Mom, we've both changed. It's a radical change for us both." Elaine raised her eyebrows. "We see the world differently now.

Our values, our priorities, they've changed. It's not about us anymore." Roger looked at her quizzically. "Christ – God – He's part of the equation. We want to please Him."

"Oh, Lord!" Elaine exclaimed testily. "Is that supposed to make me feel better? I don't want to see some religious frenzy taking over your lives –"

"Mom, that won't happen –"

"Aimee, I'm not against religion. You know that," she said. "I think everyone should have a religion," she looked at her husband, who shrugged his shoulders, "something that's good, to comfort them, give them strength – but in moderation."

Aimee took her mother's hand. "This is different, Mom. It's not religion. Not like any other religion." Her mother looked puzzled. "No, it's not. It's a relationship, a relationship with God. Christianity is different. It's not what we do to please God, it's God reaching out to us through Christ, loving us. He is God, so we can know God personally. Mom, it's unbelievable, it's wonderful –"

"Aimee, that's enough," Elaine said, withdrawing her hand. "I don't like what I'm hearing. Or seeing. That other-worldly look on your face –" she shook her head.

"It's love, Elaine," Roger interjected.

Aimee blinked with surprise, staring at her father. "Dad -?"

"Like you and Rob," he said. "I'm just explaining to your mother, that's what worship is. It's love."

"Dad –" Aimee repeated, still trying to understand.

He held up his hand. "No, no, not me. It's not for me."

Aimee patted his arm. "Dad, you do understand," she said gratefully.

"Well, I'm not completely ignorant."

"Roger, I…." Elaine shook her head. "I don't know what to make of you."

"Hey, Aimee –" Jason broke in, "that meeting you were telling about, are you coming home first, for dinner?"

"Oh, Jason!" She frowned, trying not to be annoyed at the interruption. "Yes, it doesn't start till eight."

"Then – could I go with you? I know I'm still in high school but I take college classes – do you think I could go with you?"

"You, too, Jason?" their mom asked with a worried look.

"Why not? I'm interested. Curious."

"If you're curious, just ask Aimee," she retorted. "I'm sure she'll answer your questions."

"It's Aimee I'm curious about! What would make my sister, who doesn't have a religious bone in her body, sit all afternoon on the deck reading the Bible? I have to figure this out."

Elaine shook her head slowly, staring straight ahead, her jaw set.

"Jason, yes, I'd love to take you," Aimee told him. "You would be very welcome. Rob would be glad, too. Is it okay with you?" she asked her parents. They looked at each other and shrugged their shoulders. "Jacquie, what about you?"

"No, no. This is your thing, not mine," she replied, drawing back.

"That's okay. I understand that."

"Aimee, you said this group starts at eight? What time do you end?" Elaine asked anxiously.

"Oh, eleven or so."

"You must be crazy. Rob's right, you need your sleep."

"Elaine, young people are crazy anyway. You know that. We were, remember?"

"Mom, we could be partying."

"That's true, but......"

"Say, Aimee," Roger spoke confidentially, "that code of yours, at the end – your mom and I did the same thing, once upon a time. But not three L's –"

"Dad, you'll just have to figure it out yourself. And Mom –" she kissed her mother on the cheek – "we'll be all right. Don't worry about us."

The following Friday Rob's construction site was close at hand and he decided to take his supper break when Aimee got out of work. They dropped in on Gramps for a few minutes.

"So, how are things going?" he asked.

"Oh, Gramps!" she exclaimed, throwing her arms around him. "Wonderful, wonderful news! About the wedding! We just realized we hadn't told you, we got so busy."

"Well, I can't wait to hear. Your '*wonderfuls*' are always wonderful to hear," he laughed in anticipation.

"Actually, this is Rob's story. He should tell it." She gestured to him.

"Ah – yes." He settled into a chair across from Gramps and made himself comfortable. "It's about the rehearsal dinner. I was getting pretty worried about it," he admitted.

Gramps raised his eyebrows. "What about it?"

"You know, traditionally, that's the groom's obligation. Or his family." He shrugged. "I don't have that kind of money. And what family? I sold the coins my grandparents had left and some old gold but that wasn't nearly enough."

"Dad said '*tradition be hanged',*" Aimee went on, "he said he had saved a bundle by not renting the lodge and the church didn't charge us anything because we're members. So he offered very kindly to help out with the cost of the dinner –but Rob," she smiled sweetly, "he wanted to do it himself –"

"Your dad was great, Aimee. I appreciated his offer, but this is my obligation."

"So –" she went on, "a few weeks ago," Rob continued, "a letter and a check arrived in the mail –"

"a very substantial check," Aimee added. Gramps looked on in suspense.

Rob shook his head, incredulous. "From Scott. Scott and Marie. They said, they're my family and they wanted to pay for the rehearsal dinner. Mind you, I hadn't said a word to them about it."

"They apologized for not doing it sooner," Aimee went on.

"They said if the dinner was already paid for they were sure I could find some other use for it," Rob continued. "But –" tears filled his eyes as he took Aimee's hand, "it's just the right amount to pay the bill, along with what I had," he said, his tears flowing freely. "Sometimes it –" he shook his head, "it overwhelms me. Their love. Everyone's love." He wiped his eyes as he struggled to regain his composure.

Aimee put her arm around him and kissed him. "You deserve it, honey. Enjoy."

"I'll second that," Gramps added, taking Rob's hand. "Now, you two, how's the rest of the wedding going?"

"Oh, oh, Gramps!" Aimee exclaimed. "It's all coming together! I can hardly believe it."

"I'm glad to hear! Especially after what you and your folks went through in the beginning."

"Yes. It seems that after we decided on the church, everything fell into place."

"Interesting." He nodded thoughtfully.

"Rob wanted me to have the most beautiful wedding in the world and I did too, but I wanted to keep it simple. Simple and lovely. Well, it's going to be." She smiled at him.

"You'll love that courtyard," Rob told Gramps, "since you're a '*roads and bridges*' man. It's well laid out, flagstone walks, even a little waterfall."

"So I will." He nodded in anticipation. "How's your mother doing, Aimee?"

"Well….she's agitated, of course. The closer we get to it the more things she thinks of doing. But she's got a lot of people helping her and she's taking vacation time from work. She's orchestrating the whole reception and dinner. We're doing it ourselves, my aunt and my cousin, Jacquie and Jason, and even a couple of women from the church who offered to help, along with their families. It's so amazing…"

"We're not breaking the bank," added Rob, "the Loves' or ours. Ha," he laughed, "what bank?"

"Yes, Mom said, '*no credit cards*'. Hers or ours."

"Good, good."

"So, then, we'll see you next Friday, at the rehearsal," concluded Rob.

"I wasn't planning on it," Gramps replied. "It would be too much."

"Are you sure?" they asked, disappointed.

"I'm sure. I don't need to be there," he asserted. "The guy who's pushing me, you make sure he's there, so he pushes me to the right places."

Rob laughed, "You're right, but we wanted you to have a chance to see people, visit a little. Take part in the fun."

"I'll have plenty of chances at the wedding. Isn't the rehearsal dinner at seven?"

"Right."

"See, that's too close to my bedtime. No, I'd better just stay here and conserve my strength for the wedding the next day. That will be enough. I get tired easily, you know."

"Okay," Aimee agreed reluctantly. "We'll drop in on you before we go to the church on Friday. It helps that you're close to Rob's place. We'll have Lenore with us, I'm picking her up at her apartment."

"Well, yes, you can do that. I'm always glad to see you! Speaking of being close…." He took Aimee's hand, "I don't know if I ever properly thanked you for twisting my arm to get me over here to Sunset Woods. Closer to you two."

"Oh, yes," interjected Rob, "she proposed, you accepted."

"Don't know about that. Seems to me I put up quite an argument. I wasn't going to move….."

"And then she smiled at you! With those eyes," Rob laughed and Aimee hugged Gramps.

"Ah, yes, Aimee my girl!" He patted her arm and Rob pretended to be jealous. "Yes, I looked around over here and something in me said, *'this is it'*. So Aimee, thank you with all my heart. It's been wonderful being so close to you two…."

"Our new apartment is close to you. You'll be able to visit us now, my dad and Jason are building a ramp. Rob's helping."

"Wonderful, wonderful!" he exclaimed happily, reaching over to shake Rob's hand. "That's good of them, of you all. I can't wait to visit you in your own home!" He smiled with pleasure. "I'm happy about your new place. A lot better than that concrete apartment. Now, I'd better let you get out of here so you can go about your business." They nodded. "Aimee, by the way, don't overdo it going to get Rob's mother. Couldn't Rob do it? That's a lot of driving to do on your rehearsal day."

"Oh, thanks, but it would be just as much for him. Besides, I'm used to driving."

"I don't want you to be exhausted on your wedding day. It could happen, you know."

"Don't you worry! Now, we'll tell you goodbye, and we love you."

Young people, Gramps muttered to himself, *they think they're indestructible*.

The next day Rob's job was cancelled because of a downpour. He and Aimee were spending the morning at a mall across town. In the excitement of their wedding preparations they were acting sillier and sillier, to the amusement or alarm of other customers. Rob's phone rang. "Hmm, it's Sunset Woods. Not Gramps' number. Hope nothing's wrong."

His face went white. "Gramps had a stroke."

Chapter 36

"He's at St. Luke's. That's all I know."

She clutched his arm. "Rob, you drive." She had driven her car but she knew he would race through the streets faster than she would. This time she wouldn't complain.

When they got to the hospital they made their way to a small family lounge to wait. Gramps was undergoing emergency treatment.

"Oh, honey – I didn't realize how much he means to me. It's Gram all over again. It's just not fair," she sobbed as they clung to each other. "Oh, you too," she added, remembering Rob's grandparents. He was blinking back tears. "It's okay, Rob, big boys do cry."

"Honey," he said fiercely, "I don't want to lose him! I've only just found him. And now...." He shuddered. Their tears mingled as they held each other close.

"People don't usually die of stroke, do they?" she asked.

"No – well, not unless it's massive. It's afterwards that's bad. The loss in functioning."

"It's not fair. Why Gramps? Why now? He was looking forward to our wedding. He's a good man, he honors God. And now...."

He dropped onto the settee. "I can't do it. I can't. I can't lose him! Aimee," he turned to her with an anguished look, "this must be how Gramps felt. First he loses my father, then my grandmother….no wonder he was angry." He buried his face in his hands.

"Rob, I know. It seems so unfair. I don't know why…." She put her arm around him.

"Honey," looking up, he lifted her chin. "We need to pray. Together. I know we were both praying in the car….in desperation."

"Yes, yes….but I don't know how to pray. I want God to heal him! But I don't believe in begging."

"I think we need to give him back to God. Leave him to God. Easy to say," he admitted, shaking his head.

"Yes, I feel like you do. I don't want to lose him."

"Honey," he kissed her cheek, "God is all we have. Gramps didn't have that faith, back then."

"Yes….I know God knows best. But I still don't want to lose him!"

He took her hands. "Honey, let's pray." So they did. At first they struggled, not knowing what to say. Then Rob thanked God that Gramps was in God's hands.

Aimee asked him to spare Gramps' life and that he not have any serious damage. She ended with "please, God, please. But I'm not begging."

They sat quietly, holding hands. "It's amazing, isn't it," Aimee said at last. "I feel peace."

"I know." He kissed the top of her head. "It has to be God, huh? Considering how we felt a few minutes ago. Honey, did we ever tell him we love him?"

"I'm sure we have. But let's be sure to tell him now."

They made calls, to Aimee's family, Pastor Bruce, Scott and Marie, Peter and Ming. "My mother, too," said Rob. "She can ask her church to pray." In the next hour they talked and waited impatiently until a doctor came out to talk with them.

"It was a major stroke," she said, "on the right side of the brain. That means his left-brain functions are intact, in other words, he has his cognitive abilities and speech. The good thing is, he got here fast. Before there was too much damage."

"Thank God for that!" Aimee said in a whisper.

"Yes. Remember, he is already a paraplegic. This puts a great strain on what he has left. Overall, though, he is doing well. His heart is strong. He should make a good recovery. Right now he's pretty sick. We're moving him to ICU and you can see him there. Don't be alarmed, though. He doesn't look very pretty."

They appreciated the warning. They hardly recognized him with the tubes and wires but he recognized them and acknowledged their presence. He tried unsuccessfully to speak. They told him he didn't need to.

Back in the waiting room Aimee had a sudden inspiration. "I'm going to get Howard," she said as she proceeded to call him. "It's still early enough for him to visit."

Howard was overjoyed to hear from her. He was beside himself with anxiety. All he knew was that his best friend had been rushed to the hospital. No further information was forthcoming. "Miss Aimee," he asked anxiously, "How is Allen? How is he?"

She told him what she knew. "Howard, I will pick you up and bring you here."

"I'll be waiting out front."

He was there as promised. "Thank you, Miss Aimee. Can't tell you what this means to me!"

"Howard, we knew you'd want to be here."

"Sure do. You know, the worst thing about living in a place like this is, you're stuck. Doesn't matter how nice it is. You can't just pick up and go. 'Course, I don't have a car anymore. But still, if I want to go anywhere I have to take a taxi. And wait for it."

"Today, I'm your taxi. And glad to be. By the way, he can only have family in ICU. So, you're his brother."

"Got it. '*Hello, brother*,' " he practiced.

Gramps brightened when he saw Howard. "Hello, brother," Howard told him. Aimee rejoined Rob to give them some time together.

"Hon, this is going to be an ordeal for Gramps. And for us. With the wedding just a week away….I'm going to call my boss and take off this week. He's got other guys waiting in the wings to take over."

"Oh, Rob." She considered what he'd said. "Financially…. what will that mean?"

"I still have a little savings. And I'm earning a lot more than I thought I would, so I'll make up for it when we get back. Is there any way you can get out of your house cleaning jobs? Without letting people down?" He shook his head. "You're busy enough with the museum. I don't want you to wear yourself out."

"I think so. That's a good idea. I could transfer my house-cleaning to Jacquie. You know, she was with me last week, I was training her to take over. I'm sure she'd like to earn the money, she's saving for car insurance."

"Let's do it, both of us. It will make things a little easier for us this week, and we'll be able to spend time with Gramps and each other."

"I like that. You're right. This is going to be a crazy week."

"By the way, after you take Howard back why don't you just go home? You'll be too tired to come all the way back here. I'll stay till later and catch a bus back to my place. I want to stay as late as I can."

Aimee hugged him, tears in her eyes. "Oh, darling….you're right. I'd like to stay, but I'm worn out. It will mean so much to him, to have you there. And you'll know what's going on every minute. Keep me informed about everything, won't you?"

The next morning at church she was surprised to see a taxi pull up and Rob get out. She hadn't heard from him. "Well, honey, I ended up spending the night there. He's doing as well as can be expected. Guess who came to see him?" She shook her head.

"Pastor Bruce. He'd have come earlier but he had a wedding. He came right after your family left. He stayed quite a while and we had a good visit –"

"My family? They were there?"

"You didn't know? You probably passed each other on the road."

"Maybe we did....but after I got home and ate some supper I went straight to bed. They weren't home, I didn't even think about it. I left this morning before they were up."

"They all came. They got a chance to see him, briefly. I think the staff bent a few rules. Your mom talked to the doctor; she knew what to ask. It was neat. It meant a lot to me. Pastor Bruce coming too." He gave her a kiss on the cheek.

"It means a lot to me too....I'm glad they came. And Pastor Bruce! that was good of him. I'll bet you didn't get much sleep."

"No, but I'll survive. It's not the first time. Gave me a chance to think. I had planned to go home and go to bed but then I thought, *I'd rather be here*." Aimee smiled in agreement. "Gramps was surprised to see me in the morning. It kinda made my day." He remembered Gramps' pleasure at seeing him and realizing he'd been there all night. It was a moment neither of them would forget.

In church they discovered comfort and support they had never expected. They learned that people had been praying for Gramps and for them. "It's totally amazing," Rob told Pastor Bruce. "I guess this is what you meant by the '*church family*'."

"You're finding out," he replied. "We're here for you."

"How was Gramps today?" Aimee asked Rob the next night when she joined him for a late supper at his apartment.

"He's making progress," Rob answered. "Slow but steady. He asked for you, that is, he said your name."

"Oh, honey, honey," she said with frustration, "please tell him I want to see him but I can't. They're working me to death these four days so I can be off on Friday. Imagine that!"

"The museum sure doesn't want to let you go."

"No, like I told you, I gave them four weeks' notice, but the Director told me I didn't have a right to ask for time off because

I'd only been there a few weeks! Can you believe that? I told her no, they'd had my services for eight months without pay, now could I kindly have a week off for a honeymoon? She huffed and puffed but I didn't back down! I hinted that the University would like to know whether their interns are well treated, even after they're hired on."

"That was clever, honey," he said approvingly. "Good for you!"

"I'm sorry to be dumping on you like this. It's just hard now because they're making me stay late every night to prepare for when I'm gone. The week before my wedding!"

"I don't think your advisor would be happy about that."

"No, but I'm not going to do anything about it. Rob, this meal is delicious – where did it come from?"

"People from church. I don't even know them. Then Ming came over and brought something for tomorrow."

"Why? Why would they do that?"

"Because of what I'm going through with Gramps. They took pity on me, the bachelor living alone, but they brought enough for two. They do it when there's sickness, I guess."

"Wow," she shook her head. "That is so amazing. I didn't know people did things like that anymore. In the 21st century."

"They said it was the church family, supporting us." He kissed the top of her head. "C'mon, eat up. Then I'm going to kick you out so you can go home and sleep."

"Yes, you're right. We were up late enough last night, going to the storage locker. I didn't get home until almost ten." She sighed. "It was a long weekend."

"It was rough on you, but I sure was glad to have you there."

"I'm glad I was there," she said. "I know you had intended to go alone. Well, I wouldn't have let you," she shook her head. "Too many memories. It was hard for you, I know. Besides, I wanted to see what was there."

"Right....gosh, I don't even remember packing that stuff. I told you, it was all a blur. But Ma Brannigan made me do it, go back into the house, pick out the stuff I wanted to keep. She went with me. I'm glad she did."

"I look forward to meeting her. At the wedding."

"You two will get along great."

"She was so wise, helping you pick out furniture. Now we'll be surrounded by some of your grandparents' treasured things. I love their bedroom set, and those beautiful lamps….your grandpa's recliner…."

"Right. And boxes and boxes of stuff from my old bedroom. Ugh! I'm not even going to open them. They can stay in our basement until I have the time and mood to open them up."

"I understand," she said sympathetically. "Just don't let it be ten years. Did you and Jason get it all over to the apartment?"

"All taken care of. He was able to borrow a truck and we were done by noon. We even got the furniture in the right rooms. Um, probably." he laughed.

"Ha, ha. A surprise for me. Rob – will it bother you to be using their furniture? Sleep in their bed?"

"I don't think so. I thought about it after you left. It's a good thing, I think. I'll feel close to them." He gave a little laugh. "Don't worry about me."

"Well, we're in this together. Now – I've got to go…. honey, I don't want to…."

He gathered her in his arms. "Pretty soon we won't have to say good-bye. Five more days."

"Umm…..wonderful….good night, my darling Rob."

Gramps was transferred out of ICU the next day and over to a step-down unit. Aimee was able to stop in briefly on her lunch break. She and Rob had a few quiet moments with Gramps before the doctor came in.

"He's making a remarkable recovery," the doctor told them when they were alone. "He should be back at Sunset Woods in another day. We have to credit his determination and a loving family. He talked about '*my kids*' – I guess that's you two, and his brother." Rob had been bringing Howard in every day.

"And a lot of prayer," added Rob.

"Definitely. As a physician, I see that making a critical difference."

"So, Doctor, do you think he'll be able to attend our wedding on Saturday?" Aimee asked impatiently.

"No, no. That won't happen. Don't expect it. He's still very, very weak."

She was crestfallen. "Oh – the way you talked – I thought surely –" she sighed. "You don't think so?" she persisted. "He means so much to us. I was really counting on his being there."

"Oh, my dear, I hear that all the time. Weddings, graduations. My, if love could heal a person we'd hardly have need of hospitals. No – it won't happen." She smiled. "Keep doing what you're doing. It helps more than you know."

"You've got to accept it, honey."

"No. I will keep praying. God can work miracles."

Chapter 37

They were relaxing after another late supper at Rob's apartment.

"Rob, what radical changes in our lives, since we gave ourselves to the Lord."

"I don't know," he shook his head, "I don't see that much change in you. Myself, yes. But you've always been pretty wonderful."

"Ah, love is blind. You're sweet. But there has been a radical change in me."

"Really?" he asked skeptically. "In what way?"

"A couple of things," she began slowly. "Mom has always said I could be pretty nasty when I want to be. I never wanted to believe it, but deep down....I know it's true."

"I shouldn't be surprised," he teased. "You're good at anything you do."

"Ha, ha! Smart, aren't you! Well, you might have seen my nasty side someday. Anyway, I don't want to be that way, anymore." He took her hand. "Another thing....how shall I say it? The *Queen Bee* has been de-throned." She pointed to herself.

"And replaced with what? The worker, or the drone?" He laughed, pointing to himself.

"No. By...." She thought a moment. "By the *Keeper of the Bees*."

"Hmm. Go on."

"It's hard to admit, but...I have been the *Queen Bee*. It's true, Little Sister was right. I've always known how to get my own way. I've always thought of myself as special, more so than others." She gave a little laugh. "Now that's a very painful confession, I'll have you know. Your mother taught me I wasn't."

"My mother? Oh, yes, you told me."

"Yes. I liked her from the beginning, you know that, but also, I thought of myself as above her. Superior. She saw that, and it hurt her. Thank God, she told me. I saw myself in a whole new light. I didn't like what I saw."

Rob took her hands. "I see what you mean. So, Aimee, you've been de-throned. A revolution? A new government?"

"Yes," she laughed, remembering. "When your mother told me I '*needed*' God – I resented that! I didn't need God or anybody, I had it all together. But then I realized I was needy too; that's when I came to Christ. But that's not the end of it. Pastor Bruce's sermons are helping me. I'm learning that I'm not in charge. I can't be that Queen Bee anymore."

"Ah, '*The Keeper of the Bees*'. It makes sense. So.....'*Little Sister*' was right." He nodded knowingly. " '*Little Sister*' knew."

"Yes, I told you that. What are you getting at?"

"Honey, will Jacquie always be '*Little Sister*' to you?" He squeezed her hand.

"Of course! She's seven years younger! What are you saying?" she asked with a touch of irritation.

"I wonder how she feels about being called '*Little Sister*'. She may think of it as a put-down."

"I would never put her down! Well....she's never complained. We're sisters. What do you know about sisters? You're an only child. Rob, aren't you creating a problem where there is none?"

"I think she does mind. And I know more about sisters than you might think. The girls next door, I remember their fights. Used to drive Matt and me out of the house!"

"See, Jacquie and I don't fight. But," she shrugged, "if you want me to, I'll ask her how she feels about it, my calling her '*Little Sister*'."

"If I know Jacquie, she'll say she doesn't mind. But....what do I know? I'm just a dumb guy."

Aimee sat for a moment, chin in her hands, thinking. "Do you really think it's a put-down? I know you wouldn't say something without a good reason." She sighed. "Maybe that's why she calls me the '*Queen Bee*'."

"Could be. When you call her "*Little Sister*" you're not equals."

"I never thought of that." She was quiet for a moment. "But now that she's almost an adult.... I guess I need to think of her as my equal. Is that what you're saying?" She frowned. "Rob, I trust your judgment. What do you suggest?"

"Suppose you just tell her you're not going to call her '*Little Sister*' anymore? See what she says?"

"You may be right. She's not just '*Little Sister*'. She's Jacquie. I need to treat her that way."

She took his hand and kissed it. "My sweet Rob. What would I do without you?"

"Well – I don't want you to find out! Now – were you going to say something else? I think I sidetracked you."

"Yes, yes. Getting back to changes...." She thought about it. "I'm seeing the world differently now. More intensely. It's amazing! It's a whole new world. The grass is greener, the sky is bluer. It's like when people talk about their drug experiences, except, my feet are on the ground and my head isn't exploding. Is that crazy or what?" she laughed.

He nodded in agreement. "I know. Me too. It's like – my eyes are opened."

"Yes! That's it! Now – what changes in you?"

"I'm still thinking things through. Like I told you in the beginning, it's a radical shift for me. It was always about me, what I wanted. Now, I'm trying to figure out what God wants with me, where I fit into His plan, what He wants us to do –"

"Yes, I know that. But what about here and now?"

"Hmm....There's a difference. It's hard to explain...." His mood shifted as he struggled to find the words. "There was a...a hole in my heart. I don't know how else to say it. I didn't think of it that way, but there was something missing. Gramps' love didn't fill it, and your love didn't either." He held her hand tightly. "Even though you were everything in the world to me. After I came to Christ, though – I told you I felt peace about Grandma and Grandpa – then I realized, there's more to it than that. It was like, the hole was filled."

Aimee looked at him, her eyes shining. "Rob, honey, how wonderful...."

"Pastor Bruce and I talked about it at the hospital. He said that's one reason Christ came, to heal our wounds. I didn't want to admit I had wounds. I wanted to think I had it all together.... except in those dark moments, alone. God knew, didn't He!" He blinked back tears as he put his arm around her. "Oh, baby, it's wonderful."

She stroked his face. "Anything else?"

"I want to tell the world, honey – tell people that Christ can change their lives."

"Yes, yes – I do too! I think about your mother....how excited she was to tell me about Christ, and I didn't want to hear it. But honey, she led me to Christ! Isn't that amazing?"

"You don't know the half of it," he laughed. "Never in a million years would I have expected that from her. But it tells me that I need to tell others."

"Too bad Bryan blew you off."

"No, I think he was interested. He came to Bible study. But he wasn't ready."

"Maybe you planted a seed."

"I think so. You know, I had a good talk with Joel the other day. He has a different perspective, he's Jewish, but he has an open mind. It makes me dig deep for answers. I want to talk to Pastor Bruce about it, or Peter. They can help."

"Rob, that is great! Now, how are things going with the guys on your crew? I know they found out early on that you're a Christian. So how's it going?"

"It's pretty good. They're a nice bunch. You know, at DeGeorgio's, it was so cut-throat I always had to watch my back. These guys, I feel like they have my back. Some of them are even talking with me about God."

"Do they still call you Mr. Clean?" She laughed, remembering his stories.

"Ha, ha, not as much. I think they respect me now." He shook his head and smiled. "It's unbelievable! The changes in both of us. Another thing....it still surprises me....I'm discovering creation. Like – that sunset the other night –"

"Oh, it was awesome!"

"Yes – how could anyone see it and not see a designer, an artist – God?"

"Well, we never did. We just took it for granted. Now it's like, I see God everywhere."

"Right! You know, even love is part of creation." He took her by the chin. "How could love possibly have evolved?"

"Yes....God's gift of love. What a gift!" She took his hand. "Rob....." she said thoughtfully, "Did you ever think we would believe in creation? Does that make us members of the lunatic fringe?"

"It makes us members of a very select group of people," he declared. "I've been looking things up online and I'm impressed with the caliber of scientists who believe in creation, or as they may put it, intelligent design. I remember Scott's words. He said the universe reveals order and design, by a designer, God. And he said: *'that God I worship'*. Aimee, I feel that way too."

"Yes...oh, yes, I do too. But," she frowned, "I haven't told Mom and Dad. About my belief in creation." Rob looked puzzled. "Dad would shrug his shoulders and say *'whatever'*. It wouldn't matter to him. But Mom! Rob, you have no idea. No idea." She shuddered.

"Umm....." he reflected, "I know what you mean. She would think you had '*gone off the deep end.*' "

"More than that. She would worry! Seriously worry about me. She has great respect for science. She's never been able to understand people who, as she puts it, '*deny Evolution*'. With a capital 'E', no less, it's almost sacred to her. Yes," she sighed, "that would make me, make us, members of the '*lunatic fringe*'.

"Oh, baby –" he put his arm around her, "you have to tell her someday."

She shook her head. "Not until she brings it up. She'll worry about my future, my chance for advancement, she'll think I checked my brains at the door of the church."

"She's got a point, about creation," he nodded. "It could close doors for us. Lots of people think the way she does. Most people, in fact. But I feel like, so what? Let the chips fall where they may." He nodded. "Look, honey, it's different for you, I know that. She's your Mom, and you're so close....

"I'm fine with my beliefs, until I think of Mom." She shook her head. "I'll face it when it comes. Honey.... do you still have questions? I still do, about some things."

"Oh, sure. I've been keeping Peter and Pastor Bruce busy, texting them; it seems one question leads to another – but it's good, I'm seeing things a lot more clearly –"

She looked at him with surprise, hurt in her eyes. "Rob – you never said. Why couldn't you talk with me?" *His independence!* she thought. *Is this what he means by 'independent to a fault'?*

"Oh honey...." He stopped, chagrined. "I should always talk with you first –"

"Yes. Your best friend....and I don't mean Peter," she said pointedly. "We could talk about these things together."

"Sweetheart," he shook his head, "you're right. How could I overlook you? We're in this together; we need to learn together, grow together...

"Let's remember that. Rob?" She paused, contemplating. "Do you ever wonder, why us? We owe God so much."

"I think about it a lot." He took her hands. "I feel closer to you than ever before. More than I ever could have imagined."

"Yes. There's a whole new dimension to our relationship. I now have a knight in shining armor."

"Aimee, what are you talking about?" he asked reprovingly. "Not me."

"Yes, you. Oh, I'm not a damsel in distress. You know how independent I am."

"I sure do! So what do you mean?"

"I'm learning to be dependent. In a good way. I'm dependent on your love, to complete me. Another thing. I admire you. I do, Rob, I admire and respect you. As a man! Don't be embarrassed, honey. You really are my knight."

He shook his head. "Oh, no...."

"I didn't say you were perfect."

"Ha, that's a relief! Did I ever tell you I love you?"

"Tell me again, I love to hear it," she smiled. "And I love you! Now, I've got to go home. Morning comes early."

"You're earlier tonight, I like that," Rob told her, taking her in his arms as she entered his apartment after work, carrying dinner boxes. He cleared a chair. "It's the ultimate mess. It's making me crazy."

"Yes, and soon the mess will be out of here and messing up our new apartment. I don't like that," she shook her head, frowning.

"Not to worry. Everything's under control."

"I'll find out, won't I! How's the painting coming along?"

"Almost done. Your family and I have had a great time, let's see, red, white, and blue, black and blue, neon yellow and orange –"

She screamed as she sank back into her chair. "I trust mom. She'll have it looking beautiful when we get back from our honeymoon." Her mood changed. "Honey, I told you I had bad news."

"Well....your text has me curious. Something bad about your lunch with Natasha. And your grandparents? Go ahead and tell me while I get this on the table. What about her?"

"No, no," she replied, "I must have mixed it up. I'll tell you about Natasha later. Rob, it's...." tears filled her eyes, "it's....."

"Honey, what, your grandparents?" he asked. He took her hand.

"Yes, Grandma and Grandpa Love. They won't make it to our wedding," she said. Rob looked at her with surprise. "They were due to fly in tonight. But Dad and Mom got a call today, Grandpa had something with his heart last night and he's having a pacemaker put in today." She sobbed into Rob's shoulder. "Oh, honey, they were so looking forward to being here! I can't believe they won't be here to see me married – oh, and you too, they love you too –"

"Baby, that's a shock," he replied, taking her to the couch and sitting with her. "First of all, I'm glad your grandpa got help when he did. Better at home than in the air or at the wedding."

"Yes....we thought of that. But it's really, really disappointing. They plan to come up when we're back from our honeymoon....but that's not the same."

"I'm disappointed too, not to see them at the wedding. I liked them a lot. They seemed pretty special to you."

"They are. To our whole family. Mom feels very bad about this. They've always treated her like a daughter. In fact," she gave a little laugh, "Mom used to say she hoped I had a relationship with my in-laws like she has."

"Ha, not much chance of that," Rob replied, shaking his head.

"Oh, no," she disagreed. Rob raised his eyebrows. "Marie and Scott. They're my in-laws. Marie and I have been keeping in touch, you know that."

"Ah, we're blessed, aren't we? Scott and Marie, I feel like I've known them all my life. They seem like parents to me. So, have you talked to your grandparents? How is your grandpa doing?"

"Yes, I did right away. He's feeling a lot better. I'll call tonight when I get home. Now, I'm getting hungry! Did I hear you say you were going to serve dinner?"

"I might. If you'll tell me about your talk with Natasha while I get things on the table...."

"I could do that. It helps take my mind off Grandpa. Now, about Natasha...." she rolled her eyes, "it was weird."

"Hmm, Aimee-weird I know. But Natasha-weird? What's that about?"

She joined him at the table. "I'll tell, you decide. Well," she began, "we bumped into each other carrying our trays in the food court at the Mall. I suggested we eat together, just a quick meal, I had to get back to work. She seemed a little hesitant. Cool. I thought, *did I offend her?* I had called her after graduation and asked how she was and she said, fine, she was getting over Bryan. But I haven't contacted her since."

"She hasn't contacted you either, has she?"

"No. She hasn't. She couldn't exactly say no to my invitation. I started out asking what life was like after Bryan. I asked her, '*Anything exciting happening*?' "

> *'I'm done making a fool of myself,'* she answered me. *'I never should have pushed him about marriage. If I hadn't, I'd be in Boston with him right now.'*
>
> "I thought, *what am I hearing? 'Natasha,'* I tried to be gentle. *'He told Rob he never intended your relationship to be permanent. He intended it to end with his graduation –'*
>
> " *'Oh, no,'* she interrupted me, *'That's not what he told me!'* She was angry. *'I prefer to believe Bryan,'* she said. *'Not some ugly thing Rob dreamed up.'*
>
> "I didn't know what to say to her. I didn't want to throw it back in her face. *'Well, Natasha,'* I told her, '*in any case – it's over. I hate to see you be hurt*."

'I don't need your compassion,' she said, cold as ice. *'If you hadn't filled Bryan's head with ideas about marriage before he's ready, he never would have dropped me. Besides, who says it's over? He misses me. He says we were very good together. Better than that she-cat he's with now. And when he comes back to visit his mother, well, we'll see what happens!"*

'You're talking with him?' I was shocked."

''Now don't you lecture me, Aimee Love. Of course we are, on Facebook.'

"I asked her, *'Do you think that's fair to his new girlfriend?'*

'That's Bryan's decision, isn't it? Anyway, he used to talk to his old girlfriend when he was with me. So what?'

'It didn't bother you?'

'I didn't let it bother me,' she answered. *'Bryan doesn't like possessive women, you know.'*

"I can't believe this!" Rob broke in. "It's like she has her own fantasy about what happened – some alternate reality!"

"That's what I thought too, but maybe not. Maybe Bryan was trying to let her down gently so he blamed us. Blamed me. But even so, it was weird listening to her."

"Oh, he planned this all along. He's a jerk!"

"I think you're right," she agreed. "He chose to drop her. She's not seeing that. It's too painful."

"She's got it wrong about being possessive." He stopped and thought. "No, he's got it wrong! That's just an excuse for not being faithful. If they were committed to each other, they'd be exclusive ...."

"I guess they weren't. Or, he wasn't. What if the shoe were on the other foot? Would he want her to check out her old boyfriends?"

"Not Bryan! I know him. So, what happened next?"

"I told her, '*I don't think that's being possessive. But – what are you doing now? Do you still have your apartment?*'

'*Yes,*' she said, '*My sister's staying with me until August, to help pay the bills. I intend to keep that place, it's beautiful. I just need to find the right person to live with me. People know I'm looking.*'

" '*Male or female?*' I asked her.

'*Male, for now. I'm sure I'll find the right guy by then.*'

'*Right guy' – for marriage? Didn't you want Bryan to marry you?*'

" '*Ha!*' she said. She was very bitter. '*Marriage and love are highly over-rated. It's okay for some people, you, you're almost a nun, and you found yourself a nice boy. Nice but naïve. I ought to give him a how-to book as a wedding gift.*"

"Oh…! I was ready to let her have it! I could have cut her up in little pieces. But suddenly I remembered I'm a Christian and I knew it wouldn't be right. I was speechless. I thought, '*Lord, what can I say?*' "

Rob had never seen Aimee cut anyone in little pieces but he was sure she could do a good job of it. "So, then what?"

"I took her hand. She pulled it away from me. '*Natasha,*' I said. I waited until she looked at me."

"Natasha, what do you want out of life? What are you looking for?' Rob, that's what my mother asked herself. It changed her life. She seemed startled. She thought a minute, then she said, *'I don't know. I've never thought about it. To be happy, I guess.'*

"So I told her, *'Natasha, I've found the real meaning of life. Real happiness, what life is all about –'*

"She didn't want to hear it. *'Okay, Aimee, that's enough! I don't need you to tell me how wonderful it is to be in love –'*

"No, no!' I told her, *'It's not Rob. It's not marriage.'* Now that stopped her. *'Natasha, it's knowing Christ, personally. He is the real meaning of my life.'* I could tell she was all ready with an angry reply so I went right on.' " *Natasha, it's real. Christ has turned my life around. Given me new meaning. Happiness – beyond Rob. He turned Rob's mother's life around too. She was chasing happiness, with men and alcohol, and it almost destroyed her. She let Christ come into her life and she's done a total transformation. She's learned she doesn't need a man to be happy –'*

' "She interrupted me. *'Aimee, I said that's enough! I don't want –'*

"I interrupted her. *'Natasha, you may not be ready to hear this now. But someday you may, and you can look me up.'* That was it. I smiled at her and got up. Then I added, *'Remember, if you ever need a friend, I am your friend. Oh, and I hope you'll still come to our wedding.'* Then I left. She was pretty astonished."

Rob was equally astonished. "Aimee, that's amazing. That's wonderful. I'm proud of you." He hugged her.

"But I didn't defend you," she said with dismay. "You defended me to Bryan, and here was Natasha saying horrible things about you –"

"This was different, honey. If you had, you'd have gotten into some big fight. This was much better. God put those words in your mouth, huh?"

"Yes, because I never thought of telling her about God. All of a sudden, the words were coming out of my mouth. Isn't that amazing?"

Rehearsal day at last. The wedding party was to gather in the late afternoon in the church courtyard for the rehearsal, then go to dinner afterwards.

Aimee left at noon to get Lenore. Rob had offered, but she insisted. "I want us to have some time together. Just the two of us. Woman to woman. Get to know my future mother in law in a new way."

Shortly after one o'clock he got a confusing text from her. Puzzled, he called her back. "Rob! Oh, Rob, I don't know how to tell you," she said, hardly able to talk. "Your mother's drunk. Falling down drunk. She hardly knew me."

Chapter 38

Gramps was sitting up in bed, reflecting on the last few days. He tried to shift his position but found it difficult using only a quarter of his body. *They tell me I had a stroke. A stroke! What a shock. I've known people here who had strokes, not even very bad ones, and they never really recovered. They just gave up. Too much effort. Well, I know how they feel. But – I have to recover! For Rob and Aimee's wedding. I want to go. Is it tomorrow? Or the next day? Is the rehearsal today? They were to come over, with Lenore. Amazing, how well she's doing. It will be good to see her again.*

Dear God, I don't want to miss their wedding…..I've watched those two all this year. My life has changed so much since I met them. When I think what they mean to me, they've enriched my life so much! Dear Lord, I want to see them married, see them walk up the aisle hand in hand, Mr. and Mrs. Robert Allen Carlyle, Jr. It will mean so much to me! My son's son! Can I do it? Or is it an empty dream? What can I tell them?

So, what day is today? If I ask Howard, he'll worry about me. If I ask the nurse it will go down in my chart, 'Mr. Douglas doesn't know the day of the week.' The date is written on the wall on the other side of the room in big letters, but I can't make it out. Have I lost vision from the stroke?

Are they coming today? Or tomorrow? I don't know. And what will I tell them?

Drunk? Rob didn't know what to say. He didn't want to believe it.

Stifling a sob, she went on, "Rob, we just have to forget about her for now. There's nothing I can do. I'm coming back."

"Did you call Rose?"

"Yes, first thing. I left a message. I haven't heard from her. She may be out of town."

"Well, you're right. You've got to let it go. Just come right back. I'll be waiting for you. Honey, we can't let this ruin our wedding," he said urgently.

"I know, I know. Rob, you've got to cancel her motel."

"Right. See you soon, honey. Drive carefully. Please."

An hour later a sober-faced Aimee stumbled into the apartment and fell into Rob's arms.

"Oh, Rob….what a disappointment." She started to cry.

"Aimee, Aimee, you're a bundle of nerves!" He held her close, then led her to a chair. "Let me get you a cold drink." He came back in a minute with a couple of glasses of iced tea. "You've been going through a lot lately. Worried about Gramps, and now my mother. Hey, what if you had something really big, like a wedding? Then you would be upset."

She gave a faint laugh. "Umm, I'm lucky to have you. Rob, I was thinking about this all the way back. Gram told me that some people are afraid to succeed. They feel they don't deserve to. So they relapse. That may be it."

"I don't know. Maybe you're right."

"I know all that, but," she shook her head, "why does it have to be our wedding? I hate to say it but – after all we've done for her, it's just not right!" She stopped. "Rob, I'm not thinking of you. She's your mother! How is this affecting you?"

"Ha!" He shook his head. " *'If she couldn't bother to come to my graduation, why would she bother to come to my wedding?'* That was my first thought. I remembered growing up, when she'd come to visit and my grandparents would ask her to come to my ball game or band concert – and she never did. Never. *So, here we go again*, I thought. All that old bitterness came back."

"Oh, honey…." she held him.

"I started to pace, and I called out to God, in anger. I said, '*What's going on with her? I want to understand her. I don't get it. Help me!"*

"Well, that's a prayer. In a funny kind of way."

"I guess it was. A thought occurred to me, about those old bitter experiences – back then, she was selfish. Totally. Now, she's trying not to be. I believe that. So, something else must be going on. Then I thought, she sees the world through her own eyes. Based on her experiences. It's different from ours. So, whatever she did makes sense to her. And if we saw through her eyes, it would make sense to us."

"Wow. God does speak to us, doesn't He…"

He shook his head, trying to understand. "What's really strange, I wasn't bitter anymore."

" *'Through her own eyes,'* she echoed. "That's good. It's profound. That can help me understand you, Mr. Rob Carlyle."

"Well, it helps me too. I don't always understand you, Aimee Love soon-to-be Carlyle. This can help us both. -You're right, this is profound, almost as profound as *'I do'*.'"

"Um, our promises to each other. You are so right." She put her arm around him.

"Our promises. It's kind of scary, the closer we get to it….. but in a way, kind of comforting too." They held each other close.

"Because we trust each other."

"Trust, yes. Gramps told me that one time. That our promises are based on trust. I've never forgotten it. Pretty heavy stuff, hey."

"Too heavy for me right now. I can't think at all." She leaned back into her chair. "Rob, I am so hungry! I didn't stop to eat, I came directly here. I'd love something to eat.... if you'll make it."

"It won't take me a minute." He went to the kitchen and fixed a couple of sandwiches. They ate and talked, struggling to make sense of had happened, then he pulled her onto his lap. "Do you still want to go see Gramps? Maybe you should stay here and rest...."

"I want to see him. We still have a couple of hours until the rehearsal. Oh, I hope he can come to our wedding!"

"Honey, don't expect too much from him. He doesn't have his strength back."

"I can hope," she insisted.

"Try to take a little nap, then we'll go see Gramps." He stroked her back. "Listen, honey, we've got to forget about my mom. This is our time. Tomorrow about this time we'll be man and wife." He kissed her face. "Can you believe it?"

"Oh.... I can hardly believe it...." she murmured.

"Don't let Mom get to you. Just put her out of your mind. We won't talk about her."

"Mmm...." She was almost asleep. Rob sat with her a while, then carried her to the couch and gently set her down. *Sweet, sweet, falling asleep in my arms! This is just the beginning,* he thought with anticipation.

He got himself ready for the evening ahead. After a while he kissed her.

"Umm – what a beautiful way to wake up," she sighed with pleasure, putting her arms around his neck. "Prince Charming wakes Sleeping Beauty with a kiss! I feel better now. Do we still have time to see Gramps? Do you think he'll –"

"Honey, I don't know. We'll just have to wait and see. Now, we'd better go."

"I'll be ready in a few minutes."

As they were driving there he remarked, "Something else happened today. I forgave my mom. And I figured out something about forgiveness."

"I thought you weren't going to talk about her," she said impatiently. " '*Put her out of your mind*,' you said."

"I know, I know."

"I thought you already had forgiven her. You've been pretty nice to her lately."

"Yes, but I never forgave her. I kind of expected her to mess up so I could say, at least in my mind, '*I told you so*'. I realized it today. It's like a payback for all the years she failed me."

"I'm glad for you, but I certainly have my issues with her," she said heatedly. "Didn't she realize what we've been through all week with Gramps?"

"I don't think she gave it a thought."

"Well! She should have. Why did she choose my graduation for her panic attack? And our wedding for her – whatever caused her to relapse?" she asked with increasing agitation.

"Aimee, that's not rational."

"I don't care whether it is or not!" she replied, her voice rising.

"Oh, Aimee," he said dismissively. "Besides, I thought you had it all figured out. Your Gram, what she told you?"

"Figuring it out is one thing. It still hurts. You're used to her hurting you. I'm not! It's just so aggravating!"

"You weren't going to let her hurt you, remember?" He found himself gripping the steering wheel. *How did we get into this*, he asked himself. "Look – honey, you can't let it upset you. Not today, of all days. It doesn't matter. You've got to give it up."

"Now don't get superior on me, Mr. Rob Carlyle!"

"Superior? I'm just trying to make things easier for you."

"By telling me what to do? I don't think so!"

"Aimee – I never meant –" He pulled into Sunset Woods.

"Rob, I have to work this out myself." Her tears started to flow. "And I could use a little comfort right now."

Bewildered, he stopped the car. He had never seen her like this. *God! What's wrong with her? What did I do? What do I do now,* he wondered helplessly as they got out of the car.

"Baby -what's wrong?" he asked, taking her in his arms.

She started to turn away but then let him hold her. “Oh, Rob, Rob, –” She started to cry. “Rob – I’m sorry, I’m sorry. I know you meant well. I shouldn’t have jumped on you. Why are we quarreling?”

“Oh, baby, we’re both on edge.” He kissed her face, ending with a good kiss on the lips. “We mustn’t take it out on each other. We need to back off. Relax a little. We‘ve been through so much today.” He led her towards a bench under the trees.

“What are you doing?” she protested, struggling with him. “No, we need to go in and see Gramps.”

He held her close. “Not yet, honey. Just a few minutes. We have time. You said you needed comfort.”

“No, we’ll be late! Umm...yes, you’re right...” He whispered a few words in her ear. “Oh, yes....That means so much. Oh, Rob....will you forgive me for being so snappy?”

“Well....I wasn’t very understanding. I should have been. Of course I forgive you. I always will.”

“It’s not so easy with your mother. I can’t seem to get over it. I can’t forgive her. So, what was your brilliant insight on forgiveness?”

“Not now, honey.”

“No, I have to work this out. So I can enjoy this evening.”

“Well.....we just choose to forgive her. Even if she doesn’t deserve it.”

“But it’s hard to do! I don’t feel like it. Rob, Rob. All these profound thoughts are making my head split. I need to see Gramps. I always feel better when I‘m with him.”

“Eh...what about me?”

“Oh, yes, you too,” she answered offhandedly. Seeing his hurt look she added, “Things are a little rough for me today. I‘ll be fine tomorrow.” She laughed nervously. “I have to be.”

I hope so. I sure hope so, he thought.

"Hello, Gramps!" Rob and Aimee were at his door. Aimee's smile was tense and tired.

"Hello," he said thickly. It was hard to form words. "Tomorrow – is that your wedding?"

"Oh, yes, yes," exclaimed Aimee. "Oh, Gramps, we do hope you can come," they gave him a hug and kiss.

"I don't know. Where's your mother, Rob?"

Aimee squeezed his hand. "Oh, Gramps!" Rob told the story.

Gramps held their hands. "Ah – relapse happens. There's a reason. We don't know why – but, there's a reason."

"That's the conclusion we arrived at," Rob agreed.

"Don't give up on her. But now –" he nodded his head. "Leave it alone. Enjoy your wedding." He shrugged. "Talk to her when you get back home."

"Right." Aimee gave him a kiss. "Now, Gramps, can Dad pick you up tomorrow? Just for the wedding. We won't ask any more."

"No. I can't do it," he said sadly, shaking his head. "I can't be up very long. Then I have to lie down. In fact – I have to lie down now." He pressed the button and lowered the bed.

Aimee put her arm around him, pressing her cheek to his. "Gramps, I understand. We do. We'll be thinking of you." Her tears were on his cheek.

"Hello there! Miss Aimee, Mr. Rob." Howard greeted them with a smile.

"We're glad to see you!" they exclaimed. "Howard, my dad will be over tomorrow to pick you up. At twelve thirty. He'll come to your room. You'll be sitting on the bride's side, with Mom and Dad. Because you knew me before you knew Rob." Rob rolled his eyes and shook his head, laughing.

"Oh, I'll be waiting. Wouldn't miss this for the world!"

"My dad has been wanting to meet you. Ever since he heard about you and Gramps catching the hen who laid the rotten eggs."

"Well, well, well. That's pretty nice. You tell him I'll be waiting."

"Look, hon," she pointed to Gramps, "he's asleep already."

"Yes. He's got a long way to go. Time for us to go now."

"Bye, Howard. See you tomorrow!" Aimee called. As they walked out Aimee put her arm around his waist and whispered in his ear, "Honey, the only one I'll be seeing tomorrow is you."

"Mmm...yes...Just the two of us."

A short while later they were at the church. Rob proudly introduced Aimee to Matt Brannigan and his family and Matt's mother. His sisters and their families were to come the next day.

Pastor Bruce and Aimee's parents were talking together like old friends. Aimee's aunt and cousin joined them.

Julie and Zach were there, greeting them with hugs and kisses. "Way to go, girl," Julie exclaimed, "you have a lot to look forward to! Both of you."

They welcomed Joel and Marta Greenberg, introducing them to Aimee's family who took them under their wing while Rob and Aimee were busy with other matters.

She introduced Rob to her former roommate Bridget who was there with her date. "Aimee," she whispered as they hugged, "you're an inspiration to me!"

There was a happy reunion with the Carlyle family. They eagerly introduced them to Aimee's family and Pastor Bruce, who took them into the Courtyard. Rob and Aimee and Scott and Marie remained behind.

"We'll be along in a few minutes," Rob told him.

The two couples were alone. With sad hearts Rob and Aimee told Scott and Marie about Lenore. "Ah, that's too bad," sighed Scott, "I guess it was just too much for her. Well, let's do what we can to help her." He and Marie put their arms around Aimee and Rob and prayed for her and Rob and Aimee.

"Thanks, Scott," said Rob, clapping him on the shoulder. "That helps. I think I can put this behind me. Get on with the important stuff!"

"Good lad." He looked at Aimee with concern. "How about you?"

She gave a faint smile. "I'm working on it. This has been a very hard day."

Scott patted her shoulder. "I'm sure it has been. Aimee, don't let this hurt you."

She nodded agreement.

Marie wrapped her arms around her. "Dear Aimee, you'll be all right."

Aimee smiled, then managed a laugh. "I'm better already. Thank you."

She found her parents and gave them a brief summary of what had happened with Lenore.

"But I'm all right, Mom, Dad. You mustn't worry about me." They hugged and comforted her.

"You don't look all right. You have to put all this out of your head," advised her mother. "Believe me, I know."

"I'd like to pop her one!" declared her dad, scowling.

"Thank you....thank you both. I love you. Now, don't worry about me."

Rehearsal went smoothly. Elaine had already seen the Courtyard and highly approved of it. Roger did too but, "You realize, sweetheart, if it rains you'll have to use the church. And we don't have any flowers besides what you all will be carrying."

"Oh, Dad, it's not likely. I checked the forecast. Besides, I'm praying for a sunny day. Don't you worry."

The rehearsal dinner at a nearby restaurant was a joyous occasion, marred only slightly by the absence of Gramps and Lenore. Aimee rose to announce that Rob was the recipient of a generous scholarship, as the son of a fallen Marine. Everyone cheered. From then on the evening grew more boisterous with the mingling of two families with teenagers amid the excitement of the occasion.

Aimee leaned back against Rob as she gazed around the room. "What did we do to deserve such happiness?"

He kissed the top of her head. "Pretty wonderful, isn't it... And the best is yet to come." He looked at her with concern. "You need to get home, now. You need sleep. Was it today you went out to get my Mom? It seems like a week ago." She could hardly keep her eyes open. "I'm taking you home," he whispered, "for the very last time."

He turned to Joel with a few words of explanation. "Tell everyone we'll see them tomorrow. Don't forget to come!"

She didn't protest as he picked her up and carried her out, stopping first to say goodbye to Roger and Elaine. "Oh, my goodness!" gasped Elaine. "Is she all right?"

"I'm worried. She's exhausted."

"I'm fine," Aimee murmured into Rob's shoulder. "Mom, take my car home, will you?" She handed her purse to her mother.

"Of course." Elaine looked her over quickly. "She's strong, I'm sure she'll be all right," she told Rob. "Here, take my keys to get into the house. I'll check her out when I get home."

"Don't worry, hon," Roger told her. "She's in good hands."

Chapter 39

That night Aimee slept soundly and awoke feeling refreshed. She looked out the window to see a steady downpour. "It takes more than a little rain to dampen my spirits today!" she told her mother.

But to God she complained, "Lord, why did you let it rain today? Couldn't you have given me a sunny day?"

Because of the rain Pastor Bruce called the bride and groom and the two chief attendants to the church for a quick run-through in the sanctuary. Aimee picked Rob up at his apartment and then drove to the church. They ran through the rain and met Pastor Bruce in the doorway. Entering the hallway they chatted for a minute, then he sensed all was not well with Aimee. She was near tears. "Wedding jitters, Aimee?"

"It's more than that," Rob answered for her, putting his arm around her.

"Come on in my office for a few minutes," he offered. "The rehearsal can wait."

Seated in his office, Aimee asked, "Pastor, was it wrong to pray for a sunny day? I prayed, expecting God to grant my request." Tears filled her eyes.

"No, Aimee, it's not wrong. But always remember who's in charge. He'll answer your prayer according to what is best for all concerned."

"Well....I admit it, I'm disappointed. I really had counted on the courtyard, and the flowers, and sunshine. I feel let down. I suppose it's childish....but I prayed, believing!"

"Don't let it shake your faith, Aimee. God knew what He was doing. Now..." he looked at her closely. She was still tense. "Are you okay? Is something else bothering you?"

They related the story of Lenore and her relapse. "We didn't see it coming," Rob explained. "She was doing so well."

"What a shock to you both," he said sympathetically. "And of course you've been concerned all week for your grandpa. Not to mention getting ready for a wedding."

They nodded.

"Rob, how are you taking this? I know she's hurt you before."

"I'm okay. Really I am."

"Aimee, how about you?"

"I'm doing better than I was," she replied slowly. "I'm trying not to blame her. You know, she introduced me to Christ. I owe her so much. And now this!" She shook her head, puzzled. "I don't understand it. She hurt me, she really did."

"Aimee, people will fail us," he said gently. "We fail others. It hurts. You'll have to tell her that someday. But, don't worry about forgiving her. It will come. You're doing well." He smiled at them. "The important thing now is to turn it all over to God. That will take a load off your shoulders and allow you to focus on the happiness of your wedding day. It also frees God to work. We can ask God to speak to your mother and give her true peace of mind. And you, your peace of mind too." He led them in a prayer that covered all of this.

"Pastor, that helps," Aimee told him. "I'm not going to think about this until we get back from our honeymoon."

"That's the right idea, hon," said Rob, squeezing her hand.

Leaving the Pastor's study, they walked over to the sanctuary. At the entrance Aimee stopped. "Rob – look," as she grasped his arm. "It's beautiful!" The sanctuary was filled with flowers, hydrangeas in a palette of rose and blue, interspersed with shining white snowdrops and other white flowers. "Oh

– how did this happen?" she asked, falling into Rob's arms. He called to the custodian, who was arranging chairs. He came over, smiling broadly.

"Joe – who did this?" Rob asked.

"The women of the church," he said. "This morning, early, a few of them came over. They wanted you to have flowers."

"Oh, Joe!" she took his hand. "How loving! I can hardly believe it." Now the tears came. "Thank you. And I will thank the women. The colors – they're my wedding colors!"

"Yes, they called your mother," he told her.

She quickly dried her eyes and entered into a brief rehearsal in the new setting. Catching the pastor alone, she asked, "You knew about this, didn't you?" gesturing at the flowers.

"Yes, I did. I wanted you to be surprised." He laughed. "You were, weren't you!" He had been behind them.

The rehearsal over, she and Rob walked excitedly up the aisle hand in hand in anticipation of the same walk a few hours later. They spotted two figures off to the side, in the shadows, coming towards them. They walked over.

"Mom! I didn't recognize you. You look beautiful!"

Aimee gasped, taken aback by Lenore's sudden appearance and Rob's remark.

"Surprised, huh?" replied Lenore. "Well..." She shook her head apologetically, "I haven't been a beautiful mother to you."

"Mom," he looked at her, nodding his head, "I'm glad you're here."

Aimee noticed her makeup, newly colored hair and beautiful summer dress. *Rose's handiwork?* She took a deep breath. *Oh, Lord, am I ready for this?* She squeezed Rob's hand, drawing strength from him, then introduced Rob to Rose, the woman with her.

"Rob, this is Rose Caruso, your mother's sponsor and friend. Rose, this is Rob. You know all about him."

"Rose, I've wanted to meet you. I'm glad you're here today."

"Rob and Aimee," Rose replied, "I'm so glad to be with you today!" She paused. "I wonder if we could talk with you for a few minutes? A very short talk. Is there a private room where we could be alone?"

"Well….now isn't a good time," Rob replied. "How about during the reception? We have to get ready now."

"Rob, thank you, but that can wait," Aimee interrupted. "We can talk now." *Okay, she's here, this is it,* she thought. *There must be a reason. I can go with the flow. I don't have to be in charge. Even on my wedding day.*

On their way out they almost bumped into Pastor Bruce, who was leaving. They made quick introductions. He greeted Lenore and Rose with pleasure.

"Pastor Bruce, could you tell my mom I'm going to be delayed?" Aimee asked.

"Of course. I'll be glad to."

Seated in a small classroom, Lenore began.

"I never thought I would do this to you, again," she said with a moan. "It was bad enough on your graduation, Aimee, but – your wedding? It's unforgivable." She buried her face in her hands and began to sob.

Rose nudged her. "Watch the self-pity, Lenore. Get to the point."

She looked up and dabbed her eyes. "Yes. You see, Rose was on vacation for two weeks, so I stopped going to A.A. I thought, if I can't go with her, I don't want to go with anyone else. My big mistake. Then, I started thinking about Mark –"

"Oh, Mark!" interrupted Aimee, "I should have known! I could have –"

"No, no, Aimee. It's not your job to take care of me," Lenore corrected her. "Besides, it wouldn't have made any difference."

"She's right," added Rose. "We had talked plenty. It wasn't up to you."

"So, two nights ago – it feels like a month ago," she said with a sigh, "I lay awake all night, feeling guilty for giving up Mark. I knew I was going to see him….and I was afraid," she shook her head, "I was ashamed to face him. When morning came I was out of that apartment and down to the convenience store on the corner, first thing. I got me a six pack and a bottle....and I don't remember anything until night. Last night."

Rose picked up the story. "I got home from vacation and I got your message, Aimee. I tried to call you but your phone was turned off." Rose didn't text. "I went over to Lenore's, and she was sobering up, feeling pretty bad. But she'd made up her mind she wanted to go to the wedding anyway, if I could take her. I was planning to go, but not to the reception. I suggested we come early and get some things done in the morning, then leave after the wedding. So here we are. We didn't expect to see you until after the wedding."

Lenore spoke. "I need to say something. Aimee and Rob," she began, hesitantly, her eyes downcast. "I am so sorry...so sorry for what I put you through. I – I know I hurt you." She looked up at them nervously. "I hope you can find it in your hearts to forgive me."

"Mom," said Rob, putting his arm around her, "Mom, I'm very glad you're here. It adds to our joy. I forgive you." He kissed her forehead. "And Mom, don't worry about Mark. I'm sure it will work out." She began to sob. She pulled out a tissue and wiped her eyes, smudging her makeup. There were tears in Rob's eyes.

"You can't cry now!" Aimee told him, and handed him a tissue. "Lenore, thank you." She took Lenore's hands. "It was hard," she agreed. "Hard for us. I – we -were worried about you. I'm glad you're okay now." She hugged her. "I do forgive you, Lenore."

"Rob, Aimee, there's one more thing." Taking their hands, she began nervously, "You know that I made a commitment not to drink. But I found out, a commitment isn't enough. I have to work at it every day, a day at a time." She looked directly at them. "And I will."

Rose hugged her. "You're learning."

"Now, Rose," said Aimee, "you must stay for the reception. Lenore too."

"I didn't RSVP –"

"No matter," replied Rob. "We'll see to it. One other thing. Mom, you are the mother of the groom. You'll need to be here early, about one o'clock, so you can meet the usher who will walk you down the aisle. That's the plan."

"Oh, no, no...." she dropped her head. "I don't deserve that honor. Not anymore."

"Mom, yes," he said firmly. "Plan on it. You know, you gave me birth. You gave me a start."

"Lenore, we want you there. Rose will already be seated down front. You'll sit beside her."

"Well....I guess..."

"Yes. Lenore, Rose, good bye," Aimee took their hands, "now, we're out of here!"

They hurried down the hall. Rob picked her up and swung her around. "What do you say we get married?" He stopped. "Oh – your mother will be frantic!"

"No, I think she'll understand. Now, I know we're running late. But I'm going to be ready on time. So don't you be late!"

The wedding was only a few minutes late.

Elaine rose as the music heralded the bride coming down the aisle on the arm of her father. Tears filled her eyes so that she was hardly able to see. Roger slipped in beside her and put his arm around her waist. "Oh, Roger, she's so beautiful!"

"Almost as beautiful as you when you wore that dress twenty-five years ago," he spoke in her ear.

"Roger, you say the sweetest things. But it was twenty-four years ago."

"Just rounding it off, my dear, just rounding it off."

They settled into their seats, basking in the joy of seeing their first-born wed to a young man they had come to love.

Rob and Aimee stood before Pastor Bruce, hand in hand as he read the age-old vows, '*to love....to cherish.....as long as we both shall live....till death do us part....*' Their answers rang out with conviction, "I do....I will." They repeated the marriage promises with a confidence born of their commitment to each other, "I, Rob, take you Aimee...." and "I, Aimee, take you Rob...."

The pastor then delivered a short homily ending with,

"These two young people, Rob and Aimee, who we've come to love, have made a commitment today, a commitment before God. But, a commitment isn't enough. You have to work at it every day, a day at a time."

They looked at each other, incredulous. Lenore's words, exactly! How could he have known? Rob shrugged and smiled.

There may have been some in the audience who, seeing Rob and Aimee's surprised looks wondered if they were questioning the pastor's words.

"And now, friends, I give to you Mr. and Mrs. Robert Carlyle. Rob and Aimee Carlyle."

As they made their way back up the aisle, hand in hand, the sun broke through the clouds and streamed through the windows, bathing the room in light.

The receiving line had ended and Roger guided Elaine to a quiet spot where they could sit until time for the reception. "It's driving you crazy, huh?" he asked with a sly smile.

"You know me too well," she muttered.

"Your sister told me you are not allowed in that kitchen. She's got everything under control." Elaine started to protest. "And I'm the enforcer," he said menacingly.

"I give up," she sighed as she leaned against him.

"That's more like it. This is the first you've relaxed in four months. You need it." He put his arm around her. "It was a beautiful wedding and it will be a beautiful reception. You know, from what I saw it looked like everybody worked together."

"Even my sister and I. That doesn't always happen. But yes, the women from the church – I couldn't have done it without them. They were wonderful."

"Well, they wanted to be sure you treated their kitchen right."

"It was more than that. They let me know they were doing it for Aimee and Rob, and that made me feel good." She stopped and reflected. "We have a lot to be thankful for, Roger. God has been good to us. A wonderful daughter who married a good man. That doesn't always happen."

"I don't know why we can't take the credit ourselves," he replied.

"Oh, yes, you always said she was just like you. But the rest is from God."

"Ha, ha."

"And now you have another son."

"Right. He's a good boy. A welcome addition to our family."

Rob and Aimee were enjoying the first wedding dance. "Rob, you astound me! When did you learn how to dance?"

"Surprised, huh? Well, that's my secret. Oops, sorry!" as he stumbled on her feet.

"Married people aren't supposed to keep secrets." She smiled and pinched him.

He ignored her. "Your hair is so beautiful today," he said, kissing her curls.

"Well, this would qualify as a special occasion, wouldn't it?"

"Because we're together. Any time we're together is a special occasion."

"My mom wanted me to wear it up in some Greek goddess style, but I told her no, this is my special occasion."

"Very special. Our time."

"Rob, thank you for not smashing the cake in my face."

"I had much more fun feeding it to you. And having you feed me….. Hmm, are you happy, darling?"

"I can't tell you….." Tears filled her eyes.

"Well, now," he said mischievously, kissing her tears, "it's a little late for second thoughts. I don't think we can un-marry now."

She laughed. "I cry when I'm happy. You'll have to get used to that." She wiped her eyes. "It was fun being toasted – some of those toasts were so funny!" He frowned and looked away. "Oh, honey – what is wrong?" They stopped dancing.

"Bryan should have been here today. No, no –" he squeezed her hand, "I have no regrets." She looked puzzled. "He missed out. It was his own doing. But – we've been through so much, Bryan and I. He would have done a great toast." He sighed. "I miss him. I'll probably never see him again."

"Oh, honey…."

"Hey…." he put his arm around her and kissed her cheek. "Sorry I said anything. Forget about Bryan. This is our day, our time. Our night."

"My sweet Rob." She held him close. "Honey, I know why it rained today."

"Why is that?"

"I talked to Rose a little while ago. She said they hadn't planned to see us until after the wedding. They only came to the church to check out the address, then they were going to go do other things. But when they saw my car they decided to come in. And so, we had a chance to talk before the wedding."

"Wow. Was it worth it?" He looked at her closely.

"Rob, it was fine," she laughed. "God knew what He was doing."

"I'm glad, honey. I didn't want it to upset you. Hmm, Natasha didn't come, did she?"

"Not that I saw. You didn't expect her, did you?"

"Oh – I was hoping she'd bring that book she was talking about…you never know, I might need it," he replied with an innocent look.

"Rob! I'm sure you'll do all right!" She shrieked with laughter and tried to hit him as he wrapped her in a hug. Laughing, they collapsed on to a couple of chairs. "Oh, Rob, will you look?

Dad is setting up tables in the courtyard! Let's go out for a few minutes and greet people. Maybe we can find the photographer and have some pictures out there."

"Yeah. Let's go," he replied with mock seriousness. "It's getting way too rowdy in here."

She started to get up.

"Aimee," he pulled her back and sat her on his lap. "Speaking of wedding gifts –"

"We were? Oh, yes, Natasha's gag gift – ha, ha."

"Ha! That is funny. But you know, we have the perfect wedding gifts."

"We do? What are you talking about?"

He smiled and kissed her cheek. "Aimee, the most perfect gift," he repeated. "From me to you and you to me."

"Yes, oh yes!" she held him tightly. "Worth waiting for."

"Yes....my precious Aimee. The perfect gift, each other. You know, honey, I wouldn't have had it any other way." He kissed her.

"Oh, yes....!"

"That's a down payment," he said as he lifted her up and they made their way out to the Courtyard, "a promissory note."

Chapter 40

"I'm glad you taught that boy to dance, Elaine," said Roger as he returned to the table.

They were watching Rob and Aimee dance together. "He's doing a good job."

"Just slow dancing," she replied. "I wouldn't try the other kind. I'm glad I asked him if he could dance. '*Oh, it's just walking around holding each other*', he said. Well, he got my feet a few times, '*walking around*'."

"Better yours than Aimee's."

"He learned quickly. They make a lovely couple. Roger, you can't call him a boy," she admonished. "He's not a boy anymore."

"It's just a manner of speaking."

"He was a boy. A year ago. Underneath that self assurance, he was a boy, an insecure boy. With bitterness in his heart. I was worried about Aimee, whether his anger would hurt her. But now, he's at peace with himself. He's matured. He's a man."

"Okay, he's a good man, I'll agree with that. Not a boy. Aimee found herself a good man."

"You know why, don't you?"

"No, what are you getting at?"

"He's like you. She went looking for someone like her dad. For better or worse. Not intentionally…"

"I don't see that. Rob and I aren't a bit alike."

"More than you think. You have the same good qualities." She smiled and patted his hand. "It's a compliment, dear."

"Well.…I had some help. Don't underestimate the power of love, Elaine. In my life. And in his." He gave her a wink.

"Oh, yes. Aimee's helped him."

"And maybe that religious experience he had."

"I don't know about that. I think it was Aimee. But now I'd say, he's good for her. I do believe she's learning a little humility. It must be Rob."

"Right about that. I agree, they're good for each other. They'll make each other happy. And he'll provide her a good living, he's a go-getter," he declared.

"Aimee's the unpredictable one. You know, she's the kind who would take it into her head to do something crazy, like join the Peace Corps and go halfway around the world." She frowned. "I couldn't take it."

"Oh, don't worry, Rob's too sensible for that. He'll keep her grounded. But what if they did? You followed me around the world and your mother had a fit. You remember how you felt about that."

"Now I know how she felt! If they did that to me – well –" She shuddered. "I refuse to think about this now. This is my day to be happy." A shadow crossed her face. "Oh, Roger." She took his hand. "I feel so bad about your parents, missing their granddaughter's wedding. It puts a damper on a wonderful occasion."

"But the good thing is, Pop's all right." She nodded in agreement. "Florida or here, they would have missed it. Of course, if they were here, we'd be with them."

"Yes. It's been hard, not being there to support them. It's hard on all of us. Rob too. He's missing his grandpa."

"Yes, it's a shame Allen has to miss this big day. Well.… you'll have to take lots of pictures. For all of them. Allen, and Mom and Pop." She held up her camera and smiled.

"Speaking of Rob's grandpa.…" She looked around. "Where is Mr. Grayson? Howard. We were going to have him eat with us. I don't want to leave him unattended."

"Look over there," he gestured to a nearby table. "He's doing just fine. He's found himself a group of friends....or, I don't know, maybe people he just met. He's making himself at home, they're eating together."

"That's a relief. We brought him, I wanted to be sure he's okay."

"I wouldn't worry about him." He looked around. "Not such a bad room, Elaine, all decorated. Aimee likes it. 'Course, I'd rather have had the lodge...."

"Oh, the bar. Well, you'll survive, dear."

"I'm okay. It's Aimee's party, not mine. What do you think, hon, did you ever think we'd see our daughter married in a church?"

"I'll admit I was surprised. I'm trying not to be worried about it. Does it bother you, Roger?"

"No, not at all. You more than me. I'm not one of those hard-core atheists." He shrugged his shoulders. "Maybe I'm not an atheist at all. I used to believe in God. You know that. It's just these issues I have with Him. Unanswered questions."

"Well then, talk to this preacher. He's a professional holy man. He should be able to help you."

"I've been talking to Aimee. She's thinks about these things."

She nodded. "That's probably better. This preacher has a little too much Bible talk for me." She looked around. "Oh, there's Rob's mother and her friend. I should invite them over here. I'm glad she made it, even though she did put Aimee through the wringer. Hmm....it looks like she's doing okay now." She shook her head. "I remember those times, Roger. Times I'd like to forget."

"Don't expect me to be nice to her," he said with a scowl. "I haven't forgiven her for what she did to Aimee."

"Roger, you'll do fine," she smiled indulgently. "I'm not worried."

"I think it's time Aimee danced with her old man. I'm gonna cut in."

"And I'll dance with my star pupil. Then it will be our turn, right?"

"You bet." He squeezed her hand.

"Oh, Mom!" Aimee came from behind and threw her arms around her mother's neck. "It was, it was, it was!" she exclaimed happily.

"Aimee, what on earth is a wuzzit?" asked her father.

"Dad," she frowned, "what on earth are you talking about?"

"That's what I asked you."

"I'm telling Mom," she replied with deliberation, "that it was a beautiful wedding. Beautiful, beautiful!" Putting her arms around her mother she whispered, "thank you, thank you, thank you!" She kissed her cheek.

"Rob," Roger shook his head with a smile, "this is Aimee. You'll have to get used to it."

"Used to it? Never!" Laughing, he put his arm around her and kissed her. "I don't want to get used to her. She lights up my life, and she always will. And Aimee's right –" he kissed Elaine's cheek, "it was beautiful. Thank you," he looked at Roger, "all of you."

Roger took Aimee's hand. "So, my darling daughter, may I have the honor of the next dance?"

Aimee danced with her father, and Scott, then she looked around for a particular person. Finally she spotted him. Tapping him on the shoulder she asked, "Mr. Grayson, may I have the honor of this dance?"

Surprised and pleased, he responded, "Why, sure thing, Miss Aimee, or Mrs. Rob, um, I don't remember the last name." He got up and leaving his cane behind he took her arm. With an experienced hand he guided her to the dance area. Gaining confidence, he led her around the floor with grace and ease, executing a couple of fancy turns.

"Why, Howard, I didn't know! You're quite a dancer."

"Oh, I'm not as good as I used to be. But – it helps that you're holding me up." Laughing, they returned to his table. "Haven't had so much fun in years! But I can't take too much," he admitted, eager to sit down.

"Thank you, Howard!"

Rob looked around for his mother. He had danced with his new mother in law, then with Marie, with Holly and Heather and his new sister in law, Jacquie, and with Ma Brannigan. But where was his mother? He found Aimee as she was leaving Howard's table. "Honey, have you seen my mother?"

"Yes. Take a look." In a corner were Lenore and Mark, talking seriously. They watched as Lenore took his hand.

"Best to leave them alone," he said, "they've got to work this out themselves."

She clutched his arm. "Oh, I hope!" she replied anxiously, remembering Marie's fears. "I know, we have to stay out of it. I worried about her and Scott and Marie, but they seem to have worked that out okay...."

"Right. Now, we'll stay long enough for me to dance with Mom –"

"Yes, yes. And I with Mark."

"He'll love that. Then we'll change and go see Gramps. I have a certain surprise for him, you know. A quick visit and we'll leave."

"Change? Oh, no – no, Rob. I want to go as we are. I want Gramps to see us in our wedding clothes. We can come back here and change."

"Or go to the hotel as we are. We'll see, we just need to keep it quick. Agreed?" he smiled at her.

"I can be very quick when I want to be," she replied, meeting his smile.

A few minutes later, while dancing.....

"Oh, Rob, I'm the happiest woman in the world!"

"Mom, I'm glad to hear it. As happy as Aimee?"

"Well, different reasons. But yes I'm happy. God has given me a second chance with my sons."

"How is that?" he asked as he led her around the dance area.

"Look at us! I didn't think it could happen." She looked up at him. "Rob, I know I'll never be a real mom to you, or to Mark. I realize it now. I..." she sighed, "I lost that chance. There's no going back. At least we can be friends. I love you, and I think you love me. Anyway, we're dancing. And you're the handsomest man in the world! My son."

"Yes, Mom, I love you." He kissed her forehead. *A week from now I may not feel this way,* he thought, *but today I can kiss everybody! She's right, though, I do love her.* "Mom, we are friends. It's a good beginning. Aimee and I are here for you, whatever happens."

"I know that. It's so incredible. Speaking of Aimee, I wanted to see you both before you left, but," she looked around – "I don't see her anywhere." She stopped. "Oh, Rob, I have to sit down. My feet are killing me! This is the first time I've worn high heels in twenty years." They headed towards a group of chairs. "Oh – there's Aimee."

"Yes, Mom, she's signaling us that we have to go."

"Well, I don't want to delay your honeymoon, but can we take five minutes together?"

"Sure, if it's five minutes." He looked at his watch and beckoned Aimee to join them.

"Aimee and Rob," Lenore began, "I kept wondering what to give you for a wedding gift. Then I thought, *I can give Aimee cooking lessons*."

He burst out laughing.

"What? You think I can't do it?" Lenore asked in a hurt voice.

"Oh, no, no. Mom, it just surprised me. And...." He looked sheepishly at Aimee, "she needs it. Right, hon?"

"She's right. I'm not offended. I never wanted to learn before. Now I do. Rob, your mother's a good cook. Lenore," she took her hand, "I thank you with all my heart."

"I've cooked in restaurants, I'll have you know. Next month I start a culinary arts class. So, I can teach you the fancy stuff."

"Maybe you'd better start with plain home cooking, Mom. Then you can teach us both the fancy stuff."

"Lenore, you can teach me anything you want. Rob's right, I really do need it. To save us money. No more carry-in dinners."

"Hey, I wouldn't mind doing all the cooking. But not with my schedule. It will be up to Aimee, right, hon?" She raised her eyebrows, laughing. "So it's agreed. Mom, we thank you. Now we're on our way to see Gramps for a little while."

"Tell him hello for me."

"We will. Now – we're gone!"

They were on their way to Sunset Woods. Howard was snoring in the back seat.

"Hello, Mrs. Aimee Carlyle," he told her as he took her hand and kissed her fingers. "But you'll always be my Aimee-Love."

"And my Rob-love....but Rob, we have to remember....to work at it every day. So we never take each other for granted."

"We have some good models around us, you know. Many loving couples."

"That's encouraging. Honey, something else....I could hardly wait to tell you what Mark told me when we were dancing, about your mother."

"I've been wondering."

"I came right out and asked him how things were with her. He said he was '*over her*'. He told her they could be friends, but he already had a mother and he would never want to hurt her. If she didn't mind, he would like to call her Lenore. He forgave her; he said '*alcohol makes you do dumb things*'. He didn't know if she understood or not, but it was settled for him."

"Quite a kid, huh?"

"I think he understands. I mean, this was real. That awful hurt, from your mother abandoning him, I think that is healed. I didn't think it was possible."

"Well, honey, we've seen so much healing we never thought could happen."

"Yes. We have so much to thank God for."

"I talked with her too. I think she realizes she can't be a mother to us. I hope so. That's what bothered me for a long time. She said she wanted to be a mother. It's too late for that. Friend, yes, but not mother. "Well," he reflected, "It'll be up to her to make it work. I have to wonder, though –" he hesitated, "will she ever be able to stay sober?"

"I don't know. It's not easy. I wish I had Gram to talk to. But I don't want to think about it now. This is our time!" She paused, her mood shifting. "Rob, I was so glad to meet the Brannigans and sit with them for a while! Mrs. Brannigan, and the girls, and Matt. They're wonderful people, just like you said."

He smiled with satisfaction. "I knew you'd like them. Gosh, it was good to see them."

"Too bad we couldn't visit longer. We had to break it off just as it was....ha, ha, getting interesting....."

" '*Getting interesting?*' How's that?"

"They were starting to tell stories about you. Oh, yes....." she laughed mischievously.

"Don't believe a word they say," he warned with a laugh. "Actually, I appreciated what Ma said to me. She told me I'd gotten a wonderful wife." He squeezed her hand. "Now it was my job to treat you right."

"That's right," she smiled. And I'm going to keep in touch by Facebook. I want to hear those stories!"

"Okay, okay," he laughed.

"One other thing. I want to get to know the family so they can tell me about your grandparents. Tell us both."

"Thanks, honey." His mood grew light again as he turned the car into the drive. "Now, we're here, we stay awhile, we're out!" He woke Howard, then took her by the waist as she got out of the car.

They made their way through the halls as residents and staff cheered and clapped. Most knew them well. Many were just leaving the dining area and they stepped aside as Aimee swept through in her bridal gown, Rob in his tux. Howard followed close behind enjoying the reflected glory. As they approached Gramps' room they saw a nurse leaving.

"He's expecting you. He's been waiting all day," she said.

Gramps was sitting up in bed and greeted them with a wave of his good arm. "Come in, come in!" He looked and sounded better than he had a day earlier. "Let me look at you. Mr. and Mrs. Rob Carlyle! Oh....let me fix you in my memory. Howard, you handsome dog, I never saw you in a coat and tie before."

Howard did a little soft-shoe and took a bow with a wave of his cane. Then he yanked off his tie. "You won't see it again, either!" He pumped Rob's and Aimee's hands. "Thank you for inviting me. Best time I've had in years. I'll tell you goodbye now," he said as he started to leave. "See you in church, when you get back."

"In church? Howard, that's great," Rob replied.

"Yep, a real nice couple is gonna pick me up each Sunday, starting tomorrow. The 8:30 service. 'Bout time I was back in church."

"We're glad," Aimee told him. She took him aside. "Howard, we did a new scrapbook."

She pointed to the shelf. "The blue one. Would you help him with it while we're gone?"

"My gosh, I sure will. He only has one arm now, you know, so I've been helping him out. I'll give him a hand to look at it."

"Oh, Howard, bless you! Thank you!" She hugged him and kissed his cheek.

He smiled broadly, "Bless you both, now, and goodbye." He left to let them visit privately.

"Gramps, I have a surprise for you," Rob announced.

"Hope it's some of that wedding cake. My sweet tooth is asking for it."

"Well, that too," he replied, handing him a full meal and a piece of cake wrapped separately. "I'll put the meal aside for tomorrow."

"Lenore was there," Aimee told him. "We had a good talk before the wedding. We'll tell you all about it when we get back. She says to say hello." Gramps smiled and nodded his head.

"You don't have to fix us in your memory," Rob told Gramps as he pulled a DVD out of his pocket. "Hot off the press!" He inserted it into Gramps' DVD player and in a moment a bright picture was displayed on the big screen TV. It was the sanctuary of the church, banked with flowers. Guests were being seated. Music was being played on a guitar.

"You've never seen the church, have you?" Aimee asked.

"No. But...this is almost as good as being there! It's beautiful, isn't it? My goodness – the church is almost filled. Who are all these people?"

"A lot of the church people came," Rob answered. "Most of our Bible study and couples from our couples group. Some of the older people too. Aimee's family. Friends and co-workers. From different places we've worked."

"It made us feel so good to see the church people there, supporting us," she remarked, "and pretty surprising, considering that we've only been in the church a couple of months."

Gramps nodded with pleasure. "This is amazing! All of it."

Then she exclaimed, "Gramps – look!"

The camera panned to an easel holding the photo of Rob's father at his graduation from basic training. On the side was an American flag folded in a triangle.

"Oh, my goodness! Of all things," Gramps exclaimed, smiling, tears in his eyes. "That's wonderful! It's as if he was there with you. Thank you, thank you!"

"That's what we thought," agreed Rob. "Let me fast forward. You can get the whole thing later on. We want you to see something now." To the strains of the traditional wedding march Aimee floated down the aisle on the arm of her father, radiant in her bridal beauty, to be greeted by Rob who only had eyes for the girl in white....with long dark hair.

"Ah, my beautiful granddaughter," he smiled. Aimee hugged him and kissed his cheek.

"No organ," he observed, "but that keyboard does okay."

A few minutes later they were standing in front of Pastor Bruce.

"Friends," he began, "we are gathered here today in the sight of God, to join together in holy marriage these two young people we have come to love, Aimee Love and Rob Carlyle. Most of you know the wonderful story of how Rob came to be united with the grandfather he'd never met, Robert Allen Douglas. Over the past year Mr. Douglas has had a profound impact on Rob and Aimee's lives. They want you to know that it is because of his love and faithfulness that they stand here today in the love of Christ."

He paused, then went on. "We are all disappointed that Mr. Douglas cannot be with us today because of a stroke that occurred a week ago. Many of you have prayed for him. I'm pleased to tell you he's doing better, though he's not well enough to be with us today. Aimee and Rob wish to dedicate this sacred ceremony to him, to Mr. Allen Douglas." He paused. "Who gives this woman to be married to this man...."

Rob stopped the video at that point. "Gramps, he said it better than we could. So, without getting sentimental, we want to say thank you. Then we'll take off. We have other matters to attend to!" he said with a laugh.

"Rob and Aimee. I don't know what to say." He brushed away a tear. "Thank you for–" he waved his hand – "this wonderful gift. But Rob, remember, it all began with you, your words – that I was a human being and should be treated like one. That gave me heart. It made me want to live."

"Thank you, Gramps. That means a lot."

"And the rest, they say, is history!" added Aimee, getting up to leave.

He beckoned to them. "Come here. I want to give you my blessing." He placed his hand over theirs. "Rob, Aimee. I pray for you great joy, from this day forward. Joy in the Lord and in each other. May this be the beginning of something wonderful, as you follow God wherever He leads."

"Oh, Gramps…." They thanked and kissed him. "We love you very much." Aimee put her arm around him. "Thank you for the bridal suite for tonight. What a wonderful wedding gift!"

"That was your dad and mom too."

"But thank you so much! We'll be thinking of you –"

"I doubt that," he remarked dryly.

"It sure means a lot," Rob told him.

"Now, it's time for you to leave. Out of here!"

"Oh, yes!" replied Aimee. "You don't have to tell us twice."

There was a knock on the open door.

"May we come in?"

"Who is it?" asked Gramps.

"It's Scott and Marie Carlisle," replied Scott. "Hey, you two," he said to Rob and Aimee, "don't you have something else to do? A honeymoon, maybe?"

"You bet!" exclaimed Rob.

With that there were quick hugs, "We love you all!" from Rob and Aimee, and they were gone.

THE END

Mary Ellen Blake is a licensed Professional Clinical Counselor who worked for many years with troubled children and their families – although 'it's not work when you love what you do.' Recently retired, she now has time to work on a sequel to 'The Album' which will soon be ready for publication. When she is not writing she enjoys creative cookery, church and community work, making music, taking trips with her husband and spending time with her family.

She is a frequent writer of 'letters to the Editor' plus an occasional guest editorial in her local paper in Ashtabula, Ohio. This is her first novel but probably not her last.

Soli Deo Gloria.

CPSIA information can be obtained
at www.ICGtesting.com
Printed in the USA
FFOW05n0904311217

9 781545 613283